ANGEL HEART

"Whew," she said, laying her hand over her heart. "That was something. Oh, my. That was really something. Not bad. Not bad at all."

And with those brazen words, she stepped away from him. "I'd better go back to the house," she said calmly. "Let me know when it's time to leave for Philadelphia."

Unable to speak, his pulse pounding a hot, quick race through his body, Seth simply stared her. The hunter had been caught in his own trap; the seducer had become the seduced.

She turned fearlessly into the night and walked away. She looked like an angel, an enchanted spirit, all in white with her flowing hair of silver and gold in the moonlight.

But it was no angel that he'd held in his arms—she was a dangerous, skilled seductress, with the beauty of Eve and the cunning of the serpent. And obviously, no simple country girl—and no maid, either.

Other *Love Spell* Books by Amy Elizabeth Saunders:
WILD SUMMER ROSE

AMY ELIZABETH SAUNDERS

LOVE SPELL NEW YORK CITY

To John Muldoon, with love

LOVE SPELL®

March 1994

Published by

Dorchester Publishing Co., Inc.
276 Fifth Avenue
New York, NY 10001

Printed in the United States of America.

Chapter One

It was, Laurel decided, one of the longest mornings of her life. It never occurred to her that it might be the last morning of her life.

She only knew that she was bored, bored out of her mind. Every five minutes she looked up at the Coca-Cola clock that hung over the grocery store doors, and wondered why it was moving so slowly. Maybe she'd been working at the Shop and Pack too long.

You could tell a lot about people, being a grocery checker. You could tell who had money, and who didn't. You knew who drank, who ate too much chocolate, who spoiled their kids with Fruit-Squeezies and Double-Fudge Doodles, who did their own baking.

There were very few secrets that could be

kept from a grocery checker, Laurel thought, especially one that'd been checking for ten years. It had become a game with Laurel, a way of staving off boredom. Almost like being a detective, only safer.

This customer, for instance, Laurel reflected, as she dragged a box of economy-sized detergent across the electronic scanner, she was a well-organized person. Her cart was as full as could possibly be, yet everything was stacked tidily, for maximum packing space. She probably did her shopping once a month, with a weekly stop for milk. Everything in the cart was economy-sized, no impulse items, no junk food.

"Laurel, aren't you going to say hi?"

It was Laurel's sister, Linda.

Laurel gave a startled laugh. "Oh, hi. I didn't realize it was you."

Linda looked as if such absentmindedness was beyond her.

Looking at the two sisters, a passerby would have thought how much alike they were—both of them a little taller than average, in their mid-twenties, with the heavy blond hair and no-nonsense, square faces of some long-ago Slavic ancestor. Laurel was a little taller, Linda a little heavier, but aside from that, the sisters seemed alike in almost every respect.

In reality, Laurel thought, they were as different as day and night. Linda was a planner, an organizer. Her life ran as smoothly as her Mercedes. She made lists for herself to follow, and she followed them. Laurel tried to imagine a list of Linda's life. It might look like this:

1 Graduate! With Honors, of course!
2 College! Get teaching degree!
3 Get good job, near Mom and Dad!
4 Marry Mr. Right—don't forget two kids!

"Listen," Linda began, without preamble, "I've found you a date."

Laurel sighed. "That's all I need."

Linda looked offended. "He's a nice guy. A friend of George's. An accountant."

Why was it, Laurel wondered, that married people always wanted everyone else to be paired off?

"I don't want a date, Lin. Not a date, not a boyfriend, and not a husband. Ever."

Linda looked irritated. Her carefully manicured nails tapped against the counter.

Laurel slid a family-size package of pork chops down the counter, followed by a half-case of diet soda.

"Just because you chose badly the first time," Linda argued, "doesn't mean you never have to date again. Lots of first marriages fail . . ."

"Stop." Laurel stopped checking groceries and met Linda's blue-gray eyes with a fierce look. "Linda, I'm having a bad day, and I don't want to discuss Mark. Not now, not ever. Got it? And no dates. Ever."

Linda affected a hurt look, which she had been perfecting since childhood. "Well, aren't you sweet?" she muttered.

Laurel ran a bag of frozen vegetables over the scanner, and hit "times four" on the register buttons. There must be a special, or Linda wouldn't have bought so many.

"Sorry. I'm having a really bad day . . ."

"Again?"

"I know. It's almost funny, but not quite." Laurel's bad luck had become something of a family joke. One disaster seemed to follow another, and lately it seemed to be getting worse.

"What now?" Linda leaned comfortably against the counter, eager to hear about her sister's latest catastrophe. "I have a coupon for those," Linda added, as Laurel reached for a bag of chocolate chips.

Figures, Laurel thought. "This morning," she told Linda, "I got up, and . . . well, you remember that magazine article you gave me? 'Fifty Steps To A More Organized You'?"

Linda nodded.

"Well, it said to make your coffee the night before, and set the automatic timer on the machine. So I did. Only I forgot to put the pot back under the automatic drip, and it automatically dripped all over the counter and floor."

Linda tried not to laugh.

"Then, while I was cleaning that up, the cat knocked down a glass and broke it, and then I

10

was late to work. So I stopped at the Gas-n-Go to get a cup of coffee—"

"Did you buy cigarettes?" Linda demanded with a frown.

"No. But believe me, pal, I wanted to. Badly. So guess what happens while I'm in the store?"

"Somebody stole your car." Linda had been warning Laurel that this would happen. Laurel had a habit of leaving her car running while she dashed into the Gas-n-Go.

"No, nobody stole my car." Laurel punched in the price code for broccoli. "They couldn't have. I locked my keys in it."

"Oh, Laurel!" Linda shook her head in dismay. "How did you get in?"

"Broke the window," Laurel admitted cheerfully. There had been something really satisfying about taking control.

"It's raining," Linda pointed out. "Your car's going to get soaked."

"I have plastic over the window," Laurel reassured her sister, looking out the front windows of the store. Gray sky, heavy clouds, steady drizzle. A typical September day in Washington state. She totaled Linda's purchases. "Seventy-two eighty-six, pal."

Linda took out her checkbook and found a pen. "Can you come over to dinner tonight, and meet Jim?"

"No. No, no, no. You don't listen, Linda. Not tonight, not ever. Anyway, I promised Tamara we'd go out dancing tonight."

Linda was obviously offended. She wrote her

check in silence and offered it to Laurel with the cool indifference of a stranger.

"Thanks, have a nice day," Laurel called after her sister, knowing that this mood would pass by next week, when Linda would find another date for her.

She gave the cash-register drawer a spirited push, and it promptly slammed shut on her fingers.

"Crap!" Tears sprang into Laurel's eyes, and she put her injured fingers in her mouth, taking a deep, steadying breath.

"Laurel, line two."

Laurel grabbed the phone next to her cash register, wincing as her injured fingers closed over the receiver.

"This is Laurel; may I help you?"

"Laurel, this is Bill."

Laurel cringed at the sound of her supervisor's voice.

"What's up, Bill?"

"Your landlady's on the other line. Says there's some kind of flood in your apartment, and the people downstairs are getting wet. She wants your permission to go in."

"A flood?" Laurel felt sick.

"Don't ask me."

Studiously ignoring the line of impatient customers waiting at her check stand, Laurel reached for the "Closed—sorry!" sign and thumped it down.

"What next?" she muttered. She was almost afraid to find out.

* * *

"You know we don't allow water beds on the second floor," Laurel's landlady told her in a tight, angry voice.

"Sorry." The word seemed very small and inadequate, in comparison to the 450 gallons of water that were soaking the floor of the apartment.

"And we don't allow cats. At all."

It seemed childish to say that she had been lonely, and the stupid cat had seemed like a small and harmless solution.

"I don't suppose you have renter's insurance?"

Laurel shook her head. When she shifted her weight the beige carpet squished water over the top of her shoe.

"Well," the landlady sighed, "I guess you better get this mess cleaned up as best you can, and we'll see how much actual damage was done."

Only after the woman had left did Laurel allow herself a good cry.

She spent the rest of the afternoon trudging up and down the stairs to the laundry room, drying everything that could be put safely in a dryer, throwing waterlogged books and magazines and newspapers into the dumpster.

She was standing in the middle of her wet living room, folding a load of freshly dried towels, open library books spread over the tops of her lampshades in a futile attempt to dry their sodden pages, when the knock on the door sounded.

"Laurel?" It was Laurel's best friend, Tamara, her black curls arranged to show her sparkling earrings, her face perfectly made-up, her wine red minidress showing her figure to perfection.

She stared in horror at Laurel's ripped and paint-stained sweatpants, her tear-reddened eyes, and her woebegone face.

"Oh, Laurel. Did you forget we were going out tonight?"

"Going out?" Laurel repeated.

Tamara was staring around the apartment. "Oh, Laurel . . . what famous battle was fought here? Go get your black dress on and put on some makeup. If anyone ever needed a night out, it's you."

It was always easier to go along with Tamara than to fight her. Meekly, Laurel allowed herself to be stuffed into her black dress and led out for a night of fun on the town. She felt like a Christian being fed to the lions.

They had been at the lounge for less than an hour, and Laurel was already sorry. A persistent lounge lizard was trying to monopolize her, and she was almost choking on alcohol and aftershave fumes.

Tamara, bless her heart, stepped in with a quick, "Excuse me," and neatly pulled Laurel to the ladies' room with her.

"Are you having fun yet?" Tamara asked as

the heavy door swung closed behind them.

"No." Laurel stepped back from the mirror, squinting against the harsh fluorescent lighting of the public rest room.

The mirror blurred. Better. Almost Cheryl Tiegs, only shorter. And curvier. And poorer. "Lend me some lipstick."

Tamara rummaged in her evening bag, frowning. "Do you want boring beige or go-to-hell red?"

"Boring beige. What's wrong with me? Aside from the fact that everything in my life has gone wrong, I mean."

"Your choice in lipstick, for one thing." Tamara smiled as she spoke, handing Laurel the tube. She herself chose the go-to-hell red, which suited her dark good looks.

"Seriously, Tam."

"Okay." Tamara leaned against the paper-towel dispenser and lit a cigarette in defiance of the no-smoking sign, making herself comfortable. "Honestly? Mercury's in retrograde. That's why you're afraid to take advantage of opportunity."

Laurel rolled her eyes at Tamara's image in the mirror.

"Opportunity? Where exactly is this opportunity? Have you taken a good look at the men out there?" Laurel gestured at the door of the rest room, in the general direction of the nightclub, where the bass speakers of the live band boomed in a loud, monotonous rhythm.

She had been divorced only two years but it

felt like twenty. Was she that much wiser and older, or was the selection of available men really that bad? "Did you see those two who were sitting at the bar?" Laurel demanded. "The ones who thought they were rock stars? That guy in the red zebra print uses more hairspray than you do."

"I'm not talking about those men, specifically," Tamara retorted, misting her bare throat with perfume. She held her cigarette in her mouth as she spoke, and the words came out garbled.

The smell was irresistible.

"You shouldn't smoke in here," Laurel told her best friend. "Give me a drag."

Tamara handed over the cigarette. "I thought you quit."

"I meant to." Laurel took a guilty drag, thinking of all the things she meant to do. Clean her car. Paint the bathroom. Organize her closets. Lose weight. Pay off her bills— even the ones Mark had run up.

"What about that guy from the grocery store?" Tamara demanded. "What was wrong with him?"

Laurel frowned, trying to remember. "Everything. He was divorced."

Tamara threw her hands up in exasperation, silver bracelets clattering. "*You're* divorced. *I'm* divorced. Everybody's divorced, for crying out loud."

"Yeah, well, everybody isn't paying child support for five children. Five, Tam. He didn't

16

want a girlfriend, he wanted a baby-sitter." Laurel closed her purse with a snap, pocketing Tamara's lipstick, and moved back from the mirror, checking her hem. Butt too wide, good legs, she thought.

"You look great," Tamara told her, as if she could read her friend's thoughts.

"Are you sure?" Laurel asked, envying Tamara's self-confidence.

"Sure. Anyway, who cares? You're not going to meet Mr. Right at Billy Ben's Steak and Ale."

"I'm not even going to meet Mr. You-Might-Do," Laurel retorted. "Have you *seen* those guys out there? Bruisers, boozers, and losers."

Tamara laughed out loud at Laurel's wry expression.

"Well, do you want to stay here, or look for a better club?"

Laurel considered. The reality was, all nightclubs were pretty much the same. On the other hand, almost anything was better than going back to her wet apartment and curling up on the couch with a pint of praline ice cream and the late movie. "A better club."

"Okay. Shall we head into Seattle?"

Laurel hesitated. Billy Ben's was boring but familiar.

"Come on," Tamara said impatiently, tossing her dark curls. "Get your butt out of the suburbs for a night. It'll be fun."

Laurel followed Tamara out into the smoky nightclub. It was getting crowded; people were packed on the dance floor, sweating under the colored lights. They stopped long enough to grab their coats from the backs of their chairs and wave a quick good night to the doorman.

"Leaving already? What happened to girl's night out?"

"We were having too much fun," Laurel answered, poker-faced. "It was starting to get to me."

"Too much fun," Tamara repeated with a laugh as they walked out into the parking lot. "Pull the other one, pal."

It had rained again, and the bright lights of the "Billy Ben's Steak and Ale" sign flashed against the slick black pavement. A typical September night; damp but not cold. Drizzle, steady and monotonous. It ought to let up by June.

"Okay," Laurel told her friend, "we go downtown. But please, none of those impossibly hip clubs where everyone wears black. I really hate that kind of thing."

"You wear black," Tamara pointed out, eyeing Laurel's little black dress, her standard going-out-dancing attire.

"I wear black because I need to lose ten pounds, not because I think I'm cutting-edge cool. Where are my keys?"

Tamara leaned against Laurel's little yellow Volkswagen, waiting patiently while her friend dug her keys out of the disorganized clutter of her purse.

"If you locked them in the car," Tamara

observed, "you can just take the plastic off the window."

"Why can't I get myself together?" Laurel asked, not really expecting an answer. "I'm twenty-nine, I work in a stupid grocery store, my purse is a mess, my house is a mess, and my life is a mess. I'm a disappointment to my parents—"

"Oh, you are not."

"I am, too! They just want me to get married and settle down, like Linda. It's the story of my life. I marry Mr. Wrong; she marries Mr. Right."

"Mercury in retrograde," Tamara observed sagely. She walked over to the flashing reader board in front of Billy Ben's, her high heels clicking over the wet pavement. "Dancing— Live Band" the sign said, over and over. Thoughtfully, Tamara switched the *D* and the *L*.

Lancing, Dive Band.

Tamara looked over her shoulder at Laurel for approval, her dark eyes dancing.

Laurel laughed, her search for her car keys temporarily forgotten.

"They're gonna love that," Laurel told her friend. She found her keys at last and opened the door, leaning across the car to unlock Tamara's door.

"Look," Tamara said, climbing in, kicking a forgotten cola can out of her way, "I've got it. What about a dating service?"

"No, no, and no." Laurel turned the engine

over, shifted into reverse, and pulled out onto Pacific Highway.

"Why not? What have you got to lose?"

"My dignity," Laurel suggested.

"See? See what I mean? You avoid anything that might help you meet a nice guy and you find fault with every guy you meet. What exactly do you want in a man?"

Laurel thought about that as the car moved north down the highway, past fast-food franchises and strip malls and apartment buildings. Lakecrest, Washington, home of a whole lot of nothing.

"When and if I ever get involved with someone again he can't be boring," Laurel said after a moment's thought. "Anything but boring. Someone good-looking, but someone who doesn't care about looks. Someone with an interesting life. Not just another guy in a baseball hat. Someone nice, but not a wimp. Someone . . . I don't know, Tam. I guess I'll know when I meet him."

"A soul mate," Tamara said. "When I saw my psychic last week she said that I'd find my soul mate in a tall building. What do you think of that?"

"I think you read too much Shirley MacLaine. Out of her tree, or whatever that book was."

"*Out on a Limb*," Tamara corrected.

"Whatever. And I think that your psychic is fleecing you. What if your so-called soul mate is in Paris? Or Peru? Just what are you supposed to do then?"

The headlights of an oncoming car illuminated Tamara's face briefly: her impatient frown, her furrowed brow.

"My psychic says that you should be careful around water. I almost forgot to tell you."

"She tells you this *after* my water bed spontaneously explodes. Fabulous. Did she tell you why I'm having such bad luck lately?"

"No," Tamara admitted. "I didn't ask. I was too busy worrying about me. I'm afraid that if I keep carrying a grudge against Greg, it'll affect my karma."

Laurel tried not to laugh.

"Seriously, pal. And if I don't work the anger and resentment out of my karma, I might die, and be reborn, and meet him again in another life. And then I might have to marry him again. And that would really suck."

Laurel couldn't help herself: She laughed out loud. "I think," she suggested, "that you should take that fifty bucks an hour you spend on your psychic and invest in a good therapist. You just keep paying this woman to tell you that something wonderful is coming your way and it isn't going to happen, Tam."

"Oh, Laurel. You're getting so cynical. Don't you ever wish for anything?"

"Sure I do." Laurel rummaged in her purse for a cigarette, remembered she was trying to quit, and reached for Tamara's purse, where there was a full pack. "I wish for lots of things. I wish I was eighteen again, and that my thighs quit moving when I walked. I wish I hadn't spent my last ten years married to a jerk. I wish I'd never seen a credit card, and that all my bills were paid off. I wish I'd taken better care of my teeth. I wish I'd gone to college instead of getting married, and that I had something to look forward to besides thirty more years behind the checkout counter of the Lakecrest Shop and Pack." Laurel searched Tamara's purse for her lighter, her attention momentarily distracted from the wet road. "As a matter of fact, pal, sometimes I wish I had my whole damned life to live over again."

"Oh, my God . . ."

Laurel raised her head sharply at the sound of Tamara's voice.

There was a squeal of tires on wet pavement, a flash of movement in front of them, the sound of a horn; and then, too quickly, a thump, the sound of breaking glass, and the crunch of metal.

Then nothing but silence.

The next thing Laurel heard was the wail of a siren, loud and piercing and mournful in the darkness.

For a few calm moments she listened to the sound, as if she had never heard a siren before. It seemed unusually clear and well-pitched, ringing out above the sound of hissing tires on the wet road and the crackle of police radios.

Funny, Laurel thought. *That sound usually bugs me. And now it just sounds . . . interesting. Almost musical. Weird. I should be upset. After all, that was my car that was hit, wasn't it?*

Her vision cleared, focused.

The first thing she noticed, with the same feeling of calm detachment, was that the VW was totaled. The front end and driver's side were crumpled like a child's toy that had been left in the driveway. Now that should upset her. She had fought Mark for that car during the divorce. It wasn't as if they had a lot to fight over, and it had been important to come away with something.

And now the car was totaled. It would never drive again, and it didn't matter. It really didn't matter at all.

There was another car in the road, looking almost as bad as the bug. Firemen and police officers were moving through the chaos with brisk purpose, their feet crunching over the sea of glass that sprinkled the road.

The passing cars on the highway slowed down as they passed; as much, it seemed to Laurel, to take a look at the accident scene as to avoid the scattered car parts and glass.

Tranquil: Laurel felt tranquil, like the beaming statue of Buddha that sat in Tamara's rose garden. There was no other way to describe it.

Where was Tamara, anyway? Laurel looked over the scene again, the red and blue lights flashing across the shining black pavement, the emergency vehicles surrounding the scene.

Oh, there was Tam, her black curls shining with raindrops, her face pale. She was sitting on the curb, a fireman's yellow jacket hanging over her shoulders, watching as an emergency medical technician picked bits of glass from her arm.

Poor Tamara, Laurel thought. She seems so upset. And there's no reason. Everything is all right. Everything's fine. Why doesn't she know that?

"How is she?" Tamara was asking, looking up at a police officer. Her face was very white, raindrops and teardrops mingled on her cheeks.

The police officer was shaking his head, and Laurel could see that he didn't want to answer, that he didn't want to upset Tamara.

"What? What's wrong?"

Poor Tam; she was getting all worked up over nothing.

The policeman's ruddy face was set in the same sorrowful lines as a basset hound that Laurel had owned when she was nine. A large raindrop rolled to the end of his nose.

"I think we're losing her. You never know with head injuries. I don't really like to say. The EMT is trying to get her heart started up, and then we can airlift her downtown to Harborview. That's all I can tell you."

"Oh, no. Oh, no." Tamara's voice sounded like the wail of the siren.

Laurel was baffled. Did Tam know the driver of the other car? Even as the thought occurred to her she knew it was wrong. Tamara thought that something had happened to *her*. She was over there thinking, *poor Laurel, if only I hadn't made her come out tonight.*

Laurel went to Tam, to try to reassure her.

But she had no voice.

It was the most amazing thing, really. She simply couldn't speak. And when she went to put her hand on Tamara's slender shoulder she made an even more disturbing discovery.

She had no hands.

As a matter of fact, she had no anything.

She was thinking, and moving, and watching, but, quite simply, it was as if she had ceased to be. She didn't have hands or arms or legs. She could see very clearly, but there was no question in her mind—if, indeed, she still had one—that she had no eyes, or a head to put them in.

She was, but she wasn't. Almost as if she was—

"Oh, shit," Laurel exclaimed, in her voice that didn't carry sound, "I'm dead."

The urge to fly was irresistible. Once Laurel decided that she was truly, undeniably dead, once the initial moment of shock had passed, a feeling of warm, contented peace filled her.

She thought vaguely that she really should be frantic, but she wasn't. She felt as happy and calm as she had ever felt in her life. As a matter of fact, she felt better than she ever had, alive. She had never experienced anything like the tranquillity she felt now.

She floated up above the accident scene, watching but not really caring. After all, if anybody down there was upset, one day they would be where she was now; and then they'd know how unimportant it all was.

She could see the ambulance drivers working on her body, but it didn't upset her. She watched as a detached observer. She noted, for the first time, how she looked to other people—the gold sheen of her hair, the distinct and stubborn-looking jut of her chin.

Hey, thought Laurel, *I didn't need to lose weight after all. I looked pretty damned good.*

The medics were pushing on her chest, in the hard, ruthless rhythm she had learned in the CPR class Tamara had dragged her to. ("Firemen are cute," Tamara had told her. "Maybe we'll meet somebody.") She felt a brief stab of pity for her poor, unfortunate body, and for the determined medics trying so relentlessly to force the life back into it.

Give up, fellas. Forget it. It doesn't matter.

She was floating, flying, hanging in the night sky like a star, and fingers of air flowed around her with a delicate and calming sensation, until the scene below her faded into nothingness. It was something that had happened to someone else, a long time ago.

The floating beckoned her upward, with a magical pull. It felt like golden lights and sparkling bells, warm and mystical and joyous.

She was floating through a spiral toward something wonderful.

She had never felt so perfect.

She had never been so happy.

The thought entered her mind that Tamara's psychic was on to something, with her talk of cosmic awareness and spiritual harmony. *Sorry, Tam. Sorry, Shirley MacLaine and all you other New-Age type guys I ever laughed at. You were better than right.*

A tunnel, a spiral. A force pulling her toward a brilliant and celestial transcendence.

As she spiraled into the warm wind, scenes of her life played through her mind like a slide show, a silent movie. Little things that didn't seem important—her mother, ironing and singing "Wichita Lineman," she and Linda opening Christmas presents, riding her bike around the suburban cul-de-sacs with Tamara, her first day of high school, her first boyfriend, the day she and Mark got married. . . .

And then she was at the end of the tunnel and light was washing over her in beautiful warm waves of luminous, soothing comfort.

Her heart singing with joy, Laurel stepped forward, out of the tunnel and into the light.

Chapter Two

When she first saw it Laurel thought of snow—
a vast, untainted landscape of sparkling white,
silent and endless.

After a moment she realized she was looking
at clouds.

It looked like an illustration of heaven from a
children's book—vast, fluffy expanses of white
clouds under brilliant skies, as far as the eye
could see.

A faint breeze blew, and it seemed to Laurel
that it carried the sound of bells: a faint
tinkling, sparkling sound. The breeze moved
a strand of hair against her cheek, and she
raised her hand to it, startled.

She had resumed her human shape again,
but she had never felt so marvelously healthy
and comfortable on earth. She looked down

and was happy to see her hands and legs again, looking like old friends. She was wearing a gown of sparkling white that felt like silken mists against her skin and moved like a gossamer cloud.

She drew a deep breath, looking around. "Oh, boy," she whispered. "Oh, boy. This is really weird. Really, really weird."

There was nobody in sight, no variety in the landscape of billowing white, no indication of which direction she should go.

"Well?" Laurel demanded of whomever might be listening. "What now? Do I have to go sign up for wings or something?"

There was no answer; just the soft white clouds that moved in misty formations around her.

"Okay," Laurel said. "Okay. I can handle this. I can. I can handle it."

She looked around a final time, grabbed the hem of her luminous gown, and began hiking.

To her pleasure, she found that she floated as much as she walked. A small step could propel her off the ground several feet, and if she made even the smallest effort, she floated for several yards before coming to a slow, easy descent. A running jump would lift her into full flight; that was probably the most fun she'd ever had.

After a few running jumps Laurel attempted a midair somersault, which flipped her celestial gown around her ears. It bothered her not a bit; there was nobody about to witness this undignified behavior, and she was having too much fun to care, even if there had been.

She made her way across the vast sea of clouds in this fashion, flying and flipping, unafraid and unconcerned. She was still in the grip of the incredible peacefulness that had filled her at the scene of her death when she heard the voices.

"Gin," said one.

"You're cheating," said the other.

Laurel stopped in midleap, cocking her head to listen.

"Get me an Oly, will you?" said the first voice.

"Are you going to the bingo game later?" asked the second. "Your deal."

"Grandma?" Laurel called. "Is that you?"

There was silence for a moment, except for the sound of the magical breeze that fluttered through her hair.

"Who the hell is that?" demanded the first voice.

"Nobody. It was nobody. Deal the cards."

"Grandma?" Laurel repeated. "Uncle Jerry? Is that you?"

Again, perfect stillness.

And then the clouds before Laurel billowed and parted, revealing her grandmother and her grandmother's favorite brother, Jerry.

They looked no different than they had in life. They sat at a yellow linoleum table that hovered above the ethereal ground. Grandma was wearing a hat made of cut-up and pierced beer cans, crocheted together with brilliantly colored yarns, a variety of colors that had never been seen in nature. Beneath the floppy brim, her broad, soft face regarded Laurel with an expression of stark disbelief. Her blue eyes, watery and set in deep wrinkles, blinked several times.' Her cigarette hung out of her mouth, forgotten. She held a deck of cards in her pudgy hands, resting motionless on the table.

Uncle Jerry, wizened and bald, sat across the floating table from Grandma, beaming with pleasure at Laurel's appearance. Big ears, pointed nose, his slight frame cushioned by a bulky layer of sweaters, the waistline of his pants pulled high above his natural waist, in classic little-old-man style.

"Hi there," said Jerry pleasantly. "You want a beer?"

His yellow kitchen chair floated backwards a few inches and tipped back. Jerry reached back into the mist and pulled out a frosty brown bottle.

Laurel stared at her grandmother, a smile trembling on her lips. She hadn't seen Grandma since she had been ten, when Grandma had entered the hospital for the final time, wheezing with emphysema, her skin gray and sick-looking.

Grandma didn't look like that now. Her plump cheeks were ruddy and bright, her brightly patterned blouse squeezed over her robust figure. Unlike Jerry, however, her face held no happy welcome.

"Geez Louise!" The words exploded from

32

Grandma's mouth, startling Laurel. Grandma's lit cigarette dropped from her mouth and rolled off into the clouds. She looked down, dismayed, and then back up at Laurel.

"Geez Louise," Grandma repeated, looking very agitated, "what are you doing here?"

"I guess I died," Laurel answered, for lack of a better explanation.

"The hell you did," Grandma answered sharply. "You're too damned young to die."

"She does look awfully young," Jerry agreed.

"People die all the time," Laurel answered, trying not to sound defensive. "Babies, teenagers . . . people can die at any age."

"Don't get smart with me, young lady. If I say you're too young to die, you're too young to die."

"Who the hell is she, anyway?" Jerry asked, his wrinkled face puzzled.

Laurel sighed. Apparently, death hadn't sharpened Jerry's memory.

"I'm Laurel, Uncle Jerry. Bonnie's daughter."

"Oh, yeah. Yeah. I knew that. So, you're dead, are you? You want a beer, Lisa?"

"Laurel," she repeated. "I'm Laurel."

Jerry waved a hand, as if to say it was unimportant.

Grandma straightened the cards with a swift motion and slapped the deck down on the table. "You're in trouble, that's what you are." Grandma floated up out of her chair, took the beer from Jerry's hand, and tossed it into the

33

clouds. "Damn it, Jerry, do you know who this is?"

"What, do you think I'm deaf? Of course I know who this is. This is Linda—"

"Laurel."

"Laurel, that's what I said. Laurel. Bonnie's daughter . . . oh. Oh, no. Hoo boy . . ."

"What?" Laurel demanded, starting to worry. Both Grandma and Uncle Jerry were staring at her with dismay. Something was definitely not right here.

The white clouds billowed and floated around them, while they stared at Laurel, their old faces drooping with chagrin.

"What?" Laurel repeated, beginning to panic in earnest.

"Say . . ." Jerry shook a finger at her. "You aren't supposed to be here."

"Damned right, she's not," Grandma agreed, her face dark beneath the brim of her beer-can hat. She reached into the clouds, withdrew a lit cigarette, and drew on it. Her mouth left pink lipstick stains on the butt.

"Could I get one of those from you, Gram?" Laurel asked timidly.

Grandma raised a brow. "You damned well can not. These things'll kill you. Look what they did to me."

"I'm already dead," Laurel pointed out.

"Don't be smart. You're in big trouble, young lady. Big trouble. You're not supposed to be here."

Laurel began to get impatient. "I wish you'd

34

quit saying that," she snapped, crossing her slender arms. "If I'm here, it's obviously because I'm dead; get it? And I've read all about this stuff. Time-Life books: *Psychic Voyages*. Floating, feeling of well-being, life flashing before my eyes, going down the tunnel, the whole darn kit and caboodle. And then I'm supposed to be greeted by my dear-departed relatives and welcomed to the great beyond, okay? And the book said nothing, I repeat, *nothing* about being greeted by relatives drinking Oly beer and playing gin rummy and not being able to remember my name! Get it?"

"What the hell *is* she doing here?" Jerry asked Grandma, as if Laurel hadn't spoken.

"God almighty!" Laurel exploded, throwing her hands into the air.

"Sssshhhh!" Grandma and Jerry hushed her, looking over their shoulders with panicked faces.

"You calm down," Grandma added, after a moment's thought, "while we figure out what to do with you."

"Fine. Just dandy. Take all the time you want. I'll just float around for eternity."

"Don't be smart," Grandma repeated with a sharp glance. Her yellow kitchen chair floated forward and settled comfortably beneath her ample behind.

"I just don't see how this could happen," Jerry said, his wayward brows knitting together. "How did you let this happen, Joyce?"

Grandma glared at her younger brother.

35

"Me? How did *I* let this happen? What about you?"

"I don't see what either of you had to do with it," Laurel broke in. "It was my car accident, after all."

"Car accident, hmm? Were you speeding?"

"No, Grandma."

"Oh, this is bad," Jerry said, rubbing his thin hands together nervously. "A car accident. We should have caught that."

"I must've been playing bingo," Grandma answered in defensive tones. "You know how I need to concentrate when I play."

"Aren't I supposed to be going into the light or something?" Laurel asked. The feeling of tranquil well-being was fading quickly.

"The hell you will," Grandma exclaimed, pulling another cigarette out of nowhere. "That's all we need. You just sit your butt down, young lady, while we figure out what to do with you."

"Do you play rummy, Julia?" Uncle Jerry asked politely.

Laurel sighed and wished she had a chair. Almost immediately, an overstuffed recliner appeared behind her and nudged her gently into its seat.

"Get me a beer, will you, Jerry?" Grandma asked. "Thanks. Now, as I see it, we've got ourselves a real problem. We've been sitting here drinking beer and playing cards when we should have been doing our jobs. And now we've got to get this mess straightened up, before anyone finds out."

"Yep," Jerry agreed. "Get Janice here back where she belongs. Before anybody finds out that we've been playing on the job."

"Laurel," Laurel corrected, without really caring. After all, Jerry had been unable to remember anybody's name when he was alive. "And by the way, what exactly are your jobs?"

Grandma and Jerry exchanged shamefaced glances.

"We're your guardian angels," Jerry mumbled at last, picking a lint ball off his fuzzy sweater.

"My what?"

"Clean out your ears," Grandma snapped. "He said we're your guardian angels."

Laurel stared at them, and then the truth began to dawn on her. "I get it," she said slowly. "Oh, boy, do I get it. Guardian angels, huh? This is great. Just swell."

"Watch your temper," Grandma said, but she sounded less assertive.

"We're in for it now," Jerry muttered.

"You bet you are," agreed Laurel. "Guardian angels! Hah! That's funny. It's so funny, it's killing me! No, wait, it already *has* killed me. I've been on an unbelievable six-year-long string of bad luck, wondering what I ever did to deserve it and ready to go into therapy, and it wasn't even me! *It was you!* My guardian angels, so damned busy playing rummy and drinking Oly that they didn't even take time to guard me."

Grandma and Jerry looked down at the table,

at the empty Oly bottles and discarded cards.

"Where were you," Laurel demanded, "when I got married? Why didn't you stop me?"

"When did you get married?" Grandma demanded, looking pleased.

"Oh, I think I remember," Jerry exclaimed helpfully. "Didn't she marry that nice young man? The Confederate officer who got his head blown off a couple of weeks later?"

Laurel threw her hands in the air with a cry of exasperation.

"Jerry, you idiot," Grandma snapped. "You're cattywampus by about a hundred and fifty years."

"Sorry," Jerry replied meekly.

"I married a louse," Laurel snapped. "Mark. A drinking, womanizing, irresponsible louse. And thanks to him I'll never trust another man as long as I live."

"Well, you're not living anymore," Jerry pointed out helpfully. "No great harm done."

Laurel shook her head in disbelief. "What am I going to do? I can't be dead—I have to go to work in the morning."

"You've got one thing right," Grandma agreed. "You can't be dead. They run a tight ship around here, and nobody gets in that shouldn't be. And if they find out that Jerry and I have been slacking again . . ."

"Hooo boy," Jerry finished, his wizened face puckering with worry.

Grandma reached into the clouds and withdrew an oversized straw bag. "Geez Louise," she muttered, digging through the bag. "Geez Louise. I sure hope they haven't buried you yet."

"I don't believe this," Laurel cried. "Good God!"

"Just a word of advice," Jerry said hastily. "You might want to watch your choice of words, Helen. You never know who's going to drop in."

"Here it is!" Grandma crowed triumphantly. She lifted a bowling ball from her bag.

Jerry and Laurel looked at each other.

"A bowling ball?"

"How many times have I told you not to make snap judgments? For Pete's sake, Jerry, give me an Oly."

Fascinated, Laurel stared as Grandma held the bowling ball over the table. It hovered there, suspended in midair, while Grandma passed her pudgy hands over its dark, marbleized surface.

For a moment the ball seemed to shiver; then it began to glow. The light grew brighter, and warmer, until the entire ball was blazing.

Jerry took a drink of beer and began to laugh. "It's Glynda!" he cried, "The good witch of the North!"

"Shut up, Jerry," Grandma muttered, her brow wrinkled in concentration as she stared at the glowing orb that floated before them. "You play a lousy hand of gin and you don't know when to shut up."

"I thought it was funny," Jerry muttered,

picking a fuzz ball off his sweater.

The ball flared with a brief, brilliant flame; then it cleared. It was now as clear and fragile-looking as a soap bubble.

Grandma peered closely at the crystal-clear sphere, her blue eyes anxious beneath the brim of her beer-can hat.

"Hurrah!" she shouted. "We're in luck! Three cheers for modern medicine! They haven't buried you, honey; you're just in a little coma."

"Swell," Laurel said. "I'm supposed to be happy about this?"

She floated over to Grandma's side and peered into the mystical bowling ball/crystal ball.

There she was, looking unbelievably pathetic in a hospital bed, tubes up her nose and IV wires in her wrist, machines humming around her. Somewhere in the room she could hear Linda's voice, speaking softly, and Tamara's huskier voice answering. She felt their fear, their grief, as keen and sharp as a razor blade.

"This is great," Grandma announced. "Dumb-ass doctors nowadays, can't tell when anyone's dead. We'll just send you on back; you'll wake up in the hospital and everybody can have a nice cry and say what a miracle. And," she added, snatching the crystal ball from beneath Laurel's startled gaze and tucking it back into her straw bag, "I can still make the Bingo game over at Mary Todd Lincoln's."

"You know Mary Todd Lincoln?" Laurel asked, impressed.

"She's nuts," Jerry put in. "Hooo boy, is she nuts."

"Shut up, Jerry," Grandma snapped. She shouldered her straw bag and looked at Laurel, and for a moment her eyes seemed to dim.

"Listen, you. I love you. And I'm sorry about this mess. I promise to pay better attention to you. And next time you come, I'll be happier to see you. And when you get home clean your room."

Laurel nodded, and Grandma leaned forward and gathered Laurel into her arms for a long, tight hug. Laurel breathed the familiar Grandma smells of baking bread and Oly beer and cigarette smoke and Tabu perfume.

"I love you too," she whispered. "I miss you."

Grandma stepped back, seized a handkerchief from midair, and blew her nose loudly. "Go home," she ordered sharply. "Before those fool doctors decide to operate on your brain or something like that."

Laurel nodded, wiping a tear from her eye. "How do I get there?" she asked.

"Well," Jerry told her, "you just click your heels together three times and say, 'There's no place like home—'"

"Damn it, Jerry!" Laurel and Grandma exclaimed in unison.

Jerry shrugged. "I thought it was funny. Come on, Hilary, I'll get you home. We don't want Joyce being late for her bingo game."

"I'm not Hilary, I'm Laurel," Laurel repeated softly. She turned to speak to her grandmother a final time, but Grandma was already off, her straw bag over one arm, her beer-can hat brilliant against the surrounding white clouds.

"This is it," Jerry announced, waving a gnarled hand at an opening between two clouds. "Now when you land you're gonna feel pretty lousy. Like you weigh two tons. Don't worry about it. Just take a little nap; give your body time to readjust."

Laurel nodded, looking at the airy tunnel of gossamer white before her.

"I hate to leave," she confessed. "I really do. I don't remember the last time I felt this good. So carefree. I like it here."

Jerry nodded, his rheumy eyes full of understanding.

"Yep. It's not a bad place. Not bad at all. But you can't be here before your time, and that's the way of it. So back you go."

"Well. What do I do? Just walk on in?"

Jerry looked startled. "Oh, no. Hooo boy, then we would be in a mess. No, this is the deal, Beryl . . ."

"Laurel."

"I knew that. This is the deal. You can't get back without a damned good reason. And I mean a good one. Not just that you don't want to be dead. Think of something that means enough to you, something worth living for."

Laurel thought, long and hard, and when the

answer occurred to her it was almost startling in its simplicity.

"True love."

Jerry looked startled, as if he had forgotten what they were talking about. "What?"

"True love. I've never experienced true, genuine love. The kind in movies and poems. I mean, I thought I was in love with Mark, obviously, enough to marry him. But now, when I look back at it, I know it wasn't really love at all. Fear, and insecurities, and false hope, and a lot of other stuff. I was in love with the person I thought he was; and then I was in love with the person I thought I could turn him into— but it wasn't real. And nobody has ever loved me. Not like I want to be loved."

Jerry looked pleased. "That's good. A good reason. Honey, if that doesn't get you back, nothing will. But this is the catch, honey— having made your decision, you have to follow through. You go back for a reason, you have to mean it, and do it. You go back for true love, you better find true love."

"Sure, Uncle Jerry," Laurel answered quickly, anxious to be safely back in her body.

"This is serious, hon. If you don't finish what you go back for, you don't get back in. Ever."

Jerry looked so worried that Laurel hesitated. "If I don't get back in here, where . . . ?"

"Don't ask. You remember the summer you were nine and the whole family squeezed into the station wagon and drove back to South Dakota?"

Laurel remembered an endless purgatory of flat land and dry, merciless heat, Grandma and Jerry and her mother quarreling, Linda whining, her father swearing when the car broke down in Idaho, the feeling of her thighs sticking to the blue vinyl upholstery . . .

"If you don't get in here, you go somewhere worse than that."

Laurel swallowed.

"Just a warning, honey. Don't you worry. If you go looking for true love, you can find it."

"Really? You're sure? I don't want any more mistakes made here, Uncle Jerry."

"Sure I'm sure," Jerry replied indignantly, pushing her toward the glowing tunnel. "Have a nice trip. See you in about seventy years, take care of your teeth, and say hello to Prudence for me."

"Prudence?" Laurel echoed. The air in the tunnel was pulling at her, like a magnet.

"Your sister," Jerry shouted after her.

"That's Linda," Laurel called, "not Prudence, for crying out loud."

"Whatever. Don't forget why you're going back." Jerry's voice was already faint, a sound on the horizon, and Laurel was moving, pulled swiftly, wind rushing past her and filling her ears with a dull, soft fullness.

Laurel tried to absorb all that had happened to her from the moment the car had crashed to the final farewell to Uncle Jerry. "Don't forget," he had told her. Forget what? Oh, the reason. What was it?

True love.

The words filled Laurel with a golden fire, a mystical, purposeful energy, a thrill of joy, and something else, something she hadn't felt for a long, long time. What was it?

Hope.

She had never before realized what a beautiful and perfect word it was. Not just the word, but all that it stood for. She realized that by living without hope, she had not really been alive. Hope is as necessary to a living person as oxygen or water.

Hope. The sound of it seemed beautiful to her ears, and she let the word ring through her again and again, as she slid into a warm darkness. Hope. Hope.

"Hope." Someone was saying the word aloud, very close to her ears. How odd. "Hope." It was being whispered in a delicate, childish voice.

Laurel wanted to open her eyes, but they were too heavy. She tried to lift her hand, to signal that she was alive, that she heard, but her hands were made of lead and she was incapable of the simplest movement. For a moment panic seized her; and then she remembered Jerry's words . . .

"When you first land, you'll feel lousy—like you weigh two tons. That's normal. Just take a little nap; give your body time to readjust."

Okay. Okay. Everything's going to be all right now. Just go to sleep, and you can deal with it when you wake up. I can handle this.

"Poor thing," someone murmured, far, far away. "She took a hard clout."

"She'll live. She has to." That was the small, thin voice that had whispered next to her ear.

The flow of voices grew fainter, and for a moment she thought she heard the distant *blip . . . blip . . . blip . . .* noise of a heart monitor, and she smelled the sharp, medicinal smell of a hospital room. Then she slipped away from it, into a dark, heavy slumber.

She opened her eyes easily, so easily it was surprising. She felt none of the heaviness, the leaden lethargy she had felt earlier . . . was it yesterday?

Instead of the sterile white hospital ceiling she expected to see, she saw wood.

Dark, rough boards, with slashes of sunlight coming through.

Laurel closed her eyes, then opened them again.

The ceiling was the same. Unfinished, dark boards sloping to a sharp peak. And she could smell the wood, too, the pleasant, rich smell of sunlight heating the boards.

Briefly, she wondered if she had indeed died and her body was temporarily being stored in some toolshed, but she rejected the thought almost instantly. A hospital morgue would be a cold, sterile place, full of tile and steel. Laurel watched TV; she knew what a morgue looked like.

Not like this.

She lifted herself on one arm and stared at the room, her heartbeat quickening and her breath coming in rapid, unsteady beats.

This was no hospital room.

The wooden ceiling sloped down to rough wooden walls, windowless. The only light in the room came through the many cracks in the ceiling, and warm sunlight lay in speckles across the broad planks of the floor. Against one wall a railing guarded a hole in the floor. Next to the opposite wall a pile of pumpkins, ripe and orange, provided a hill of color against the unrelieved brown of the wooden walls and floors. Strings of onions hung from the exposed beams. An attic of some kind.

"Damn it, Jerry," Laurel whispered. "I'm in the wrong place." Where was the hospital bed, the IV pole, the sterile tile? Linda and Tamara, with florist bouquets of carnations and helium balloons bearing cheery get-well messages?

"Fabulous," Laurel muttered. She sat up, and a brief pain shot through her head.

She was in a narrow bed, low to the floor. The sheets were rough but clean. She swung her legs to the floor and noted with interest her nightgown, a voluminous garment of linen, high-necked and full. Better than a hospital gown, she supposed. The only thing to do was get out of bed, figure out where she was, and phone home.

She froze at the sound of approaching footsteps. Someone was coming up to the attic. Laurel swallowed nervously, wondering how she would explain her presence.

She stared at the attic entrance as a small hand appeared and gripped the railing.

The child that followed appeared to be about eight or nine years old, sturdy and fair.

Her blond hair was pulled off her round face and covered with a ruffled white cap; her small, stocky body was clothed in a long dress of deep blue, a stained white apron firmly tied around her waist. A miniature Martha Washington, Laurel thought. A little girl dressed for her school pageant.

But even as she thought this, she knew that it was wrong. The costume was too good, from the rough linen of the cap to the worn, square toes of the heavy shoes. Too real. Not a quick costume run up on some sewing machine. Real.

And the child was staring at her, surprise evident all over her solid little face, the round, blue eyes, the childish mouth open in shock.

Say something, Laurel thought. *Say something quick, because I can't.*

"Hope," said the little girl, and her face began to glow as she smiled.

"Hope," she repeated, her voice rising, "you're alive. I knew you wouldn't die. Oh, Hope, I've been so afrighted, thinking you would die. Lawful heart, Hope, I've been crying for two days, now. I did think my eyes would fall right out. Father said not to worry, that it was in God's hands, and I should not question, it was not fit; but I couldn't help it. Oh, Hope, I am so glad. . . . What's the matter, Hope? Why do you look like that? Hope? Can't you speak?"

Laurel stared aghast at the happy, trembling child, whose plump little hands twisted in her apron as she spoke. She looked again around the warm attic room and at her feet, bare and slender against the rough floorboards.

"Hope, can you speak?"

"This," said Laurel, almost choking, her voice quivering, "this I can not handle. Bursting water beds, yes. Broken car windows, yes. Cat poop on the floor, yes. Death, yes. But not this. I can not handle this."

"Hope, don't afright me," the child said, and anxious tears shone in her blue eyes. "Does your head hurt, still? Are you addled?"

"I don't know," Laurel answered honestly, and she wondered if she looked as frightened as the little girl did. More than likely. "I really don't know. Tell me something—what's your name?"

The child began to cry, tears welling up in her blue eyes and pouring over her pink cheeks. "Prudence," she snuffled. "I'm your own sister, Prudence, and you don't even know. Oh, Hope, I'm that agrieved. What has happened to you?"

Laurel fought the panicky feeling that was threatening to overwhelm her and managed a sickly smile. "Don't cry. All right? Please don't cry. I'm just a little dizzy, all right? Honest. Let's just stay calm, and everything will be fine."

The crying child wiped her face on her apron, snuffling. "Truly?"

"Truly, Prudence."

"Now you sound more yourself," Prudence observed with an unsteady smile.

"Myself," Laurel whispered. She reached up to touch her head and felt her hair, longer and heavier than it had ever been, hanging in a thick braid. She drew it over her shoulder and stared at it, running her fingers over the thick plait, staring at the bright gold of it. Thicker; and brighter than her usual color.

"Myself," she repeated. "It's almost funny—but not quite." She stared around the room once more, at the rough wood, the low bed, the little girl in the Martha Washington clothes. From outside the room she heard the call of a bird, a rich and warbling song. "Prudence," she said, trying to sound calm, "I'm a little . . . wobbly. How long have I been ill?"

"Two days," Prudence answered helpfully.

"And what day is it now?"

"Why, 'tis the tenth of September, Hope."

Laurel took a deep breath before asking the next question. "And the year?"

Prudence gave an unsteady little laugh. "You've only been down two days, Hope. 'Tis still the year of our Lord 1777."

Laurel lay back into the smothering depths of the featherbed and closed her eyes.

"Uncle Jerry," she whispered. "This is a major-league screwup."

Chapter Three

Living in another person's body, Laurel thought, was much like staying in the house of someone you didn't know very well. They might say, "Make yourself at home," but you really couldn't. Every time you showered in a strange shower, dried yourself with an unfamiliar towel, or opened an unknown cupboard, there was a feeling of intruding, of being an interloper. It was a guilty, uncomfortable feeling.

Laurel stood outside the kitchen door, examining her new hands—thin, and marked with hard work. There was a half-healed burn mark on one palm. What had Hope Garrick done to herself? Laurel wondered. A scar from cooking on an open fire, perhaps. The sounds of voices from the kitchen interrupted her thoughts.

" . . . wits are addled. Can't remember a thing."

"Poor Thomas. Prudence is too young to be of much help. Is poor Hope really so bad?"

Laurel leaned against the rough wall of the stone house and closed her eyes tightly. *Don't cry,* she told herself. It seemed that she had spent the past four days in tears.

She tried to remain calm, but the hopelessness of the situation was frightening. A hundred times a day panic would seize her; strangling, nerve-racking panic. And then the tears would follow, hot and bitter, flooding over her cheeks until her eyes felt bruised.

Don't think about it, she told herself fiercely.

She concentrated on the sounds of the voices coming from the kitchen—a woman from a neighboring farm, Mistress Cranmer, who came by the house each day, was speaking to another neighbor, who had dropped by with a gift of sausages. Laurel, unwilling to bear their scrutiny and sympathy, had run for the back door.

She could picture the neighborwomen as they spoke, their doleful faces beneath their white caps, standing at the rough trestle table in front of the kitchen fireplace.

"It's worse than bad, Sally. The chit has plain lost her wits, and there's no getting around it. She's blabbing all manner of nonsense and she's helpless as a babe. Can't be trusted with the simplest of tasks. She let the fire go out twice yesterday, and when I scolded her for it she cried and prattled a lot of gibberish. Talking to someone called Jerry and swearing till the air turned blue. Not at all like our Hope."

Laurel took a deep breath and stared at the brilliant blue sky. From where she stood she could see fields of ripening corn and pumpkins surrounded by thick, leafy forests. In the middle of a field, Thomas Garrick was methodically gathering beans from their bushy plants. Thomas, whose sour, suspicious face greeted her each morning. The man who thought he was her father.

"Mayhap her wits will improve as time passes." This was the sausage-bearing woman.

"Law, Sally! It's been four days since the girl opened her eyes. Betwixt us, I don't hold much hope. That's how it is, with some folk. Remember Widow Jeffery's son, that struck his head during the barn-raising? He was like a baby for the rest of his life."

"Does poor Hope drool?"

Offended, Laurel glowered at the back door, held open by an iron hook to let the nonexistent breezes cool the stifling kitchen, where the fire never quit burning.

She felt a soft pressure on her hand and looked down to see Prudence, her pink cheeks bright in the heat of the day. Prudence took Laurel's hand with her own small, plump fingers and held tight.

"That's wretched," Prudence whispered. "You don't drool, Hope. You just . . . are a little funny."

That's about all that's funny, Laurel thought. For four days she had been trying to maintain her sanity. By listening to Prudence, who tended to chatter, she had discovered many things.

She was in the body of a girl named Hope Garrick. Hope and her little sister Prudence had gone, one hot, fateful day, down to the river to do some fishing. Hope had apparently fallen on some slippery rocks, struck her head, and fallen unconscious. Through careful questioning, Prudence had also disclosed that Hope was eighteen, that she was engaged to a man named Ephraim Shrimpton, and that their mother had died in childbirth seven years earlier, along with her infant son.

Laurel recited everything she had learned over and over again to herself. She was in Pennsylvania, near the town of Chadsford. It was 1777. There was a war going on, and the British and American forces had clashed only days before, a scant few miles from here. The Americans were retreating toward someplace named Chester, and she, Laurel, was in serious trouble.

"I've got to get out of here," she whispered, the words slipping out before she could stop them. "I've got to get back."

"Hope!" Prudence whispered, tugging at her hand, "you're doing it again."

"Sorry," Laurel responded automatically.

Inside the kitchen, the neighborwoman's voice rose in self-righteous tones.

" . . . and I said to Thomas, I will not be ill-used. I will do my Christian duty, and gladly help until Hope is well, but once she is on her feet she must pull her own weight. I can't spend my days waiting on a great lug of a girl. She must shift for herself, and if she cannot remember, she must be taught."

"Come on, Prue," Laurel whispered. "Let's go for a walk."

"But the work," Prudence argued. "We've got to peel the pumpkins to dry, and take in the beans and onions, and grind the corn for supper, and tighten the bed ropes—"

"Too damn bad," Laurel interrupted. "I'm not in the mood." The worst thing about this place, she reflected, was the work. It began at sunrise and continued until it was too dark to see. Even little Prudence was expected to work and did. Even she, considered a recovering invalid, was allowed no respite.

Every day before sunrise she had to go down the attic stairs—which were more of a ladder than proper stairs—and build up the fire. Then water for cooking and cleaning had to be heated, which meant hauling heavy buckets down to the stream and back, and filling the weighty iron kettle that stood directly in the fire, on its stubby legs.

Then breakfast must be cooked. Laurel longed for cornflakes and toaster pastries and Dunkin' Donuts with hot cups of coffee to go, please.

Instead, following Prudence's whispered,

anxious directions, she boiled lumpy pots of corn and stewed pumpkin and served bitter mugs of hard cider. The cider, which seemed not to affect Thomas or Prudence, was strong and intoxicating, and by the time she had drained her mug Laurel's tears would start again.

"What ails you, girl?" Thomas had asked abruptly, frowning above his grizzled beard at his hapless "daughter."

And Laurel, feeling the effects of a full pint of strong alcohol before the sun was up, answered honestly. "I'd like a double cappuccino to go, and a pack of Marlboro Light one-hundreds, please," and promptly burst into semihysterical laughter at the sight of Thomas's horrified face.

Oh, for a cup of coffee and a fragrant, slender cigarette! And a hot, steaming shower! And a cushioned couch and a color TV and a little plastic microwave box of fettuccine and a blissful hour of idleness!

How many times had she seen pictures of this era? The founding mothers and fathers of our country, staring up at her from the pages of her history books, stiff and formal, white-capped women and bewigged gentlemen in buckled shoes. But the people around her weren't pictures in a book. They moved, they spoke, their buckled shoes tracked dried grass and dust over the wide planks of their floors.

"Hope! Don't leave me behind!"

Laurel, startled out of her reverie as she stalked across the grassy fields, stopped and turned, the unfamiliar weight of her long skirts dragging around her ankles. Prudence was following, panting in the sun like a round-eyed puppy, wisps of white-blond hair straggling from beneath her white cap.

Little wonder the child looked hot, Laurel thought. She herself was sweltering under the heavy linen gown, the layers of petticoats, the slip—smock, Prudence called it—that she wore. Thank God it wasn't Sunday, and they were able to dispense with the long, scratchy stockings and cumbersome, clumsy shoes. *I've got to get out of here*, Laurel thought. The thought repeated itself in her head at least a hundred times a day. *I've got to get out of here; I've got to find a way back.*

"Father said not to go awandering," Prudence reminded her. "There may be soldiers about. They are camped at Brandywine Creek, Hope, and at the meetinghouse."

"Fabulous. Do you suppose they've got coffee?"

Prudence wiped a plump hand across her forehead. "Not the British soldiers, Hope. They still have tea."

"Losers." Laurel hiked her skirts up over her knees and climbed the stone fence that bordered the hayfields of the Garrick farm. "Hey," she exclaimed, feeling a rare rush of pleasure. "Hey! Would you check out these legs?" Oblivious to Prudence's horror, she pulled her skirts higher, examining her new thighs with approval. "I look great! Yeah!

Good-bye, cellulite! Jane Fonda, eat my dirt! Yes, folks, we're tired, we're oppressed, we're undernourished and overworked and we haven't brushed our teeth in a week, but, by God, do we have thighs!"

"Hope . . ."

Laurel, perched on the stone fence with a bare leg extended like a panty-hose add, turned to Prudence.

The child's hands were twisting in her grubby apron, her soft bottom lip caught between her teeth. She stared at her older sister, tears trembling on the rims of her china-blue eyes.

"Hope . . . you're acting addled again."

Laurel sighed and pulled her heavy skirts down over her bare legs. "Sorry. Really, I am." Poor little Prudence, who led such a drab and comfortless life. It was obvious that she had adored her older sister, and now even that had been taken from her. Now the poor little girl was stuck with a babbling bundle of nerves. And Laurel was painfully aware that her own incompetence in housewifery had added to Prudence's workload.

"It's hot, isn't it?" Laurel decided to stick to a safe topic. "Muggy."

Prudence brightened. "Direful hot for September," she agreed. "But we should be thankful that winter's still far off."

Winter. Laurel shuddered. By winter she wanted to be long gone from this place. She stared up at the blue sky, into the cloudless, brilliant emptiness.

Grandma . . . Uncle Jerry . . . Do you see me? Do you know what's happened? Help me out of this!

As usual, nothing happened. Laurel dropped her head to her hands and let out a long, shuddering breath.

"Hope? What's amiss?"

"Probably a good game of gin rummy. Or a bingo game. Too much Oly. Who knows?"

Prudence looked at her with blank, worried eyes.

"Sorry, Prudence." Her words were automatic, absentminded. How could she get hold of Grandma and Jerry? She thought of Tamara's psychic and what she might do. Sit in a corner like a pretzel and meditate, probably. Briefly, Laurel wished for the Ouija board that she had owned as a child. She and Tamara, when they were eleven, had tried unsuccessfully to make contact with Abraham Lincoln, for some unfathomable reason. If only she knew for sure how she had gotten here . . .

"Prudence," she exclaimed suddenly. "Where was I when I hit my head?"

"Down at the river."

"But where, specifically? Will you take me there?" It was a long shot, but it might work. After all, there wasn't much that seemed too far out of the realm of possibility these days.

"Why?" Prudence asked bluntly, her blue eyes fastened with suspicion on Laurel's hopeful face.

"Because . . . because . . . Well, look: You

know how I've been . . . not myself?"

Prudence nodded.

"Well, it happened when I hit my head, and I thought that if I hit my head again, I might be myself again."

Prudence twisted her little mouth in a disapproving fashion.

"Come on, Prudence, it's worth a try!"

"What if you die? Or what if you get even more addled?"

"Impossible," Laurel assured her. "Please, Prudence."

Prudence cast a longing look over her shoulder at the Garrick farmhouse. She looked back at Laurel, obviously torn. Predictably, her eyes began to fill.

"Don't you want me to be as I was before?"

Prudence wiped her nose on the back of her hand and shrugged. "I don't know, Hope. I . . . I vow I loved you dearly before, but now . . . I like you very much. You seem stronger. Braver. And you never make me wear the stiffening board strapped to my back anymore."

"That barbaric damned thing," Hope muttered. She had almost cried the first time she had seen Mistress Cranmer strapping the heavy board to the child's back. "To make her grow straight," the woman had explained. Hope had suggested that Mistress Cranmer herself might strap the board to her own head and see if it didn't straighten her out. Then, to the good woman's dismay, she had flatly refused to allow the offending device within her sight again.

"And you don't scold me for eating too much, and you don't make me pray as often. Not that I minded," Prudence added hastily, wondering if she had gone too far. "I like who you are now, Hope. You never scold me for talking too much."

Pleased and embarrassed, Laurel smiled at Prudence.

"Don't you miss anything at all about the way I used to be?"

Prudence considered. "Aye," she admitted, her cheeks turning pinker. "I don't mean to be sour, but I mightily wish you could do your work. I'm fair tired out, trying to carry my load and yours."

Laurel felt ashamed. She hated to burden Prudence, but there was so much that she simply didn't know how to do. How did one card wool? make a twig broom? heat the brick oven? Where was the grease kept to fill the betty-lamp? the soap to scour the pots?

"You see, Prudence, it's too much. Just too much for you. We've got to try, all right?"

Prudence stared up at her addled "sister," perched on the stone fence, searching her face as if looking for an answer.

"If you're certain, Hope . . ."

"I am; I swear."

"Oh, don't! Don't swear! Please, Hope, 'twould be a sin!"

Laurel laughed and pulled Prudence toward her. "Silly! Let's go to the river."

Mournfully shaking her head, Prudence

clambered over the fence and led her sister into the leafy woodland, toward the banks of the Brandywine.

It was one thing to think about intentionally dashing one's head against a rock; it was quite another to do it.

As a matter of fact, Laurel discovered, even if you worked up your courage and tried to fall on a rock, you couldn't do it. The human body, which occasionally demonstrates greater sense than the mind, automatically does what it needs to do in order to break the fall.

"Shit," she muttered after her fifth ineffectual attempt. She climbed back up the bank and sat beneath an ancient oak next to Prudence.

"I knew you couldn't do it," Prudence murmured drowsily. The humid air of midday was taking its toll on the child; her eyes drooped.

Who could blame her? Laurel thought, leaning her back against the oak. Prudence did the work of a grown man, and the chances for rest were rare to none. Thomas Garrick thought of idleness with horror. Idleness was a sin, a trap to lure one off the godly path, into the ways of Satan.

Thomas Garrick was not Laurel's favorite person. It was nice to be away from his suspicious stare, his disapproving frown. Laurel smiled at Prudence, whose sleeping head had fallen to her shoulder, and relaxed.

The sluggish river wound its green way into

the leafy forest. A swarm of gnats flew by, and somewhere nearby Laurel heard the rattling whirr of a cicada, a sound that had frightened her the first time she had heard it.

Born and raised in the cool, pine-scented air of the Pacific Northwest, Laurel was amazed at the humidity of the East. It was like walking into a steamy bathroom, only there was no walking out. The long days stretched ahead of her, days that promised only relentless toil, sweating beneath the sultry sunlight, working harder than she ever had before.

She settled comfortably next to Prudence and let her eyes close. As she drifted off to sleep, she wondered, as she always did, if she would wake up in the twentieth century. The saunalike heat of the day lulled her into a half sleep, and she drifted in and out of consciousness.

Images chased each other through her mind—the lush green and damp heat of the Pennsylvania forests; Thomas Garrick's sour, mistrustful face; Tamara sitting on the curb at the accident scene; Grandma's worried face, the soft wrinkles around her eyes. She dreamed of a hospital room, and her sister Linda sitting in an olive-green chair, nodding as someone explained that she had to make sure Laurel's hands didn't curl up, that comatose patients needed to have their muscles moved. For a moment Laurel felt the dull pressure of air being forced into her lungs, the rhythmic push of the respirator, and she could hear Tamara saying, in a carefully cheerful voice, " . . . hell of a way to lose weight, pal."

"Who was that?" Prudence asked, her voice drowsy.

Real. Laurel was awake instantly, her heart thudding, her hands shaking.

Forest. The sluggish river, and Prudence, stirring from her sleep.

"What was what, Prudence? What did you hear?"

"Someone swearing, I thought," Prudence mumbled, rubbing her eyes with her fists. "Something to do with weight, I think."

Despite the heat of the day, Laurel shivered. "Oh, my God," she whispered. "Oh, Prudence, you heard it! It was true!" Wildly, she looked around. Perhaps there was a sign, a clue, a way back. Perhaps this location was the key.

"What was it?" Prudence asked, her bottom lip beginning to tremble. "Hope, don't frighten me! Listen, there it was again. . . ."

Laurel froze, listening.

She could hear something—the murmur of voices over the sound of the river and the birdsong.

But not Tamara's voice, or Linda's. These were the low, deep voices of men.

"Look," Prudence whispered. "Soldiers!" Her small, callused hand sought the safety of Laurel's.

The glint of gold shone through the shrubs on the opposite riverbank, followed by a flash of red.

" . . . sending Continentals to harass our left flank."

Laurel stared, scarcely able to believe her eyes, as two British soldiers came into view.

They stood on the opposite bank of the river, white-wigged and perfectly uniformed despite the heat of the day. Gold buttons gleamed against brilliant scarlet coats; white stockings and breeches clung like kid gloves to muscled legs.

"And where did he hear that? Does he have a man in Washington's camp, Howard?" The man speaking was unusually tall, Laurel thought, compared to the other men she had seen since her arrival. His white wig made his chiseled face seem even more tanned than it was. His voice was low, with a country burr to it, compared to the other man's more clipped reply.

"Of course he has a man in Washington's camp. Major General Grey is no fool, Goodwin."

"No, of course not." The one called Goodwin, the tall one, was taking a flask from his belt as he spoke. "If Washington intends to harass our left flank, Grey's spy must have been in camp yesterday. Was he?"

Prudence was pulling Laurel back into the bushes, her hand tight with tension. Laurel could see why. She hadn't expected to feel the fear that raced through her at the sight of the enemy. Their guns, long and narrow, hung casually over their shoulders. The bayonets, cold and deadly-looking, reflected in the sun with a dull light. It made Laurel sick to think that those bayonets had probably been covered with American blood only days before.

"You're awfully interested in Grey's plans, aren't you, Goodwin?" The soldier's voice was casual, but there was a dangerous gleam in his narrow eyes as he glanced at his tall companion.

"Of course I am." The one called Goodwin knelt on the riverbank and rinsed his flask in the green water. "I'd be a poor soldier if I didn't care, wouldn't I?"

Laurel and Prudence, unnoticed in the leafy undergrowth, watched as the soldier called Howard circled behind his tall companion. His mouth twisted in a sneer.

"A good soldier, are you, Goodwin? Or mayhap . . . a good spy."

Goodwin tensed, but only for a moment. "I'm no spy, Howard. Just a man who believes in king and country, and—"

His words broke off abruptly as his fellow soldier brought a rock down on his head.

Laurel and Prudence flinched at the sickening crack, and Prudence brought her hand to her mouth, stifling her soft cry.

Goodwin wavered, his eyes blurring, his face blank with shock. The silver flask fell from his hands into the depths of the Brandywine.

To Laurel's surprise, the blow didn't fell Goodwin; he began to stand.

"Bastard spy!" The soldier called Howard sputtered in panic and rage, and he seized

Goodwin around the neck.

His teeth clenched, Goodwin attempted to dislodge the smaller man from his back, staggering backwards and trying to slam the red-coated man against the riverbank.

Despite Goodwin's superior size and strength, Howard had the advantage of surprise on his side, not to mention the blow on the head that Goodwin had already taken. His arm tightened around the larger man's neck, and he refused to be dislodged.

"Dung-eating Colonial! Did you think I didn't know?" Howard's voice was taut with fury.

The man called Goodwin attempted to speak, but no sound issued from his constricted throat. He gave a mighty lurch, trying to throw his opponent.

Laurel cringed at the sounds of helpless rage, the furious struggle. She had never seen hatred like that which she saw in the gleaming eyes of the soldier called Howard. She wondered, fleetingly, if she should make a sound—alert them to her presence, see if she could give Goodwin a moment's advantage.

Even as the thought occurred to her there was a mighty splash, and the struggling men tumbled into the green depths of the Brandywine.

For a moment it looked as if Goodwin might prevail. He leaned backwards, forcing the treacherous Howard beneath the surface of the water as his fingers sought to dislodge the ever-tightening arm at his throat.

Howard surfaced in a shower of water, his

face dark with rage, and gulped in huge mouthfuls of air. His eyes blazing, he tightened his death grip on the other man's neck.

"Please, Goodwin . . ." Laurel's whisper went unheard in the splashing and fighting. She wanted the man to live, wanted him to win . . .

Goodwin's handsome face began to turn a dark shade of purple. His fingers slipped from Howard's strangling arm.

With a shout of triumph, Howard leapt on the weakening man with all his weight, and Goodwin's head slipped beneath the dark surface of the water.

Frozen with horror, Laurel felt as if she were trapped in a nightmare. Time seemed to move very slowly. She noticed, as if in a dream, the full-throated song of a nearby oriole over the sound of Goodwin's futile splashing, and Prudence, her face unusually pale, a corner of her apron stuffed in her mouth. Horrified, she saw Goodwin's white wig floating away, and the way his dark hair floated in black ribbons beneath the surface of the water.

Howard's laughter echoed across the river. It was an evil sound; the sound of a man who is killing and enjoying it.

Goodwin's hand broke the surface of the water, reaching out with a supplicant's gesture, asking for help that wasn't there. It was an oddly graceful hand for such a large man; a musician's hand, or a painter's, the fingers long and slender, with a peculiar but definite beauty.

The hand fell back into the river, and Laurel choked at Howard's cry of triumph. *No,* her mind shouted. *No, not fair.*

But Howard was dragging Goodwin's body from the river. The handsome face was blue and lifeless and he was limp in his murderer's grasp.

Laurel felt sick. Beside her, Prudence was quivering, her face buried in her apron.

Panting, Howard dragged Goodwin to the riverbank only a few feet away from where the two girls sat, and reached into the pockets of the lifeless man.

It was more than Laurel could bear.

"Murderer!"

She hadn't meant to shout, but the word seemed to burst from her throat with a raw, fierce sound.

It startled Howard as much as it startled her, and for a moment their gazes locked and she was staring into his piggy eyes. She felt as if her hatred might burn him.

She sprang to her feet, mindless with rage, fury pounding through her veins, heat blazing behind her eyes.

After one startled moment Howard ran, underbrush crackling beneath his wet boots.

Without thinking, Hope let him go and rushed toward Goodwin's lifeless body. Wrong. It was wrong that such a strong, vibrant man could die, so quickly, so unjustly.

She rolled the man to his side and pushed as hard as she could against his lungs. Water poured from his mouth and nose as his lungs emptied.

"Hope!" Prudence's cry was horrified and confused.

Laurel laid her head against the breadth of the man's chest, cold against her cheek.

No sound.

Automatically, her hand slid beneath his neck and tilted his head back. His mouth fell open; a wide, generous mouth with a deep shadow beneath the lower lip.

"Lawful heart, Hope!" Prudence fluttered on the edge of her vision like a plump little blue-bird.

Filling her lungs, Laurel bent her mouth over Goodwin's cold lips and filled his silent lungs with two hard, full breaths as she pushed aside the wet fabric of his red coat.

She pushed gently, and heard the air leave his body. Her fingers sought the hard line of his ribs, the soft, vulnerable skin where they joined, and she gave a fierce, ruthless push, then another.

"Live," she whispered, pushing hard. "Live."

"Mercy God," Prudence whispered. Laurel could tell she was crying, but she didn't care. Later, she could deal with Prudence. Right now, all her concentration was on the man who lay beneath her hands on the riverbank, and the fierce motion of her hands as they thrust against his chest.

" . . . Twelve, thirteen, fourteen, breathe." Again, the cold lips beneath her warm ones, the full strength of breath from her own lungs into his. *Live, Goodwin. Live.*

And again, pushing beneath the sternum, one, two, three, four . . . Prudence staring with horror at her sister, surely gone mad . . . ten, eleven, twelve . . . wondering if she was hurting him and *breathe* again.

"Jesus, have mercy." Poor little Prudence was genuinely terrified; Laurel could hear it, but all her energy, all her effort, all her care was concentrated on the dark-haired man on the grassy slope.

"Live. Breathe, damn it."

Push and breathe. Depress two inches, count, breathe. Fill his lungs, hard. They must be big lungs, thought Laurel. Such a strong man. Push and breathe. Force the life-giving air in, from your body to his. Give him life. Listen as the air leaves. Push, again. Fifteen times. Don't stop until help arrives.

And then she felt it. A surge of energy, a whisper of movement in the still body.

Push and breathe.

He drew breath. A weak thump in his chest; and then another.

"Christ in heaven," Prudence screamed, seizing Laurel's arm, and staring at her sister with terrified eyes. "Stop this, Hope! He's dead! What are you doing? He's dead!"

Laurel stared as the rugged face began to gain color, saw the lips move as the God-blessed air moved between them.

"Not anymore," she whispered and sat back on her heels. She lifted a hand to her face and realized that it was wet with tears. "He's not anymore."

Prudence was, for the first time in her short life, speechless.

The man on the riverbank drew a few hard, ragged breaths, coughed a few choking coughs, and opened his eyes.

For a few moments there was absolute silence. He stared, looking dazed, at the golden-haired girl before him.

"Angel," he whispered, the word sounding almost like a question. His hand, with its long, beautiful fingers, reached up to touch Laurel's long braid, gleaming gold in the sunlight, and his mouth curved into a soft smile. "An angel," he repeated, his voice barely audible. His dark brown eyes caressed her for a moment before they closed.

Prudence sat on the grass, threw her apron over her face, and promptly burst into noisy tears.

"I'll bid . . . nine." Jerry beamed over the top of his cards at his sister.

"Geez Louise, Jerry. You're either stupid or cheating." Grandma glared across the table at him, but Jerry just beamed back, looking like a good-natured mole emerging from his burrow of woolly sweaters.

"Bid," Jerry reminded her.

Grandma treated him to another glower,

reached back into the pristine clouds, and withdrew a lit cigarette.

"Five," she said at last.

"Hooo boy. One of us is going under, this hand," Jerry said with relish. "And it won't be—"

"Excuse me."

Startled, Grandma and Jerry turned with one motion. A stranger was walking toward them through the sparkling mist, an elderly man dressed in an elegant frock coat and breeches of white brocade, his perfectly combed white wig and cravat competing for snowiness.

"Who the hell is that?" Jerry demanded. "Hey, who the hell are you?"

"So sorry to intrude. I'm Nat Goodwin. I was to have met my grandson Seth today and I can't seem to find him. Have you seen him about?"

Grandma, resplendent in a crocheted cap with a pom-pom and a sweatshirt with the words WORLD'S GREATEST GRANDMA emblazoned in gold on it, shook her head.

"No. Do you play gin?"

"No, I'm afraid not." The stranger looked vaguely uncomfortable, then turned to Jerry. "I was told that you were at the entrance to 1777 a while ago. Did you see anyone?"

"Nobody but us here," Grandma answered for him. "And we haven't seen anyone, have we, Jerry?"

"Nope," Jerry agreed. "Nobody here but us chickens. You want an Oly?"

The stranger looked confused, either by Jerry's chicken joke or the cold brown beer bottle that floated toward him through the air.

"No, thank you," he murmured politely. "Sorry to have bothered you."

Jerry and Grandma watched as the man floated away, looking disturbed.

As soon as he was out of sight, Grandma turned on Jerry.

"Okay, Jerry, what's going on?"

"Nothing. The guy's nuts. I was nowhere near 1777. Hoo boy, is he nuts. Hey! Hey! Joyce, what are you doing with that bowling ball? Put that damned thing away!"

Grandma set the bowling ball into a midair spin, glaring at Jerry as it flared into light. "Like hell I will. Seeing that old fart reminded me—I better check on Laurel."

"Why do you want to do something like that? She's fine."

Grandma frowned at her brother. "Jerry . . ."

"Okay, okay. But I tell you, everything's fine. I sent her back just like I told you."

The bowling ball flared into gold fire, then cleared.

"Oh, Jerry. Oh, no. Jerry."

"What?"

The two old heads bent over the crystal-clear sphere, and their eyes met in horror as they saw the image in the ball.

"Who the hell is that?" Jerry asked uncertainly.

"That's Laurel, you old fool!"

"Doesn't look like Laurel. Well, a little. The coloring. Taller, though. Are you sure?"

Grandma's jowls quivered in rage. "Jerry, you dumb ass. You sent Laurel to the wrong damned body! That's not her body in the hospital, that was her body two hundred years ago! And I'll bet money that's Goodwin, next to her! The guy that was supposed to show up today! Damn it, Jerry! Do you have any idea what kind of trouble you've started?"

Jerry gave a weak smile and picked a fuzz ball off his sweater. "Hoo boy. Hooo boy. This is tricky, isn't it?"

"Tricky from the git-go," Grandma agreed. "And getting trickier every minute."

Chapter Four

"Father won't like it." Prudence's solid little face was set in determined lines, her lips turned firmly down. "He told us to stay away from soldiers."

"Too late. We should at least wake him up before we go. Howard might come back and find whatever he was searching for in Goodwin's pockets. As for . . . Father, he doesn't like anything."

Prudence's mouth tightened. "'Tis already getting late, and we've yet to start supper."

Laurel looked down at the sleeping man on the grassy riverbank. His breathing was easy and strong, his pulse steady. He looked better. As a matter of fact, he looked damned good. Too good to leave lying here.

She looked up at Prudence, who sometimes

resembled an old woman as much as an eight-year-old girl.

"I think we should wake him up at least. I'd feel responsible if Howard comes back to search him. After all, I saved his life." *And as soon as he's out of this place,* she added silently, *I'm coming back, to try to find my way back to the twentieth century.* She had been so close! She had actually heard Tamara's voice, smelled the medicinal odor of the hospital room.

And then you came along, she thought, gazing ruefully at Goodwin.

Prudence, following Laurel's gaze, shivered. "He was dead," she whispered. "I saw it, Hope. He was dead and you brought him back to life." Awe and fear shone in her pale blue eyes. "Mercy, Hope, how did you do that?"

Laurel shrugged, avoiding Prudence's gaze.

They both jumped a little as the sleeping man on the grass stirred and opened his eyes.

He sat up, shaking his thick, dark hair back from his face. It had dried in the sun, and now it hung in shining waves down over his collar to his shoulders. His eyes, a rich, warm brown, never left Laurel's face. His wide mouth was smiling a little, but the smile didn't reach his eyes. They were wary, questioning, waiting.

Sitting up, he was much taller than Laurel, and she moved back a little. He reached out with one of his oddly graceful hands and took her wrist in a firm grasp.

"What happened?" he asked. His voice was low and husky, his tone urgent.

78

"You were dead," Prudence burst out, less intimidated than eager to spread the news. "That fellow Howard held you beneath the river until you died; and then he hauled you out, all blue and dead. And when he went into your pockets Hope shouted at him; and he took fright and ran. That way," Prudence added helpfully, pointing a stubby finger.

Still holding Laurel's wrist with one hand, Goodwin reached inside his red uniform jacket with the other, searching. Apparently whatever he sought was still there, for the relief showed on his face. "And then?"

Prudence was enjoying herself now. "Then Hope brought you back to life. It fairly frightened me to death, myself. She pushed on you and pushed on you and told you to breathe. 'Breathe,' she kept saying, and she . . ." Prudence reddened and dropped her voice confidentially. "She put her mouth over yours and she breathed life into you. And she kept saying, 'Live,' and you did."

For a long time Goodwin said nothing. He stared into Laurel's face with an intense, searching gaze, until she dropped her eyes. "Is that true?" he asked finally.

Laurel stared, fascinated at his mouth when he spoke. A movie-star mouth, perfect and strong. The thought of touching her own lips to it made her shiver. "Yes," she answered. "It's true."

He didn't seem surprised.

Laurel remembered the scene of the car accident, and how she had viewed it at the moment of her own death, floating above, looking down. Had he done the same?

"Howard thinks I'm dead?" The question was abrupt.

"Yes."

Goodwin appeared deep in thought. "Good. Good." He looked at Laurel again, with the same dark, piercing gaze as before. "Well, mistress, it would appear that you've saved my life, though by what means I can't say."

Laurel felt like a stupid teenager beneath his gaze. She blushed and her heart fluttered. "No big deal," she murmured; and then she blushed again at what a stupid thing that was to say. She tried to pull her wrist from his grasp, but he caught her hand as it slid away, and for a long moment her hand was held tightly in his. Strong, warm fingers. A thrill of heat in her hand, rushing through her veins, tingling in her face. Surprised, she looked up at him. His eyes were riveted on her face, and a moment of understanding passed between them. He knew what she felt and his dark eyes echoed the feeling back at her.

"Are you really a spy?" she asked, changing the subject abruptly.

His eyes went carefully blank. "How much did you hear?"

"Oh, everything," Prudence burst in. "From the time you came down the bank. Hope was over here trying to hit her head, and she—"

"You were trying to hit your head?" Goodwin's dark eyes were on her, and Laurel blushed.

"Aye, she was," Prudence explained. "She hit it last week, purely through mishap, and she's been off the path ever since. Just as silly as can be. Not quite mad, but almost."

"Thanks, Prudence. You're a real peach."

"You see what I mean? I'm not a peach, or an apple, or any such thing. And we thought that if she hit her head again, she might get better."

Goodwin looked from one sister to the other with an inscrutable expression.

"It worked on 'Gilligan's Island,'" Laurel muttered.

Prudence gave Goodwin a knowing look.

"Excuse me," Laurel interjected. "Excuse me? May I say something?" She struggled to her feet and looked sternly at her two companions. "I am not crazy. Get it? I know it's hard to believe, but I am not crazy. There are things going on here that I can't possibly explain to you, because if I tried, you'd think I was nuts, so you're just going to have to trust me on this. When I hit my head last week something happened. And I may be different, but I'm not crazy. Get it?"

"Say yes," Prudence advised Goodwin.

Goodwin nodded hastily.

Great, Laurel thought. *I've finally met a great-looking guy and he thinks I'm loony tunes.*

"Listen," she implored him. "Do you remember when Howard was holding your head under water?"

81

Slowly, he nodded.

"Do you remember what happened after that? Floating, and realizing that you were dead, and going into a tunnel?"

He was shocked; Laurel could see it. His jaw tightened almost imperceptibly and he blinked, then pulled back a little. And then a careful mask descended over his rugged features.

"I've no idea what you're speaking of, mistress."

He was lying. Laurel wondered why. Maybe it frightened him that she knew what he had experienced. Or perhaps what he had gone through was so contrary to everything he had been taught that he was unable to handle it. Or maybe he didn't want to be thought of as crazy.

"Hope . . ." Prudence was standing nervously, twisting her apron in her hands. "We have to go."

Reluctantly, Laurel stood. "Well, see you around. Nice saving your life." She hated to leave him. What was it that made him so attractive? Maybe it was the combination of the very civilized and very rugged—the strong, almost craggy lines of his jaw and cheekbones and the large, soft brown eyes, as thickly lashed as a woman's. And the obvious strength of his body, the muscles of his chest and shoulders beneath the formal red and gilt-braid coat of the British army.

She followed Prudence up the riverbank, suddenly aware that she had worn the same brown dress for four days, that she needed a shower, that her eyebrows probably needed plucking, and—

"Hope?"

She turned quickly and looked down the hillside at him.

He stood, a bemused smile on his dark features, the golden twilight glowing on his dark hair and sparkling on the brass buttons of his uniform.

"I don't know your surname," he said awkwardly.

For a moment Laurel didn't either.

"Garrick," Prudence said helpfully. "Thomas Garrick's daughter, Hope Garrick."

"I'm Seth," he answered, offering his name as if it were a gift. "Seth Goodwin. Thank you, Angel."

Prudence was unusually quiet on the walk home. No wonder, Laurel thought. The poor little girl was probably confused beyond belief, seeing a man apparently brought back from the dead. And yet she didn't seem frightened. She looked up at Laurel thoughtfully from time to time, and after a while took Laurel's hand into her own.

"Betwixt us," she said softly, "I'm glad you saved his life."

Laurel smiled. "I am too."

"He's uncommon comely," Prudence added, and Laurel laughed aloud at the quaint expression.

"Uncommon comely," she agreed. "A definite babe."

Disaster awaited them at the Garrick house. The neighbor, Mistress Cranmer, had left a piece of beef on the spit, assuming that Laurel or Prudence would be there to turn it. Now one side of the meat was burned to a black crust, filling the kitchen with smoke. The opposite side of the meat was a sickly-looking gray. Some ears of corn that had been cooking near the ashes had roasted into brown, shriveled sticks, and smoke curled out from the edges of the oven, a hive-shaped door built into the brick of the fireplace.

Laurel opened the door of the oven, and grabbed the long wooden paddle she had seen Mistress Cranmer use to insert bread pans. It was an unwieldy operation at best, but at last she managed to scoot the paddle beneath the pan and pull it out. Clouds of black smoke billowed out with it, revealing what might have been the remains of a loaf of bread or a pudding or a brick.

Prudence took one look and burst into tears. "Lawful heart, Hope! We've burnt the dinner and Father will beat us for certain!"

"Like hell he will," Laurel muttered. She went to the fireplace, which was big enough to park her VW bug in, and surveyed the damage. Laurel attempted to turn the crank of the spit with a long iron toasting fork and succeeded only in knocking one end of the spit off the lug pole, the long, central bar that crossed the firepit.

For a moment the grisly-looking roast wobbled; and then it rolled off into the hot coals and ashes.

Prudence's cry of dismay and Hope's four-letter exclamation rang out simultaneously.

"Damn, damn, damn." She impaled the sizzling meat with the toasting fork and dragged it through the ashes and out onto the clean planks of the kitchen floor. It left a trail of grease and ash in its wake.

Prudence took a good look at the ash-covered, steaming lump and, predictably, burst into fresh tears.

"Oh, Prudence! For crying out loud! Would you quit? I can handle this, all right?"

Prudence raised her apron to wipe her face, her sniffles subsiding. "How?"

"How?" Laurel looked around the kitchen; at the heavy iron pots suspended by their s-hooks over the fire, the gleaming pewter displayed above the mantel, the piles of clean vegetables on the scarred trestle table. "Good question."

"We could wash the ash off," Prudence suggested.

"Right. Then we'll cut the black part off and cut up the rest, and make it into stew."

Prudence brightened. "I vow, Hope, that's clever! Father won't ever know, will he?"

"No, not if we don't tell him." Laurel hefted the meat to the table and reached for a knife.

She wiped a damp lock of hair from her forehead, cursing the heat, and began sawing at the unfortunate roast. "Get it?"

Prudence beamed and clambered up on a stool, her cheeks rosy beneath the ruffle of her cap. "I get it," she agreed happily, and the modern expression sounded so funny in the childish voice that Laurel laughed.

"And then you should change," Prudence added, "Before Ephraim arrives."

Laurel raised her head abruptly. "Who?"

"Ephraim. Ephraim Shrimpton, Hope. You're to marry him, after the harvest is in."

"Oh, no. Oh, no, I won't. I can handle a lot, but that's going too far." Laurel looked around for a suitably large kettle. A huge black pot with stubby iron legs stood in the corner of the fireplace. With some effort, Laurel dragged it to the table, and began tossing in the pieces of beef.

"But, Hope—"

"Forget it."

"But, *Hope*—"

"I mean it, Prudence. Not another word."

Prudence looked as if she wanted to speak, but thought better of it. She gave a heavy sigh and a mournful look at the giant kettle.

"Here," Laurel said, offering Prudence a knife. "Cut some vegetables." A trickle of sweat ran down her spine, and she cursed Uncle Jerry silently as she hacked away at a pile of carrots.

*   *   *

Against Prudence's advice, Laurel took a cold bucket of spring water up to the attic and attempted to wash herself before changing. The strong lye soap, brown and pungent, stung her skin and made her eyes water, but it felt so good to be clean that she didn't care.

From the heavy wooden chest in the front room—the keeping room, Prudence called it—Prudence produced a dress that was almost a pleasure to wear. It was pale blue cotton, with a darker blue stripe and a pattern of white-flowered vines alternating between the stripes. Unlike Hope's everyday brown dress, which Laurel had been wearing since her arrival, this garment seemed to be somewhat carefully made and fitted.

First, Prudence offered her a lace-trimmed chemise to wear beneath the dress. It looked like a low-necked nightgown, with wide ruffles at the elbow. Then came the skirt of the gown, tightly gathered on a drawstring waist. Over that came the bodice, a stiff, tight-fitting affair, lined and padded in white cotton. At first, Laurel thought that there were strips of metal sewn in, but Prudence informed her that they were reeds.

The bodice simply laced down the front of the stomach, and the laces and exposed chemise were covered with an inverted triangle panel of fabric that Prudence called—appropriately—a stomacher. Once fastened on with its ribbons, its seams hidden by the ruffles of the low-necked bodice, the entire ensemble seemed to be made in one piece.

"You look like a gentlewoman," Prudence said, offering Laurel a lace-trimmed cap.

"I feel like a sausage stuffed into its casing. Could we loosen the laces a little?"

Prudence looked shocked. She held out a pair of knit stockings and Hope's heavy leather shoes. Examining the latter, Laurel saw that there was no difference between the left or right shoe.

Laurel sat on the low bed while she pulled the stockings up her legs, and again she thought what a pleasure it was to have eighteen-year-old thighs.

"The stew smells wonderful," she told Prudence with an appreciative sniff.

"Aye, it does." The little girl was changing her grubby apron for a fresh one with a ruffle and smoothing her white-blond hair beneath a fresh cap.

"You have such pretty hair—it's a shame to hide it."

Prudence looked startled and blushed a deep crimson.

"You shall make me vain," she mumbled, hanging her head but looking pleased. It occurred to Laurel that Prudence was unused to receiving compliments. Poor little thing. It would be hard to leave her.

"This is a pretty dress," she remarked, smoothing the full skirts. "Who made it?"

"You did some of it," Prudence told her with

a worried look. "I wish you could remember. But I did most of the bodice and sleeves."

"Prudence! Did you really?" Laurel looked down at the miniature stitches, the carefully bound holes where the ribbons laced, the artfully shaped and ruffled neckline. The dress was a masterpiece of skill and artistry. It was hard to believe that such work could have been from the fingers of a nine-year-old girl.

"Aye, I do most of the sewing. I have a knack for it. Don't you recollect my sampler? Father made me take it down."

"No." Laurel shook her head, mystified. "Why?"

Prudence went over to the bed the girls shared and got down on her knees. She reached beneath the bed and, after a minute, withdrew what appeared to be a folded sheet. Carefully, with a solemn expression, she reached into the folds of fabric, withdrew her sampler, and offered it to Laurel.

The piece of heavy linen was about two feet square and so heavily encrusted with stitches that it resembled a heavy tapestry.

Laurel drew a deep breath of admiration, lifting the work closer to her eyes for a better look in the darkening room.

The central figure in the tapestry was a woman in a rose-colored gown, her golden hair flowing. She had one hand raised in an almost admonishing manner, and she seemed to be speaking to the two golden-haired girls at her side—probably meant to be Hope and

Prudence, Laurel realized.

The trio sat beneath a lush and fruit-laden apple tree, each branch and leaf picked out in careful, meticulous stitches. Around them flowers in a rainbow of colors bloomed, and rabbits and deer stood nearby, as if they hesitated to intrude on the tender familial scene. And across the pale blue sky, framed within a lush pattern of vines and flowers, Prudence had painstakingly stitched a verse. It took Laurel a few moments to decipher the strange, archaic spelling:

> God did see fitte
> Your life to take
> And for you will I ever pine
> Myne comfort is the vow you spake
> Of love forever myne.
>
> Prudence Garrick,
> 1776

"That's beautiful, Prudence." Laurel's voice was soft in the quiet attic.

Prudence folded the sampler carefully, her bottom lip caught firmly between her teeth. After a quiet moment she spoke. "Do you think that it's true, Hope? What Mother promised? Do you think she can truly look down from Heaven and see me? Do you think she still loves me?"

"I know it's true. I know it. And of course she loves you. Who could help it?"

Prudence blushed happily as she put the sampler back into its hiding place. She sent Laurel a tender smile as she descended the attic steps.

Laurel sighed. As anxious as she was to return to the twentieth century, she regretted having to leave Prudence. She hadn't expected to come to love the child so much in the few days she had been here.

"Hope!" Prudence was calling her name up the attic stairs, a note of excitement in her voice.

"Hope! Father and Ephraim are coming—and Seth Goodwin is with them!"

A rush of unexpected pleasure heated Laurel's face.

Grow up, she ordered herself. *You've done stupid things, and you've done stupid things, but getting a crush on some ye olde hunk that's been underground for two hundred years is way beyond stupid.*

All the same, she was grateful for the dress of delicate cotton that Prudence's nimble fingers had shaped and she patted her hair carefully before descending the steep staircase.

If she had tried to imagine a more revolting fiancé for poor Hope, she couldn't have done it, Laurel thought. Ephraim Shrimpton was a small, thin man who smelled strongly of unwashed hair. When he smiled at her his teeth were uneven and blackened at the edges, and some were missing. Despite the careful appearance of his waistcoat and breeches, Laurel was pretty sure the man hadn't bathed in a while.

Standing next to Seth Goodwin, he looked even worse.

Some of her horror must have shown on her face, for Thomas Garrick gave his addled "daughter" a stern look.

"Daughter, have you no proper greeting for Mr. Shrimpton?"

Laurel swallowed, and she glanced at Seth Goodwin before answering. His dark eyes were curious, and for a moment she saw a glint of humor in them. "How do you do?" she managed, trying not to look at Shrimpton's teeth.

"And this is Mr. Goodwin, of Philadelphia. He was separated from his regiment, and we have offered him our hospitality until he rejoins them."

This time Laurel's smile was genuine.

"My daughter Hope; my daughter Prudence," Garrick announced. Prudence gave Goodwin a timid smile.

Thomas Garrick showed his guests into the keeping room, the front room of the house, and they settled themselves into the hard wooden chairs that offered the only seating. Laurel thought how small and crude the room looked with Seth Goodwin in it. Even without his white wig, the scarlet and gold British uniform gave him an elegant air, and his height dwarfed the other two men.

"Daughter!" Thomas Garrick's voice was sharp, and Laurel jumped.

She blushed as she realized she had been

staring at Goodwin. All three men were watching her—Goodwin with amusement; Garrick and Shrimpton with stern disapproval.

"Perhaps our guests would like a tankard of beer?"

"Oh. Oh, sure. I'll get right on it." As she had earlier, Laurel felt clumsy and tongue-tied in front of Seth Goodwin. Damn, he was good-looking. As she entered the kitchen, she almost knocked down Prudence. The child had already filled three pewter tankards. She offered them to Laurel, her eyes dancing with suppressed excitement.

"He's here, Hope! Goodwin is here! Did you ever think he'd dare?"

"Not in a British uniform. Does Father know he's a spy for the Americans?"

Prudence looked shocked. "Mercy on us, I hope not."

Laurel hesitated at the heavy kitchen door, balancing the three pewter mugs. "Why, Prudence?"

"Oh, Hope, you know Father's a loyalist!"

"He's *what?* Of all the stupid, shortsighted, asinine things I've ever heard . . ." Laurel took a deep breath and shoved the door with her shoulder.

The three men looked up expectantly as she came in, and their conversation ceased abruptly, leaving her certain they had been discussing her. She gave them their beers with ill-concealed irritation, her ire rising at the sight of Thomas Garrick's disapproving gaze,

Shrimpton's assessing one, Seth's curious.

"Drink up," she said abruptly. "Cheers."

Ephraim Shrimpton took a sip of his beer before addressing Garrick. "I'm sad to see that Hope is doing so poorly. In truth, she seems quite crack-brained."

Laurel bristled. What nerve!

"Nay, not at all. 'Tis merely her manner of speech that's afflicted. You may be sure that she will make you a good and obedient wife."

Laurel's jaw dropped at Thomas Garrick's words. Why, the rotten old liar! He merely wanted to get rid of her as quickly as possible. Laurel struggled not to speak. *Calm down,* she told herself. *Tonight you can head down to the river, and you'll be back in 1994 before you know it. One more night.*

"Is it true that she cannot work? I'll not have a wife who is useless."

"Idle gossip," Thomas assured his guest. "Hope will do exactly what she is told to do. I can assure you that she will be subservient to your will in all things."

Ephraim looked pleased. "And she is as pleasing to the eye as ever. Despite the gossip, I'll consider taking her as wife."

Laurel wanted to pummel the pompous little twerp. Poor Hope Garrick! Had she really been engaged to this gruesome specimen of manhood? "Oh, thanks," she snapped. "That's just too generous of you. Unfortunately, I won't consider it."

Thomas Garrick turned white and stared at

his "daughter" with a face like thunder. "You will do as you are bid."

"He's not my type."

Thomas Garrick was speechless at this defiance. Ephraim Shrimpton choked on a mouthful of ale, and Goodwin raised his dark brows.

"And what is your 'type,' Mistress Garrick?" Shrimpton asked carefully.

"Ideally, someone good-looking and intelligent," Laurel answered, not bothering to mince words. "Failing that, I'd prefer someone who knows how to brush his teeth."

Shrimpton's face flamed, and he closed his rattrap of a mouth over his sparse teeth.

Thomas Garrick's face was red. His jaw worked, and his nostrils flared.

Prudence forestalled the explosion. "Supper's done." Her voice quivered, and she reached up to take her sister's hand, pulling her toward the kitchen. "What are you doing?" she hissed, her face drawn with fear.

Laurel resisted the urge to laugh. After all, what did she have to lose? After dinner tonight she would slip out of the house, down to the river, and away from this place. Failure never occurred to her; deep inside her was a certain knowledge that she would succeed.

Prudence had set the table neatly, with bowls of heavy ceramic, and silver spoons. There were only four chairs in the house, and Laurel was wondering what to do, but Prudence apparently had dealt with this before. She simply waited until the guests were seated and stood to eat.

Laurel had left the back door wide open, and the shuttered window as well, hoping to catch some sort of breeze, but in vain. The golden twilight was heavy and stifling, not helped by the heat of the kitchen fire.

She sat silently across from Goodwin, bowing her head as Thomas Garrick asked God's blessing on the meal. Laurel added her own prayers, silently. *Please, please, let me go home tonight. Please, let the way out be at the river, please let Prudence not miss me too badly, please—*

"Daughter, we're waiting."

Laurel jumped. "Oh. Oh, sorry." Again, a suspicious look from Ephraim, an amused look from Goodwin.

She used a heavy towel to cover the handle of the stew pot and hefted it to the table with great effort. Then she took the iron ladle that Prudence offered her and loaded Thomas Garrick's waiting bowl.

The stew was purple.

Or not precisely purple. More of a deep, dark, bluish-purple. The meat and carrots had turned an indistinguishable gray-blue, the parsnips and potatoes a brilliant violet-blue, and the beets a rich, vivid magenta.

There was dead silence at the table.

Laurel stared into the pot, at the purple and blue vegetables swimming in the purple-black broth.

"Ummm. Hmmm. Well . . . it's . . . ummm

96

. . . purple," she offered at last. "Most definitely purple."

Seth Goodwin's face disappeared behind his linen napkin. His eyes danced merrily over the top. Ephraim Shrimpton looked horrified; Thomas Garrick's face was turning a shade of color similar to the red-purple beets.

"I like purple," Laurel assured the present company, ladling stew into one bowl after another, wondering what could have happened. "Purple is good. Nothing wrong with a little purple. Ninety percent of all purple foods contain vitamin C; did you know that?"

"Daughter—" Thomas Garrick's voice was tight with fury. "*Why* is the dinner purple?"

Good question, Laurel thought. She looked down the table at Prudence, whose eyes were like blue saucers. The child's hands fluttered, and she seemed to be wavering somewhere between laughter and tears. She glanced nervously at Laurel before speaking.

"She . . . she cooked it in the dye pot," Prudence managed. "Where we boiled indigo last month. I tried to tell her . . ."

Seth Goodwin gave a bark of laughter.

It was all Prudence needed. She dissolved into giggles, covering her mouth with her small, capable hands.

Laurel dropped the ladle into the stew and stepped back, a reluctant chuckle escaping her.

Prudence shook with helpless laughter. "Oh—your *face*," she gasped, looking at Laurel. A fit of giggles rendered her speechless.

Laurel had to admit that she probably had looked pretty funny. Seth Goodwin was laughing silently into his napkin, but Ephraim Shrimpton was staring with horror at the purple mess in front of him, as if he suspected poison.

Thomas Garrick was furious. His mouth tightened until it became a small, hard line, his face dark.

And then, unexpectedly, he rose from his chair. His arm snaked out, seizing Prudence roughly.

"Will you mock me?" he bellowed. "In my own home, at table? You disobedient little wretch!"

He punctuated the end of his sentence by slapping Prudence across the face, a violent clout that sent the child reeling into the wall.

Laurel's breath left her and she stood frozen with disbelief.

Prudence clambered unsteadily to her feet and went to stand back at her place at the table, her head bowed. Her plump cheek was brilliant red where it had felt her father's hand. A small trickle of blood ran from her nose.

She didn't look up. She simply stood, as still and silent as winter, the laughter gone from her face.

To Laurel's horror, neither of the men present moved to defend Prudence. Goodwin lowered his gaze, his mouth tightening with disgust, but he spoke not one word. And Ephraim didn't even raise a brow. As a matter of fact, he looked somewhat satisfied.

"That was unnecessary." Laurel was angry—angrier than she could ever remember being before.

Thomas Garrick lifted his head, startled. "Cease your prattle," he ordered Laurel. "How dare you?"

"No, how dare you? How dare you strike a child, simply for laughing? It's . . . barbaric. Ignorant." Laurel's voice shook with fury. "Children shouldn't be hurt."

"Cease your scolding," hissed Garrick, "or I warn you, I shall beat you. I have been patient till now but you push me too far."

Ice-cold fury gave Laurel courage. "Beat me, you old son-of-a-bitch, and it'll be the last thing you ever do."

Prudence gasped aloud, and Ephraim choked on his beer. Goodwin stared at Laurel with surprise and a little admiration.

"Nobody beats anybody; not when I'm around," Laurel declared. "Not Prudence, not me. Nobody. I will not tolerate it. Get it? Never."

Thomas Garrick looked as if he was strangling.

Bravely, Laurel turned her back on him and placed a gentle hand on Prudence's shoulder. "Come on, sweetie. Let's get you upstairs and clean you off."

With a frightened glance over her shoulder, Prudence allowed Laurel to lead her from the room.

"I will be master in my own house," Thomas Garrick shouted after them. "I will not be defied."

"Oh, shut up and eat your purple dinner," Laurel muttered. Her hands shook as she helped Prudence up the stairs.

Laurel rose from her bed in the darkest part of the night, trying not to disturb Prudence, who slept solidly beside her, dried tears on her soft face.

Moonlight streamed a silvery path across the floor, and the silence of the night seemed to beckon her.

Now. It was time to go. The air seemed full of magic, the moon lending its luminous light to guide her.

She looked back at Prudence, sleeping soundly, and winced at the sight of the dark bruise on the child's cheek.

"I'm sorry," she whispered. "I'm sorry I have to leave you. I love you."

It hurt. Her throat felt hard and tight and her eyes stung with tears, but she turned her back on the sleeping child and made her way through the silent house, out into the warm night and toward the river.

Chapter Five

Seth Goodwin sat at the table in the Garrick kitchen, writing. The single candle at his elbow cast a circle of light in the dark room. His quill moved cautiously over the paper before him, scratching out words with meticulous care.

He stopped, blew the ink dry, and reread the message. If anyone should read the letter, the words must seem meaningless, vague, but not so nonsensical as to arouse suspicion.

From my bed beneath the stars, I can spy many constellations in the sky. I imagine that you can see the same from your camp. At this point, I have no plans to travel and am content to enjoy my rustic vista.

The horse I bought from you is somewhat balky, and I find that I must strike him

*occasionally. I have also noticed a scar on his
left flank. I trust that this was a minor injury,
or you would have informed me of it before my
purchase.*

Good enough, he thought. He leaned back
in his chair, listening carefully. From the bedchamber beyond the keeping room, Thomas
Garrick snored once and muttered in his sleep.
Outside the open kitchen shutters there was the
soft, rhythmic song of crickets, a comforting
sound in the indigo night. Aside from that,
nothing.

Silently, he withdrew a heavy sheet of paper
from his breast pocket. There were no words
on it, but simply holes cut at intervals. He
placed it over the insipid words he had just
written and permitted himself a small smile
of satisfaction as words appeared through the
strategically placed cutouts.

spy

in   *your*

camp

plans to

strike

on   left flank.

Satisfied, he folded the papers and placed
the letter in his haversack. The paper with the
holes he consigned to the fire. He watched as
the slumbering coals glowed against it. The
edges turned black, then burst into flames.

Only when he saw that the paper was completely consumed did he turn to go. Even now, he knew, Washington would be leading his troops in a northwesterly direction, avoiding Philadelphia. It would only be a matter of days until General Howe led his red-coated soldiers into the city. The British were hungry for Philadelphia. It was the fairest of American cities, a model of prosperity, the birthplace of the revolution.

And Seth Goodwin intended to reach his home before the British did. Time enough to receive his new assignment, to put his house in order, and maybe even to get a little work done.

He looked with distaste around the crude farmhouse kitchen, comparing it unfavorably with the elegance and comfort of his Philadelphia townhouse.

Thomas Garrick was not a successful farmer, by any stretch of the imagination. The chairs and benches of his house were sparse and crude, the food at his table meager and poorly cooked. There were no objects of beauty or decoration to be seen—no display of silver plate, no embroidered cushions or wall hangings. Everything Seth saw confirmed his opinion of Thomas Garrick—a harsh, joyless man, stingy of pocket and spirit.

And if that had not been enough to damn him, the man was a royalist.

The sound of a soft footfall on the stairway startled him. Without a sound he pinched the candlewick between his fingers, extinguishing the flame, and flattened himself against the wall.

He wasn't surprised when Hope came into sight. Pretty, mad Hope. At least, she behaved like a madwoman. What was she doing, wandering through the dark house? She looked like a spirit, clad only in her white nightrail, her pale hair loose and gleaming in the moonlight.

"She has lost all sense," Thomas Garrick had lamented, after Hope had left the table. "My daughter has gone and in her place is a prattling, demon-tongued idiot."

Idiot? Somehow, Seth found it hard to believe. Despite the fact that her speech was sometimes nonsensical, there was a keen and piercing light in her gray-green eyes, a look of intelligence. She carried herself with the dignity of a woman and not the giddy air of the eighteen-year-old she was. No, she didn't strike him as an idiot. Was she perhaps feigning madness to avoid marriage?

And there was something else about her, something he couldn't put his finger on. Perhaps, he reminded himself, the fact that she called you back from death, like a sorceress. The thought made his spine tingle. "Do you remember?" she had asked. "Do you remember floating above your body? Flying, and going down a tunnel?"

He did remember. He remembered clearly.

And though he considered himself an intelligent man, and a modern one, and though he would scoff at anyone who claimed a belief in witches, he was more than a little unnerved by Hope Garrick.

He pressed against the wall as she glanced around the dark kitchen. She didn't see him, in the shadows of the corner. If their positions had been reversed, he would have known someone was there. The sound of a breath, the smell of freshly burned paper in the air, perhaps just the sixth sense a spy needed to live—he would have known.

But Hope Garrick, witch or no, was unaware that he stood, watching her.

She looked out the window and the moonlight poured over her hair and shoulders. She took two deep breaths, and spoke to the darkness.

"This is it," she whispered, so quietly that he knew she spoke only to herself. "This is it. I'm going home. Good-bye, little Prudence. I'm sorry to leave you alone with that old jackass."

And with those mystifying words, she padded across the floor on silent feet, and silently slipped out the back door.

She didn't look back as she crossed the rutted farmyard.

Mystified, Seth was unable to resist following her. Witch, madwoman, or wily maid slipping out to meet an illicit lover—he needed to know Hope Garrick's

secret, or it would trouble him forever.

She was sure that she was in the right spot.
The river wound before her like a black ribbon,
the moonlight sparkling a luminous trail across
its liquid surface.

Funny, how much louder the night sounds
were, without the noise of cars and modern
life to muffle them. A distant owl, the faint
breeze . . . it even seemed that she could hear
the water moving.

It seemed that the night was alive, waiting.
There was magic in the air.

Carefully, Laurel picked her way down the
riverbank, until she found the rock that Prudence had identified earlier as the place where
Hope had fallen.

She settled herself onto the rock and ran her
hands over its rough surface. It was still warm
from the heat of the day.

She closed her eyes tightly and wished.

For a long time she sat that way, breathing
in the night air and the cool, green scent of the
river, feeling the breeze on her cheeks. Like an
Indian Yogi, she tried to empty her mind of
thoughts, to let the universe take its course.

After a while the sounds of the night drifted
into a pleasant blur, and Laurel felt an almost
drugged calm blanket her. She couldn't tell if
she was awake or dreaming, and she didn't
really care. She dreamed of the brilliant stars
in the black sky above her, and it seemed that

they swayed toward her, that they almost spoke her name.

"Oh, this is bad," she heard Uncle Jerry murmuring. "Hooo boy, have we ever messed this up . . ." and she could hear her Grandma's answer, impatient and muttered, ". . . true love, my foot. What the heck good is that going to do anyone?"

She dreamed of her hospital bed, far away through time; and Tamara offering Linda a cup of coffee in a brown-and-white paper cup. "I just believe that she's still in there," Tamara was saying. "You know?" and Linda ran her fingers through her frosted blond bangs, her blue eyes almost gray with pain. "I hope you're right, Tam," she whispered. "Because I need her . . . I really need her."

A heavy, leaden feeling. Trying to move, trying to open her eyes. An image of Linda's face; and then, oddly enough, Linda's 27-year-old face became Prudence's eight-year-old one. Laurel could clearly see the little girl, her fingers held against her bruised cheek, her face tight with grief. "But I need you . . ."

Prudence's grief was cold and sharp, like a knife piercing through the fog in which she floated.

"I'll stay."

The words were out of her mouth before her eyes opened. And then the magic was gone, the dream images were gone, and Laurel was sitting on the rock, staring at the dark, inky river. Her breath rose and fell in shaky rhythm and her hands trembled slightly.

The night around her felt peculiar and unnatural in its silence, like a room that had been full of people who vanished the minute the door was open. No trace of them remained, only their essence.

Laurel buried her face in her hands. Had she actually been in the hospital room with Linda and Tamara, or had she only dreamed it? And had she really sacrificed her return to care for Prudence? Or was there something more?

"Crap," she said, and dashed a tear from her cheek.

The sight of the tear startled Seth as much as the profanity. Hope Garrick hadn't struck him as the crying type.

Without thinking, he stepped forward. "Hope?"

She gave a small shriek and scrambled off her rock. When she turned to face him her gray-green eyes were wide with fear.

"It's Seth. Seth Goodwin."

She let her breath out with an audible gasp. She stood there a moment more, her hand over her heart, and then her entire body seemed to sag with relief. "Oh. I . . . didn't expect anyone." She sat back down on the rock and turned her back to him.

Odd. She didn't offer an explanation, nor did she seem embarrassed at being caught out in her nightrail. Mad or brazen? Seth wondered. He disliked things that weren't explainable.

Experience had taught him that there was a reason for everything and it was part of his job to know—to observe people, to discern their motives, to analyze their behavior. He was usually very good at it, but Hope had him befuddled.

"Why did you sneak out of the house?" He made his way down the grassy bank of the river and sat beside her on the wide, smooth rock.

She looked annoyed, whether by his question or his presence, he couldn't tell. Her brows, which were very straight and dark, drew together, and her mouth tightened.

"I was thinking about Prudence," she answered after a while.

A half-truth if he had ever heard one. "And do you always leave the house in your shift and wander alone through the night to do your thinking?"

She shrugged, surprising him again. She seemed not the least abashed that he had pointed out her half-naked state. Did she know that the moonlight shone through the fine linen? Did she know that the lines of her slender body were plainly visible? He ran his eyes over her slender waist, the long, lithe lines of her legs, the curve of her breasts, high and firm . . .

He looked away, shaken by the sudden heat that flooded through him.

"I want to leave," she said suddenly. "I want so badly to leave. But I just can't abandon Prudence. Did you see the way he hit her?"

Her eyes blazed with fury. "Somebody should do something about it."

Seth laughed softly. "What do you suggest?"

"Well . . . *something*. It can't be legal, can it? Beating a child?"

"Legal?" Seth wondered what she meant. "Of course it's legal. A man may do as he wishes with his property. He may beat his bound servants or his wife or his dogs or his children as he deems fit."

She looked horrified, as if she had never heard of such a thing. Her mouth opened and closed abruptly, as if she wanted to argue but couldn't think of the words. At last she crossed her arms, her face dark with displeasure. "I like that," she said. "The way you list *wife* right in between servants and dogs. This is a hell of a place."

He raised his brows at the profanity. She looked so sweet and lovely with her hair streaming down her back, silver and gold in the moonlight.

"Poor Prudence," she added. "Isn't there any way to keep that old coot from beating her?"

Seth almost laughed aloud. Where did this country maid learn such language? Certainly not from her father, or from Ephraim Shrimpton. She must have a secret lover, one of dubious quality. It would explain much— her salty language, her pretended madness, her sneaking out into the night, clad like a wanton.

"Prudence is not beaten so badly," he told

her, steering the conversation safely back to conventional realms. "I was beaten much more than that as a child."

She looked so genuinely horrified that Seth was embarrassed. "Do all parents beat their children?"

"It wasn't my parents who beat me. It was the joiner that I was apprenticed to. My parents didn't care enough to beat us, and they 'prenticed us out to the first place they could." Oh, those had been dark days. Beaten regularly, usually hungry, turning the greatwheel to operate the lathe, sanding piece after piece of oak, cherry, or maple, drilling holes with an ancient bow-drill. He had tried to ignore the abuse, and tried to save himself by becoming the best boy in the shop.

And slowly, despite the regular beatings he had to endure, he had learned to love his craft. He remembered with pride and affection the first piece of furniture he had made on his own, start to finish. It had been a simple bench of fine, flexible oak, made without pins or nails, sturdy enough to last a hundred years. . . .

"And it's legal to beat your apprentices, as well?"

Startled, he glanced at Hope. "Legal, yes. Some apprentices have been beaten to death. But not all tradesmen are cruel to their charges. In fact, some are better off in their training than they were in their homes. Especially if they have a fine skill; then they are much valued by their masters. In Philadelphia,

I know a woman who runs a dressmaker's establishment, and she treats her apprentice girls so well that they cry when their years are up."

Hope was staring at him with an almost startled look.

"What's this woman's name?" she asked. "If I was to go to Philadelphia, where would I find her?"

"Mistress Kimball, on Front Street," he answered. "But don't you think you're a little old to apprentice?"

"For crying out loud, I wasn't thinking of me. I was thinking of Prudence."

"For crying out loud," he echoed. "What manner of oath is that? Where did you hear it?"

She blushed, with a guilty look. She had heard it somewhere she shouldn't have; that was obvious.

Seth knew how to question people: when to push ahead and be direct, and when to withdraw and bide your time. He changed the subject swiftly, to give Laurel time to relax.

"Do you think Prudence has skill enough? Mistress Kimball has the finest establishment in the city."

"I think so. Of course, I don't know, but it looks good to me." The diversion worked. She turned to him, meeting his eyes with a gaze of almost disturbing directness. "How exactly does one become an apprentice?"

Seth studied her face carefully before

answering. There it was again: the unexplainable. She looked a man in the eye as if she was his equal, and at the same time asked a question that any child should know the answer to. It was unsettling, disturbing. Eighteen-year-old country girls didn't look strange soldiers directly in the eye; they blushed and fluttered with shyness, or the bold ones pretended to.

"If you're serious about getting Prudence an apprenticeship, you must take her to her prospective mistress and let her judge for herself the child's potential skill. If she accepts Prudence, you pay the fee."

"Is there always a fee?"

Seth shrugged. "In unusual cases, it can be waived."

Laurel brightened at that, and he thought how charming her face was when she smiled. Her cheeks curved into a pleasant roundness; her teeth were very straight.

"And you, Hope?" he asked abruptly. "You have decided how to get Prudence out of her father's house, but what of you? Do you have a plan? A place to go?"

The smile faded abruptly from her eyes, and the look on her face confounded him. Fear. Sorrow. Secrecy. Not the look of a girl who planned to elope.

"I can handle it," was her vague answer.

"And what of your lover? The one you sneaked out to meet tonight?"

For a moment her face was blank; and then

her laugh rang out, as merry as church bells on Christmas Day. "Is that what you thought? Oh, for crying out loud! That's all I need. Who did you think I was meeting here? Ephraim the Toothless Wonder?" She laughed again, and for a second time he marveled at her directness. No simpering maid, hiding her dainty giggles behind graceful hands; Hope threw her head back and laughed with strength.

He liked it.

He liked it, and he found himself thinking that a man would always know where he stood with Hope Garrick. There would be no elaborate comedies of manners and farces of coy flirtation.

Unbidden, the thought occurred to him that she would probably make love the same way she laughed—with strength and pleasure, without false modesty or maidenly blushes.

To his surprise, she shoved his shoulder. Again, it was the gesture of an equal, the horseplay of an affectionate comrade.

"Yuck!" Her voice was full of mingled disgust and laughter. "Did you really think I'd sneak out to meet Ephraim? That's so disgusting. If I was sneaking out to meet someone, it wouldn't be anyone like that."

Then who? Seth wondered, but didn't say.

For the first time she seemed to notice that he wasn't wearing his British uniform, that he was clad in the dark, rough clothing of an ordinary citizen: a simple vest over a white shirt and dark breeches that buttoned at the knee.

"You're out of uniform. Are you going to join the Americans?"

An innocent question? Or something more? "No. I intend to go back to my home in Philadelphia. I've business that needs attending to, before the British take the city."

She nodded, and seemed to consider his words. "And when the British take the city? Will you go to White Marsh, and on to Valley Forge?"

If a sudden snowstorm had begun to fall in the hot summer night, he would have been less surprised. For a few moments he was unable to believe what he had heard. Where would a country girl, half-mad and living in a loyalist household, acquire such information?

She looked at him with a face of innocence, as if she had no idea that her comment had knocked the wind out of him.

"Who told you this?" he asked, and his voice was calm and silky, despite his misgivings. "What do you know about White Marsh? Or Valley Forge, for that matter?"

She shrugged, and appeared to be thinking over his words. "Ummm, Valley Forge," she answered at last. "The turning point of the Revolutionary War. Washington and his troops stay at the camp through the winter of seventy-seven and seventy-eight." She wrinkled her brow and raked her hand through her long hair. "And then that German arrives to drill the troops . . . and . . . ummm . . . the British take the winter off."

115

"They what?" He could hardly believe what he was hearing. She knew about Von Steuben, "that German." She knew too much to be a simple, half-mad girl. And why was she letting him know it? And this, about the British . . . Was it a trap?

"The British are taking the winter off. You know . . . taking it easy. They're just going to live it up in Philadelphia until spring comes. It's a pretty dumb-ass way to fight a war, if you ask me; but it's not my problem."

She was speaking the truth, or thought she was.

Seth was doing his best to remain calm, but it was pointless. "Where did you hear this, Hope Garrick? By whose tongue? By whose word? Where did you come by this knowledge?"

She was startled by his sudden interrogation. Her eyes widened and she drew back. A guilty flush stole over her cheeks. "I read it someplace."

"What else did you read? Where did you read it?" His hand was gripping her shoulder, and even in his panic he was aware of the warm, bare skin beneath the thin fabric.

"I don't remember." Her voice quavered. Afraid, or lying? "Forget I said anything, all right?"

"I will not." Was she a fool, or did she think him one? "What think you, that you can play the idiot for me and I'll pretend along with you? No, Hope Garrick, you know a little more than naught. By God, you will tell me where you learned these things!"

He had seen grown men quake before his anger and he waited for her to break, to burst into tears and confess. Her lover was a spy; it was no accident she had met him on the river; she was in league with Howard . . .

"Back off!" Her voice resounded with a sharp bite, loud in the quiet night.

He was so startled that his hands dropped from her slender shoulders. What audacity she had!

She was furious, and her eyes sparkled with anger. "Look here—I have had it! Get it? I am sick to death of people telling me what I will and will not do. That damned Thomas Garrick, and now you! I've had it! Just because you're a damned man doesn't give you the right to order me around!"

"It most certainly does," Seth answered indignantly.

She looked completely flabbergasted. Her jaw dropped, and she took several deep breaths before she spoke.

"Well, when did God die and leave you the job?" she demanded in churlish tones. She left her perch on the rock and stamped away, up the riverbank.

Seth followed, undaunted. "Where did you hear this information? Where did you read it?"

She had the most stubborn chin he'd ever seen. Infuriating, really. And to think, only that night he had been pitying her. Poor, pretty country maid, lost her wits from a blow on her head! Poor, sweet Hope Garrick, can't even cook a simple soup. And, he remembered with fresh indignation, he had eaten that purple slop, out of pity.

And she was a spy, or in league with one! She had fooled him, befuddled him with an acting skill that could have taken her to the London stage. Acting the fool, the innocent maid; while all the while she was sneaking from her bed in her shift and trading secrets with her lover, who even now might be in the American camps. Who was he? Seth wondered.

To whom would she pass her information? And why was she telling him? It wasn't just a slip of the tongue, an innocent mistake. No, she was after something, letting him know just how much damage she could do.

"What do you want from me?" Perhaps she would lay her cards on the table, and in so doing, she might tip her hand.

"What?" She looked startled by his question, but he was no longer fooled. Clever little spy, sly little cat.

"Come, Hope. Don't take me for a fool. What do you want? I want to know where you heard your information, and I'm asking you your price."

She stood stock-still and tilted her head as she thought. The moonlight lit her hair, and he remembered his first glimpse of her, bending above him on the riverbank as he drew air into his pain-racked lungs. He had thought her an angel, golden and shining in the sunlight.

"Take me to Philadelphia."

He hoped he had heard wrong. "What?"

"Take me to Philadelphia. And Prudence, too. I want her taken on as an apprentice, in that dress shop you told me about. If you can do that, I'll tell you how I know what I know. And more. I promise."

Damn! Three days or more on the road with this conniving witch-angel. Was she setting a trap for him? Would he be captured, arrested, hanged for treason?

Not if he was careful. And simple pride told him that he would not be outwitted by a slip of a girl playing at espionage.

"Very well. You'll go to Philadelphia, if that's your wish. And your sister, as well. And I shall write a letter of introduction to Mistress Kimball, for Prudence. But I warn you, if her skill isn't equal to the job, Mistress Kimball will turn her out."

He was utterly taken by surprise at her reaction. It wasn't the cool triumph of a card player who had thrown down the trump. No smug smile, nor the smirk of a wily manipulator.

Instead, her face broke into a smile as brilliant and direct as sunlight streaming through a window. Her laugh rang through the quiet night like golden chimes, and to Seth's complete shock she threw her arms around him.

It was a gesture of careless abandon, utterly without device. Seth was almost knocked off balance, as much by the surprise of it as the motion. Hope was laughing and thanking him as if he had done her a wonderful favor, as if she hadn't blackmailed him. The manipulative little witch, he thought, half amused. And now did she think to seduce him?

What else could a man think? After all, when a young woman dressed only in her shift throws her arms around you and presses her body against you, a man could only come to a certain conclusion.

He tightened his arms around the laughing girl and drew her tightly to him.

"Such a simple trick," he whispered to her. "But so effective, Hope. I would hate to interfere with your careful plans. . . ." Intoxicating, he thought, more than simply effective. The feeling of warm skin beneath the fine linen of her shift, the silk of her hair spilling over his hands, the soft breasts crushing against his chest . . .

But he was no green youth, no novice of intrigue to be so easily seduced and duped. Hope Garrick had better learn that swimming out of her depth was dangerous, that she was in over her head.

He tipped her head back with a strong hand, tangling it in the thick richness of her hair, and took her mouth beneath his with a fierce purpose. He plundered the softness of her lips with his own, kissing her relentlessly, over and over again. Oh, young Hope would be sorry that she had tried to undo his wit . . .

He employed none of the slow maneuvers of seduction, none of the gentleness he normally would have taken; but let his hands stroke her body as they would, and let the heat of his kiss take its own willful path, into the satin softness of her mouth, tasting her clean, sweet tongue at will . . .

She was kissing him back.

It was the last thing he had expected. She didn't faint, or tremble, or turn to jelly in his arms. It was unthinkable! That this simple young chit, this bumbling little spy could withstand a kiss that would have burned the lips of a seasoned Jezebel!

Not only withstood it but was kissing him back with a skill he had never known, her soft mouth dancing like magic around his own, her tongue moving over his lips like quicksilver, heating his blood to fire . . .

Her slender body was twining around him like a vine, exquisitely soft and warm. Her fingers played along his neck, like the touch of a butterfly's wing, incredibly seductive. Ah, the way she leaned into a man, the almost naked heat of her body, with only a thin covering of fabric between them. . . .

She pulled away and tilted her head, looking up at him, her eyes shining blue-green secrets at him.

Shaken, Seth drew a deep breath as reality hit him.

By God, she had turned the tables on him!

He had meant her to be shaken, to teach her

what was what, to give her a taste of what was good for her . . .

And there she stood, the little witch, meeting his kiss like a seasoned French courtesan, seducing him like a sorceress, with a skill that should be far beyond her years or knowledge; and laughing up at him with nothing but pleasure in her pretty young face.

She laughed again, a shaky little laugh, and brushed her hair off her smooth forehead.

"Whew," she said, laying her hand over her heart. "That was something. Oh, my. That was really something. Not bad. Not bad at all."

And with those brazen words she stepped away from him. "I'd better go back to the house," she said calmly. "Let me know when it's time to leave for Philadelphia."

Unable to speak, his pulse pounding a hot, quick race through his body, Seth simply stared at her. The hunter had been caught in his own trap, the seducer had become the seduced.

She turned fearlessly into the night and walked away. She looked like an angel; an enchanted spirit, all in white, with her hair flowing silver and gold in the moonlight.

But it was no angel he'd held in his arms— she was a dangerous, skilled seductress, with the beauty of Eve and the cunning of the serpent. And, obviously, no simple country girl— and no innocent maid, either.

"Be ready to leave in three days," he barked after her. "Take only what you can carry easily.

And I'll have no shilly-shallying, no tears or nonsense on the road." There, that made him feel a little better, a little more in control of the situation.

From the dark riverbank above him came a sound that sounded annoyingly like a snort.

"As if," Hope Garrick snapped. And if her words were meaningless, her tone was not.

Seth stood, seething in the moonlight, until the sound of her footsteps died away.

Three days. That would give her time to contact her cronies, whoever they might be. Time to arrange a trap, time to plot his capture.

But what Hope Garrick didn't know was that he wouldn't give her three days. They would leave on the following night.

"Sorry, sweet Hope," he whispered. "This journey shall follow not your scheme, but mine."

Chapter Six

"I've got a surprise for you," Laurel whispered to Prudence as they gathered the breakfast dishes from the trestle table.

The kitchen was bright and warm with sunlight. It shone on the pewter mugs and on the wide plank floors, and lit Prudence's blond head to a glowing halo.

The sounds of early morning floated in the kitchen door—the full-throated birdsong and the farmyard sounds of waking animals. Somewhere in the yard, Laurel heard Thomas Garrick's voice, low and measured, and Seth Goodwin's deeper reply.

"What?" Prudence demanded, her eyes bright with curiosity. The dark bruise on the silken cheek made Laurel's heart ache, but Prudence seemed unaware of it.

125

"We're leaving," Laurel whispered. "We're going to Philadelphia. There's a dressmaker there, and Seth Goodwin thinks that she'll take you on as an apprentice. She's good and kind, Prudence, and Seth says that her apprentice girls love her."

Prudence stood stock-still, her rosebud mouth open, her china-blue eyes wide.

"Lawful heart," she whispered after a moment's thought. "To the city, Hope?"

"Yes. Isn't it exciting?" Laurel squeezed Prudence's rough little hand, desperately wanting her to agree. "Just think, Prudence—you'll live in a fancy house and learn to make beautiful gowns, and you'll have a skill. You'll be able to make money, and not have to depend on anyone when you grow up. And nobody will ever hurt you again."

Prudence looked out the kitchen window, her eyes wide. "What will Father say?" she demanded, her voice squeaking.

Laurel smiled, a hard, tight smile. "*Father*," she replied, "won't know."

Prudence was speechless.

"Don't say a word. Not a single word. We just carry on like nothing's going on, and in three days we'll leave. Get it?"

Prudence swallowed and turned to gather a load of heavy pewter dishes from the table. When she turned back her eyes were bright with excitement. "I get it," she agreed, and the look of trust on her round little face touched Laurel's heart.

* * *

She wanted a bath. She wanted tweezers, and a good bottle of hair conditioner. She wanted a blow dryer, and a dishwasher, and a microwave.

Most of all, Laurel wanted coffee, brown and fragrant and rich, in a smooth ceramic cup, and a cigarette to go with it.

She wanted to smoke so badly it hurt. She tried not to think of it, and thought of it anyway. She thought about the way an unopened pack felt in her hand, the caress of the silky cellophane, the way it opened with a little pull. She dreamed about the gleaming silver foil, wrapped as beautifully as a Christmas present, and how you opened the symmetrical folds to reveal the contents of the coveted pack. Cigarettes, perfect little cylinders of white, sometimes with a golden stripe around their filtered ends. The way they rested between your fingers, the sweet taste of the golden tobacco . . .

While she was picking beans from their curling green vines and heating water in great iron kettles and scrubbing linens in steaming pots of stinging soap, Laurel was thinking about smoking. She recited, in her head, a litany of her favorite cigarettes—the first one of the day, always combined with a cup of coffee; the second one, smoked while putting on makeup, the third, in the car on the way to work. . . .

By the time she had counted up to her after-dinner cigarette she was crying, large, salty tears that rolled down her face and splashed into the pot of stewed turnips she was cooking.

"Grandma!" Laurel hissed, turning her face to the vast blue sky outside the window. "Uncle Jerry! Will you two dips get me out of here?"

As usual, the sky remained placid. There was no mysterious breeze, no whispered message, no sign. As far as the eye could see, the green forests and golden fields shimmered beneath the blue skies, unchanged.

Each night, after dinner, after Laurel and Prudence washed the dishes, the Garrick family gathered in the keeping room and Thomas read to his daughters from the Bible. As far as Laurel could see, it was the only book in the house.

It had been the routine every night since she had arrived and, she assumed, every night before that. She and Prudence sat silently in their hard wooden chairs, Prudence usually with some kind of mending in her hands, and they listened as Thomas Garrick droned on and on.

"And the children of Israel did secretly those things that were not right against the Lord their God, and they built them high places in their cities . . ."

Richard Burton he ain't, Laurel thought, listening to his reading. It was stilted, awkward, and without emotion, like the reading of a child who has only begun to learn and isn't comfortable with the words.

Tonight's routine was, thank goodness, rendered a little more interesting by Seth Goodwin's presence.

Dark and silent, his tanned skin and dark eyes set off to perfection by the brilliant scarlet jacket of his British uniform, he sat on a hard bench, leaning against the creamy plaster of the wall.

Whenever Laurel looked up he was watching her, his dark eyes solemn and observant.

" . . . they would not hear, but hardened their necks, like to the neck of their fathers," Thomas Garrick read. Laurel wondered what it meant. Certainly Thomas was giving no clue by expression or inflection. Perhaps he didn't know, either.

Prudence stitched away, her tiny fingers skillfully reworking the bodice of an old gown of her mother's.

And Seth Goodwin never took his eyes from Laurel.

She tried to keep her composure but it wasn't a simple thing. It made her think of junior high school, and how a boy she had had a crush on had sat behind her in social studies class. Whenever she'd moved to pick up her pencil or open her bookbag or moved her head, she had been acutely aware of him sitting behind her. The excitement had been unbearable. Did he like the way her hair looked when she tilted her head? Did he notice the blue of her new sweater? Was he looking at her at all, or was she just another back sitting between him and the chalkboard?

She felt the same way now. Ridiculous, really. She was almost thirty years old and should know better. Or were Hope Garrick's eighteen-year-old hormones playing havoc with her mind?

The idea struck her as funny, and she stifled a laugh. How many times had she wished for an eighteen-year-old body to go with her thirty-year-old mind? And now she had it.

"Daughter," Thomas Garrick said slowly, looking up from the heavy book in his hands, "is there something humorous about the children of Israel?"

Laurel jumped. "No. No, not at all," she assured him. "Most definitely not. Not a comic bunch, by any means."

Thomas swayed slightly and hesitated before speaking. "Then I advise you to keep your merriment to another time and place."

Laurel shot a quick look of resentment at Seth Goodwin, who had provoked all this by staring at her.

Thomas's voice droned on and on, and Laurel stared at her hands. Hope's hands. Borrowed hands.

She wondered if Jerry and Grandma knew where she was. She wondered if they were working on getting her back. She worried about her other body, back in the twentieth century. What if her family decided that her coma had gone on long enough? "Pull the plug," she tried to imagine her mother saying. Thank goodness, she couldn't picture it.

And then—as awful as the thought was—it occurred to her: *What if she never got back?*

What if she was stuck here forever?

Oh, crap—I'm going to die here. I'm going to end up Mrs. Ephraim the Toothless Wonder. I haven't been immunized against anything. I'll never see a bottle of roll-on antiperspirant again. I'll never have another cigarette, or have cold pizza for breakfast. I'll never—

"Hope."

Startled, she looked up.

Thomas Garrick had fallen asleep in his chair, and Seth had caught him as he slid to the floor. He took the Bible from the sleeping man's hands and offered it to Prudence.

"Be ready to leave within ten minutes."

Laurel stared at him in disbelief.

"What happened to him?" she demanded as Thomas Garrick's mouth fell open.

"I drugged him. He'll sleep most of tomorrow. It gives us a better start. We're leaving tonight."

Prudence sat frozen, her silver needle poised above her fabric.

"Tonight?" Laurel repeated. "Why tonight?"

Seth carried Thomas from the keeping room and into his bedchamber. When he came back he folded his arms across his broad chest and met Laurel's eyes sternly.

"Why?" he repeated, his voice cool. "Why, you ask? Because, Hope Garrick, I am no fool.

Do you think I am such a simpleton that I could be duped by an empty-headed, prattling chit of a girl, still wet behind the ears?"

Apparently, it was a rhetorical question, for he continued without waiting for an answer.

"We will leave within the hour and we will do so because I say, and you will remember that I am in charge of this damned journey, and you will follow my orders. No wool-headed, simpering little twit will be my undoing."

Laurel rose to her feet, her face hot with anger.

"Well, since we're sharing, let me say this: No self-important, overbearing chauvinist is giving me orders. You better figure that one out right away. I'm only going with you because I want Prudence out of here before she's seriously hurt. But that doesn't give you the right to order me around, just because you're a man."

"I wish you'd quit saying that." Seth raked a hand through his dark hair, looking extremely put out. "I do have the right. Man has been set above woman as her superior. It's the law of nature and the law of God." His tone of voice on this last inferred that this was the final word on the subject.

Laurel tried to think of a clever response. "Oh, yeah?" she finally managed. It wasn't the sort of reply she had had in mind, but it succeeded in making Seth look irritated.

"Come on, Prudence. Let's pack."

Like a trusting puppy, Prudence followed her obediently from the room.

*   *   *

During the night the green forests were black and shadowy. Their footsteps seemed very loud, and the occasional breaking branch cracked like a shot in the silence.

Laurel pretended to be brave for Prudence's sake, but she wondered to herself how Seth could tell where they were going. By the stars, she guessed.

She stumbled over a rock on the forest floor and silently cursed her heavy skirts.

"I don't see why we aren't taking the road."

"Because the roads are full of British soldiers," Seth snapped over his shoulder. "As far as they know, I'm quite dead, and it's to my advantage to let them think so."

Laurel digested that. Prudence's small hand was warm and solid in her own, and she gave it a reassuring squeeze.

Hope's shoes were heavy and awkward on her feet, and she could tell she'd have blisters before long. Though it must be two in the morning, the night was hot and humid.

"When do we stop?" she asked.

"When I say," Seth answered.

"When I say," she mimicked under her breath. She stumbled again and would have fallen if he hadn't caught her. For one brief, dizzying moment, she felt her breasts against his chest, his strong arm around her waist. Then he pushed her firmly away.

"Try to pay closer attention," he ordered.

Mad enough to spit, Laurel concentrated on

feeling her way through the dark. *Think of Prudence*, she told herself. *Prudence deserves a safe, loving home, a future, the chance to learn a skill so she won't have to depend on arrogant men like this.*

She shifted the weight of her knapsack to her other shoulder and blindly pushed ahead, remembering with affection her favorite pair of Levi's, torn at one knee and softened with age, and her cross-trainers, perfectly shaped to her foot from wear.

It was almost dawn when they stopped, and Prudence was leaning heavily on Laurel's arm, only half awake. The forest was gray, and a heavy fog swam through the trees, giving Laurel the feeling of being in a rain forest.

She spread her hooded cape on the ground and collapsed beside Prudence, kicking off her shoes.

The last thing she saw before she fell asleep was Seth Goodwin, leaning against the sturdy trunk of a sumac, his rifle across his knees.

It was a comforting sight. She slept immediately, knowing that he was awake and alert for danger. As long as he was there, no harm would come to her.

It was a feeling she'd never had before.

"Well, isn't that just great? Isn't that special? Isn't that just too sweet?" Grandma grabbed her floating bowling ball and stuffed it back into her oversized straw handbag. The ball floated out again. Grandma shoved it back in with a glare and zipped the bag closed.

Jerry smiled, a tender expression in his faded eyes.

"I think it's kind of nice, Joyce. I think she's going to fall in love with him."

"Jerry, you idiot. Of course she is. That's the problem. He's supposed to be dead; she isn't. At least, Laurel isn't. Hope is. We're dinking around with history, Jerry, and you know that's against the rules. What if they fall in love? Have children?"

Jerry looked thoughtful. "Hmmm. Maybe nothing. Or maybe one of their descendants will perfect cloning. Or invent a master race that will destroy the world." He gave a wheezing little laugh at his sister's horrified expression.

"Just a little joke, Joyce."

"Well, I'm not laughin'." She wasn't, either.

"Neither am I," announced a voice, and Jerry and Grandma jumped as Nat Goodwin came striding through the clouds.

He looked perfectly composed in his silver-and-white-brocade waistcoat and his perfectly powdered wig, but there was a dangerous gleam in his eye and a threatening lift to his brow.

"Hey, stranger," Jerry said, "you want a beer?" His voice was a little weak, his smile a little shaky.

A frosty brown bottle floated toward Nat Goodwin, stopped abruptly at the sight of his face, and vanished back into the clouds.

"You . . . you . . . bumblers. You want-wits! You . . . celestial twits!"

"Hoo boy," Jerry muttered, rubbing the end of his pointed nose. "Hoo boy."

"Jerry, you idiot," Joyce snapped. "Now see what you've done?"

Nat Goodwin turned on her, fire in his eye. "And you! You were at a Bingo game!"

"I won, too. A hundred and fifty. And you know, that pushy Amelia Earhart expected me to split it with her, just because she watched my cards while I went to the john. Well, I told her—"

"I don't care what you told her," Nathaniel Goodwin snapped. "If you think—" He broke off abruptly as he read the sparkling letters across the front of Grandma's sweatshirt. SHIT HAPPENS, it said.

Grandma beamed down at the message across her broad bosom. "Kind of says it all, doesn't it?"

Nathaniel Goodwin sagged as if he'd been defeated. A lion-legged Chippendale chair floated out of the silken mist behind him and he sat down with a heavy sigh. The chair floated him up to Grandma's yellow linoleum table, and for a moment he simply sat there, looking beaten.

"I . . . I think I'll take that beer," he said to Jerry. "And then, perhaps, we can discuss our next move. It seems that my grandson's destiny has been altered, and it seems that your grand-daughter was the cause. Now, I haven't spoken

136

to anyone about this, but you know there are rules that we can't change. We have to get Seth here, and there's no way around it."

"And Laurel can't get in," Grandma pointed out, "until she's good and in love. And then she's got to go straight home, before anyone goes pulling any plugs on her other body."

"The question is," Jerry said, his wizened face puckering, "Can we do both those things without hurting anyone?"

The three sat silently around the table while the sparkling mists flowed and floated around them.

"Hooo boy," Jerry muttered at last. "Anybody for a game of gin?"

"It sounds like the perfect diversion," Nat pronounced, lifting his white head.

"Deal me in," Grandma said. "And throw some good cards this way. I could use a little luck."

I could, too, Laurel thought, half asleep. She tried to adjust to a more comfortable position, but the forest floor was hard and rocky.

For a moment she couldn't remember where she was or how she got there. She had been dreaming, something about Grandma and Uncle Jerry, but the dream had been vague, and their voices had sounded far away.

She opened her eyes and saw Seth Goodwin. If he had moved from his position at the foot of the sumac, she couldn't tell. He still sat there, his long rifle resting across his knees, his dark eyes canvassing the sky.

Laurel sat up slowly, following his gaze upward.

What time of day it was, she couldn't be certain. The typically blue sky was still shrouded with dark gray, and heavy, dark clouds rolled and boiled above the trees.

The air felt heavy, dense with moisture.

"What time is it?" she asked, trying not to wake Prudence, who still slept solidly beside her.

"I'm not sure," Goodwin answered. "Noon, I would guess. Mayhap a little later."

Laurel pushed her hair off her neck. It felt damp and sticky. Her brown dress .clung uncomfortably to her back. She glanced down at Prudence and noted the sheen of perspiration on the child's sleeping face.

Since she had arrived in Pennsylvania, she had never seen a cloudy day. Maybe a little fog in the morning, but that was all. The sun always appeared well before noon, one brilliant day after another. Not like this. This sky was threatening, ominous.

She looked at Seth and wondered if he was worried.

You couldn't tell by looking. His rugged, tanned face was inscrutable, his dark eyes unreadable.

"Is it going to rain, do you think?"

He looked at her as if she had said something remarkably stupid.

"No, I don't think it's going to rain. I think

the sky's going to open up and unleash the mother of all storms on us. There's a difference, you know."

Even as he spoke, a warm, heavy wind moved through the forest and the trees shivered. A few loose leaves, their green just touched with gold, came loose from their branches and flew like feathers through the sky.

Far away, Laurel heard a rumble of thunder.

Another wind, heavy with moisture, gusted through the green trees, and leaves began scurrying across the forest floor, as if brought to life.

"Should we try to find someplace dry," Laurel suggested, "until it passes?"

Seth rose to his feet abruptly, nodding. The wind caught a few strands of his dark hair and tossed them over his forehead. "Aye, we should. Wake your sister. I don't like the feeling of this."

Laurel knew what he meant. The air felt alive, dangerous. The sky felt almost as if it were pressing down upon them.

She shook Prudence awake, gathering her neatly tied bundle of clothing at the same time. Prudence woke quickly, her blue eyes wide and startled at finding herself beneath a canopy of swaying trees instead of in her attic room.

"We'll have to move quickly," Seth told them, "if we mean to find shelter before the storm hits. There is a German settlement not far from here, if I remember correctly. We may reach it in time."

Laurel shouldered her pack, nodding. The wind was picking up, and it tossed her heavy skirts around her ankles. "Come on, Prudence. There we go." She picked her cape up off the ground and shook the dirt and twigs from its folds.

Another gust of wind rushed through, stronger and faster than before. Small branches began to blow around them, and a twig stung Laurel's cheek as the wind flung it against her.

Behind them through the trees, she could see the horizon darkening to a sooty black. She could almost smell the rain approaching.

Despite the humid warmth of the forest, she shivered.

"I'm afraid," Prudence confessed, a slight quaver in her voice.

"Afraid of what? Don't worry, Prudence, it's just a little wind and rain. At the very worst, we get wet. And that's not so frightening, is it?" Laurel kept her voice carefully cheerful. She was afraid, too. "Don't be a wimp, Prudence. It's kind of exciting, when you look at it that way."

Prudence offered her a shaky smile as she lifted her bundle, and Seth Goodwin sent her a quick look of grudging admiration as he led them quickly down the forest paths.

Not for the first time, Laurel wondered how he knew his way. He followed the natural paths of the forest as if he knew them intimately, as if he was certain of his direction.

Laurel followed, trying not to think of her tired legs, her blistered, throbbing feet, the sticky, itching feeling of her dress clinging to her back. She hadn't eaten, and her stomach rumbled. She didn't allow herself to think of coffee.

Instead, she watched Seth Goodwin, and the way he moved, like a cat, like an animal who knows his territory. His haversack hung over one broad shoulder and rested comfortably in the small of his back. The wind blew the white folds of his shirt around his lean body and loosened his dark hair from the black ribbon that held it at his neck. Unbound and streaming in the wind, it gave him a dangerous, primitive look.

His legs moved tirelessly in long and even strides, up and down the wooded slopes, and Laurel followed him almost as if hypnotized, the wind whipping the heavy folds of her skirts around her legs and tossing the fabric of her cape around her shoulders.

The forest seemed to go on and on, stretching endlessly, swaying branches of green as far as the eye could see. Laurel wondered if he really knew of a nearby settlement. It seemed impossible. They must be miles away from anyplace civilized. It felt as if they were the first people to ever traverse these primeval forests.

At Laurel's side, Prudence puffed and panted as she hurried to keep up with her longer-legged companions. Her face was red and shining with perspiration.

Laurel had no idea how long they walked like that, trying to outrace the approaching storm. Most of the morning, she estimated. It became a rhythm, a mindless act, one foot in front of the other, Prudence huffing and puffing at her side, Seth in front of her, his long rifle like an extension of his arm. Up hills and down, twigs crackling beneath their feet, ducking beneath branches and climbing over fallen logs as the sky grew darker and heavier above them.

When the first clap of thunder sounded Laurel almost fell. It was deafening, powerful. The forest floor shook with the strength of its roar. The sky darkened to a deep charcoal.

Then the storm began in earnest.

The first raindrops began to pelt them, heavy and large and warm. They struck Laurel's face and the top of Prudence's round white cap. They made dark marks across the back of Seth's wind-whipped shirt.

The forest seemed alive. The trees moved and swayed beneath the force of the wind, their branches creaking and moaning, leaves and broken branches racing across the ground like small green animals. The whisper and clatter of leaves was punctuated by the sharp, quick tap of raindrops.

A falling branch struck Laurel's shoulder and she winced at the hard blow, almost knocking Prudence over as she recoiled from the impact.

Lightning crackled across the sky, and for a moment everything was illuminated with a brilliant, electric-blue light.

Laurel glanced at Prudence, whose face was pale and stricken.

"It's all right. It's just lightning." She urged the child forward.

When she looked up she saw Seth glancing over his shoulder at them. His face was set, determined. He said something, but his voice was lost in the sound of the wind and rain.

Even as the sky opened up and rain began streaming down, Laurel couldn't help but notice what an incredibly sexy man he was. The rain soaked his shirt to the shape of his body, revealing the taut lines of his chest, the powerful muscles of his arms and the long, smooth line of his stomach.

Laurel wished she looked half so appealing in her shapeless brown dress, but she knew she more likely resembled a drowned rat than a windswept immortal.

A gust of wind whipped her wet skirts against her ankles and almost knocked her off balance. She grabbed Prudence's arm as she heard the child cry out and steadied her.

The rain was hammering down on them, the drops striking her face and head almost painfully. Branches were waving wildly around them, and sharp cracks rang out when they broke. They either fell to the ground or were flung by the wind.

If one of those branches hits us, we're dead, Laurel thought as a mighty arm of oak went crashing to the forest floor. She pulled Prudence closer to her, urging her to walk faster. She focused on Seth's back, hoping he truly knew where he was going.

At least it was warm rain, she told herself. A summer storm. It could have been worse.

Her skirts tangled on a pile of twisted branches, and she swore as she bent to free them. Rain streamed down her neck and over her bare forearms. Out of the corner of her eye she saw Seth turn to look at them, and she felt, rather than saw, his impatient expression at her predicament, her sodden skirts knotted and tangled in the thorny branches.

At her side, Prudence hesitated.

"Go on ahead." Laurel had to raise her voice to be heard over the wind and rain. "I'll be right with you."

Prudence gave her an uncertain look and then started for the top of the slope where Seth waited. Poor Prudence, Laurel thought. The child looked miserable, wet and frightened. Her cap had been lost in the wind and her white-blond hair was loose from its braid, hanging in wet strands around her face.

Probably wishing she was home, where all she had to worry about was a nice, safe beating, Laurel thought.

The wind blew her hair in front of her eyes. She was clawing the wet strands away from her face and bending to pull her skirts when she heard the noise.

It was a strange, heavy groaning, unlike any sound she had ever heard before.

Startled, she looked up.

It was a tree. A huge oak, ancient and massive. Despite its size, the power of the wind was moving it, and its branches were rubbing together, producing the eerie, almost human moan.

And it was falling.

Time seemed to move very slowly. Laurel was very aware of the giant tree, pushed beyond its endurance, leaning farther and farther into the wind.

And then it gave another sound, a kind of muffled tearing as its roots appeared in a shower of dirt, as if some giant, unseen hand was ripping it from its bed.

And it was falling toward Prudence.

Prudence lifted her face toward the falling tree, her mouth falling open with horror.

Laurel moved. She heard her tangled skirts ripping; she felt her feet touch ground, once, twice, saw the giant tree rushing toward her, saw Seth turning and a brief glimpse of terror on his face.

And then her body collided with Prudence, hard and fast, and they both went flying to the ground as the tree fell.

Chapter Seven

The tree came down where Prudence had been standing only a second before.

It landed with a thundering noise, branches crashing and clattering. The ground shook beneath the impact. It landed so close to them that Laurel could feel the branches as they whisked past her cheek, almost touching it.

For a moment she couldn't breathe. She simply lay on the wet dirt, one arm around Prudence, hardly daring to believe they were alive.

The rain poured over her, plastering her dress to her shoulders and dribbling onto Prudence's still, white face. The child lay motionless, her eyes dilated with fear.

Laurel tried to speak and couldn't. Her stomach felt hollow and unsteady.

"Are you hurt?"

Seth Goodwin was bending over them, his face ashen beneath his tan. Rainwater dripped from his hair. His fingers, long and graceful, reached for her wrist, played over her pulse. Behind him, the green trees and gray sky poured water.

"I'm fine." Laurel's voice was weak, barely audible above the sound of the wind and rain. She swallowed, and tried again. "I'm fine. Prudence . . ."

"Unhurt, I think." Seth's fingers were gently rushing over the girl's limbs, checking for broken bones.

Laurel tried to stand. Her knees shook, and the wind tangled her wet skirts around her legs. She grabbed at the branches of the fallen tree and pulled herself upright.

Seth helped Prudence up, and Laurel caught the child's arm as she swayed.

She looked like a drowned kitten. Her normally pale hair was dark with rain, streaming in wet ribbons over her small shoulders. Her hands shook as she clutched her bundle. Her china-blue eyes stared straight ahead.

This is my fault, Laurel thought. *My fault. I should have left her at home, instead of dragging her out into the wilderness.*

"We've got to find shelter," she said, "quickly. I think she's in shock." She put her arm around the little girl's shoulders. "Come on, Prudence. Let's go. We want to get out of this storm."

Prudence stared but didn't move.

"Please, sweetie . . ."

Prudence stood as if turned to stone, her shaking fingers curled tightly around her bundle.

A large branch came crashing near them, and Laurel's heart flopped with fear. The rain poured from the sky in sheets, one following the other.

"Come then, Prudence," Seth said, and his voice was gentle, with none of his usual arrogance. "Let's go find a dry place, and something to eat." He balanced his long rifle at his side and bent down. He picked Prudence up and shifted her weight over one shoulder. He took her bundle and handed it to Laurel.

"Move fast," he said.

Laurel followed the order without question, following him into the endless forest. The rain pounded and breaking branches cracked and clattered around them. The wind howled like an injured animal.

Laurel stared straight ahead at the tall man carrying the terrified child, the sodden blond head next to the dark one. She put one foot in front of the other and followed him through the storm.

"Not much longer," he shouted over his shoulder.

Against all reason, Laurel felt better.

Perhaps there had been a house there, months ago.

Quite obviously, there had been a fire, as

well. All that remained of the house was a pile of blackened timbers, soaked and dripping in the driving rain.

Laurel felt something crumble inside her, and Seth let loose with a streak of profanity that would have done a truck driver proud.

They stood in the middle of green fields, bordered by split rail and stone fences, staring at the ruin of the house, the wind buffeting their hair and clothes. Across the field a bolt of lightning shot from the black sky, sizzling and singeing its brilliant trail to earth.

Laurel thought she could feel the electricity through her feet. She wondered what would happen if lightning struck her. Perhaps that was the plan, the way to return her to the present.

She turned, looking around them. "Look!"

Down the slope of the hill was a shed, built with thick stone walls and a sturdy roof.

Seth sent her an unexpected smile, bright with relief.

"Come on," he shouted.

Laurel followed him down the slope of the hill, her feet sliding in the muddy grass. The heavy door swung open at her touch and Laurel moved to step in.

She almost fell.

Instead of the firm dirt floor she had expected, there was nothing, a hole leading down into blackness.

She steadied herself on the door frame and

looked over her shoulder at Seth, still carrying Prudence.

"There's nothing there," she explained, raising her voice over the sound of the storm.

Seth looked puzzled. "Is the ladder gone?"

"Ladder?" Laurel looked down, and there was a ladder at her feet. "How did you know?"

The look he gave her told her that she had slipped. She should have known this.

"It's a springhouse," he said simply, in a voice that said he shouldn't have to tell her that.

"Oh. I knew that." Laurel wondered what the hell a springhouse was.

"Carry my rifle," he said. "I can't manage it and your sister both."

Laurel took the rifle gingerly and began her way down the ladder and into the darkness below.

She soon knew what a springhouse was.

It was deep and cold. A sort of cellar, for storing food. Ye olde refrigerator. Not the best place to warm up. It was also very dark and damp.

She took her shoes off immediately, and gasped with relief at the touch of the cold, hard-packed earth against her bruised and blistered feet.

She heard Seth coming down the ladder, his progress slowed beneath the weight of the child he carried.

"Here," he said, when he reached the bottom

rung. "Look through your bundle and try to dry her if you can."

Laurel, shivering in the cold, tried to move quickly. She could feel Prudence trembling in the dark next to her. Far above them the storm howled, and stray branches crashed against the roof of the springhouse.

She could hear Seth rummaging through his haversack, and after a few minutes she saw a spark strike in the darkness, and then another.

"What's that?"

"Tinder," he said, after a brief pause. "I'm trying to light a candle."

Relieved, Laurel said no more.

Soon a slight flame glowed; and then a candle sputtered and caught. The light revealed a room the size of an elevator, with a hard-packed earth floor and walls.

Laurel turned back to the open bundles before her. In the middle of one she found a dress that was not too wet.

"Here, Prudence. Change into this."

For the first time since the tree had fallen, Prudence sprang to life. "Oh, Hope! Oh, Hope. I can't!"

"Enlighten me," Laurel suggested, trying not to sound impatient.

Prudence stared at Seth with round eyes.

"Oh, for crying out loud, Prudence. He'll turn his back. Let's get real, here. If somebody was to offer me something dry right now, I'd strip down in front of the whole British army."

Seth gave a surprised bark of laughter, and Prudence burst into tears.

"We're going to die," she choked out. "I know it, Hope. I'm hungry and I'm frightened. Oh, this is all our fault, Hope. We defied Father; we broke the Commandments." A fresh wave of tears stalled her, and she snuffled loudly before resuming her lamentations. "We're going to be punished, Hope. God sent this storm to punish us."

"Oh, Prudence! I don't believe it. Look, if we die, Mr. Goodwin will die, too. And he didn't run away from home, did he? It must be raining on hundreds of people and not *everybody* could possibly be running away. See? Please, Prudence, just put on a dry dress, and we can eat something and you'll feel better, I swear it."

"Prudence?" Seth Goodwin's voice was quiet beneath the howl of the wind. "Here, will this help?" He reached into his leather haversack and drew out apples and sausages, along with a crusty round of bread.

At the sight of the food Prudence's sobs ceased.

She allowed Laurel to change her into a dry dress while Seth turned his back. Laurel spread their damp capes on the hard floor, covered them with the clothing from their bundles, and wrapped Prudence in a blanket while she ate.

At last the child stopped shivering. She sat, looking around the tiny room with wide eyes, listening to the storm above them. The candle flickered and threw eerie shadows on the wall, and the wind howled like a lost wolf.

Seth leaned silently against a cold wall, his eyes accusing Laurel. *All of this is your fault,* he seemed to say. *The storm, the crying child . . . all of it.*

The storm raged above them, and debris banged against the roof, until Laurel thought she might go crazy.

"Prudence," she said at last, "have I ever told you the story of Cinderella?"

Prudence looked startled. "No, Hope. Is it a Bible story?"

Laurel smiled. "No. No moral; just fun. Listen: Once upon a time there was a beautiful girl, and she worked very hard. Just like you do . . ."

Prudence listened with wondering eyes, and after a while they forgot the storm. When Cinderella was finished Laurel moved on to Rumpelstiltskin, and then to the Frog Prince.

By the time she was halfway through Sleeping Beauty, Prudence was asleep, nestled in her warm cocoon of clothing and blankets. Then they sat, silently listening to the storm raging above them.

"Have you run out of stories?" Seth asked.

Startled, Laurel looked at him. He was sitting on the other side of the room, leaning against the wall. He had been silent for what seemed hours. He had wrapped a heavy blanket of wool around his shoulders. Laurel wished she

154

had one, but her blanket was wrapped around Prudence.

"You're joking, right?"

"No." He smiled, a short, quick smile. "I'd like to hear another story. Try this—I'll start, and you can finish it. Once upon a time there was a farmer's daughter. She was so beautiful that many men loved her, but her beauty was only a disguise. The farmer's daughter had a deep, dark secret. You see, everyone believed that she was crazy, and she pretended along with them. And the reason was . . ."

Laurel took a deep breath. To her surprise, tears stung her eyes. Oh, how she wished she could tell the truth. But even if she did, he would never believe her.

"The farmer's daughter," she said, keeping her tone light and mocking, "pretended to be crazy so that she wouldn't have to marry some toothless creep that made her sick to her stomach. Instead, she ran away from home, was never seen again, and they all lived happily ever after. The end."

Seth raised a dark brow and folded his arms across his chest.

Laurel, studiously ignoring him, tipped her head back and stared up through the dark emptiness, up to the doorway high above them.

"How long do you think the storm will last?"

He shrugged. "Maybe through the night."

Laurel passed her fingers over the candle, trying to warm them. It only reminded her of how cold the rest of her was. Her legs and feet felt like ice; her breath showed in smoky puffs when she spoke. It made her think of cigarettes. Cigarettes made her think of coffee. Coffee made her think of her apartment kitchen, clean and warm and easy. What an effortless thing it was, to load a dishwasher and push a button. To push the top of the electric coffee grinder and have the warm room fill with the scent of freshly ground beans. To get a little chill and turn up the furnace.

"Are you crying, Hope Garrick?"

She blinked rapidly and hugged her knees. "No." Damn Seth Goodwin and his piercing stare. He was always watching her, his beautiful dark eyes never wavering. As if he was waiting . . . but for what? For her to slip, for her to reveal herself . . .

"Are you homesick?"

Even that simple question was hard to answer. *Yes, I'm homesick, for something two hundred years away. No, I'm not homesick for the Garrick farm.*

"No, not homesick. Just cold."

He gave her an appraising look. "But you won't take your blanket from Prudence. Interesting."

"She's a child. I'm an adult."

"Some would say that was all the more reason that she should sacrifice her comfort for yours. You treat her as if she was more important than an adult. Interesting."

Laurel shot him a sharp look. "Would you

stop that? *Interesting. Interesting.* It makes me feel like a rat in a maze."

He looked confused, and Laurel realized that it was probably an expression he had never heard before.

"You *are* interesting," he said at last. "Very much so. You're very brave. It surprised me, today, when you pushed Prudence out of the way of the tree. You didn't cry or complain along the trail. And I can see that your feet are in sorry shape. Most women would have cried."

"Says you," Laurel snapped, irritated by the generalization.

He tilted his dark head and studied her for a moment more. "When the tree fell you didn't hesitate. You rushed into its path. When the branches were falling around you, and the lightning crashing, you didn't panic. You scarcely reacted. Almost as if . . ."

"As if what?" Laurel asked.

His eyes were piercing. "As if you didn't fear death."

"I don't," Laurel said simply. Funny, that he should have noticed, when she herself hadn't consciously realized it. But it was true. She no longer feared death.

"And what about you, Seth Goodwin?" she demanded. "You were dying, weren't you? You were doing the whole floating, going toward the light trip, weren't you? Are you afraid of death?"

His expression was guarded, cautious. He

seemed to weigh his words carefully before he spoke. "I believe that there is a logical and explainable reason for everything. One has only to search long enough to find it. Even that which appears unexplainable."

"Hah," Laurel said. She put her hands over her mouth and puffed against her cold fingers. It didn't help.

Seth watched her like a hawk. "Again, you make no sense. There you've been sitting, for likely three hours, shivering like a leaf. Yet it never occurred to you to complain of the cold."

"Well, what good would that do? It's not as if we could build a fire or anything. I'm sure there isn't a dry piece of wood within fifty miles."

"Interesting," Seth repeated. "Did it ever occur to you that if you complained, I'd be obliged to give you my blanket?"

"You would?"

He smiled again. His teeth looked very white in the dark of the room. "For a price."

"What price?" Laurel asked. She wondered if he'd ask something indecent, and what she would say if he did. Maybe it would be something simple: a kiss. She could handle that. She stared at the shape of his mouth and thought about the time he had kissed her by the river, the dark, flooding heat of it, the way her knees had trembled. . . .

He held out the wool blanket like a gift, his eyes mocking and bright. "Tell me where you got your information."

"Oh, for crying out loud," Laurel exclaimed. She laughed, and the sound was hollow in the empty cellar. "I thought you were going to ask something indecent."

He looked shocked by her bluntness, and by her laughter. He raised a reproving brow at her and tightened his heavy blanket around himself, as if for protection.

It made Laurel laugh even harder.

"You're a hardheaded jade," he said at last, sounding very surly. Laurel wasn't sure what a jade was, but she was pretty sure it wasn't flattering.

"Whatever. Do I get the blanket?"

"Do I get the truth?" he shot back.

Laurel wavered, cold and miserable. "I told you, I read it someplace."

"Half-truth," he snapped.

"So, do I get half a blanket?"

He glared across the cellar at her, his eyes glittering and dark.

And then he sat up and lifted one side of the wool blanket. "Come, then. Half a blanket, if you dare."

Laurel stopped short, her breath catching. Did she dare? Oh, to curl up next to his warm, hard body, to be pressed against him . . .

To be warm.

"You bet your butt I dare," she muttered. She lifted her chin and met his gaze, her spine stiffening at the challenge in his expression. Oh, he was handsome. Oh, the way his eyes glittered over his slanting cheekbones, the strong, firm line of his jaw.

With as much dignity as she could manage, she crossed over to his side and sat next to him.

He enfolded her into the warmth of the wool, his long arm closing around her shoulder, pulling her shivering body next to his warm one. For a moment Laurel resisted; and then she wrapped both arms around him and buried her face into the heat of his chest.

She wondered if he, too, felt the surge of desire that flooded through her body. After a moment he gave a long, ragged sigh. They were both perfectly still.

"You should sleep," he suggested, "while you can." His voice sounded strained.

If I can, Laurel added silently. She was painfully aware of the feeling of his warm skin beneath his shirt, the scent of his damp hair and sweat, the feeling of his breath against the top of her head.

Don't think about it. Think about anything else. Think about how cold you are. Think about the storm. Think about high school. Just don't think about sex. You can handle it.

It was a long, long time before she slept.

The year he was eight, he had met his grandfather, Nathaniel Goodwin, a clockmaker. He remembered going into his grandfather's workshop and seeing an open clock on his table, its works exposed, its key in place. He had turned the key around and around, fascinated by the inner workings of the machinery, the way the springs and cogs had moved and tightened as a result of his touch.

Typical of a child, he thought, to continue a motion without thinking through to the consequences.

He had been fascinated by the mainspring of the clock, watching it tighten and tense; until he gave one too many twists of the key and the entire works seemed to explode.

He felt much like that mainspring now. Tight, tense, tested beyond reasonable endurance.

He had forgotten to think through to the results of his action. For other men, it was stupid; for a spy, deadly.

But he had looked across the cold floor of the springhouse, and the sight of Hope had moved him to act illogically.

He wondered if she had done it intentionally. She had looked so pathetic—her hair loose from her braid and falling in golden waves around her face. She had seemed pale, fragile. Her shivering had made him feel like a brute, cozily rolled up in his army-issue blanket. And the way she had sacrificed her own blanket to her frightened little sister, without even hesitating . . . She seemed not to notice her skirts, ripped and gray with mud, or the leaves tangled in her hair.

Beautiful, like a pagan goddess decorated with earth and leaves. Fearless, like a sorceress for whom death holds no mystery.

And damnably dangerous. Just like the child who had wound the clockspring with no thought of the consequences, he had offered her the warmth of his body and blanket.

The consequences were painfully uncomfortable.

She had fallen asleep hours ago, the little witch. She was quite comfortable and happy.

Seth was in agony. He had never been so tempted by a woman. She was sleeping close to him, the top of her head resting against his throat, the gold silk of her hair caressing his bare throat with every breath. Her arm lay across his torso; her soft hand had fallen to his hip bone. It was impossible not to think of that hand moving back, and down a few inches. . . .

She had flung her leg across his lap, and that was the worst of all. The heat from her thigh burned against him like a fire, making him imagine all too clearly what might happen . . . say, if she was to move in her sleep, or if she was to awaken and shift that thigh fully over the top of him, and let him bury himself in the heat between her slender legs.

He cursed her silently, cursed himself for a fool, and tried to think of things that had nothing to do with golden-haired witches with hot, silken thighs.

He thought of his shop in Philadelphia, and a secretary he was building of gleaming walnut, with careful patterns inlaid. A design of swags, perhaps of white pine? Or a simple Grecian-inspired geometric across the front? Both?

In his arms, Hope Garrick sighed, a hushed, rich noise. She shifted her weight so that her sweet young breasts pressed against the front of his shirt, and all thoughts of secretaries and highboys and walnut and lathes fled his mind. All he could think of was the heat of the young woman in his arms, the way her body felt next to his, the warm smell of her, soap and clean hair and woman.

Hard, hot, and miserable, Seth Goodwin swore again, and began counting to a hundred. He wondered how long it might be till morning.

When Laurel woke up her body was hot with desire. It had been years since her divorce, since she had slept next to a man.

Her thigh was flung over Seth's lap, his hand wrapped around it in a familiar way, like the hand of a lover. His body heat radiated against her; his scent filled her nose. His arm around her shoulders felt perfect, comforting and protective.

Across the cellar, Prudence stirred and made a sound in her sleep.

Laurel pulled away from Seth as if she'd been burned, yanking her skirts from the tangle of legs and blanket.

He woke with a start. "What's wrong?"

"Nothing. Just waking. Look, I think it's morning."

Chinks of daylight shone above them, around the frame of the door and through small cracks in the ceiling. Laurel stumbled to the ladder and began climbing toward the door. She could hear birds singing. There was no sound of wind. The storm had passed over.

"Where are you going, Hope?" Prudence's voice was thick with sleep.

Laurel clung tightly to the rungs of the ladder, anxious to reach the sunlight. "I'll be right back," she called over her shoulder. "I really have to take a pee."

In the darkness below, silence greeted her; and then she heard Prudence ask, "Take a pea from where? What for, Hope?"

"Never mind," she called down. "It's an expression."

She pushed open the springhouse door.

Sunlight burned her eyes, brilliant and blinding. She blinked and waited for her eyes to adjust, before climbing out into the morning.

It was a beautiful day. The surrounding hills and meadows were a tapestry of greens; dark, rich greens and pale golden greens, and every shade between, sparkling in the sunlight. The sky above was clear and bright. It was hard to believe that only yesterday it had been black and heavy.

But the storm had been there. Everywhere Laurel looked she saw fallen branches and downed trees balancing against their stronger brothers. And everything was wet, sparkling and freshly washed in the morning light. The air smelled clean and fresh. The sunlight poured over Laurel, warm and golden. It felt like a blessing.

She stumbled over her skirts as she made her way to a leafy grove. Green; she had never seen a place so green. She waded through a patch of glossy green vines and relieved herself, feeling a little self-conscious.

When she made her way back up the slope Seth and Prudence awaited her. Prudence was eating an apple and holding Seth's hand.

"You look like a couple of vagrants," Laurel called. She was unable to resist laughing. Both of them were covered with dirt and dried mud, their hair flattened and tangled by yesterday's rain.

"You aren't so pretty yourself," Seth pointed out.

Laurel laughed again, looking down at her dress. The brown homespun had never been pretty; now it had crossed the line to downright appalling.

It was ripped from hem to knee and gray with mud, and green moss decorated the knee. A few twigs were tangled in the tattered hem.

"I don't know; it's kind of attractive, don't you think? The homeless look."

Seth smiled at her, and to Laurel's surprise her heart skipped a beat and her pulse raced.

"Never have I met a woman who cared so little for her looks," he said, and he made it sound like a wonderful quality. "You're a strange woman, Hope Garrick."

"Only since she hit her head," Prudence added. "Before that, she was as meek as a lamb."

Seth looked down at Prudence, surprised. "Was she, indeed?"

Prudence nodded.

Seth looked at Laurel again, his dark eyes searching. There was curiosity there, and suspicion, and something that hadn't been there before. Desire, and admiration.

Laurel felt a hot rush and met his eyes without flinching. A flicker of understanding passed between them.

"What?" Prudence demanded, looking from one silent adult to the other. "What's amiss? What are you thinking?"

"That we should get moving." Seth turned away and moved toward the bundles of clothing that lay against the stone wall of the springhouse. "We should reach Haverton by this evening if we make good time. There's an inn there where we'll be safe. Fine, clean beds."

A clean bed sounded like a luxury. Laurel grabbed her bundle and offered Prudence hers. "Let's go."

To her surprise, she found herself wishing that Philadelphia was farther away, that she could travel with Seth Goodwin forever, through the green and sparkling forests.

Her thoughts were broken by a distant sound, a crackling, popping noise somewhere in the distant green hills.

"What was that?"

Seth gave her an impatient glance. The laughter was gone from his eyes, his mouth tight and grim. "Gunfire," he answered, the words short and sharp. "And not too far from here. We'll have to be watchful."

"Whose gunfire, I wonder?" Laurel had no desire to walk into the makings of a future historical site.

"Good question, Hope Garrick. Whose do you want it to be?"

Laurel flinched at the cold look in his eyes, the suspicion with which he regarded her.

He checked the leather bag of shot balanced over his lean hip and inspected the horn of powder that hung next to it before turning his back and crossing the grassy field.

Laurel took Prudence by the hand and followed, her tattered skirts dragging across the sparkling grass.

In the distance, gunshots rang out, echoing under the endless blue sky.

Chapter Eight

She noticed the itching at about noon.

It started around her ankles and slowly began to spread. She stopped walking long enough to scratch, and wondered if the wool in Hope's stockings was giving her an allergic reaction.

Slowly, the itch began to creep up her legs: a persistent, irritating prickle. She scratched through her skirts, shifted her bundle and pulled her skirt up, and scratched again. The itching grew worse.

"What's amiss, Hope?" Prudence stopped and looked over her shoulder as Laurel fell behind.

"Nothing." It had to be the knitted stockings. Laurel tugged them down to her shoes, where they gathered in bulky gray doughnuts around her ankles. Lovely.

She hurried to catch up to Prudence and Seth, who never slowed his pace.

"Look," Prudence said softly, pointing.

A deer stood, as still as a statue, in a grove of birch. It regarded them with huge, startled eyes, and then leapt gracefully away, branches and brush crackling beneath its hooves.

Enchanted, Laurel stared after the wild creature, captivated by its grace and beauty.

"Hope!"

Laurel turned quickly at Prudence's admonishing tone.

"What? Oh, sorry." Without thinking, she had hoisted her skirts up around her thighs and was scratching at her legs. Prudence was staring at her as if she had done something truly depraved.

"I think I walked through nettles or something," she explained. "I've got some kind of rash and it's driving me insane."

"We've been nowhere near any sort of nettle," Seth replied. He sounded as if she was personally insulting him. "I know better than to lead you through nettles."

"Well, we've been near something. Would you take a look at this?"

Laurel lifted her skirt and held out a leg for their inspection. It looked even worse than she had imagined.

Angry red bumps covered her legs. Around her ankles, the lumpy rash blazed scarlet, tapering off to rosy pink bumps around her thigh.

"Oh, Hope . . ." Prudence stared, aghast.

Seth looked at her as if she was the stupidest woman in the world. "You've walked through poison oak. It looks like you did it intentionally."

"Oh, right." Laurel scratched furiously. "As if. I don't even know what poison oak looks like." She had heard of it, of course, but there wasn't any in Seattle.

Seth rolled his eyes heavenward. "Pray, Hope, don't take me for a fool. Any half-wit knows poison oak."

"Well, I don't." She bit the words out through clenched teeth. She was miserable, itching and miserable, and that arrogant man thought she had done it on purpose. The heat of the day was on them, and sweat began to drip down her back.

Seth was glaring at her as if she were a child. "You expect me to believe that you don't know poison oak when you see it?"

"I don't particularly give a rat's rear end what you believe," Laurel snapped, hurling her bundle down. Now her behind was itching, and she resumed her frantic scratching, oblivious to what Seth and Prudence might think.

Prudence's mouth dropped into a shocked *o*, her cheeks scarlet.

"What the devil did you do?" Seth demanded, his eyes narrowing. "Lift your skirts and sit in it?"

Laurel froze. She remembered that morning, hiding behind the trees, wishing for a roll of toilet paper as she relieved herself in a patch of glossy green leaves . . .

"Oh, for crying out loud. I did."

"You did what?"

"I lifted my skirts and sat in it."

Seth stared at her, his dark brows drawn, his face blank.

Laurel twisted and itched, her teeth clenched. "How do you make it stop?"

Seth looked very tired. He dropped his head and rubbed at his eyes, as if he was developing a headache. He took a deep breath and raised his eyes heavenward, as if asking for help from on high.

"Forget it," Laurel advised him. "I've been trying that for days and everyone's busy."

"I told you she was a little mad," Prudence put in. "Now will you believe me?"

His eyes darted from Prudence to Laurel, as she squirmed and scratched, and back to Prudence. He appeared to be thinking.

"I don't know what the hell to believe!" His words were sharp and startling, and both girls flinched.

After a minute he appeared to regain control. "Come on," he ordered, turning back to the trail. "There's a stream not too far ahead. I think mud will help."

"Thank heavens." Laurel picked up her bundle.

He glanced back over his broad shoulder,

shaking his head in disbelief. "I'm a fool," he muttered in tones of resignation.

"That's good," Laurel told him, not bothering to sound anything but nasty and impatient. "They say that the first step is admitting you have a problem."

The scorching look he sent over his shoulder told her that her humor was less than appreciated.

The creek was only a foot deep in the center, clear and sparkling over its bed of rock and sand. There were no tangles of mysterious weeds, no murky hiding places for God knows what.

Laurel, without hesitating, sat down in it. The water was almost lukewarm, but it still felt good against her itching, burning skin.

Prudence stared for a minute, then discarded her shoes and stockings and dangled her feet in the water. She looked almost guilty, as if even such a small pleasure might be sinful.

Seth kicked his pack beneath some shrubs and leaned his rifle against a tree. He emptied the water from his barrel-shaped canteen and filled it from the stream.

"That's what you were doing the first time I saw you," Laurel remarked. "Right before Howard hit you on the head."

He looked up at her, his eyes dark and sharp over the proud line of his cheekbones. "That was a woeful day for me." There was such a mournful sound in his voice that Laurel laughed, even though she felt insulted.

173

"You're alive, aren't you?"

"So far."

"Then you're doing better than I am. Don't complain."

Prudence waded happily into the stream, humming a little tune under her breath. She wandered downstream, dragging a branch through the water and watching the resulting bubbles.

"Don't go far," Laurel cautioned her. "Stay within sight."

Prudence sent her an agreeable smile.

"She looks happy, doesn't she? I think that's the first time I've actually seen her playing." Laurel rubbed a handful of sand over her itching ankles. "That jerk Thomas Garrick never gave her a minute to herself. That poor child worked from morning till night."

When she looked up Seth was staring at her bare legs, as if mesmerized. When he saw her looking back he averted his gaze.

"Work is good for children," he said, after a pause. "What good could come from letting a girl run wild and do as she pleased? She would turn rotten, spoiled and lazy."

"What a bunch of hooey. Play is very important psychologically. When children play they're usually acting out certain behaviors and responses. Like when they play house, they're experimenting with adult behaviors. Exercising control over their environments, so that they . . ."

She had lost him. He was giving her that

what-in-the-hell-are-you-talking-about look.

"Didn't you ever play?"

He looked appalled. "No. I was apprenticed when I was very young. I was too tired to play."

Laurel thought about that. "That's why you're so sour."

Seth looked mortally offended. "Sour?"

"Well, serious. Maybe not sour, but very serious. Don't you ever laugh?"

"There's a war going on, in case you haven't noticed," he reminded her. "And war is serious business. At least, it is to me."

"It should be. You're in a dangerous business, being a spy. Does your family know?"

"I don't have a family. Or perhaps I do; I haven't seen them since I was seven."

Laurel was horrified. She forgot her itching legs and stared at him. "Why not?"

He shrugged. "I don't care to. They were glad enough to be rid of me. They apprenticed me out to the first place they could and didn't really care about the man's reputation. They never even checked to see if I was alive. When I was fifteen I left Trenton. Ran away to Philadelphia and began working for myself."

"What do you do?" Laurel was fascinated. "When you aren't spying, I mean."

"I'm a joiner."

"A what?"

He looked at her, puzzled. "A joiner; a cabinetmaker. I build furniture. I have a shop in the city."

Laurel nodded. "Do you like it?"

He laughed. "I like it well enough," he said, and the smile that played around the corners of his mouth told her it was an understatement.

"I'd like to see your work," she told him, and she warmed at the sight of his smile.

"Would you? When we get to the city I'll show you my shop. Unless you have other plans, of course."

"Other plans? No, I plan to leave Prudence and go back to Chadsford."

"You do?" Seth stared at her, mystified. "I'd not have thought that you'd want to go home. I can't imagine that your father will be too pleased with you."

Laurel didn't know how to answer that. All she knew was that the key to returning to the twentieth century was there on the riverbank where she had met him. There was no way she could explain it all, so she turned her attention to her itching legs.

"We should get moving," Seth said after a few minutes, "if we intend to reach Haverton by tonight."

Laurel sighed, looking around at the sparkling little stream, the lush vines and verdant growth, the trees overhead. Downstream, Prudence was sailing a flotilla of leaves in a race, her round little face relaxed and happy.

"I hate to leave. My feet feel good for the first time since we left."

"This was your idea," Seth reminded her.

"Not mine. I'd be to Philadelphia by now if not for you."

"You'd be dead, if not for me," Laurel pointed out.

She turned to see what he thought of that.

He was staring at her with the same studious, preoccupied look he with which always contemplated her. Laurel found herself wishing for one of his rare smiles, so that she could watch the sharp and solemn angles of his face soften. If he was handsome when he was solemn, he was incredibly beautiful when he smiled.

"What were you doing, down by the river, Hope Garrick?" he asked quietly. "Did you know that Colin Howard and I would go there?"

Laurel shook her head. "No. It must have been fate."

Her words were spoken carelessly, but the moment she spoke them they seemed to increase in importance. They felt heavy with significance. For a moment the forest sounds seemed to stop. The birdsong halted; the waters of the stream seemed to still.

A chill chased down Laurel's spine. And suddenly Uncle Jerry's voice sounded in her head, as clearly as if he stood in the clearing with them. . . .

"You go back for true love, you better find it. Otherwise, you don't get back in . . ."

She stared at Seth, seeing him as if for the first time—the way his dark hair shone in the sun, and the high set of his cheekbones. She stared, mesmerized, at his nose; the sharp, fine line of it, the slight hook in the center, the way his nostrils flared, the way his heavy brows slanted toward it, as if he had spent too much time scowling. His beautiful mouth, an impossibly perfect shape, full and beautifully colored, and the way the corners turned down. . . .

He said something, but Laurel didn't understand the words. Her head was buzzing, her spine tingling. And then again, she thought she heard Uncle Jerry speaking, his voice muffled by the humming in her ears. He sounded very far away.

"It's no good, Nathaniel. He'll never understand her, and that means he won't trust her. Can't have love without trust."

And then Grandma—*"You got that right. Can't win for losing, as they say. Deal the cards, Nat."*

Another voice answered Grandma, presumably the unknown Nathaniel. *"Then he must learn to trust her. As long as they're stopping at the stream, I say we go with Plan C, immediately. But mind you, I don't want Seth hurt too badly. I care a good deal for that boy."*

The buzzing in her ears increased; her vision clouded black and red, as if she was going to faint; and then, abruptly, it cleared, and she was sitting in the middle of a bubbling stream, her brown skirts floating around her itching, rash-covered legs, staring at Seth Goodwin.

"Who the hell is Nathaniel?"

He stared at her, his dark brows narrowing. "What?"

"Nathaniel. Somebody named Nathaniel. Someone who loves you. Somebody who died . . ."

He paled beneath his tan. "Why?"

Laurel felt a little hysterical. "Damn it, who is he? Please, please, tell me he's sensible. Please tell me he's not the kind of guy to do something stupid. He's not the kind of man who'd make a huge mess of something, is he? 'Cause we need all the help we can get."

Prudence, still watching her fleet of leaves embarking, looked up, her round face worried.

"Well, whoever Nathaniel is, I hope you were nice to him while he was alive, that's all I can say, because he's about to start Plan C."

Seth leaned forward, his dark eyes almost snapping with intensity. "What do you mean?"

"Plan C!" Laurel shrieked. "That's what! Plan C! Let's just assume it comes after Plan B and before D! That's all I know, damn it!"

Seth looked at Prudence. "Does she often get this way?"

"Only since she hit her head," Prudence answered, and launched another leaf. "Sometimes she talks to people who aren't there. I've never heard of Nathaniel before."

Laurel buried her face in her hands. For some reason Plan C made her stomach clutch. Foreboding; that's what it was.

"How long does she stay hysterical?" Seth was asking Prudence.

"Oh, don't mind me," Laurel reassured them. "I'm just having a little nervous breakdown here. Nothing to worry about at all." She clambered out of the stream, her wet skirts heavy and slapping unpleasantly around her ankles.

"What are you doing?" Seth asked, as she picked up her bundle of clothing.

"I'm out of here. Gone. History. And if you have the brains of a chicken, you will be too. I don't know who Nathaniel is, and I don't know what Plan C is, but I'm not in the mood to hang around and find out."

Prudence hurried out of the water and grabbed her own bundle.

"Now wait a minute here," Seth snapped. "I mightily advise you to think—that is, if you have any wits left about you. You cannot just go off into the woods alone. You don't know where you're going. You don't have any sense of direction. You don't have any food."

"Then come with us," Laurel urged. "Let's go, before this Plan C action starts."

He stared at her, bemused.

"Do you even know who Nathaniel is?" she demanded.

"Perhaps," was the grudging reply. "But more likely it's just happenstance, just a name plucked out of the air, the thought of a madwoman."

"Mr. Logical," she muttered. "Fabulous. I'm living in the twilight zone, and who do I get stuck with? Mr. Logical."

180

"I think he's nice," Prudence put in, softly.

"Nice? *Nice?* Listen, honey, nice has nothing to do with anything. Trust me, I've got this feeling that something awful is about to happen, and the sooner we get away from here the better. Got it?"

"No," Prudence answered, tears springing to her eyes.

Laurel took a deep breath, wondering how to explain. And then she saw Seth looking at her, pity in his eyes.

"Never mind, never mind. You think I'm a couple sandwiches short of a picnic, and nothing I do or say is going to make a difference."

"I don't know what to think of you," he confessed after a long pause. "Every time I convince myself that you're not mad you do something to disprove me."

Laurel drew a deep breath, wondering how she could ever explain herself. She decided that half the truth might be digestible. "All right. Listen. Sometimes, I hear things. Okay? And I just heard someone named Nathaniel talking about you, and saying that as long as we were at the stream, he was going to start Plan C, and that he didn't want you hurt too badly. Now I don't know Plan C from a hole in the ground, but whatever it is, I say we avoid it."

Seth rose to his feet. "You really believe this, don't you?"

"Hope . . ." Prudence tugged at her arm.

"Darn right I do."

"And you really believe that we're in some

kind of danger if we stay here."

"Darn straight."

"*Hope . . .*"

"And you expect me to believe you."

"Well, that's the general idea. Unless you think I'm standing here babbling for my own pleasure."

"Hope!"

"What is it, Prudence?" Laurel whirled to face the tearful child, and looked in the direction of her pointing finger.

Four British soldiers stood there, scarlet coats brilliant against the green trees, gold braid sparkling. Their muskets were trained on the three travelers.

"Oh, great." Laurel sat down on the ground, heaving a tired sigh. "This is just swell. This is all I need."

"Step forward and keep your hands in sight." One soldier gestured at Seth with his pistol.

Seth stared at Laurel, his eyes hard and cold. "You knew about this," he whispered. "You knew, damn it."

"Not in the way you think," Laurel protested, but Seth was turning his back on her, his mouth set in a bitter, hard line.

Laurel thought of Seth's rifle, leaning against a tree only yards away. Even if he could reach it, it wouldn't do him any good now.

Seth stepped forward, his hands upraised, looking absolutely unconcerned. "What can I do for you, gentlemen?"

"What are you doing here?"

Seth didn't miss a beat. "I'm escorting my cousins to Philadelphia. They've been orphaned."

Mr. Soldier-in-Charge rolled that one around in his mind. "Mmmm-hmmm."

"It's true," Laurel put in.

"Quiet, wench." The soldier was watching Seth with suspicious eyes. "Digsdale," he barked, and one of the other men jumped to attention. "Search their belongings."

Laurel's and Prudence's bundles lay in plain sight on the banks of the stream. Laurel thought of Seth's leather haversack, hidden beneath the shrubbery. What was in it? The British uniform he had worn? The papers Colin Howard had been searching for?

Digsdale, a pale young man whose wig sat askew beneath his tricorn hat, untied Laurel's and Prudence's packs. He scattered the contents: wooden combs, petticoats, spare dresses, Prudence's sewing kit, a wooden bowl, gray woolen stockings, some squares of flannel and a packet of salt for cleaning their teeth.

"Nothing, sir."

"Mmmmm-hmmmm." The soldier in charge had deep wrinkles around his eyes, as if from squinting. He was squinting at them now, as if he could read their thoughts.

"Traveling alone, are you?"

"Yes, sir," Laurel answered. "Alone together, that is."

He gave her an impatient look. "Are you traveling alone?" he demanded again, pointedly ignoring Laurel and Prudence and addressing Seth.

"We are."

"You're not a soldier of the colonial army?"

Seth shook his head. "No, sir. I'm a farmer, just waiting for this mess to be over."

"Funny, you don't look like the type of man to straddle a fence. You look like the type of man who'd be in the thick of things."

Seth didn't reply to that. There didn't seem to be anything to say.

"Take him," the commander said after a moment's thought. "I think he's lying. We can search him, question him later, back at camp."

Prudence shrank back behind Laurel, her trembling hand seeking the safety of Laurel's larger one.

Digsdale produced a length of rope from somewhere and bound Seth's hands behind his back. He tested the rope and, satisfied, took the other end firmly in his hand.

"What about the wenches, sir?"

The commander gave Laurel and Prudence a careless glance, as if he had quite forgotten them.

"Leave them. Let them find their own way home, if that's where they're going. They're of no importance to me."

Laurel stood still, feeling as if someone had kicked the breath out of her.

"Sir . . ." Seth spoke at last, and his voice sounded tight and strained. "Perhaps you could provide the ladies with an escort to the inn at Haverton. I'm afraid they're unfamiliar with the area."

"His Majesty's soldiers have more important things to do than toadying to colonial guttersnipes."

Laurel felt a flush of anger.

"Company, forward!"

Seth cast a hard, sharp glance over his shoulder at her. His eyes glanced at the shrubbery where his leather pack lay hidden, and then back to Laurel.

Almost imperceptibly, she nodded.

The soldiers began marching, Seth sandwiched between Digsdale and another soldier, each holding an end of the rope that bound him.

"God go with you," Prudence called, her voice catching.

He didn't look back.

As soon as the soldiers reached the crest of the hill and disappeared into the dense trees, Laurel began to move. She dove for Seth's pack and tossed it to Prudence.

"Hurry; pack our things." She picked up Seth's rifle. It was as tall as she was and felt heavy and awkward in her hands. She thought of how he carried it, as if it was an extension of his body; how his odd, graceful fingers caressed it.

"Oh, Hope." Predictably, Prudence was near tears. Her hands shook as she gathered up their belongings from where the soldiers had scattered them. "Oh, Hope. Will they kill him? Oh, poor Mr. Goodwin. What will we do, Hope? We'll die here; we're lost—"

"Forget it. I have a firm policy against dying more than once a month." Laurel slung her bundle across her back and pulled Prudence to her feet. "Hurry, Prudence. We don't want to lose them."

Open-mouthed, Prudence stared. "Lose them, Hope?"

"Damn right. We're going to follow them, and we're going to get Seth back."

Laurel set off in the direction in which the soldiers had gone, Prudence trotting behind her. Itching legs and aching feet were forgotten. She was going to save Seth, before something terrible happened.

"Get him back? Lawful heart, Hope! However shall we?"

"I don't know yet. All I know is that we will." The consequences of failure were too horrible to imagine. She tried not to picture herself and Prudence, lost in the wilderness, slowly starving.

She paused at the crest of the hill, breathing hard. Far ahead she caught a brief glimpse of scarlet in the green trees.

"I can't believe those twits haven't considered camouflage. Why don't they just leave a trail of bread crumbs for us to follow?"

Prudence stared up at her, her round face already gleaming with perspiration. "What if they see us, Hope?"

"They won't. We'll make sure of it. Besides which, they don't expect us to follow. Didn't you hear that guy? 'Let them go; they're of no importance.' He thinks we're stupid or helpless, get it?"

"We're not, are we, Hope?"

"No, we're not. I'm going to make him eat those words."

"Lawful heart," Prudence exclaimed again, and she looked up at Laurel with eyes full of awe and admiration. "You are the bravest person I know, Hope. Are you going to shoot them?"

Laurel laughed, warmed by the child's praise. "Not if I don't have to. I don't have the faintest idea how to shoot this thing. Let's go. And remember, if we have to talk, we whisper."

Prudence nodded, and the two set off into the dense and endless forests.

Chapter Nine

"Why weren't you traveling by the road if you were on your way to the city?"

Seth wondered how long they would continue interrogating him. "I told you; my cousin had wandered into poison oak. We left the road to find the stream. We thought that some mud might ease the rash."

"What day did you leave Chadsford for Philadelphia?"

"The fifteenth, I think." They were searching for the holes in his story.

"Why aren't you serving in His Majesty's forces?"

"I told you; I'm a farmer, not a soldier."

The major sat back, dissatisfied. He looked across the darkening campsite, where Digsdale was stewing a rabbit in a pot over the fire.

"Digsdale, some tea, please."

Seth tried the ropes that bound his wrists behind a young sapling. It was tightly knotted. The British were taking no chances. They had taken his boots, and they were giving him no food or water.

The major accepted the tea from Digsdale as graciously as if he was sitting in his own drawing room, instead of a clearing in the forest.

Seth assessed his position. Digsdale and the other two soldiers would take turns standing guard for the night. Unless the reconnaissance team was surprised by a stray group of colonial militia, he didn't stand a chance.

He wondered if Hope would be able to find the main road. He thought of the way she had looked when they had led him away, her eyes dark with shock, her golden hair lying in tangles across her shoulders, her ragged dress wet and hanging in tatters. And little Prudence, her face still with horror, tears in her eyes. "God go with you," she had called.

He would need that blessing. And so would Hope and Prudence Garrick, wherever they were now.

They would never find their way out of the forest. And he would never be able to help them. He knew all too clearly what his fate would be.

If the British didn't get the answers they wanted, they'd march him to the nearest prison and keep him there until they could verify his story. Then, when they discovered he had lied, they'd hang him.

Or they might decide that it wasn't worth the trouble, and hang him here. That seemed more likely. Not a pleasant choice, either way, Seth reflected.

The smell of the stewing rabbit over the fire made his stomach growl. He wondered if Hope and Prudence had found something to eat. Not likely. He wondered if they would panic when darkness fell. There was flint and candle in his pack, if they had the presence of mind to look.

He strained his ears to hear Digsdale and the man next to him speaking as they bent over the fire.

" . . . hang him before we leave," the soldier was murmuring.

Digsdale nodded. "What's one colonial more or less?"

Seth closed his eyes, leaned his head back, and prayed. It was the only alternative left to him.

Over the crest of the next hill, Laurel and Prudence were packing up the contents of Seth's haversack. The sun had sunk beneath the rise of the next hill, and the shadows of the trees were long and dark around them. Soon, Hope knew, it would be completely dark. She suppressed a shiver at the thought, and fastened the clasp of the pack, drawing the straps tight.

"Now, are you sure you can do this, Prudence?"

Prudence nodded.

"The worst part will be sneaking up on them. We can't make one noise. Not until you actually speak."

Prudence swallowed and nodded again.

"What if this isn't what we think it is?" she asked, holding out the corked vial of blue glass they'd found in Seth's pack.

Laurel didn't want to think of that. "It has to be. And if it isn't, we'll think of something else."

Far in the distance, she could see the light of the British fire.

"I think it's dark enough. Let's go." She took the blue medicine bottle from Prudence's hand and tucked it firmly into the deep cuff of the child's sleeve. Her stomach was a tight knot; her heart beat a quick, fierce rhythm against her chest. She had never been so frightened in her life. She held Seth's rifle across her chest, against her heart, as if she were holding part of him.

Seth was leaning against the sapling, his eyes closed, when he heard Prudence's voice.

"Please . . . please don't shoot me."

His eyes flew open and he stared in disbelief as Digsdale dragged the frightened child into the circle of firelight. Alone. His eyes immediately raced around the dark clearing. Where was Hope?

"Look, sir, it's the little wench from this afternoon."

"I have eyes; I can see that." The major rose from his folding wooden stool, the deep lines at the corners of his mouth growing deeper. "Where is your sister, child? What are you doing here?"

Prudence was crying, her eyes and nose swollen. "She broke her leg. She fell over some rocks. She told me to go get help."

Seth's stomach gave a sickening lurch.

"Damn!" young Digsdale exclaimed. "What do we do, sir?" His boyish face showed concern. Seth had met his kind before—young, genteel, more comfortable in a drawing room than an army.

The major shrugged, uncaring.

"I got lost in the dark." Prudence's voice was thick, and she choked on her sobs as she spoke. "I saw your fire and thought you might help me. Please, don't let Hope die." She raised the corner of her apron and wiped at her eyes. "I'm so hungry," she added pathetically. "Please, may I have some food?" Her eyes wandered to the fire and the fragrant pot of stewed rabbit that bubbled there.

"I don't see what it could hurt, sir," Digsdale said.

"She's alone, certain enough," added one of the other soldiers, who had made a round of the campsight, torch in hand.

"Oh, all right," snapped the major.

Prudence dropped her bundle to the ground

as Digsdale offered her a bowl. She took it eagerly and rushed to the fire without waiting for assistance. As she dipped the bowl into the stew, Seth saw a glimmer of blue glass in her hand, then saw her drop something into the fire.

For a moment her eyes met his. And then recognition struck him. It had been the bottle of opiate—the same one he had used to drug Thomas Garrick the night they had left Chadsford.

He looked away, afraid that the soldiers might see the hope and relief in his eyes. There had been enough drug in that bottle to knock out an entire regiment, much less four men.

Prudence sat happily by the fire. Seth noticed that she had managed to fill her bowl before she had drugged the stew. She ate with her fingers, her tears drying on her face. The major looked away, offended.

"You've had your supper; now go," he snapped, the minute her bowl was empty.

Wide-eyed, Prudence stared at him. "In the dark?"

"Damn it, yes! We're not nursemaids, we're soldiers! I've no doubt you'll find your way easily back to your sister. Go on."

Prudence twisted her hands in her apron. "She said not to come without help."

The major lifted his brows. "She did, did she? Well, just you go on and tell her that help is on the way."

"Is that a lie?" Prudence asked, owl-eyed.

The major rounded on the child. "Damn, but you're an impertinent child. How dare you accuse an officer of His Majesty's army of lying?"

"I think you are," Prudence informed him.

"I don't care what you think. Get out of here at once."

Prudence cast a sad look over her shoulder at Seth and turned to go. "If I get lost in the woods," she added, with a pathetic tremble in her voice, "and starve to death, or get killed by wild animals, or go over a cliff in the dark, will your conscience hurt you?"

The officer turned three shades of red and an odd kind of purple. He turned away and found the eyes of his men on him, accusing and condemning.

"God's nightshirt!" he bellowed. "Stay, then. But you're gone at the first light, and you'll keep silent and out of my way till then."

Prudence brightened. "Thank you, sir. I'm sorely afraid of the dark. Are you?"

The officer turned back to his camp table and folding stool. He adjusted the flame of his lantern and studied the papers in front of him.

"Shall I make myself useful?" Prudence ventured timidly. "Shall I serve supper?"

"I don't give a hang what you do, so long as you do it silently," the major replied through gritted teeth.

Prudence smiled sweetly and began ladling rabbit stew into the men's army-issue bowls.

Seth noticed that she gave the major an extra-large serving.

He put it to the side of his papers with an impatient gesture. It sat there, untouched, while he continued to read.

"Busby, more tea." The major adjusted the spectacles on the end of his nose and made a careful mark on the map before him. The untouched stew sat cold beside his maps and papers.

"Busby! Hop to it, man!"

When no answer was forthcoming he twisted impatiently on his folding stool, holding out his cup.

"He fell asleep," Prudence said. She looked down at the sleeping soldiers, lying like abandoned toys next to the fire. "They all did. Would you like me to bring your tea?"

"The devil, you say. Wake them up."

"I don't think it will work. They seem passing tired."

"I said wake them up. Oh, never mind. Digsdale!"

There was no answer from the posted sentry in the dark forest, and the major's thick brows narrowed.

"Digsdale!"

The major stood and took a few steps toward the circle of firelight, squinting into the darkness.

Seth hardly dared to breathe. He was certain that Digsdale, too, had succumbed to the effects of the drug Prudence had slipped them. Whatever his part in this escapade was, it must be coming soon.

Suddenly, Hope was there, stepping into the firelight, his rifle in her thin hands. She pointed it at the major's head. She looked like a witch, her gown stained with mud and dirt, hanging in tatters around her slender forearms and bare ankles, her hair matted with twigs and leaves.

"Everybody down," she barked out in ferocious tones, "or the fat guy gets it in the head." Her hands were tense and the gun shook in her white-knuckled grip.

The major froze, his hands raised.

Prudence frowned at her older sister. "They're already down, Hope. They can't get any lower."

Wild-eyed, Hope looked around at the sleeping men. "Oh. Oh. Well, I thought it was the thing to say. I'm pretty new at this." She gestured at the major with the point of the rifle. "Get down, and keep your hands where I can see them. Try anything and I'll blast your head off." She paused and fixed him with a frosty, steel-eyed stare. "Go ahead," she added, in dry, measured tones. "Make my day.

"I've always wanted to say that," she added cheerfully, casting Seth a smile. "Prudence, get a knife and untie Mr. Goodwin."

Prudence almost tumbled over her own feet in her haste to obey.

"Hope Garrick." Seth thought he had never seen a sight as beautiful as the tangle-haired,

197

ragged girl clutching his rifle. "Witch or angel, I could kiss you. God bless you."

Prudence sawed through the ropes binding his wrists, and he sprang to his feet as the ropes fell away.

"You'll not get away with this," the major warned, from the dirt where he lay.

"Get a grip." Hope raised an exasperated brow. "We've got a gun, you're on your face in the dirt, and you're telling me we won't get away with it?"

Seth bound the major's wrists and ankles with the same ropes that had lately trussed him. He stood flexing his hands as the blood began circulating through them again.

He looked down at the firmly bound man, and then took his rifle from Hope's hands.

"You little fool." His voice was like a caress. "It isn't even loaded."

She laughed softly, gazing up at him. Tears shone like stars in her great green-blue eyes, made all the brighter in contrast to the dirt smeared across her dimpled cheeks.

Seth hesitated only a moment; then he held her stubborn chin with his fingers and drew her face toward his. He covered her rosy, laughing mouth with his own, and felt the sweet heat of her lips melting into the kiss.

Once, twice, three times, he moved his mouth over hers, and their tongues met with a honey-sweet fire. Her hands touched his cheeks, as soft and seductive as a summer breeze, and her body melded into his with a rush of heat.

"Mercy on us!" Prudence gasped.

They broke apart immediately, suddenly aware of the wide-eyed child staring at them, the scowling British officer at their feet, and the unconscious soldiers lying motionless around the campsite.

"I take it you saved my pack," Seth said after a minute.

"Yes. It's right over there, in the bushes."

He took a deep, steadying breath. "Then let me find my boots and we'll be off."

Hope nodded and took Prudence by the hand. "By the way," she added, with a stern look down at the firmly trussed officer, "the next time you tell someone that they're of no importance, you remember this: You may be a man, but you're not a very smart one. Trying to sneak through the forest in a bright red coat banging drums and blowing bagpipes has got to be on the list of top-ten stupidest moves in history. And by the way," she added over her shoulder, "you're going to lose."

Seth thought how sure she sounded. "You're a hardheaded little patriot, aren't you?"

She looked pleased by his remark. "I guess I am." Seth shouldered his rifle, and they started off into the forest, just as they had before—except that now she walked at his side, her hand tucked securely beneath his arm.

*   *   *

"Haverton," Seth said softly. "What think you, little witch?"

The town seemed asleep, except for the faint bark of a dog and an occasional candle glowing in a diamond-paned window.

But it was a town, just the same. The road was of hard-packed dirt, still slightly muddy from the storm. Tidy houses with stone fences and smaller cottages with shuttered windows lined the dark road. Flowers bloomed beneath dark windows, a few silent shops displayed their signs, and the tall, steepled church sat in silent vigil above the village green.

"It's beautiful. Civilized. Perfect."

Seth smiled down at her and shifted Prudence against his other shoulder. The sleeping child didn't even stir. "Perfect? Wait till you see Philadelphia. Look ahead, to the crossroad. There's the inn."

Laurel almost cried with relief. It was a three-storied structure, built of sturdy stone with a steep, gabled roof. Candles glowed in the lower windows, and she could hear the faint sound of voices; she could smell food cooking.

"We'll have to take a good look before we dare go in. We don't want to take any more risks than we have to."

As they approached the building, the front door banged open, spilling light across the wide wooden porch.

Seth halted in the street and put a warning hand on Laurel's arm.

The young man who stepped out into the evening air looked neither menacing nor dangerous to Laurel. With his pleasant face and longish golden hair, he would have looked right at home in the twentieth century, except for his buckskin vest and knee breeches. He took a deep breath of the fresh air and shook his head as if to clear it.

Seth laughed under his breath. "We're in luck. You must have a guardian angel looking out for you."

Laurel almost choked.

"What's this, Stephen?" Seth called out, moving forward into the innyard. "Too much ale already? It can't be much past twelve."

The golden-haired young man peered uncertainly into the darkness; and then the pleasant curve of a smile brightened his face. "Hellfire! Is that you, Goodwin?"

"It is, that. What's the situation?"

"Damn!" exclaimed Stephen, shaking his blond hair from his eyes. "I don't believe it. We expected you three nights ago, at least. Thought you might have gone down at Brandywine, or Paoli."

Seth stiffened, and Laurel saw his eyes darken. "What of Paoli? I've had no news."

Stephen shook his head, his pale eyes darkening. "Nothing good, my friend. They slaughtered us. Kicked our sorry arses. They say General Washington swore until smoke came out of his ears."

"That I can believe."

"Cornwallis's troops are mean bastards. Good fighters, though. And they say Howe's going to take Philadelphia within the week. Congress packed up and moved to Lancaster, last I heard."

Seth swore quietly. "Then it must be true. Do you know where Washington's troops are now? Can you get a message through?"

Laurel didn't move, unable to believe that she was hearing this, that these men were discussing Washington as if they knew him— and they did.

"Now?" Stephen laughed. "Tonight? Not with the amount of beer in my belly. I doubt I could sit a horse. Perhaps Gordon could. Come in, Goodwin, and get off your feet. You look like you've had a bad night or two. Who are the girls?" he added, as if noticing Laurel and Prudence for the first time.

"They're on their way to the city," Seth said, not really answering the question. "And we'll need a room for them, right off. This little one's heavy."

Stephen tossed Laurel an easy smile and held open the door for her as if she was a lady, instead of a bedraggled, mud-covered wreck.

The first thing she noticed in the large common room was the smell of burning tobacco. The past two nights had been so frightening that she had almost forgotten how badly she wanted to smoke. But now she remembered. Everywhere she looked, men were smoking, pipes were blazing, pouches of tobacco lay open on tables. Beer and smoke. The smell of taverns hadn't changed in the past two hundred years.

"Damn, Goodwin! We thought you were dead!" The man coming toward them was obviously Stephen's brother. He had the same pleasant, curved face, the same mild smile. His hair was darker, but the resemblance was striking.

"That's what I told him," Stephen informed his brother. "Listen, Gordon: Can you get through to Washington's troops, do you think?"

Gordon looked less than enthusiastic. "Why me? I'm just a poor innkeeper, minding my own business."

"And I'm King George," Stephen retorted.

Gordon shrugged and gave an agreeable smile. "I guess I make as good a target as the next man, though I think you make a better one."

The smells of roasting meat and strong beer were making Laurel dizzy, and she swayed slightly.

Seth caught her arm. "Let's find Mistress Garrick and her sister a room first, shall we? Then we can sit down and discuss it over a beer."

Gordon took a ring of keys from his belt. "Of course. Sorry. You'll all have to share. We're full up. People leaving the city, people going to the city. Everybody thinks they're going to avoid the British, but they just keep coming, like a damned plague of locusts."

He gestured at Laurel, and she followed him up the wide, dark stairway, Seth carrying Prudence behind her. Gordon held a candle aloft in an iron candlestand, lighting their way down a long, narrow corridor.

The room that he showed them was simple, but after the Garrick farm and three days on the road it seemed luxurious to Laurel.

There was a high bed, canopied in a heavy cream lace, with a matching coverlet, a simple but lovely table by a window, and a handsome wardrobe with gleaming brass handles against one wall. Silver sconces held fresh white candles against the pale plastered walls; the floors were bright with polish.

Bending, Gordon pulled out a smaller bed from beneath the high one, and Seth deposited Prudence there on the clean quilt that covered it.

Laurel was so tired, she wanted to cry with relief.

Seth leaned forward and took her hand, concern written on his rugged features. "Will you be all right? Do you need anything else?"

"Food. And a bath." The words tumbled from her lips without hesitation.

"At this hour?" Seth looked surprised.

"It's not a problem," Gordon said agreeably, lighting the candles. He took the door key from the ring at his belt and offered it to Laurel. "I'll send the maids up. Pay them no mind if they grumble."

Laurel smiled her thanks.

"I'll see you soon," Seth added over his shoulder, and he left the room with their host.

Laurel collapsed onto the featherbed, and when the maids arrived they had to knock twice before she staggered to the door to let them in.

One girl, rosy-faced and white-capped, carried a plate of steaming food, which she set on the desk. She regarded Laurel's tattered dress and tangled hair with interest.

"No wonder," she remarked, as another maid dragged a wooden tub into the room. "I guess I'd want a bath, too, did I look like that."

She gave a good-natured smile that took the sting out of her words.

"I'd be a lot more understanding if they were on the first floor," grumbled the other maid.

"Give over; you've been well paid." The first girl turned her toothy smile on Laurel. "That's your sister, is it? Poor little thing. Shall we wake her up and let her eat?"

Prudence was stirring even as the girl spoke, her nose twitching like a rabbit's at the scent of the food. Her eyes grew very round at the sight of the pretty room and the two maids, one hauling buckets of steaming water in with ill grace and dumping them into the tub.

Laurel pulled back the linen towel that covered the tray and sighed at the sight of the food: stewed chicken and vegetables swimming in golden gravy, fragrant with herbs; a bowl of custard sprinkled with nutmeg and a loaf of perfect bread; pots of jam and honey and butter nestled by its side. Bowls of white glass and linen napkins and silver spoons.

"Mr. Goodwin said you'd be hungry," the first maid said. "I reckon he was right," she added, as Prudence reached for the bread and ripped a piece off with her dirty fingers. "Here, poppet. Let me get you a chair and fill your bowl, and you can eat like a proper lady."

Prudence stared as the girl pulled a ladder-back chair to the table and filled the spotless bowl for her. She held the silver spoon in her hand and traced the simple scroll design of the handle as if she'd never seen anything so lovely.

She probably hadn't, Laurel realized. Compared to Thomas Garrick's mean and stingy farmhouse, this inn probably looked like a castle to Prudence.

The food was as good as it smelled, and Laurel ate with pleasure, wondering if anything had ever tasted so wonderful. The simple custard seemed incredibly rich, and when she uncovered the blackberries baked in its center she sighed with delight.

The smiling maid laughed out loud. "You must have had a rough trip. I've never seen anyone take on so about a custard."

"It's the best custard I've ever had," Laurel announced.

"Well, if you want anything else, you must say so. Mr. Goodwin said you were to have whatever you wanted; spare no expense." The maid looked dreamy-eyed. "Would that a man who looked like that would say that to me. Do you want anything else?"

Laurel thought about it. Between the food, the almost full tub of steaming water, and the featherbed, she was in hog heaven. Still, anything she wanted . . .

"Soap? A bottle of good wine?"

"Right away." The maid was untying their bundles and shaking out their dresses. She laid out a clean nightrail for Prudence and threw their spare dresses over her arm. "I'll take these down and iron them for you. Be right back with the soap. Do you like rose or lavender?"

Prudence let her breath out with a sigh at the thought of such luxury. "Oh, Hope, say rose."

"Rose is good."

Ten minutes later, Laurel lowered her naked body into the steaming tub, while Prudence stared with a combination of awe and horror.

"Oh, Hope, however do you dare?" Prudence seemed to think that washing was a quick road to death, and that an all-over naked bath was not only a direct route to pneumonia, but sinful as well.

"I dare, all right." Laurel scrubbed the bar of soap into her hair and dunked her head beneath the water. She emerged laughing, and reached for the glass of wine next to the tub. "Ah, this is good."

Prudence dipped a piece of bread in the jam and ate, a thoughtful expression on her face. "Hope, do you suppose it's this grand in Philadelphia?"

Laurel lathered her hands and scrubbed her neck. "Grander. Seth says it's the most beautiful city in the world."

Prudence shook her head in wonder.

"And Prudence, that's why I'm taking you there. If you can learn a trade and learn to take care of yourself, you can live like this. Forever. Good food and nice clothes and pretty furniture."

Prudence seemed dazzled by the thought. "But what will you do, Hope?"

Laurel froze for a moment and turned her attention to washing her bruised and blistered feet. "I haven't decided yet," was her noncommittal reply. Thank heaven, the child seemed to accept it.

There was a knock on the door, and the rosy-cheeked maid returned, bearing their freshly ironed dresses and a stack of clean towels. She laughed at the sight of the empty tray and bid them good night as she carried it from the room.

"Just think," Prudence mused. "To have eaten all that, and not have a single dish to wash."

"Amen," Laurel agreed, climbing from the tub and drying herself. She would have stayed in all night gratefully, but the water was cooling and, afraid or not, Prudence was going to bathe too.

The rose-scented soap proved enticing

enough to ease Prudence's distrust of bathing, and within an hour the child was scrubbed, in a fresh nightgown, and asleep in her trundle bed.

Dressed in a clean shift, Laurel sat beside the sleeping child, working a wooden comb through the tangles of her hair. Prudence's innocent question had disturbed her more deeply then she liked to admit.

What would she do when she left Prudence in Philadelphia? Make her way back to Chadsford and find her way back to the twentieth century? Of course; it was the only answer.

But it would be hard to leave Prudence. And harder still, she admitted, to leave Seth Goodwin.

She closed her eyes and buried her face in her hands, not wanting to acknowledge what was becoming more and more obvious with each passing day—that in Seth Goodwin, she had at last found the man she'd dreamed of.

Jerry and Nathaniel sat side by side on an overstuffed sofa, a bowl of potato chips floating between them. Jerry was wearing a pair of fleece-lined bedroom slippers; Nathaniel's white wig was resting on the arm of the couch, revealing his own thin hair.

They both stared with glazed eyes at the blaring TV in front of them.

On the screen, a smiling game-show host

beamed at his contestants. "Spin the wheel or solve the puzzle?"

A helmeted Viking stroked his beard. "Spin!" he bellowed. "Come on, big money!"

"Four hundred."

Jerry, his eyes never leaving the TV set, pulled a beer from the clouds and offered it to Nathaniel. Nathaniel took it and flipped the cap over his shoulder into the white mists.

"Solve it, lack-wit," he shouted at the Viking on TV.

"Can you solve the puzzle, Mr. Erickson?" the TV host asked.

"A stitch in time saves none!" roared the Viking, shaking his sword. The studio audience groaned.

"Miss Ross?"

The cheery colonial woman smiled at the host. "I should know this one, Pat. A stitch in time saves *nine*." The studio audience burst into delighted applause.

"Turn it off!" Grandma bellowed, and the TV set beat a hasty retreat into the white clouds.

"Hey!" Jerry exclaimed, "I was watching that!"

Grandma waved a piece of paper at them. "Look at this! Just read this, would you?"

"We can't, unless you quit waving it around," Nathaniel pointed out.

Grandma glared at them both. "Fine. Listen to this. 'Inventory problem in your area. Possible late arrival. Please facilitate census and return results ASAP. Peter.'"

Jerry and Nathaniel looked stricken.

"Facilitate," Grandma repeated, scowling at the note. "Fancy-schmancy. He can't say 'do,' like everyone else; he has to say 'facilitate.'"

"Joyce, be nice."

Grandma scowled, and straightened her beer-can hat. "I can't help it, Jerry. That Peter gets on my nerves, with his holier-than-thou attitude."

"He *is* holier than thou," Nathaniel pointed out. "The man's a saint."

"That's more truth than poetry," Jerry agreed.

"Fine. Mr. Fancy-schmancy aside; does anyone have any ideas of what we should do?"

"Is Laurel in love yet?" Nathaniel asked, straightening his cravat.

"She's butterflies in her stomach in love, but not head over heels. Any ideas on speeding things up?"

"Sex is good," Jerry suggested helpfully.

"How would you know? You can't remember that far back," Grandma said rudely.

"Hey!" Jerry said, looking offended.

Nathaniel guffawed.

"Well, if that's the plan, we should definitely get Prudence out of the way," Grandma said after a moment's thought. "Children and passion just don't work well together."

"The sooner they get to Philadelphia, the better," Nathaniel agreed.

"Done. And we'll just pretend we never got the note. We ought to get at least two late notices before they call the Boss." Grandma crumpled the offending paper in her hand. "But we'd better get moving. I don't want a demotion."

"We'll get right on it," Jerry promised, and Grandma bustled away into the sparkling mist, satisfied.

Jerry and Nathaniel exchanged glances and settled back onto the couch.

The potato-chip bowl flew obligingly up to them, and the TV scooted forward and turned itself on.

"And our next contestant is here from the beautiful city of St. Petersburg; let's give a warm welcome to Mrs. Alexandra Romanov! Tell us a little about yourself, Alexandra!"

"Well, Pat, in addition to being an empress, I'm a mother of five. I collect tiaras and religious icons, and in my spare time I enjoy shopping and oppressing the masses."

"Hoo boy, she's a bright one," Jerry said. "You want a beer?"

"To be certain. Shouldn't we get to work? Or should we wait till the show's over?"

"Wait. And after this is 'The Young and Relentless.'"

"Wonderful," Nathaniel said, and took a handful of chips.

Chapter Ten

She thought she heard Grandma and Jerry bickering, but the sound was faint and far away, and she knew it was just a dream. Laurel was sleeping, a rich, warm sleep, and for a moment she was reluctant to leave it, but the sunlight was insistent and bright against her eyelids, calling her back to the waking world.

For the second morning in a row, Laurel woke up with Seth's arm around her. She knew without opening her eyes that it was him; she knew by the scent of him, by the heat and weight.

He was curled around her body as if they had always slept like that, as if his arm belonged wrapped around her shoulders, as if his hand was supposed to be lying against her stomach.

The morning air was warm and damp, the

chest against her back warm with a sheen of moisture.

She gave a languid stretch and nestled her body closer to the heat of him. He made a contented sound in his sleep, and his hand tightened against her stomach and pulled her more tightly against him.

Bliss. The feeling of his long legs behind hers, and how perfectly she fit against him, and the possessive touch of his hand against her belly, and the heat of his breath against her neck, and how it warmed her blood. She wriggled closer to him, and sighed as she felt him growing hard against the pressure of her thigh. His lips pressed against her neck and . . .

"Hope?"

She froze, and her eyes flew open.

Prudence was sitting up on the trundle bed, fully dressed, her clean hair gleaming white in the morning sunlight. She was staring at her older sister with interest.

"You're sleeping in the same bed as Mr. Goodwin. Are you going to marry him?"

Seth's hand, which had been moving in a slow, sensuous pattern over Laurel's belly, stopped dead.

"No." Laurel pulled the heavy coverlet farther up over her shoulders.

"But I thought that—"

"Hey, Prudence, aren't you hungry?"

The child blinked, then smiled. "Oh, yes. Do you smell the food? It smells like ham, doesn't it?"

214

"Why don't you go downstairs and have breakfast?"

Prudence beamed and jumped to her feet. "May I?"

"Go ahead. I have to talk to Mr. Goodwin about something. I'll be down in a little bit."

Bright-eyed and curious, Prudence rushed out the door, eager to see the workings of an inn, her sister's compromising position already forgotten.

The door closed behind her with a solid bang.

Laurel lay without moving for a moment, suddenly aware of what she'd done. She'd sent Prudence away to be alone with a man. He probably thought she was a tramp.

She turned her head to look at him. How strange, that he already seemed so familiar. He lay as if asleep, one arm thrown over his head, his skin dark against the white sheets. A day's growth of beard darkened his jaw, giving him a disreputable look.

As if he felt her gaze upon him, he opened his eyes. He said nothing; just looked at her with his deep brown eyes, as if weighing her thoughts.

Laurel swallowed, suddenly nervous. "What time did you come in last night?" she asked, and the words sounded funny, modern, the kind of question a wife might ask her husband.

"Late." His voice told her nothing; his expression was inscrutable. His hand was heavy against her waist, but he made no move to take it away.

They were close, so incredibly close that she could feel his breath against her cheek. Her pulse was quick and unsteady, and her lips trembled a little as she leaned forward.

"Hope . . ." There was a slight note of warning in his voice, but Laurel ignored it. She kissed his mouth very softly, tasting the warm skin. She traced the full, rich curve of his bottom lip with her mouth, and feather soft, touched a kiss to the slight downward curve at the outer corner and rubbed her cheek against his.

She pulled back and waited.

His dark eyes were full of light and heat. "Witch," he whispered, and the word was like an endearment. He reached out and took a handful of her hair, letting the gold of it slide across his fingers. "Oh, Hope. Do you know what you're doing?"

"You bet I do."

He looked surprised at her quick response; and then he laughed a little. "Then, by all means, don't stop."

Laurel sat up, raking her heavy hair off her shoulders. She was suddenly very aware of the way the sunlight shone on it and through the thin cotton of her nightshift. And most of all, she was aware of Seth's eyes on her, hot and hungry.

"One minute." She slipped from the bed and padded across the floor to slip the bolt into place. When she turned back to the bed he was sitting up on one arm, watching her.

"You're a bold wench," he murmured, but a dimple played at the corner of his mouth, as if he liked bold wenches.

"Am I?" Laurel asked, leaning against the door. Good; she felt bold. She felt seductive and wanton and hungry for him. The desire in his eyes heated her blood, encouraged her to go farther.

"Suppose I was to do this . . ." She bent down with an easy motion, lifted the thin fabric of her nightgown, and pulled it over her head. "What would you think then?" She shook her hair out and felt it tickle her back and hips. She tossed the nightgown aside.

The morning sunlight streamed through the window and lit her slender body with incandescent light. It shone in her hair, glittering like spun gold, and Laurel felt the heat on her skin as keenly as the heated blood that flickered through her veins.

And Seth, dark and powerful-looking against the white sheets of the bed, stared at her with hot desire, passion and surprise mingling in his eyes. "I'd say you were the most forward and wanton little witch I've ever seen." His gaze rushed over her from head to foot, and she shivered at the intensity of it. "And," he added softly, "you're as beautiful as you are bold. And well you know it. Come to bed, Hope Garrick, and show me what else you know."

Shameless and seductive in her nudity, Laurel made her way back to the bed, suddenly very aware of the sway of her own hips and the graceful line of her slender arms, and the way the sun lit her hair. She felt the power of her own sexuality more keenly than she had ever felt it before, and saw it reflected back at her from the smoldering depths of Seth's eyes.

He grasped her waist the second she was within reach and tumbled her to the bed beneath him, kissing her with hard, burning kisses, gently biting her neck.

Their mouths met, hungry and hot, their tongues mingling in a satiny embrace that turned Laurel's blood to a hot liquid, and she arched against him.

"Temptress," he whispered, and his breath was hot against her ear. His hand traveled over the soft skin of her shoulders and covered her breast. She stiffened and arched into his touch. She almost purred beneath his body as she rubbed against him like a cat.

He raised himself away from her, watching her with hot eyes. "You surprise me, Hope Garrick. You're no simple little country girl, who hides her eyes at the sight of a man's body."

Laurel laughed softly, running her hands over the firm width of his chest, the taut skin of his stomach, and up again over the sleek muscles of his shoulders. "Hide my eyes from this? You do think I'm crazy, don't you?" Her hands slid down to his hips and she felt the fabric of his breeches. Unable to resist, she reached for him, boldly, and closed her hand over the hot, hard length of him.

He let out his breath with a long, shuddering sigh, and swore softly. Then he bent over her and took her mouth beneath his own with a savage, fierce hunger.

Laurel met his kisses with equal intensity, her pulse pounding a dark, fierce rhythm through her body. Each touch of his hands burned a hot magic through her body, every kiss drew her deeper into the sweet delirium that darkened her mind.

Their kisses were fire-hot and fierce and their hands were hungry and desperate, as if this was their only chance to feed the long-smoldering fires of their passion.

And then Seth peeled his breeches from his fevered body and pinned her beneath him, his hand shaking as he stroked her flushed, damp cheeks. "Hope," he murmured, his voice husky. "Little witch. I don't know what man taught you these wanton's tricks, but by all that's holy, I swear I will drive him from your mind."

Laurel, shaken by the possessive fire that burned in his dark eyes, didn't protest. She simply smiled and arched her hips beneath his slender, strong ones, opening to him. She could feel his hardness, hot and demanding, lying against the heat of her body, and she welcomed it.

He drew in a long, sharp breath and pushed into her.

Hope Garrick was a virgin.

It had never occurred to Laurel, lost in her

desire for this beautiful, hot man, that Hope might be a virgin. As a matter of fact, she had become so used to being Hope that she had ceased to think of them as separate people.

Seth seemed as shocked as she was. He froze, staring at her with something between disbelief and betrayal.

"You're a virgin," he said, sounding horrified.

"I forgot."

"What in the hell do you mean, you forgot? How can a woman forget something like that? If I had known, Hope—"

"Shut up," Laurel said, her voice husky with passion. "Just shut up." She wrapped her long legs around his and thrust herself up with a fierce, hungry movement.

For a moment she was stunned by the burning sensation, the pain. She wondered if it had felt like that the first time she had lost her virginity and she had simply forgotten. She wondered if she was the only woman in the world who'd had to think about that.

And then Seth made a sound—a low, soft groan deep in his throat—and she reached up to touch his face with trembling fingers.

He stared at her with eyes dark and soft with tenderness and gently kissed her cheeks, her forehead, and her mouth, until her blood began to race again and she began to move beneath him. Her body quivered at his touch; her hips rocked her against the smooth, hard length of him, seeking the release she knew would follow.

Stunned by her ready passion, lost in the tight, hot softness of her body, Seth Goodwin forgot his resolve to treat his virgin seductress gently and thrust into her body with hot, rapid motions, over and over again, until she cried out beneath him like a woman gone mad and his own world exploded into blackness and brilliance, like a lightning-filled sky.

He was more confused than ever.

Hope had been virgin; that was indisputable. He had felt the barrier, felt the tearing; her virgin blood was dark across his own body and smeared across the pristine sheets of the bed. He had felt the incredible tightness, heard her release her breath in a hiss of pain.

And yet, her behavior had not been that of an innocent. The way she had flaunted her body in the sunlight, clean and gleaming ivory and gold, and the way her hands had played over him, the bold way she had stroked and fondled him . . .

Hardly the actions of an inexperienced girl. But where had she learned such things?

He rolled over in the bed and raised himself on one arm. Hope was dressing, doing her hair in the mirror, unaware of his observation. Good. Seth had learned that when people think themselves unwatched their motions and behavior are most revealing.

She was examining her own reflection with

a bemused expression, tilting her head this way and that. Her blue-green eyes were dark and solemn. There was no vanity in her expression, even though she was enchantingly lovely. Instead he saw concern, and a dark, brooding look that had no place in a face so young and lovely.

She noticed his scrutiny and smiled over her shoulder, a satisfied cat smile. Not the look of girl who'd just lost her virginity.

"No tears, Hope?"

She looked confused. "Tears? I thought it was wonderful."

"What about the loss of your maidenhead, Hope? Does it mean nothing to you?"

"Oh. That. Well, no. Not much, I guess." She turned back to the mirror. She tried several times to pin her hair up, but it kept sliding down her neck. After a few attempts she began to braid it.

Seth found himself becoming worried by her apparent lack of concern. "You don't think I'll marry you, do you? Because I won't."

She raised her dark brows and gave him a cool look. "Excuse me? Excuse me? I have absolutely no intention of getting married, to you or anyone else. Ever. The end." She turned her back and muttered something under her breath that sounded inexplicably like *butt face*.

"Don't be ridiculous. Of course you'll marry. What else is there?"

She looked at him as if he had said something stupid.

"Try this: As long as I'm not married, nobody can louse up my life. I'm in charge of my own life. I'm the captain of the ship; I'm the commander-in-chief; I'm the big cheese—"

"I was with you up until the cheese part."

"Whatever. The point is, I don't want to get married. Nothing personal, you understand. It just doesn't float my boat."

"I see," Seth said, feeling oddly insulted. Float her boat, indeed. What utter nonsense. He reached for his breeches on the floor with as much dignity as he could muster. Somehow, he felt like the wronged virgin instead of the ravishing villain.

"Look here," he said, after a moment's reflection, "women simply can't go around sleeping with men and refusing to get married."

Hope was lacing her gown, the blue-and-white cotton with a floral stripe that accented the blue of her eyes, the gold of her hair. She looked up from her task and met his eyes. "Why not?" She wrapped her golden braid into a knot on the back of her head and pinned it there with brisk, no-nonsense motions.

"Why not?" Seth repeated. "Why not? Because it's immoral, for one thing. Only a harlot would ever consider such a thing."

"So, does that make me a harlot?"

"No. I mean, yes, if you were to continue such behavior."

"Let me get this straight," she said with a gleam of mischief in her blue-green eyes. "A woman who sleeps with a man with no intention of marriage is a harlot."

"Correct," Seth agreed.

"So, what does that make you?"

Seth felt a vein pulse in his forehead. "A man, damn it. After all, I had no idea you were a virgin. You certainly didn't act like one."

"Oh, and you're an expert? Just how many virgins have you deflowered, Mr. Morals Expert?"

"Two," he snapped. "You and my wife."

She went white and the hairbrush fell from her hand and clattered to the floor. She bent to pick it up, her head down, her expression hidden. The sunlight coming through the window was brilliant against the top of her head.

"Hope."

She looked up, and Seth felt cruel. Her soft mouth was set in a hard, tight line, her eyes dark with grief. She looked like she'd been kicked.

"I'm sorry. That was unkind of me. Jane has been dead for four years now."

She exhaled softly. "I'm sorry," she said. "Was it horrible? Did you love her? How did she die?"

Seth reached for his shirt and pulled it over his head. "How odd you are," he commented. "Did your mother teach you nothing? You should say, 'Forgive me if I have mentioned something that causes you grief,' or, 'My condolences on your loss,' or some such thing. Instead, you ask me questions as if you have a right to know."

She said nothing to that, simply walking to the window and staring out at the innyard. "Sorry."

Seth dressed in silence, thinking of Jane. He had been barely twenty when he married her, young and idealistic and mad to possess her. Little, quiet Jane, with her doelike eyes and modest behavior. She had cried with horror when he took her virginity, her eyes closed and her hands curled into fists. He had tried to be gentle; he had promised her that it would get better.

It never did. She hated the marriage bed; she always lay still and tense beneath his body. It made him feel like a brute, like an animal, and after a while he ceased his unwanted attentions.

Soon it seemed as if they led separate lives beneath the same roof; Jane and her church meetings and sewing circles, he and his shop and his furniture. A travesty of a marriage, a sham. And then she had succumbed to influenza, and she slipped out of life as quietly and modestly as she had lived. She died almost politely, as simply as if she had walked into the kitchen and never come out.

And he had felt only guilt and relief. By the time she died, Jane was a stranger to him.

"Hey." Startled, Seth looked up. Hope reached down and stroked his cheek, her eyes as tender as her gesture. "I'm sorry. I really am."

He caught her hand and pressed his lips to her wrist, feeling the warm pulse beneath his lips. Sweet, crazy Hope. Beautiful, wild, lusty Hope.

How different marriage would have been with a woman like this.

Like a thirsting man drawn to water, he found himself drawn to her lips. He kissed her softly, his tongue finding the warmth of hers and slipping over the satin heat, feeling her breath mingling with his. And she kissed him back, with a hunger that matched his own perfectly.

There was a sweetness, a perfection in their shared kiss that almost frightened him. It was as if their souls had touched and, having touched, could never be complete without the other.

Seth reminded himself that he wasn't a fanciful man. It was hard to remember, when he felt as if he had been caught in an enchantment.

"There you are!" Prudence sat at a table in the common room, empty plates littering the table before her.

Laurel sat down next to her, reaching for a basket of rolls. "These look so good."

"They are. Everything is." Prudence beamed across the table. "Isn't it exciting? Isn't it wondrous? Will we be staying here long, Hope? When will we leave for Philadelphia?

226

Are you going to marry Mr. Goodwin?"

"Where did you get that idea? I'm not going to do anything of the sort."

"Then you could stay in Philadelphia," Prudence said, her eyes pleading and anxious, "and be near me."

Laurel toyed with the hard roll in her hand. She tried to imagine herself staying here, trussed into stiff dresses and pinched shoes, never being able to jump in a shower. Heating water over a fire every time she wanted to wash her hands in warm water, emptying chamber pots every morning. Horrible.

And she tried to imagine herself leaving Seth and Prudence.

Was it just as horrible, or worse?

"You look a sight better this morning than you did last night."

Startled, Laurel looked up. It was Stephen, who had been on the front stairs when they arrived last night.

"That's not saying much," she pointed out, thinking of how she had looked, tattered and muddy, with her hair in mats and tangles.

Stephen laughed at her wry remark; and then, to Laurel's delight, he said the most wonderful words she'd ever heard.

"Would you like some coffee?"

"Yes. Yes, more than I want air to breathe."

It was bitter and weak, but it tasted better than imported Italian beans to Laurel. She drank it black, not bothering with her normal dollop of cream and two spoons of sugar, and

227

was just draining the last of the mug when the front door of the inn flew open with a crash.

A young boy stood there, maybe seven years old at the most, his breath coming in hard gasps, his cheeks flushed. His eyes darted around the room until they lit upon Stephen, standing by Laurel's table, pot of coffee in hand.

"Soldiers, Stephen. Ten of 'em. Father said to run and tell you, quick."

Stephen set the iron pot down with a dull thud.

"Where?"

"Just past our farm. I ran like the devil was on my heels to get here."

"Damn." Stephen's usually mild eyes were sharp and dark. He grasped Prudence's shoulder. "Run upstairs and tell Seth. We'd better move while we can."

Laurel watched as Prudence raced out of the room and up the stairs, her white-blond braid bouncing down her back. Stephen crossed the room with quick strides and spoke to a group of men smoking pipes by the bar. They dispersed quickly, grabbing hats and jackets from the backs of chairs.

One of them turned to look at Laurel briefly, his face puzzled, as if he knew her and couldn't place her. She wondered if this might be someone who had met Hope. Had she seen him before? Thin, pointed nose, small, piggy eyes, very pale face under a head of sandy hair.

And then the man was gone, leaving her

with the feeling that she should have recognized him.

The boy who had delivered the news ran from the room, back out into the sunshine.

Laurel tried not to panic. What did it mean? Would there be a fight in this peaceful town, or were the soldiers simply passing through? With a final look at the steaming pot of coffee, she gathered her skirts in her hands and rushed toward the stairs, trying not to trip on the bulky fabric.

Seth was already halfway down the stairs with Prudence behind him, hastily gathered bundles hanging from his arms, his rifle hanging over his back.

"We're going," he greeted Laurel.

"Gee, I kind of thought so." She grabbed her pack from him and fell into step beside him.

"Can you ride?" he asked her abruptly.

"No. Never have in my life."

"Damn." He crossed the main room of the inn with long, hurried strides, and Laurel and Prudence clattered behind him, out into the sunlit innyard. "Would you like to learn?"

"Do I have a choice?"

He gave her a quick smile that didn't reach his eyes. "Not unless you plan on spending another evening with our companions of yesterday. And I don't think they'll give us another opportunity to escape them."

Laurel thought of the soldiers she and Prudence had drugged, the colonel she had left bound in the forest. No, they probably weren't too pleased with her. "Are they the same soldiers?"

"Mayhap. I hear there are ten of them, and that's more than we met by the creek. But there's a chance. And I don't take chances. The sooner we're in Philadelphia, the better off we will be."

The stables of the inn were a long, low building, open along one side, and Stephen was leading two horses out, already saddled.

The animals looked huge to Laurel, their hooves and mouths enormous.

"God go with you, Goodwin. May we meet again soon."

Seth gave Stephen a brief smile. "And you. I hope your brother's back within a fortnight. Keep your ears open."

Stephen sent them a carefree smile. "Who, me? I'm just an innocent innkeeper."

There was a hard look in his eyes that gave the lie to his merry words, and Laurel shivered, suddenly conscious that she was riding away with an American spy, into British-occupied territory.

She was in the middle of a war, and people died in wars.

And then she felt a thrill of excitement unlike anything she had ever known. She was part of history; she had saved an American patriot from an unjust death and helped a message go through to General Washington. Perhaps she had helped shape the world a little differently.

The road ahead suddenly beckoned like an

unopened book, and her eyes sparkled with excitement as Seth offered her his hand. His eyes brightened with approval at her smile, and her heart turned over at the sight of him, his dark hair shining in the sunlight, his rifle at the ready over his arm, ready to face danger and death for a cause he believed in. Handsome. Brave. And, even if only for a moment in time, hers.

"Beats slinging two percent at the Shop and Pack," Laurel remarked, and if nobody else understood, it didn't really matter.

Chapter Eleven

It was almost night when they neared Philadelphia, a balmy and sea-scented twilight, with
clouds of fog beginning to drift around the
treetops. Occasionally, Laurel would see the
electric-green sparkle of fireflies in the brush,
a sight that had shocked her the first time she
saw it.

There were no fireflies on the west coast;
they were something she had read about in
books. She hadn't expected them to be so
brilliant, like a startling display of miniature
Christmas lights. They started next to the
ground, randomly twinkling in the thick
grasses, and then gradually floated toward
the treetops, where they decorated the dark
trees with their magical sparkle.

Magical, she thought, like the entire day.

They had ridden through the day, through lush green forests and over covered bridges, past inns of stone with sparkling windows and older buildings of logs with steep-pitched roofs. They had passed by farmhouses surrounded by fields of ripening corn and bushy green tobacco leaves. The September sun was hot on their backs, but there was a hint of autumn in the air, a gold cast touching the fields and leaves, a haze in the air that hadn't been there a day before.

Laurel didn't think about past or future. She was living in a dream, riding on horseback through an enchanted landscape. Seth's eyes lit on her every few minutes, full of admiration. She had climbed fearlessly onto the horse and was handling the reins like a cavalry soldier. When Prudence had shown fear Laurel had laughed it away, making their first day on horseback seem like a great adventure.

And there was admiration in Seth's eyes for her beauty, as well. Laurel felt beautiful; she forgot about the way her dress pinched her waist and the stiffened reeds sewn in the bodice jabbed at her hips and underarms. She felt slender and graceful, and when her skirts billowed around her ankles she felt like a little girl playing dress up, a princess in a fairy story.

Prudence, riding behind Laurel, her arms around her sister's waist, caught the mood of excitement, and she chattered happily about the great city and the sights they might see there.

They had stopped for lunch at a German farmhouse, and Seth had lifted her off the horse, his hands large and firm against her waist. She shivered and leaned forward, and they stayed locked like that, their eyes soft and glowing at each other, until the farm woman had said something in German, rolling her eyes and laughing.

By the time they reached the outskirts of the city, Laurel felt as if she and Seth had been lovers forever. Her heart fluttered with every move of his graceful hands, the way he shifted his rifle, the way creases appeared around his dark eyes when he smiled.

And he was smiling a lot. Whenever Laurel looked up and caught his eye the memory of the morning was there between them, and she would start to smile. He would shake his head, looking a little dazed, and his smile would start, slow and bright.

As soon as they were out of British-occupied territory, he had seemed to change. He relaxed; his gestures became looser and easier. And when they rode into the city of Philadelphia he seemed like a different man.

He loved his city; it was obvious. He rode at Laurel's side, and their horses' hooves made a pleasant sound on the cobblestone streets as he pointed out the sights to them. Great churches with spires reaching into the night sky and the wharves that were the center of the ship-building trade and fine brick houses. He pointed out a house and told her it belonged to Dr. Franklin, and Laurel realized with a jolt that he meant Benjamin Franklin.

The streets were lined with shops—booksellers and dressmakers and silversmiths and toyshops and tobacconists and apothecaries—and Laurel wished that she could go in and marvel at the goods.

She stared with delight at passing carriages and horses, and felt like Prudence, stricken silent with awe at all the new sights and sounds.

They turned down a tree-lined street of brick buildings, tall and narrow and close together, and Seth pointed out a handsome building with gleaming white shutters.

"My home," he said quietly. "We'll stay here tonight, and I'll take Prudence to Mistress Kimball's in the morning."

He helped Prudence and then Hope to slide down from the horse's back, and he held her hand as she stared up the brick walk at the front door, at the candle burning in front of a many-paned window.

"My housekeeper's here," he said softly. "I'll tell her you're a cousin. It's easier to explain that way. Do you mind?"

Laurel shook her head. "Not a bit."

"Good. Welcome to Philadelphia, Hope Garrick."

Laurel smiled up at him and felt a dreamlike rush of heat as his eyes shone down at her. "I'm glad to be here," she told him, and followed him up the front walk, her hand still clutched in his.

The house was a marvel of craftsmanship, from the carefully turned spindles on the staircase to the gleaming parquet floors. Graceful chairs with richly brocaded seats sat next to gleaming tables of cherry and rosewood, and soft candlelight warmed the rooms with a golden glow.

The rooms were small but beautiful, and everywhere was the gleam of wood-carved mantelpieces, doorways, curved and shining moldings, all bright with polish and fragrant with the smell of oil.

They ate in the brick-and-plaster kitchen, under the suspicious eye of Seth's housekeeper, Mrs. Avery, who had greeted Seth's story of orphaned cousins with a lifted brow but had said nothing.

Despite the woman's doubtful look, Laurel liked her. She had a round, pleasant face, and she spoke gently to Prudence and hastened to make everyone comfortable, fussing over their travel-worn, dusty clothes, and demanding to know who had eaten properly and who had not, and insisting that they eat again, immediately.

Laurel had the uncanny feeling that she had been in the house before, that she had felt the gleaming banister beneath her palm, that she had sipped flowery-scented tea from the china cups and sat across the polished oak table from

Seth, watching the firelight play on his hair and shadow the hollows beneath his cheekbones, listened to his voice as he spoke quietly to Mrs. Avery.

It was a rich, contented feeling, and she wondered what it would be like to live in such a house, to have such a man for a husband, to wake each morning in his arms and hear the sounds of the passing carriages on the cobblestone streets.

I could do it, she thought. *I could stay here, and Prudence could live with us, and I could just stay here and be with him forever. I'd like that.*

The moment the thought came to her mind, she felt a low, persistent buzzing in her ears, and her vision began to cloud red and black. Very faintly, she could hear her Grandma speaking.

". . . get her back to the river. She's got to get home, and damned quick, or we're on our way to the smoking section."

The china cup in Laurel's hand fell to the table, and tea spilled in a shining stream across the oak. She swayed, dizzy and feeling sick.

"Hope?" Seth was at her side, steadying her swaying body with an arm around her shoulders. "What happened?"

Unable to speak, she simply stared at him with eyes of blue-green sorrow.

I'm going to lose him. I've made love to him only once and I love him, and I'm going to have to leave him.

He stared at her with troubled dark eyes,

and his fingers stroked her cheek once before he spoke.

"It's been a long day. Perhaps you should go to sleep."

"That's a good idea." Her voice was unsteady. The touch of his hand on her face was feather-soft and warm. She wanted to press her face into it and forget about everything else—forget about Grandma and Jerry, forget about her poor, comatose body in the hospital bed, forget about her parents and her friends . . .

"I guess I'll be making up the beds," Mrs. Avery put in from across the room, where she was putting freshly polished silver onto already full shelves. "Will your cousins share a room, sir?"

Laurel met Seth's eyes, and a rush of longing passed between them.

"Separate rooms, I think," he answered, and turned away before anyone could see the hot desire on his face.

Laurel exhaled a breath of mingled sorrow and longing.

One more night, she told herself. *What harm could there be in one more night?*

She opened the shutters and stared down at the moonlit streets, hardly able to believe what was happening. It was like living on a movie set or walking through a museum, only vibrant and alive, where museums tended to be formal and impersonal.

She stared down the cobblestone street and

tilted her head up, to look past the treetops to the star-sprinkled sky. Without the electric lights of the twentieth century to dim the night sky, the stars seemed huge and brilliant.

Unreal. Beautiful, but unreal. Like a dream that had to end too soon, before you were ready to wake up. She thought of the first few days she had spent in the past, moping around the Garrick farm, wishing with all her heart to be back in the twentieth century.

And now she wished the opposite. Laurel slammed the shutters and turned back into the simple bedchamber—simple but perfect, like all of Seth's house. Everywhere she looked was evidence of his taste, his skill with fine cherry and mahogany and walnut. She stroked the satin-smooth polish of the headboard, marveling at the gold of lighter wood inlaid in a scroll pattern, almost too perfect to have been done by hand. His shop was in the basement, he had told her. He would show her tomorrow.

Tomorrow—the day they would take Prudence to Mistress Kimball's. The day she would return to Chadsford and try to find the way to get back to her own body, lying helpless and full of tubes in a tiled hospital room over two hundred years away.

"Like my body ever had so much fun," Laurel muttered, thinking of that morning in the inn. Oh, the way he had tumbled her beneath his body, and the warm scent of his skin against hers, and the way his breath had shuddered when he finally found relief in the grasp of her body . . .

"Seth Goodwin," she whispered. "Seth Goodwin, Seth Goodwin." She whispered the name like an incantation, as if by saying it she might bind him to her.

As if he could hear her, she heard his footsteps in the hall, and she felt herself tremble at the sound of the gentle tap on her door.

"Hope?" He opened the door, his voice soft and husky in the quiet house.

"Come in. I'm awake."

He entered the room, and his generous mouth curved into a smile at the sight of her in her thin nightgown, her hair unbound and hanging down her back.

She held out her arms to him and he crossed the room in two quick strides and gathered her to his chest with a ragged sigh. She could feel his lips against her hair, his breath warm where he kissed her.

"Mmmm." She burrowed against his body as easily as if it was something she had done a million times, reaching up to feel the warmth of his neck, the steady pulse that beat there, the soft curls at the back of his neck that weren't long enough to be tied into the black ribbon.

He bent his head to her and she tilted her head back, her mouth parted in invitation, as if with a life of its own.

His tongue slid against her own with a silken heat; she drew in his exhaled breath as if it were her own; their lips touched again and again with a sweetness that made her dizzy.

"Angel." His whisper was shaky against her cheek, and he pulled her tightly against his chest. She rubbed her face against the white cotton of his shirt, breathing the musky scent of clean man and sweat, the faint odor of horse-flesh still on his clothing. Earthy, intoxicating. The scent of Seth Goodwin, like the scent of no other man on earth.

"Hope." He reached down with his long, tanned fingers and tilted her face up to his. She stared at him with marveling eyes, scarcely able to believe that he wanted her—this beautiful man with his dark, rough-hewn features and elegant hands, his dark, piercing eyes and broad shoulders.

"Sit down for a moment, Hope. I need to speak with you, and I find I can't hold you and think at the same time."

"Who wants to think?" Laurel asked with an uneven laugh, but she reluctantly pulled away from his arms and settled herself on the edge of the bed. She watched him with adoring eyes, the straight, strong lines of his neck and the dark sheen of his hair, the slender lines of his hips. *Beyond babe*, she thought, and felt her cheeks dimpling at the words.

"Stop looking at me like that," he ordered softly, his eyes sparkling at her. "I can't think when you do that."

"You're having some serious thinking problems," she observed. "I think I like it."

His eyes glowed and he exhaled a long,

unsteady breath. "Be serious, for once, and let me get on with it. I've been thinking—"

"But not easily."

"Hang it, Hope, be still! I've been thinking. In the morning we can take Prudence to Mistress Kimball's, and from what I've seen of her work she'll have no trouble being accepted. She's a skilled little girl, and clean, and eager to please. That's not a problem. But when Prudence is settled in we're left with you."

"Are you implying that I'm a problem?" she demanded, doing her best to sound indignant.

"Damn implying, young woman; I'm saying it outright. Yes, you're a problem. You're a double-tongued, baffling, headache of a problem."

"How do you figure that?"

He drew his dark brows together and raked his dark hair from his forehead with an impatient gesture. He settled on the bed next to her and took her shoulders in his strong hands, turning her to meet his dark eyes.

"Where do I begin? It's an uncommonly long list, for such a slip of a girl. First of all, there's a goodly chance that you're not quite all there; that you did, indeed, send your brains askew in a fall. You're quite disconcerting; the things you say, the opinions you hold, the words you use. Secondly, there's a good chance that you may have information that nobody outside Washington's inner circle should have. I'm damned if I know where you got it, but I tell you this—if you're a British spy, you're a damned poor one. If you're not, which I strongly suspect is the case, there still leaves the question of where you got your information. Unless, of course, you're a witch, and that's too ludicrous to consider."

"Ludicrous doesn't begin to describe it," Laurel put in. "And if you get any smart ideas about burning me at the stake, I'm going to be really pissed off."

"Would you cease! This is 1777, you know."

"Oh, believe me, I've noticed. And you think you have problems."

"I do! And this is the third problem—"

Laurel let out a cry of dismay and tumbled backwards onto the bed, clutching a pillow to her head. "Hey! Hey! How long is this list? I'm a tired pup." She pulled the pillow from her face, blew a wayward strand of hair from her mouth, and winked at him. "I liked it better when you were having problems thinking."

He tried to hide a smile and failed. He made an effort, cleared his throat, and took the pillow from her hands, tossing it aside. "Thirdly, there's the problem of you wanting to return to Chadsford. It can't be done."

"What do you mean, *can't?*" Laurel sat up on one elbow, suddenly serious. "I don't have a choice. I have to."

"Be sensible. The British are closing in; they're surrounding the city from here to God knows where. I wouldn't risk it, and I can't have you traveling alone. Think, Hope: what if you were taken? Do you want to be hanged? Imprisoned? I can't allow it."

"Now see here, bucko—"

"No, you see here, you little madwoman. It's ridiculous, dangerous, stupid. Do you want to die?" His mouth was set in a tight line, his eyes dark with anger. "There's only one agreeable solution to this problem, if you think about it. Stay here in the city."

"And just how am I supposed to live? What am I supposed to do? I can't cook. I can't sew. I'll never find a job. I don't know a damned person here. Am I supposed to beg on the street? Sit on a corner with a sign that says 'Support your local crazy woman; please leave donations'? What about food? What about a place to live? What about—"

"What about marriage?" He grasped her wrist and pulled her into a sitting position, looking at her with eyes dark and searching.

Laurel sat still with shock.

"Marriage to whom?" she demanded, after a long, tense pause.

He looked at her as if she was stupid and gave an impatient glare. "Me, you fool."

Laurel felt as if the wind was knocked out of her. He was serious. He wasn't joking. "You?"

"Do you have any other offers that I should know about? Of course, me. After all, be logical. I'm a good man. I make a very good living. We can afford to hire a cook, and you can have your dresses made. God knows, you need some. And I did take your virginity, Hope. I should like to do the honorable thing."

She stared at him, openmouthed.

"It's logical," he repeated.

"Logical?" she echoed.

"Yes, very. After all, I can tolerate your little madnesses, and if you're my wife, I'll be able to keep an eye on you. If you're involved with any espionage, I'll be the first to know."

"Well, isn't that cute? Isn't that special? Isn't that the best damn reason for getting married you ever heard in your life?" She punched his shoulder lightly. " 'Marry me, darling, so I can keep an eye on you, and if you do anything wacky, I can take it.' Seth Goodwin, how awful! What a terrible reason to propose!"

She was joking, but there was a bitter note in her laughter.

His hand dropped from her shoulder and caressed her cheek, and his eyes were tender when he spoke. "The fourth problem is this: I adore you."

Laurel sat silently, wondering where her breath had gone. Fear rushed through her, a tremble of uncertainty, disbelief; and then, slowly, her heart made a peculiar movement, a soft flutter like a butterfly, like a rose opening under the sun. "Don't be funny."

"I'm not." He leaned forward and his lips brushed hers softly before he finished speaking. "I wouldn't joke about something like that. This morning . . . this morning at the inn . . . it was something special. Not because you were a virgin. My first wife was a virgin, and the experience was damned unpleasant. Because it was you. The way your mouth felt with mine, the way you touched me . . . oh, God, the way you touched me. The way you took me into your body, and the way you moved beneath me. I've never felt anything like it. I'll never feel anything like it again."

He cleared his throat. "I'm not saying that it was just the act of bedding you. But I felt as if you were made for me. You're strong and beautiful and bad-tempered, and . . ." He stared into her eyes, and his hand brushed the hair from her neck and laid there, warm and strong. "I love you."

Laurel's breath trembled and sweet, hot tears filled her eyes. *I love you.* Words that she had never thought she'd hear again, words that she had sworn she would never speak to any man.

"I love you," she whispered, and it was as simple as drawing breath.

They sat in the silent room, their eyes glowing dark and brilliant, and she laid her hand on top of his, the simple gesture as full of grace as a miracle.

Marry him. How easy it would be, how simple the words. To make love to him every night and wake up in his arms each morning. To stay here forever . . .

Never to go home.

She suddenly thought of her sister, far away, watching her lie in a hospital bed. Linda, who she had shared everything with for thirty years. And her parents, practical and steady, with their weekend trips to the coast and well-ordered lives, who had always been there when she needed them. And Tamara, her best friend. Funny, brash Tamara, who always seemed to know what she was thinking even before she said it. What were they doing now? Were they sitting around her hospital bed at Harborview, watching her waste away in a coma? What would happen if she decided to stay? Would her body simply linger on, or would it expire?

She had a brief, awful image of her mother crying, making funeral arrangements, cleaning out her chaotic apartment.

And Grandma and Jerry, probably the worst guardian angels in the history of the world— what would happen to them? *There are rules we have to follow . . . Don't want to get sent to the smoking section . . .*

She felt her heart contract, a hard lump in her throat. She stared up at Seth, at his rugged, handsome face and impossibly beautiful brown eyes.

"I can't." The words were tight; they hurt to say.

"Why the devil not?"

"I just can't." She took a deep, shuddering breath and turned away from him. "Don't ask me to explain, because it's just too much. You'd think I was crazy."

"That's never bothered you before."

She laughed softly. "Trust me on this. It's not possible."

He appeared to weigh her words, to consider

what she was saying. "I see absolutely no reason why you shouldn't marry me. And until you give me one, I simply refuse to accept the answer. Unless, of course, there's somebody else. That would be the most obvious explanation."

Laurel considered lying. It would be an easy way out.

He chose that moment to take her hand in his, and his long, tapering fingers fondled hers, stroked the palm of her hand with a tender, loving motion.

"No. There's nobody else."

He leaned toward her, the candlelight glowing gold in the reflection of his eyes, and her mouth moved toward his as if by instinct.

Heat and light. The satin feeling of his lips over hers, the clean, warm taste. Slowly, softly, their lips stroked and moved together, until she was dizzy.

"Marry me." His whisper was warm against her cheek; her arms moved easily around his neck. His chest pressing against hers seemed like the most perfect sensation in the world.

"I can't." His hands were running down her spine, over the curve of her waist, and hot desire poured over her, sweet and dark.

"Can't be damned." His mouth moved against her neck, kissing the hollow at the base of her throat, moving in a slow, sweet trail to the tender skin beneath her ear.

Laurel tried to speak and couldn't. Her hand glided across his shoulders, feeling the muscles beneath warm skin. His hand moved to the back of her neck, then through her hair with a silken, firm touch.

He pulled her face to his again, and their mouths met again, searing and hungry, hot kisses that made her shudder and warmed her blood to an incandescent glow. Her fingers shook against his shoulders, and the touch of his hand against her breast made her cry out softly, a raw sound of hunger.

"Oh, sweetheart . . ." He pushed gently at her shoulders, leaning her back into the soft depths of the featherbed. His hands traveled over her breasts, warm through the thin cotton of her gown, and a new wave of heat flooded through her at his touch.

She touched him just as eagerly, feeling the strong, hard lines of his chest, the perfect curves of his upper arms, the lean curve of his hips. His mouth sought hers as if he was starving for her, and she kissed him back with equal fervor.

His hands tugged at the hem of her nightgown and traveled softly up her long legs, playing over her thighs and seeking the very center of her desire, hot and aching for his touch.

She arched against his fingers, unabashed in her need, and the low, soft moan he made in his throat was the sweetest sound she had ever heard.

She pulled her nightgown over her head and flung it aside, eager for the touch of his skin against her own. He stared at her with brilliant, bemused eyes as she reached for the ties that fastened his white shirt at his throat and loosened them. The buttons that fastened over the hips of his breeches were next, and the dark ribbon that bound his hair at his neck.

"God help me, Hope . . ." His voice was ragged; his hands stroked her slender ribs and the soft curve of her waist. The heat of the humid night bathed their bodies with a faint sheen. They glowed in the candlelight, golden and shining, dark against the white sheets.

He discarded his clothing quickly, his intense, glittering eyes never leaving her body and face. He drew in his breath sharply as Laurel's hand closed over the hard length of him, hot and velvet smooth.

She was trembling with the intensity of her feelings—not just the unrestrained desire, but the almost sacred awe she felt for his beauty, the way the candlelight shone over his long, hard body, the way his thick hair fell wild and dark over his shoulders . . . the most beautiful man she had ever seen. And his eyes, dark and soft with passion beneath his thick brows, the way they glowed at the sight of her . . .

"I love you," he whispered, and his voice was low and almost fierce. "I love you, love you . . ."

He pulled her body beneath his with a possessive, quick gesture, and she opened herself to him without resistance, wrapping her legs around his.

Heat and strength sinking into her, making her body part of his own, their mouths blending together, their shared breath mingling. . . .

"I love you," she gasped, when his mouth left hers. She stared up at him as he leaned over her, delirious and shaking with the feeling of his body inside her own. It was perfect, it was good; nothing had ever felt so right.

They moved together as if they had been doing so forever, since the beginning of time. She matched each thrust of his body with equal passion, arching to meet him again and again. She lost her sense of time; he was driving every thought from her mind with each sure, hot stroke of his body. Nothing mattered, nothing in the world except that she was here, and he loved her, and every touch of his fingers and mouth were making her his.

She reached her peak with a hotter and more blinding intensity than she had ever thought possible, crying out with her mouth pressed against the soft hair of his chest, breathing in the scent of him, her arms wrapped around the warm, silken skin of his back, pressing his body against her heart as if she could melt into him.

"Sweetheart . . ." She heard his voice faintly through the roaring in her ears, dark with passion and wonder, and then he thrust hard into her, twice, three times, and flooded her body with his own hot release.

"I love you," he whispered, his mouth warm and wet over hers, as he withdrew from her body. He kissed her again, and pulled her against his chest as he lay back into the soft featherbed.

She lay there, still trembling with the beauty of it, listening to the sound of his racing heart as it slowed and steadied. They gazed at each other with the eyes of lovers, bright with wonder and joy, shaken by their own feelings.

His hand stroked the soft skin of her shoulders; he planted a tender kiss on her brow before he closed his eyes.

"Marry me," he murmured, his eyes still closed, his voice husky with sleep. "Never leave me."

"I never want to leave you," Laurel whispered back, her heart aching with love. "Ever."

As soon as his breath steadied into the pattern of sleep, she cried quietly against his chest, afraid of what the future might hold.

Chapter Twelve

"Hope! Come in, sweetheart." Seth looked up from his worktable with a brilliant smile, his eyes lighting at the sight of her hesitating in the doorway of his shop.

She had dressed in the blue-flowered gown that seemed to be the only decent thing she owned—he would have to see about getting her some new things, he realized—and her hair was unbound, streaming down her slender back in golden waves, heavy and bright in the morning sunlight that shone through the high windows of the half-basement room. The thought crossed his mind that during his entire marriage, he had never seen Jane with her hair unbound. She had worn it in a tidy roll during the day, covered with modest caps, and in prim braids at night.

It would never have occurred to Jane to wander through the house with her hair loose, any more than she would wander around naked. For that matter, he had never seen Jane naked. She changed her clothes in private, and the times that she had submitted to her wifely duties, she had done so in her nightgown, in complete darkness. Not like Hope.

"What are you thinking about?" Hope demanded, a knowing smile playing around her lips, as if she knew full well what he had been thinking about.

He watched as she stepped around the room, her eyes wandering to the neatly arranged rows of awls and hand drills, the shining saws in various shapes and sizes, the tidy piles of new wood, stacked according to type and size. She stopped and ran her hands over a finished chair of deep mahogany, touching the elaborately pierced and scrolled back, perfectly symmetrical and without flaw, ready to go to the upholsterer's and be fitted with a seat.

She found his mark on the inside of the seat support, a neat *SG*, the letters intertwining, and ran her finger over it. She lifted her head and smiled at him, her eyes bright with admiration. "Beautiful," she said.

Seth was surprised at how much her approval warmed him. He watched as she walked over to the other finished pieces in the room, running her hands over a walnut sewing table, a black cherry sideboard, and a matched set of chairs with more elaborate carving than he personally preferred.

Hope stopped in front of a wardrobe that stood against the far wall, and raised her brows at the massive piece, the elaborate swags that festooned the edges of the doors.

The wealthy of the city liked their furniture to mimic the more traditional European designs, but Seth loved the simpler, cleaner lines that the American craftsmen were leaning to. He was pleased to see that Hope seemed to share his tastes.

"So, this is what you do when you're not being the James Bond of the American Revolution," Hope said quietly, almost as if she was talking to herself.

Puzzled, Seth looked up from the mahogany drawer front on the table in front of him. "James Bond? Should I know him?"

"No, and neither should I," Hope said with a light laugh. She tilted her head to the side, reading the titles of the books that lined the shelf above his desk.

"The Gentleman's or Builder's Companion. Cabinet Maker's Guide. Designs for Chinese Buildings, Furniture, Etc. . . ."

"Who taught you to read?" Seth asked, impressed by the ease with which she spoke. It was not something he had expected, from a girl raised in such backward circumstances.

She looked up at him, startled and a little guilty.

"My mother," she said after a short pause,

257

and the way she said it made him wonder if she was lying.

He decided to let it pass. "Did you sleep well? Have you eaten?"

"Yes and yes. We ate some sausage turnovers with Mrs. Avery in the kitchen, and she's taken Prudence to the market with her. What are you working on?"

"A drawer front, for a secretary. I'd like to have it finished before I receive my next orders." He nodded at the graceful piece, made in the clean, unbroken lines he favored. It stood against the wall, still unvarnished, empty holes where the drawers would be. "You see, I'm working on the inlay now. I gave it a lot of thought. Satinwood, in the shape of a sun. It's pleasant work. Careful, but pleasant."

Hope stood next to him, her shoulder touching his, and ran her fingers over the empty shape he had been painstakingly carving out—a half sun, its rays radiating from a half circle in graceful curves.

She smiled up at him. "I like it."

Had Jane ever noticed his work? Not that he could remember. He didn't think she had ever come into his workshop. Hope's blue-green eyes were fastened on his face with admiration, and he actually felt a little embarrassed.

"It's not really my design. I copied it, from the back of the chair General Washington uses when he's at the State House. It's a fine piece of work."

"I'd like to see it finished."

"I would, too. I pray I might, before the British arrive. Then things will be mightily dangerous. I shall likely have to leave the city."

Her face tensed, and she drew a deep breath. "And go where?"

"It depends on my orders. If I haven't received any notice by then, I'll report to General Washington."

Hope's face was tight, her fingers flexed with a nervous motion. "I'll miss you."

There was such sorrow in her voice that Seth was startled. "Miss me? I should think you would. But you need not worry. You'll be safe enough here. I'll enjoy coming back to my pretty wife."

Her eyes widened, and she lifted her hand to touch his cheek. Even that simplest of gestures warmed his blood.

"I can't marry you, Seth Goodwin."

She wouldn't meet his eyes, and he gave an impatient sigh. "Can't or won't? Come, Hope, be frank with me. You give me your body, you say that you love me—"

"I do! More than you can imagine!"

"Then I fail to see the reason for your refusal. It's simply not logical."

"Life isn't always logical, you know." She turned away, biting her lower lip, and he caught the gleam of tears in her eyes.

"Hope, sweetheart . . ." He took her shoulders and pulled her back against him, holding her tightly against his chest.

He dropped his mouth to the side of her

neck and kissed her gently, breathing in the scent of freshly washed skin. She sighed, a long sorrowful sound.

"What is it, Hope? That you were pre-contracted to Ephraim?"

"Ephraim who?" she asked, and her tone told him that she knew very well and would have just as soon been contracted to a beetle.

He laughed softly and buried his face into her soft hair, nuzzling her neck until he felt her breath quicken and her pulse race against his lips.

"Then why not—"

"Oh, be quiet," she whispered, turning her face to his and rubbing her cheek against him. Her arms lifted and slid around his neck. "I don't want to talk about it. Can't you think of anything else to do with your mouth?"

Her lips moved over his, stilling any lukewarm protest he might have offered, and he found himself kissing her until they were both mindless with the pleasure of it.

He was only a little shocked when she shifted herself onto his worktable and wrapped her long legs around his hips, her fingers fumbling at the waist of his breeches. Shocking, wicked behavior for a respectable young woman, his logical mind told him. And yet, she was so honestly beautiful and frank in her passion that he pushed her skirts above her waist and took her there in broad daylight, tumbled across his worktable with the curling pieces of satinwood lying around them, as pale and bright as her hair.

They made love with a desperate, furious hunger, and his carving tools rolled from the table and clattered to the floor, forgotten.

"Marry me," he repeated, later that day. They were walking with Prudence to Mistress Kimball's, to see about her apprenticeship. The cobblestone streets of Philadelphia were busy this sunlit afternoon, and Laurel kept bumping into Seth as she craned her neck to look at the sights of the bustling city.

Every detail fascinated her—the slender and tightly laced gentlewomen out doing their daily marketing, followed by maidservants with baskets over their arms, the strings of their white caps untied and falling over their shoulders, the apprentice boys standing in the doorway of a printshop in their ink-stained aprons, the cameo and silver filigree buttons on the waistcoat of a gentleman leaving a tavern, a sheaf of papers clutched in his pudgy hand.

The scent of burning tobacco wafted past Laurel's nose, and she turned to watch two young men walking by, silver-tipped walking sticks held gracefully in their hands, long curved pipes smoking. One of them raised his brow at her ill-concealed interest.

Seth gave her hand an impatient tug. "And what is so uncommonly interesting about those royalist pups?"

"Are they royalists?" Prudence asked, her

eyes lighting with interest. She seemed to have forgotten that her own family had raised her in that tradition. "How can you tell?"

"Because I know. Are you going to answer me, Hope?"

The jealous note in his voice made Laurel laugh. "Their pipes. I wasn't looking at them; I was thinking about their pipes." Oh, how nice it would be to sit down beneath the shade of a tree and hike her skirts over her knees and light up a cigarette. . . .

"Marry me," Seth whispered into her ear, for what must have been the fiftieth time since that morning.

"Knock it off," Laurel whispered back. Seth looked puzzled, and Prudence made no attempt to pretend that she hadn't heard.

"Knock what off, Hope? What did Mr. Goodwin say to you? Oh, look! Look, Hope! Oh, Mr. Goodwin, what is that place, pray?"

Seth smiled as he followed the excited child's pointing finger.

Laurel looked up at the handsome brick building, two-and-a-half stories and topped by a spired cupola in gleaming white and gold. White cornices and railings, gleaming steps of white marble, and sparkling, white-framed windows proclaimed the structure as a place of importance.

"That, young Prudence, is the Pennsylvania State House. Not so long ago, the greatest men of this country sat in that building and signed a paper declaring our independence from England. Ah, but that was a day."

Hope felt a thrill of disbelief as she stared at the building. Independence Hall. There it stood, exactly as it would be standing two hundred and fifteen years later. Almost exactly. She took Prudence's hand.

"Look, Prudence. Do you see the bell, hanging in the tower? That's the Liberty Bell." Uncracked, she added silently. What a strange thing to think, that she would be the only living person in the United States who had actually witnessed such a thing.

"The liberty bell?" Seth repeated. "That's a good name for it, isn't it?"

"Well, what do you call it?" Laurel demanded, wrinkling her brow and wishing she had paid better attention in her history classes.

Seth gave her a bemused smile and tugged at the string of her white, lace-trimmed cap, straightening it. "We don't call it much of anything. We just ring it."

"Well, ring it carefully," Laurel advised him, and took a last look at the state house before following him and Prudence down Chestnut Street toward Mistress Kimball's.

Mistress Kimball was a handsome woman of about forty, her hair still dark and glossy beneath the white lace of her cap.

Dressed for success, circa 1777, Laurel thought, admiring the carefully draped and fitted dress of dove gray silk, the graceful but simple lace that adorned the round, low neck and tight, three-quarter-length sleeves.

She sat at a long, wide desk, very obviously the queen of her domain, her round spectacles perched on the end of her nose as she looked over a line of figures in a tidy ledger.

All around her, shelves stacked with a rainbow of fabrics and ribbon lined the walls, sketches of Parisian dresses neatly framed and displayed for the customer's convenience.

A tidy young assistant in a simple black gown was waiting on a fashionable young woman and her mother, displaying what could only be a ball gown for their approval.

Laurel heard Prudence catch her breath at the sight of the offered dress, a vision of heavy champagne-gold silk, the hem of the skirt encrusted with a pattern of embroidered roses in deep, rich pinks and wine colors, climbing up the sides of the dress to form an almost striped pattern. Around the low-cut shoulders, more roses, made of silk and velvet, perfectly mimicked real blossoms, and here and there brilliants sparkled like dewdrops among them. Green velvet leaves and tighter wine and rose buds trailed down the pointed bodice, and more velvet blossoms and leaves decorated the embroidered sleeves.

The young woman being offered the dress appeared displeased. "I wanted pink," she said in petulant tones, shifting on her damask-covered bench to look at her tired-looking mother.

The shop assistant cast a pleading look at Mistress Kimball, who didn't look up from her ledger. Only a tightening of her mouth indicated that she had heard.

"It is pink, poppet," the mother reassured her in a weary voice. "Look at the roses. Aren't they pink?"

"No. They look almost red. I don't want it."

"But, sweeting, I've already paid for it. It looks exactly like the picture—"

"No, it does not. The roses were pinker. Oh, it may do for right now, but soon the British lords will be in the city, and I simply must look perfect. English gentlemen aren't like these colonial bumpkins, Mama. And as soon as they arrive, the really grand parties will start, and if I attend looking like a milkmaid—"

The ledger was closed with a sharp bang, and the previously staid Mistress Kimball sprang into action, moving like a sudden storm.

"Out! Out with you! I've customers aplenty; I don't want your business."

The white-skinned miss stared up at the dressmaker, her face still with shock. "Very well," she retorted after a moment. "I don't want to shop here anymore. Have the dress wrapped and sent around this evening, and consider it done."

"I will not. Your money will be returned to you, and you will leave the dress. Take yourself and your impudence elsewhere."

The agitated mama wrung her hands. "Pray consider, Mistress Kimball—"

"I have considered, and my decision is made. Madam, there is the door."

The young assistant was already carrying the enchanting dress away, her nose in the air, her eyes sparkling with delight. As the curtained rear door of the shop opened, Laurel caught sight of two more young girls peeking in with interest, their fabric and needles poised in their hands.

"But, Mistress Kimball—"

"Out!"

The much-insulted young woman rushed by Laurel without even looking in her direction, her hand-wringing mother hot on her heels. The door banged behind them.

"Back to work," Mistress Kimball called in sharp tones, without even looking over her shoulder. There was a flurry of movement behind the curtained doorway, and a soft giggle.

The good proprietor of the shop cast a sharp glare at the shop door and returned to her seat, muttering under her breath about brainless young women who had no sense of style or politics.

She sat, took off her spectacles, rubbed her eyes with a tired sigh, and replaced them. Then she tilted her head and regarded the three spectators standing by the front door.

She smiled a gracious and warm smile, as if the previous scene had never occurred. "Seth Goodwin! How are you, young man? It's been some time, hasn't it?"

"It has. I'm pleased to see you haven't changed, in your business or your politics. You're a woman to be reckoned with."

Mistress Kimball regarded the handsome man with a shrewd eye.

"What do you want?"

Seth laughed, throwing back his dark head. He reached out a hand and placed it on Prudence's shoulder. "Come, Prudence. This is Mistress Kimball. Mistress Kimball, my cousin, Prudence Garrick, recently orphaned and left to make her way in the world."

"How did I know?" Mistress Kimball asked, of nobody in particular. She made a gesture with her hands, as if to say it was all too much for her, and returned her forgotten quill pen to the silver inkstand on her desk.

"Come here, Prudence Garrick," she added, and Prudence scurried forward, her blue eyes wide.

Mistress Kimball examined her as carefully as if she were a bolt of new fabric, from starched white cap to carefully cleaned buckled shoes. The worn blue cotton of Prudence's Sunday dress earned a small frown; the painstakingly stitched white cuffs earned an appraising lift of the brow.

"I need another girl as much as I need a British regiment camped in my cellar. Did you bring any work to show me?"

Almost trembling with fear, Prudence nodded and produced the heavy sampler she had carried from Chadsford with her. Mistress

Kimball examined the work with the eagle eye of a woman who knew her business, taking note of each graceful lily, each meticulous letter, every careful leaf that branched across the azure sky.

Laurel watched silently, her hand at Seth's elbow, remembering the first time she had seen the sampler in Thomas Garrick's comfortless attic. How it had moved her—poor, lonely Prudence, working her sorrow and love into a careful tapestry, turning her grief into an object of beauty.

Myne comfort is the vow you spake
Of love forever myne.

"Do you think it's true, Hope? Does Mother still see me? Does she still love me?"

"Of course she does. Who wouldn't? Love doesn't die, Prudence. It goes on forever."

Mistress Kimball cleared her throat and looked at the flaxen-haired, trembling little girl before her. The look in her eyes was soft and compassionate, and she no longer seemed like the hard-eyed businesswoman who had shown her loyalist customers the door.

"And did you make this with your own hands, Prudence Garrick? No help from your sister?"

Prudence gave a startled little laugh. "Oh, none at all. Hope was never very good with her needle, and since she hit her head she can't sew at all."

Mistress Kimball gave Laurel a quick look that expressed her lack of estimation for such ineptness.

"Very well, little Prudence. I shall be honest with you. There are a hundred girls that would like to work for me. Some sew as well as you; others do not. Why should I take you?"

"Because I'll work harder than anyone else," Prudence answered, setting her chin at a determined angle. "And I can cook as well, and clean—"

"My girls don't cook," Mistress Kimball answered abruptly. "They don't have time. We wake at five, we're at our tables by six, and we don't stop until sundown, excepting meals. You have one afternoon a week to yourself, and Sundays, of course—and I expect my girls to attend church. I shall expect you to behave with modesty and gentleness, and to keep yourself clean and attractive at all times. When you leave here you shall be as accomplished a seamstress as any in Europe. Do you think you're equal to the work?"

Prudence nodded eagerly.

Mistress Kimball smiled, the stern lines of her face softening. "Very well. As a favor to Mr. Goodwin, you may stay. I think I shall put you to work at the embroidery table."

Laurel felt a pang of sorrow as Mistress Kimball took Prudence's hand in hers. Oh, Prudence would be happy here, no doubt, and learn a skill that would serve her all her life. She'd be better off here than at Thomas

Garrick's, no question about that. But it would be hard to say good-bye.

And there was one less obstacle between her and her return home.

Mistress Kimball glanced over her shoulder. "Sarah! Will you come here, please?" A pencil-thin girl of about thirteen entered the room so quickly that Laurel knew she must have been listening.

"Sarah, this is Prudence Garrick. She's going to be staying here. Will you show her your room and help her to make up the spare bed? Explain the rules to her, and introduce her to the others. She'll be working at the embroidery table for now, but you may take the rest of the afternoon to show her around."

"Yes, Mistress Kimball. Prudence?"

Prudence looked at Laurel with wide, uncertain eyes.

"Go ahead," Laurel said. "I'll be back to see you tomorrow, if you like."

Prudence swallowed and held her arms out to her sister, and Laurel held the little girl tightly, giving her shoulder a reassuring pat.

"Don't worry."

Prudence nodded, blinking back tears. "Tomorrow, Hope?"

"Promise."

Prudence followed Sarah from the room, her eyes already wandering to the stacks of glorious fabrics.

Mistress Kimball gave Laurel a comforting smile. "Don't fret. It's always a little hard on them at first, especially when they're loved at home. But they adjust quickly. They're busy and happy, and the other girls are kind. I don't tolerate mistreatment under my roof."

"Thank you," Laurel answered, surprised to find tears in her eyes.

"And you, young man," Mistress Kimball added, with a stern look at Seth, "you owe me."

"I had no doubt but that I would." Seth didn't look too worried about the prospect. "I'll start repaying you by bringing you some new business. My cousin Hope needs some new things. A few things for around the house, and something to wear to the Williamses' party tonight."

"What party?" Laurel demanded, startled.

"Tonight?" Mistress Kimball repeated. "I'm a businesswoman, not a magician! I can't possibly make something by tonight."

"Nonsense. I imagine you have the perfect thing already. Perhaps something that another customer didn't want . . ."

Mistress Kimball lifted her dark brows. "You surprise me, Mr. Goodwin. I always thought of you as a thrifty man. The only thing I have equal to the Williamses' affair is very expensive. And adjustments might be necessary."

Seth shrugged. "A man needs to be a little extravagant every now and again. And I'll not have Hope looking like a country cousin."

"She doesn't look much like a cousin of any sort, if you ask me," Mistress Kimball returned evenly. She turned her back before anyone could answer and left the room in a rustle of silk, calling for her assistant. When she returned she was carrying the champagne silk dress with the incredible roses. "Better for you than some brainless little loyalist," she announced, holding the dress up by the shoulders. "Give me an hour and we'll have a good fit. Can your stays be laced any tighter?"

"Not if I want to eat," Laurel answered.

"Then starve. It'll be worth it. Go about your business, Goodwin, and come back in an hour. And don't think I'll give you a discount, because I won't."

"Perish the thought," Seth murmured, and he made a graceful bow before he left the shop, leaving Laurel in the authoritative hands of Mistress Kimball and her assistant.

"I hate commercials," Jerry informed Nathaniel, "just hate them. There are some places that commercials just aren't needed, and this is one of them."

"I like the one with the windup rabbit," Nathaniel replied, opening a plastic bag of cashews and dumping them into his hand. "I never see it coming. You think you're going to have to hear about acid indigestion or toilet paper, and merry! Here comes the little pink bunny."

Jerry gave a derisive wave of his hand. "Hooey. I can see it coming a mile away."

Nathaniel ignored this, loosened the buttons

272

on his waistcoat, and settled back into the couch cushions, chewing his cashews. "Did I get a package from the home shopping channel?"

"Don't know. Haven't checked the mail." Jerry picked up the remote control and began flipping through the stations. "All right. Here it is."

Both men leaned forward, their eyes riveted to the TV screen.

"Get a little closer, will you?" Jerry asked, and the TV scooted a few feet closer on its stubby legs.

The film they watched showed a stately house, filled with gentlemen in waistcoats and white wigs and women in panniered skirts with flowers in their hair and sparkling fans in their hands.

"Ah! Ah! There they are!" Nathaniel shouted, pointing.

"Where?" Jerry demanded, opening a bottle of beer. "Where the hell are my glasses?"

The missing glasses floated out from the clouds and settled on the edge of his pointed nose, crooked. Jerry muttered, and straightened them.

"There! Coming in the door." Nathaniel beamed at the TV. "That's my Seth. Handsome boy, isn't he?"

Jerry nodded, his eyes never leaving the TV screen.

Laurel and Seth were entering the crowded room, laughing softly at some shared joke.

Laurel was as enchanting as a fairy-tale princess, her golden hair looped up and pinned with wine red roses and ribbons, hanging down over one smooth shoulder in perfect golden ringlets. She was wearing a dress of golden-cream silk, festooned with silk and velvet roses and heavy cream lace. Her waist was laced to an impossibly small circumference, her arms slender and glowing beneath the frills of lace that frothed at her elbows.

Her hand rested nervously on the deep blue velvet arm of Seth's frock coat. The camera moved in for a close-up, catching the worried look in her blue-green eyes.

"What if I do something wrong? What if I eat with the wrong fork, or trip on my dress?"

Seth laughed again, his eyes adoring as they traveled over her face and the exposed skin of her bosom. "Stop it. You won't do anything gauche, I promise you. You're absolutely perfect, sweetheart. Perfect. Just answer politely, keep your more radical opinions to yourself, and have a good time."

"I can't breathe."

"Then how will you dance?"

"I can't dance! I've never danced in my life— at least, not like that. Are you nuts? I can't even move."

"Then it's time you learned. After all, I simply can't have the good people of Philadelphia saying, 'We just cannot invite the Goodwins. Bad enough that the woman is mad, but she can't

274

even dance a simple minuet.' "

"Oh, for crying out loud," Laurel said, rolling her eyes. "Enough with 'The Goodwins' routine. I told you that as soon as Prudence was settled I was going home, and I meant it."

Seth appeared unconcerned. "You seem to have forgotten something, sweetheart."

"Oh? And what's that?"

Seth smiled and lifted a dark brow. "You promised that as soon as we got to Philadelphia, you'd tell me where you got your information. That and more, you said. Had you forgotten?"

"I guess I did." Laurel's face was pale; her eyes dropped.

"You forget the most crucial things," Seth pointed out. "It's a mystery to me. And a mystery, by the way, that I intend to solve. I'm holding you to your word, sweetheart. And you're not going anywhere till you keep it."

Laurel fumbled with her fan. "And if I keep my word? If I tell you everything?"

Seth was silent for a moment; then he reached out and touched a loose golden curl that lay against her cheek.

"Then, sweetheart, we get married and live happily ever after. Just like the stories you tell Prudence."

Laurel smiled a bittersweet smile. For a moment her eyes shone with a faint glint of tears. "Fairy tales. And fairy tales don't come true."

"What in the name of Jiminy Crickets are

you watching?" Grandma demanded, her sudden appearance causing Jerry and Nathaniel to jump.

Jerry hastily switched channels. "News. Lookee there, Joyce. Floods. Water all over the darn place. Hoo boy, what a mess."

"What a mess is right," Grandma snapped. "We're in serious trouble and you two are lumping around watching some maudlin miniseries."

Jerry and Nathaniel exchanged quick glances. "Oh, it wasn't that bad," Jerry muttered.

"Good costumes," Nathaniel agreed. "Nice sets."

"Oh, get over it. Turn that idiot box off."

The TV set went blank and scurried into the clouds.

"Now, you two clowns listen to me. I went to pick up the mail, and you wouldn't believe what was in there."

Grandma stood, glaring, her hands on her ample hips. Her sweatshirt announced, in bold letters, that she would rather be playing bingo. Jerry and Nathaniel both wished that she was.

"Well? Can you guess what was in the mail?"

Nathaniel tugged at his cravat. "Perhaps an electric juice-maker from the home-shopping network?"

"Geez Lou-ise!" Grandma exclaimed. "What haven't you ordered? No, and it wasn't the automatic food dehydrator, and it wasn't the

Franklin Mint commemorative plate, either."

Nathaniel looked disappointed.

"I like that decorative plate. And it's a limited edition."

Ignoring him, Grandma reached into her bulky handbag and withdrew a pile of letters. "Trouble. Nothing but trouble." She ripped one open and began to read aloud. "Warning— this is your last notice. Unless you respond to our previous notices we will be forced to turn you over to a higher authority for legal action regarding the matter of Laurel Behrman, also known as Hope Garrick, who apparently entered premises without validation on 9-7-1993.

"Also please respond to matter of Seth Goodwin, scheduled to report on 9-12-1777, unaccounted for. Please respond to our office within ten days with explanation or settled account." Grandma tossed the letter into the clouds, her lips turning down with disapproval. "And guess who that's from?"

"Peter in accounting?"

"Of course it's from Peter in accounting, you idiot! That know-it-all Mr. Fancy-schmancy holier-than-thou—"

A deep rumble of thunder sounded in the distance, and Grandma ceased her tirade immediately, glancing over her shoulder.

"Keep it down, keep it down," Jerry muttered. "Hooo boy, Joyce, one of these days you're going to go too far."

"We already have, no thanks to you."

Nathaniel threw the empty cashew bag over his shoulder and raked his fingers through his white hair, leaving it standing up in tufts. "Pray don't start, you two. I beg of you. It won't advance our cause and it gives me a wretched headache. Let's sit down and begin sorting out a plan. That way, when we're called up to the office, we'll be able to show them that we're working on it, and at least making some progress."

"Now that sounds like a plan," Grandma agreed. "Okay: The first order of business is getting Laurel back to Seattle before anything goes seriously wrong with her body. Unfortunately, that means we have to take Hope out. And we have to do it kindly. Any suggestions?"

"Is there a kind way to take someone out?" Jerry asked, picking a fuzz ball off his sweater. "That's the damned thing about death. Unless you're ninety and lie down for a nap, it's all pretty unpleasant."

"Oh, it's not that bad," Grandma snapped.

"How was Hope supposed to have died, anyhow?" Nathaniel asked. "According to the rules, don't we have to stick to the original method?"

"Rules, schmules," Grandma retorted. "If anyone here cared about rules, we wouldn't be in this mess, would we?"

"She hit her head on a rock on the riverbank," Jerry said, addressing Nathaniel. "She was supposed to slide on down into the river

278

and drown, but that's when Laurel moved in."

Nathaniel loosened his cravat, a thoughtful look on his lined face. "Odd. In almost the exact same spot Seth was supposed to have died, a few days later. It makes you wonder, doesn't it?"

Grandma waved her hand. "Oh, you know how these young souls are. They get all worked up into a passion about each other, and they keep trying to meet. Sometimes it works, sometimes it doesn't."

"I know!" Jerry jumped up off the couch, his eyes bright with excitement. "Let's take them both out at the same time! And then, we can turn time backwards and send them someplace where they were together. That way, the next time all this comes up, it never will have happened!"

"Geez Lou-ise, Jerry! That's the stupidest idea you've had yet!"

"The hell it is!"

"The hell it isn't! If they'd ever gotten it right before, do you think they'd still be trying so hard? Think about it—just where exactly would you send them back to?"

Jerry rubbed his pointed nose, considering. "What about the fifteenth century?"

Nathaniel turned on him, fire in his eye. "Oh, no! What are you thinking of, man? All that trouble with the Plantagenets, and then the bubonic plague, to boot! It took my poor boy almost two weeks to die!"

"And poor Laurel shutting herself up in a

convent," Grandma added. "Yeah, that was a good life, Jerry. Try again."

"I forgot about that. Okay, what about India?"

"Laurel died in a flood," Grandma reminded him.

"And Seth was trampled by a herd of elephants," Nathaniel put in.

"Okay! Okay! Hoo boy, you two are critics. Everything has to be perfect, doesn't it?"

"Anyhow, I think we've caused enough trouble with the time element. Let's just get this together and get it over with." Grandma looked over her shoulder, and an overstuffed armchair covered with a crocheted blanket rolled out of the clouds. She settled herself into it and thought.

"Is Laurel in love? True love?"

"Let me think . . . What are the rules on that?" Jerry mused. "Love suffers long, is kind . . ."

"Beareth all things, hopeth all things, believeth all things," Nathaniel added. "Maybe not in that particular order, but close. Aye, I'd say that Laurel has reached that point."

Grandma gave her companions a sharp glare. "That's just swell, but let's not forget—love ain't a one-way street. What about Seth? He can bear a heck of a lot, and hope he's got coming out his ears. It's that 'believeth all things' that's going to cause problems. Laurel's got a lot of explaining to do. Will he believe it?"

"We'd better hope he does," Nathaniel answered softly.

"It ain't over till it's over," was Jerry's philosophical observation, and he went to find himself another beer.

Chapter Thirteen

Partygoing had never been Laurel's favorite thing—she was not one of those social creatures who immediately felt comfortable around crowds of strangers. She'd much rather spend an evening watching TV with Tamara or Linda than getting dressed up and going to a glitzy party. And making small talk in the twentieth century, awkward as it might be, was far easier than chitchatting in eighteenth-century Philadelphia.

Laurel was in a daze. Everywhere she turned, she was being introduced to people—Seth's friends, Seth's business acquaintances, relatives of Seth's late wife.

It hardly seemed real, Laurel thought. She wondered if Cinderella had really had such a good time as people said—or did she feel like an impostor, dressed up in an unfamiliar dress?

The women murmured soft greetings and waved their fans as gracefully as if they were extensions of their hands; the men bent their white wigs as they bowed over her hand.

They spoke of music she didn't know, of dances she'd never learned, of towns and villages she had never heard of. And always, everyone spoke of the war.

The impending invasion added an almost forced gaiety to the evening, a tension that crackled through the air.

Over and over, she heard the words Fort Stanwix, Freeman's Farm, General Howe, General Burgoyne, the landing at the Head of Elk, and Washington, Franklin, Jefferson . . .

Next to Laurel, a woman in a gown of bronze-colored silk shot her a rueful smile. "It's a shame, isn't it?" she asked. "Everyone leaving the city? Think of it . . . who can tell when any of us shall see each other again? Tomorrow the city will be half abandoned. How odd it will seem."

Laurel stared, uncomprehending. "Why? Are the British really so close?"

The woman whose name Laurel couldn't remember gave a soft laugh. "My heart! Have you really been so far out in the country? Yes, of course. It's a matter of days, even hours. General Howe is determined to take our city at any cost, and we don't have the numbers or strength to fight him. Are you leaving or staying in the city?"

"I don't know just yet," Laurel replied. She tried to untangle her fan from the lace on her sleeve. "Crap," she muttered, and the woman in the bronze silk gave a soft gasp, her own fan fluttering up to cover her mouth. She looked at Laurel with wide, shocked eyes.

"Excuse me, please," she murmured, and made a hasty retreat, her powdered white curls bouncing over her shoulders.

Laurel shot a nervous glance at Seth, wondering if he had heard. To her relief, she spied him across the room, deep in conversation with two solemn-looking men. Talking about the war, probably. He looked so fierce and handsome in his velvet frock coat, his dark brows drawn. Unlike many of the men in the room, he disdained to wear a wig, and Laurel thought how much more attractive it made him, somehow more masculine-looking than the powdered and curled gentlemen he spoke to.

Laurel attempted a graceful wave of her fan and hit herself squarely on the lip with a loud smack. *So much for the womanly art of fan fluttering*, she thought, tucking her fan away hastily and hoping that nobody had seen.

All across the crowded room, people were chattering to each other, greeting each other. They all seemed to be completely at ease. Laurel felt like an impostor, dressed in another woman's gown. She crossed the room, trying not to trip on her sweeping skirts, and leaned against a wall.

A passing matron in deep blue looked shocked, and Laurel straightened her spine immediately. Apparently, leaning was simply not acceptable.

Her tightly laced corsets were giving her a backache, digging in to her hips and ribs. She wondered how the other women in the room could bear it. Maybe, after being tightly laced all their lives, they'd simply lost all feeling in their upper bodies.

She looked around for a chair, but they all seemed to be taken. Damn! If she didn't sit down soon, she was going to pass out cold.

Trying to look at ease, she made her way across the crowded room, nodding politely to people she'd been introduced to. The woman in the bronze gown quickly turned her back when she saw Laurel, suddenly engrossed in another conversation. The two women she spoke two gave Laurel quick, appraising glances, and Laurel heard the murmur, " . . . Seth Goodwin's cousin."

Eager to be out of the way of their curious eyes, Laurel made her way through the room with an air of studied indifference and escaped through some partially opened double doors at the far end of the room.

She almost sighed with relief to find herself alone. All she needed was a minute to compose herself; then she'd rejoin the party, before Seth noticed she was missing.

Fascinated, she studied the empty room. The ceiling was high, painted with murals of the sky. The draperies and upholstery were in the same tranquil shades of blue, cool and restful in the soft light shed by several fresh candles, and a little fire burned in a gleaming, marble-fronted hearth. Carefully arranged chairs surrounded a silent piano-type thing—a spinet, maybe? A harpsichord?

Delighted to be alone, Laurel couldn't resist touching the keys of the instrument and listening to the quivering notes. She made her way to the fire and plopped herself into an empty wing chair. Her silk skirts were slippery beneath her, and she almost slid to the floor. The furniture here, she discovered, was more decorative than comfortable. Nobody relaxed in a chair; they perched on them in genteel postures.

Laurel looked over the fireplace, where there was a portrait of a pale man with dark rings under his eyes, looking curiously flat.

"What I want," she told the flat portrait man, "is an E-Z Boy recliner and a pack of Marlboro Light 100s. And my Levi's. That's all. Is that too much to ask?"

The flat portrait man didn't look as if he would have approved.

A spark crackled in the fire, and Laurel pulled her skirts away, glancing down in alarm.

And saw the pipe.

A long-stemmed ivory pipe, with a silver tip on the mouthpiece, brimming over with bright, golden tobacco.

Unsmoked.

"This," Laurel said quietly, "is my lucky day."

The pipe lay on the stone hearth, as if the owner had come in for a smoke, loaded his pipe, and been suddenly called away. Next to the pipe lay a pair of silver smoking tongs, the tips blackened by use. Laurel had seen smoking tongs used many times since her arrival—the owner would simply pick them up, take a coal from the fire, and hold it to the end of his pipe until it was lit.

"It's not my usual brand," Laurel told the sour-looking painted man in the portrait, "but thank you, I think I will."

She glanced around the room once more, to make sure she was alone. Aside from the empty chairs and silent spinet, she was.

She bent down and picked up the pipe, almost sliding off the hard seat of the chair. Impatiently, she lifted the bulk of her skirts over her knees and braced her feet on the floor. Grabbing the pipe in an eager hand, she lifted it to her nose and sniffed the familiar scent of tobacco.

Despite the ease with which she had seen the task performed, getting a coal from the fire into the smoking tongs was more difficult. The heat from the fire made her flinch, and when she at last secured a burning ember she dropped it twice.

Leaning forward over the hearth, and being careful not to hold the burning ember over her silken skirts, Laurel at last managed to bring the glowing coal to the end of the pipe she clutched in her teeth.

With a furtive glance over her shoulder, she drew in.

It was nothing at all like she expected. The smoke was hot and bitter and harsh, biting at her throat.

She coughed violently, tears flooding her eyes. The smoking tongs fell to the hearth as she gasped and hacked, pounding her chest.

"Damn it!" she exclaimed, holding the pipe at arms' length. "Either the taste of tobacco's changed in the past two hundred years or I'm out of practice." She blinked back tears, dizzy and feeling a little green around the gills.

Should she give it up or try again?

To be frank, the whole experience brought back memories of her first cigarette, smoked behind her parents' suburban house, in order to impress an older and more sophisticated cousin. The experience had left her short of breath, dizzy, and light-headed. And yet . . .

There it was, the familiar feeling of nicotine running through her veins, the call of the smoker to answer his bad habit, the memory of a million blissful smokes with as many steaming cups of coffee.

"Nothing like being an addict," Laurel informed the flat man in the portrait, and settled back in her wing chair for another drag.

She didn't cough at all on the second pull of the pipe, and the third was even smoother.

By the time she was on to the fifth, Laurel was a happy confirmed smoker again. She sat in front of the fire, her slippery skirts bunched around her waist, her cotton petticoats covering her thighs, her long legs crossed comfortably, and enjoyed her pipe.

She wondered if she could get away with taking the pipe, decided against it, and debated how she could best go about getting one of her own.

She had seen a tobacconist's shop on the way to Mistress Kimball's earlier that day. Perhaps she could ask Seth for some money—tell him she needed some ribbons or something—and go buy a pipe and a little pack of tobacco. She could sneak out of the house on the pretext of going to the outdoor privy, and that would be it, clean and simple. She'd be smoking again.

True, it was a little harsher than she would have liked, but there wasn't any help for that. A girl had to do what a girl had to do. And if anybody didn't like it—

"Mercy on us!"

Laurel's eyes, which had been shut in blissful contemplation of her tobacco-filled future, flew open in horror.

Apparently, it was time for the "musical portion" of the evening to begin, and the Williamses' servants had thrown open the double doors to admit the guests—and the guests were there, in droves.

Laurel sat, still with shock, the smoking pipe still in her mouth, staring.

A hundred sets of eyes stared back. Ladies with careful coiffures fluttered their pale hands over their paler faces; gentlemen in stiff waistcoats and cravats regarded her with stiffer expressions. A collective murmur of dismay and disapproval ran through the gathering crowd.

Laurel tried not to think about what she looked like, with her beautiful skirts bunched around her knees, slumped in the chair with a pipe hanging out of her mouth.

"Seth Goodwin's cousin . . ." she heard someone whisper, and she felt her face flushing a brilliant red.

She dropped the pipe with a clatter and tugged her voluminous skirts down.

And suddenly, Seth appeared out of the crowd, his face set in tense lines, his dark eyes gleaming with a dangerous light.

"Excuse me . . . excuse me, please . . ." He made his way across the room with quick, purposeful strides and seized her hand in a none-too-gentle grip, pulling her to her feet.

"What in the devil are you doing?" he hissed beneath his breath.

Laurel offered him a weak smile.

"Never mind." He began to pull her from the room. The crowd parted silently as they made their way, as if making room for a leper. The women drew their skirts away as she passed; the men avoided her eyes.

Laurel wished she could disappear through the floor.

Seth was making weak apologies—they had to leave early, his cousin didn't feel well, the recent shock of her parent's death, and things like that. Beneath his dulcet tones, Laurel could hear plain, cold fury.

She didn't know whether to laugh or cry.

He was silent all the way out the front door and halfway down the street, never releasing his firm grip on her elbow.

She darted a quick look up at him and looked away immediately, unnerved by the sight of his glittering eyes, his tightly set mouth. She decided to be grateful for his silence.

It was over too quickly.

"What in the devil did you think you were doing?" The words were an explosion, loud in the quiet street, and Laurel jumped, stumbling on her hem.

"Well? What was that? What possible excuse in God's realm could you have! What were you doing? What? Tell me, please, because I'm completely befuddled! What was . . ." He gestured back at the house with an erratic, impatient thrust. *What was that?*"

Laurel scratched at her shoulder, where the stiff lace and artificial roses were making her itch. "I found a pipe," she offered in a feeble voice.

He dropped her elbow then and covered his eyes with his hands. "You found a pipe," he repeated quietly. "You found a pipe."

"Well, yes. It was just lying there. I guess somebody forgot about it."

He dropped his hands and regarded her with stark disbelief. "And?"

Laurel gave a weak shrug. "I guess . . . well . . . I guess I felt like having a smoke."

"You felt like having a smoke."

"Well . . . yeah. I mean, I didn't think anyone would find out. I just . . . felt like it."

Seth looked around, as if checking to make sure the street was still there, or the sky was still overhead, or maybe to see if they were still on the same planet.

"You felt like it," he repeated softly. "She felt like it," he explained to an invisible audience. "She just saw a pipe, and she just felt like it. No great matter, nothing odd at all; she just felt like it. That's all."

Laurel nodded in hasty agreement.

"*Have you lost your bloody mind?* What do mean, you felt like a smoke? You can't do that! What in the devil came over you, Hope Garrick? I take you to one of the finest houses in the city, I introduce you to the people who'll be your neighbors and friends, and you decide to take up a pipe? Do you have any idea what those people must think?"

"They think I'm crazy?"

"Yes, they think you're crazy. And what's more, they're right. What possessed you, Hope?"

Unable to think of an adequate answer, Laurel shrugged.

"Is this a habit of yours?" The words were sharp, spoken in the kind of tone you used to a

293

disobedient child or a not very bright dog, and Laurel felt her temper rise.

"Yes. Yes, it is," she retorted in defiant tones. "There. I'm a smoker, and I haven't smoked in weeks, and I've just been dying, and there was the pipe—"

"Women don't smoke! It's simply not done. Are you trying to tell me you were smoking on that godforsaken farm of yours?"

"Well," Laurel said, struggling to keep up with Seth's furious stride, "no. Not there. But before that, I smoked."

"*Before that?* What do you mean, before that? You were born on that farm; you've lived on that farm all your life. What do mean, before that?"

Laurel rushed along at his side, wondering what had possessed her to say such a thing.

If she could only tell him how difficult it was for her, the constant pretense, the incessant fear that she would somehow embarrass herself. And what if he knew that she was from another world? What would he think? Would he love her, she wondered, if he knew she was a thirty-year-old divorcée, or was he simply infatuated with Hope Garrick's youthful charms? She might never know.

He glared down at her with a quick, hard glance, and something in her face caused him to stop and look again.

"What do you mean?" he repeated, more softly this time.

"It's . . . kind of hard to explain. Almost

impossible, as a matter of fact. And if I did, I don't think you'd believe me. I know I wouldn't."

She stared up at him, surprised by the sudden sting of tears in her eyes. What would he say if she told him the truth? She laid a hesitant hand on his shoulder, wishing with all her heart that she was simply what she pretended to be, an eighteenth-century farm girl, and that she could simply marry him and stay in Philadelphia until the day she died. But she wasn't Hope, she was Laurel, and she would never fit in. She would always be living a lie, worrying about doing or saying the wrong thing.

"Tell me, sweetheart . . . what is it?"

His unexpectedly tender question caught her off guard. He was so handsome, with his dark, rough features and graceful height, that her answer caught in her throat.

Tell him. If he loves you, he'll have to believe you. And you can't keep lying forever, she told herself.

But what if he thinks that you're nuts? What if it's just too much for him to swallow? What if he changes his mind about loving you?

She'd have to take her chances. Perhaps his response would be the deciding factor and she'd know whether to stay in the past or make her way back to Chadsford, and to the future.

"How far are we from your house, Seth?"

Curious, he reached out to brush a disheveled curl from her temple. "Only a few moments' walk. Why?"

"Because I think you'd better be sitting down when I tell you the truth."

He didn't seem surprised by her words. "All the truth, Hope?" he asked.

Laurel took a deep breath. "Every last damned bit. And let's start here. My name isn't Hope. I'm Laurel. Laurel Behrman."

What a strange relief, to say it out loud. She suddenly felt like a whole person again.

Whatever it was he had expected to hear, it obviously wasn't that. He simply stood, staring at her as if he had never seen her before.

A cool breeze moved down the street, carrying the faint scent of autumn with it. The leaves on the trees above them shivered, and Laurel did too, suddenly wishing that she could take back the words she had spoken.

Seth glanced at the trees and held his hand out to her, his face unreadable.

"Come then, Laurel Behrman, if that is indeed who you are: Tell me your story, and we'll see what's to be done with you."

Silently, Laurel placed her hand in his and followed him down the quiet streets, their shoes loud against the cobblestones.

"It's simply too much to be believed. Too much." Seth leaned forward, his elbows resting on his knees, and stared at the fire. The flames cast dark shadows beneath his high cheekbones and reflected gold in his dark eyes.

"Tell me about it," Laurel retorted. "I told you you'd never believe me. Hey, half the time I don't believe it myself. But here I am, and here you are. How do you think I knew about Washington's position? About Whitemarsh, and Valley Forge? And I know more, too. The war will end in October of 1781. Cornwallis is going to surrender at Yorktown. So there."

Seth looked over at her, sprawled across the four-poster bed in her white shift, her golden hair loose and gleaming in the candlelight.

"I got mostly As in history," she added. "The first president of the United States was George Washington; his term ran from 1789 to 1797. Then John Adams, till 1801. After that, Thomas Jefferson. Then comes James Madison, then James Munroe, then John Quincy Adams. After that, Andrew Jackson, Martin Van Buren, and William Harrison. I can keep going, all the way to Carter-Reagan-Bush-Clinton, if you like. Forty-two of them, unless I've missed something at home."

Seth leaned back in the armchair and stared at her, silent. His eyes never left her face.

"Hey! How the heck do you think I revived you, after Howard left you for dead?"

Seth spread his hands in a helpless gesture.

"Ha! I'll tell. Cardiopulmonary resuscitation, that's how. CPR. I took a class. I could teach you how. Kind of like jump-starting a heart that's stopped. It's a very common medical practice."

Seth was shaking his head slowly. "It's just a lot to swallow."

"Well, it's the truth. The whole, stinking, honest-to-God truth. If you believe me, fine. If you don't, there's not a lot I can do." She leaned back against the pillows and crossed her arms. "But if you think you're confused, think how I feel. One minute I'm driving down the road with Tamara, listening to Bruce Springsteen and on my way to get a beer, and then boom! I'm dead. In the prime of my youth. Well, maybe a little past the prime of my youth. I'm thirty, you know."

"You are?" Seth sounded surprised. Surprised and maybe . . . maybe, just a little, as if he believed her.

"Yep. Thirty, divorced, and single. I work at the Shop and Pack. I'm a grocery checker. I have a sister named Linda and a cat named Wiley, and I did drive a little VW bug, but it looked pretty bad the last I saw it. My parents are Bonnie and Lou Behrman. I was born in West Seattle General Hospital; May 14, 1963. My best friend is Tamara Peterson, and we graduated from Lakecrest High in 1981." To Laurel's surprise, a tear rolled down her cheek, and she dashed it away.

"And I'm stuck here. And I'm supposed to go back. And I'm not sure I want to. See, I thought I'd just get Prudence settled away from that Thomas Garrick and I'd be able to walk off. But

I didn't count on you. I didn't think I'd fall in love. I thought I was done with all that stuff."

Seth leaned forward and took her hand in his own. He turned it over and ran his long fingers across her palm. "And . . . supposing all you've told me is true . . . how are you supposed to get back to wherever it is?"

"Seattle. Seattle, Washington. The forty-eighth state. Pacific Northwest."

He shook his head, trying to assimilate this.

"I'm not sure exactly how, but I know it's got something to do with the river. The same place I met you. That was where I came in, I think, after Hope hit her head."

"Inconceivable."

"I told you. I told you it was hard to believe. But how else do you explain everything?"

"I can't." He rose from the chair and crossed the room, and stood looking out the open window. "I can't explain any of it. And you sound as if you're telling the truth. At least, you believe you are. And if you've been making up any of what you've told me in the past hour, you're the greatest storyteller ever born. If you told me you'd been to the moon, it would be easier for me to believe."

"Well, I haven't, but someone has. And you know what's there?"

Seth looked over his broad shoulder at her, his face blank. "I haven't a clue."

"Nothing. Rocks and craters. That's it. Not much gravity. Watched it on TV. 'One small step for man,' and all that. Neil Armstrong, the first man to walk on the moon."

Seth stared back out the window, up at the moon. He gave a long, tired sigh, and shook his head again. "It's all too much."

"Hey," Laurel said, and a teasing note crept into her voice, "does this mean you don't want to marry me?"

He turned abruptly and looked over at her lying across the bed. She was propped on one elbow, the thin skirt of her chemise tangled around her knees with her usual lack of modesty, her golden hair streaming across her shoulders. Despite the teasing smile on her mouth, her blue-green eyes looked close to tears.

"God help me, Hope, or Laurel, or whoever you are. I don't know what this means. But this I know. I still love you. And what I intend is this—I want to marry you, and hold you in my arms every night, and wake up and make love to you every morning for the rest of my life. And I will never, ever, let you anywhere near the banks of the Brandywine, as long as there's breath in my body."

"You believe me." The words were whispered, quiet in the softly lit room.

"I must. There's nothing else to think."

Laurel held out her arms to him, wanting the reality of his body pressing against her.

He shed his waistcoat and shirt and lay next to her, holding her tightly, as if he was afraid she might melt away. He rained soft kisses over her brow and cheekbones and across the warmth of her neck, until she moaned with the sweetness of it.

"Never leave me," he whispered.

"Never."

"Promise." His hands slid beneath her shift, over the silken skin of her thighs and up over her slender ribs, stroking the soft curves of her breasts.

She touched him with a hunger that awed her, marveling at his strength, the clean feeling of his hair in her fingers, the way his mouth fit over hers, the way their shared breath mingled when they kissed; perfect, sweet, made for each other.

The only sound in the room was that of their breathing, and the soft whispers of their clothing falling to the floor and the soft creaking sound of the bed ropes that supported the featherbed.

When she reached for the smooth, hard length of him and drew him into her body she shivered at the sound of desire he made, low and soft in his throat, and she cried out softly as he entered her and their bodies became one.

"Promise me," he repeated, his breath hot against her ear. He lifted off of her and lay looking down at her, golden and pale beneath him.

She drew a shaking breath and stared up at him, poised above her, with his eyes hot and hungry, his hair falling dark and wild across his chiseled face.

"I love you, Seth Goodwin . . . forever."

He threw his head back, his hair tossing like a stallion's mane, and he drove into her with a furious, possessive heat, riding her until she cried out with a wordless sound of passion and love, until her body shook with waves of white-hot desire, one after the other, blinding and beautiful in their intensity.

That night, when Laurel slept in his arms, she felt for the first time as if he was holding her real self, instead of Hope Garrick.

Chapter Fourteen

Heavy. Her eyelids had never felt so heavy. Leaden and dry, as if she'd been drugged. Laurel tried to move her arms, but they, too, felt like lead weights.

She wondered, as if through a fog, if she was sick. That must be it. Sicker than she had ever been before. And something had changed; something felt different.

" . . . breathing on her own for twelve hours now." The unfamiliar voice was very far away.

"That's a good sign, isn't it?"

Was that her mother's voice?

"It means she's breathing without the respirator, and that's good. It means her lungs are beginning to function normally." The unfamiliar voice was cool, professional.

She must have been sick. She was in a

hospital. She could smell the sharp, sterile scent of clean tile and professionally bleached sheets. She could hear the rhythmic *bleep ... bleep ... bleep* of some kind of medical machinery.

What in the heck was going on?

She struggled to speak, but the effort was too much.

"Of course it's a good sign! How could it not be?"

That was Tamara's voice, and her familiar smell of coffee and Giorgio perfume nearby.

Oh, that's right ... Tamara, the car accident ... and Pennsylvania, and Prudence, and Seth. ...

Oh, God ... Seth ...

"Seth!"

Harsh and strained, his name rose from her throat as if it had been torn from her heart.

"Seeeeth!" Blind with pain, her heart twisting with grief, she came struggling out of the dense fog that surrounded her, struggling against the leaden inertia, fighting to sit up. ...

"Hope!"

Her vision cleared, and he was there. She was safe. She was in her four-poster bed in Philadelphia, and the cool light of early morning was filling the room, and Seth was there.

She sat gasping, her heart pounding, tears hot against her eyes.

"Good God, Hope, what happened?" Even as he spoke, he was gathering her into his arms. She closed her eyes and laid her face against his chest, feeling the soft tickle of his dark hair against her cheek, breathing the warm, early morning scent of skin, listening to his heart beat.

Alive. Still hers.

"I thought I was gone. Gone home." Her voice shook. "I *was* gone, I swear it. I was in the hospital. I could hear it, Seth, I could feel it. My mom was there, and Tamara, and I thought I'd never see you again."

His hand moved through her hair, stroking the back of her neck with a soothing motion. "A dream, angel. Just a dream."

Laurel shuddered. "No. No, it wasn't. It was real."

"And yet, here you are."

She pressed closer to him, inhaling the scent of his skin, and the smell of the room, oiled wood and clean linen and fresh beeswax from the candles. The featherbed was soft and warm against her bare skin, and she thought of the firm, hard hospital bed and shuddered.

"You don't believe me."

Seth's fingers, gentle and warm, tousled her hair. "I believe that you believe it. Isn't that enough?"

"I guess so. After all, I'm not sure I'd believe me. But I know it was real." She tilted her head back and ran a trembling hand across the proud line of his cheekbone, across his mouth. "Oh, Seth . . . what if it ends, just like that? What happens if I just wake up one day and I'm two hundred years away from you?"

He believed her enough to look horrified by the idea.

"Impossible," he stated. "It's absolutely impossible. It was only a dream."

"But, Seth . . ."

He kissed her softly, his lips gentle against her forehead. "It was a dream," he insisted. His hand traveled down her side, stroking her ribs, the curve of her waist, her hip, and his mouth moved over hers.

"You're a dream," Laurel whispered, moving her body closer against him through the tangled sheets, until his hands and mouth banished all thoughts of the future and she gave herself to him with a fierce hunger, as though his body could keep hers there, simply by the intensity of their love.

She laced herself into one of her new dresses from Mistress Kimball, a pale yellow cotton patterned with scrolls of darker gold and sky blue flowers, grimacing as she tugged the laces through the steel eyes. A piece of fitted fabric covered the laces down the front of the pointed bodice; a stomacher, Mistress Kimball had called it. Sky-blue ribbons descended down the front of her gown, from the deep rounded neckline to the pointed waist.

Not bad looking, for armor, Laurel thought, admiring herself briefly in the mirror. She braided her hair in a single plait, secured the end with a ribbon, and went down the narrow staircase to the kitchen to join Seth.

He wasn't alone. Sitting across the kitchen table from him was Stephen, from the inn at Haverton. His simple clothing was stained with dirt and his battered tricorn hat sat on the table next to him. He looked tired, as if he had been traveling a long time.

He smiled his pleasant smile at Laurel. "Good to see you. You look better than you did the last time we met. City life must agree with you."

Laurel smiled, casting a quick glance at Seth. The memory of the morning was still fresh in her mind, and her cheeks warmed at the tender look he gave her. "Oh, it agrees with me, all right. What brings you here, Stephen?"

"This and that. Nothing King George would approve of, you can be assured." He smiled again, a strained smile that didn't reach his eyes. "Last night, for example, we had a bell that needed to be moved."

Seth set down his heavy mug of coffee with a soft laugh. "What, the state house bell?"

"Gone. Vanished." Stephen shrugged. "I don't know a thing about it—except that the damned lobsterbacks will have to find their own damned bell to ring. They may move their sorry pampered asses into our state house, but damned if we'll make it easy for them. Cleaned the place out last night. They'll find scant welcome."

"How close are they?" Laurel asked.

Seth stared into his mug for a moment before answering. "Any closer, angel, and

307

they'll be sitting at the table. They're not close; they're here."

Laurel's heart skipped a beat. "What, in the city?"

Stephen nodded. "Aye. They came in like they owned it. A few shots were fired, but nothing to speak of. We don't have the troops to resist."

"Bastards," Seth muttered. "They think we'll just give them our land. But they've underestimated us. We'll fight them down to the last man, if we must. I'll not live under Mother England's bitch thumb."

"Amen," Stephen agreed. "It'd have made you sick, Goodwin, to see all the folk lining the streets, cheering the damned troops like they were heroes."

"It's going to make me even sicker," Seth added, "when I go out and join them." He gave Laurel a bitter smile. "As far as anyone's concerned, we're loyalists now. Until I have orders to leave the city we have to blend in. It makes my stomach turn, but we're going to go cheer the mighty invaders, sweetheart."

Stephen shook his golden head. "Not for long, you're not. Here." He reached into his shirt pocket and withdrew a folded paper. "Orders, Goodwin. From Whitemarsh."

Seth took the paper and unfolded it. "Ah, so Gordon made it through the lines, did he?" His dark eyes scanned the paper once, then again. He stood and walked to the brick fireplace, tossing the paper in and watching while it burned. He turned to look at Laurel, his face solemn.

"Damn. I'd hoped to finish that secretary before I left. I hate to leave a piece unfinished."

"What is it?" Laurel asked, her stomach tightening.

"I'm to report to Whitemarsh, and soon. Time to put on a uniform and join the troops."

Laurel looked around the kitchen, at the smooth plaster and brick walls, the shelves of gleaming silver and pewter, the polished copper pans. "And me? What about me? Do I stay here and wait?"

"That would be safest." Seth's voice was soft.

"I don't know, Goodwin." Stephen looked thoughtful. "After that little episode by Haverton she's a wanted woman. The odds of her being recognized aren't as small as you think. She's pretty, and she has a distinctive way about her. And she humiliated that British officer so beautifully. By the time his men woke up and untied him he was good and furious. You should have heard him when he showed up at the inn. He wanted to kill her. And you, too."

Seth looked thoughtful. "That's true. I'd hate for her to meet him, walking down the street. And the British will be headquartered here for a while."

"At least all winter," Laurel pointed out.

"I say you should take her with you. There are plenty of decent women with the army. Wives, laundresses, cooks . . ."

"I don't like it," Seth objected. "It's dangerous."

"It's dangerous here," Stephen argued. "It's dangerous everywhere. What if she was recognized and imprisoned while you were at Whitemarsh? You couldn't help her, and would she even be able to get word to you?"

"But what if the British attack? I don't want her anywhere near the front lines."

"The British aren't going to attack," Laurel reminded him. "Not all winter. Whitemarsh is safe, and they won't attack Valley Forge. We may freeze to death, or starve to death, but we won't be attacked. That I know for a fact."

"Are you sure, Hope?" Seth's eyes searched her face for any hesitation, any sign of doubt. "You're asking me to believe that which is inconceivable to me, that which is impossible. Are you absolutely sure?"

Laurel met his eyes with a firm gaze, hoping that he could see the truth there. "I swear on my soul. I swear on anything. Everything I've told you is the truth."

The last glimmer of doubt vanished from his face.

Stephen's smooth brow wrinkled. "Why do I get the feeling something's afoot that I'm not privy to?"

"You wouldn't believe half of it." Laurel stood up, trying not to stumble on her skirts, and faced Seth, laying her hand on his shoulder. "Now you listen to me, Seth Goodwin. I'm going with you, and you'd better get used to the idea. I'm not going to risk losing you. Neither of us really knows how much time we have left, or what's going to happen. And I'm not going to waste a single moment. Where you go, I go. I promised, remember?"

They stood, their eyes locked together, and Laurel reached up to touch his cheek and the dark stubble that shadowed the clean line of his jaw.

"I remember," he answered softly. "But I won't hold you to it, if you change your mind. I love you, angel."

"Then I'm going with you."

He bent and pressed his lips against her forehead.

"Looks like love to me," Stephen commented. "Should I leave?"

"No, don't be dumb," Laurel answered, stepping away from Seth. "When do we leave, Seth?"

"Today or tomorrow, at the very latest. I'll have to figure out a way for us to leave the city without arousing suspicion."

"Quakers," Stephen said.

"What?"

"Leave dressed as Quakers," Stephen suggested. "Everyone knows that the Quakers won't take sides. It's perfect."

"It's a damned good idea," Seth agreed. "I'm surprised at you, Stephen. You're more devious than I would have wagered."

"Who, me? I'm just—"

"Yes, yes, an innocent innkeeper. Save your story for the British."

"The next time I speak to the British I won't give them a story," Stephen said, his face darkening. "I'll give them a bullet in their arrogant heads, damn them all to hell."

Laurel turned to look at Stephen, surprised by the bitter hatred in his voice. When she met him he had seemed so lighthearted and careless, almost as if the war and espionage were a fine joke, a merry adventure.

"Will you be joining Washington's troops as well, Stephen," Seth asked, "or heading back to Haverton?"

Stephen drained the coffee from his mug and regarded it for a moment before answering. "Actually, Goodwin, that's one of the reasons I'm here. Do you still own a British uniform?"

"Yes. Why?"

"I'll need it," Stephen answered in determined tones. "My brother was taken prisoner yesterday, and they intend to try him as a traitor and a spy. I intend to bring him out before they can hang him."

Laurel thought of Gordon, and how kind he had been to her and Prudence at the inn. "Oh, Stephen . . ."

"You're mad," Seth said bluntly.

"The hell I am," Laurel replied with indignation. "I thought we'd cleared that up."

"Not you, sweetheart: Stephen. You can't

possibly infiltrate the British camps. You haven't the experience; you haven't the skill. You'll be hanged yourself."

"Damn, Goodwin! Do you expect me to leave my brother to die without even trying to help?"

Seth set down his mug with a sharp bang. "No, you idiot. I expect you to stay here and let me do it. I've spent the last year in British uniform without being caught; I expect I can manage it one last time."

Laurel shivered, despite the warmth of the kitchen, and reached out for his hand. "Seth, are you sure? I'd die if you were captured."

"I wouldn't offer if I wasn't sure. Besides which, Stephen could never get away with wearing my uniform. I'm a full head taller than he."

"Not quite a full head," Stephen objected. "I'm taller than I look."

Seth gave him a doubtful look.

"I am."

"Be that as it may or may not, I won't allow it. It would be suicidal for you to try. Do you know where Gordon's being held?"

"Right here in the city. I stood in the crowd and watched the prisoners being marched in. He doesn't look well, Goodwin. I think the bastards beat him."

"But he's able to walk?"

"Aye, he was."

Seth nodded. "Then I'll bring him out, my friend. And we'll leave the city together, immediately after. The British will be too concerned with the taking of the city to try anyone for a couple of days, so he'll be safe enough till nightfall."

Laurel tried not to think of Seth failing, of his being recognized, tried, and hanged. Her hand tightened over his. "Oh, Seth, be careful."

He turned and gave her a careless smile, the small lines around his dark eyes crinkling. "Don't worry, sweetheart. It's not the most dangerous thing I've ever done."

"Oh, really? What was?"

He lifted his brows, as if straining to remember. "Ah . . . that would have been . . . let me see . . . Was it copying General Burgoyne's paper while he slept five feet away? No. Maybe carrying a message through to Washington at McConkey's Ferry? No, that isn't the worst. I think the most terrifying thing I've done was agreeing to escort you to Philadelphia. I honestly didn't think I'd survive the experience."

Laurel rolled her eyes. "Oh, you're funny."

Seth gave her shoulder a quick squeeze. "I've never been more serious in my life."

"Women are dangerous things," Stephen agreed. "I'd rather face the entire British Navy than one angry woman. Particularly a pretty one," he added, giving Laurel a teasing smile.

Seth stretched and shook his hair back from his eyes. "Very well; now that that's settled, we have things to do. Stephen, you head into town and find out exactly where the prisoners are being held and who's in charge, and anything else you can. It won't do for me to be seen on the street today. Laurel, I mean Hope, can you find your way back to Mistress Kimball's?"

"I think so. It wasn't that far."

"Good. Don't speak to her in front of anyone; tell her that it concerns a delicate matter. Use those words exactly. A delicate matter. Do you understand?"

"No, but I'll say it anyway."

"See that you do. And tell her that we need clothing suitable for a Quaker couple that will be leaving the city tonight. Mind that nobody overhears you."

Laurel nodded. "Anything else, boss?"

Seth thought. "No. That should be enough. Oh, you may want to speak to your sister. Don't tell her anything, of course. Just that you're leaving the city, and that it may be a long time before you see her again."

A chill raced down Laurel's spine, a superstitious tingle that made her shiver. "Got it."

"As for me," Seth added, "I'm heading into my shop for the rest of the day. I intend to finish that secretary. There's nothing that annoys me so much as leaving an unfinished piece, and God knows when we'll return."

If we return, Laurel thought, but didn't say aloud. As she went upstairs to put her hair up and find a proper cap, she couldn't shake the eerie feeling that this was her last night in Philadelphia.

Don't worry about it, she told herself sternly. *Even if you're right, there's not a thing you can do about it, except handle it.*

And before she finished the thought she heard her Grandma's voice in the empty room, as clearly as if she was standing there.

"Bingo," Grandma said.

Stephen accompanied Laurel to Mistress Kimball's shop, carrying a basket and walking a few steps behind her, as if he was a servant. "No need to call attention to myself," he observed. "Nobody looks twice at a servant."

Laurel saw the point in that and was glad of the company. The streets of Philadelphia seemed different today; red-coated soldiers were everywhere, laughing among themselves with the confidence gained of an easy victory.

Everywhere she looked, brass buttons were shining against scarlet uniforms, black boots were banging against the cobblestone streets, sabers rattled from hips. Perhaps it was her brief encounter in the forest with the British reconnaissance team that had taken Seth prisoner that made her shiver at the sight. Perhaps it was the reminder that she was smack-dab in the center of a war.

Or maybe, she told herself logically, it was simply the change in weather. Autumn had laid her cooling hand over the city. The first golden leaves were blowing through the streets; the sunlight seemed dimmer and touched the streets with a gentler light.

"Storm brewing," Stephen said from her elbow, as if he had been following her thoughts. "We'll have rain tonight, I shouldn't be surprised."

Again, Laurel felt a superstitious shiver of fear, and she glanced up at the sky before they stopped in front of Mistress Kimball's shop. "No, I wouldn't be surprised either," she agreed, and took her basket from Stephen's hand before entering the shop.

"Clothing for a Quaker couple by tonight," Mistress Kimball repeated, sounding indignant. "I'm a seamstress, not a magician. That Goodwin! He thinks his handsome face and figure will get him anything he wants."

Laurel glanced around the empty shop. "Well, will they?"

Mistress Kimball gave her a stern look through her round spectacles. "You're an impudent piece of baggage, young woman. Not at all like your sister." She lifted a waistcoat of pale blue from the table in front of her, examining the seams with the exacting eye of a card shark, and made a noise in her throat that could have meant anything.

"Too bad you're so much taller than his first wife," she added. "Anything Jane wore would have passed in a Quaker meetinghouse. Timid as a mouse; no sense of style. I suppose," she went on, changing the subject abruptly, "this Quaker couple is tall. Of the same height as you and Goodwin, would you guess?"

Laurel met the sharp eyes without flinching. "I think so."

Again, that noise that might have meant

anything. "Very well, then. I'll have something sent around before dark. Is that all?"

Laurel took a deep breath. "No. That is, I'd like to see Prudence. I mean, I know she's working, but I really would like to tell her good-bye."

Mistress Kimball's eyes were suddenly soft behind her round glasses, and she gave Laurel's hand an awkward pat. "Of course. Of course you may. After all, these are trying times, aren't they? One never knows what might happen."

"Exactly," Laurel agreed. "You can say that again."

Mistress Kimball folded the blue waistcoat carefully, examining the porcelain buttons, each one painted with a delicate country scene and framed in gold filigree. "You need not fear for your sister, Mistress Garrick. I give you my word that she'll be kept safe and happy, for as long as need be."

The usual acid tone was absent from her voice. She spoke very softly and kindly.

"Thank you," Laurel answered, trying to keep her voice from quivering. "I appreciate it."

When Mistress Kimball looked up she wore her usual stern face. "Very well; go see young Prudence. She's through the back door there. Try not to keep her from her work overlong, and don't upset her unneedfully."

"No, of course not," Laurel agreed, and made her way through the curtained doorway at the back of the shop.

Laurel was startled at the amount of activity

behind the quiet showroom of the shop. An older woman was supervising the cutting tables, three young assistants were fitting garments on mannequins, and everywhere a rainbow of fabrics and threads were in motion.

Relief washed over her as she caught sight of Prudence. The little girl sat at a long table with two other, slightly older girls.

She looked as happy as if she had unearthed Solomon's treasures. A rack of fine thread stood before her, skeins of shining blues and roses and violets and greens, and a length of primrose yellow silk was stretched on a wooden frame. Prudence was laughing softly at something one of the other girls had said and threading a shining needle with a length of emerald green. She looked freshly scrubbed and, like her companions, was dressed in a simple black dress, with a delicate wide collar of fine white lace draped over her shoulders and tied in a simple knot below her collarbone.

Far from looking somber on the child, the black of her dress seemed to highlight the pale cornsilk color of her hair, the rose in her plump cheeks. She looked well-rested, clean and, best of all, contented.

"Nice dress," Laurel greeted her, and Prudence jumped up from her chair, beaming.

"Oh, Hope! This is the most wonderous fine place! May I stay, truly?"

"What, you don't miss me?" Laurel laughed at the embarrassed blush on her sister's face.

Funny, how easy it was to think of Prudence as her sister.

"I didn't mean that, Hope. Not a bit. But just look, do you see what they've trusted me with?" Shining with pride, Prudence indicated the primrose silk. Laurel leaned in and smiled at the sight of Prudence's work—a pattern of ivy leaves and blue morning glories against the light fabric.

"This will be along the hem, and where the skirts divide *a la polonaise*," Prudence announced grandly, eager to show off her new knowledge. "And if I do well enough, I may embroider the stomacher, as well."

One of the other girls at the table smiled. "She does well, for a little thing," she admitted. "Better than I did. But by the time she gets round the bottom of that hem, she won't think it's such a treat."

The other apprentice girl—the tall, thin one who had shown Prudence her way in on the day she arrived—laughed merrily. "No, she won't. She'll be saying, 'Please, please, send me back to the farm!' "

"Oh, no, I will not," Prudence argued. "I shall stay here until I'm grown, and then I shall open my own shop, and you can come and work for me, and I shall send *you* back to the farm, Sarah."

The older girls laughed with delight at the idea, until a warning cough sounded from behind the curtained doorway, followed by the sound of jangling bells as the front door of the shop opened.

"Now we have to whisper," Prudence informed Laurel, lowering her voice. "Customers in the shop."

Laurel nodded solemnly. "Listen, Prudence, Mistress Kimball says that I may speak to you for a few minutes. Is there somewhere else we can go?"

"Take her to our room, Prudence," Sarah suggested kindly. "But don't be too long or Mistress Kimball will put you in a pot and have you for dinner."

"As if," Prudence disclaimed with scorn, and Laurel smiled, recognizing her own expression.

She followed Prudence up two flights of narrow stairs, catching a glimpse of Mistress Kimball's private sitting room after the first— an elegant, well-appointed room with handsome, graceful furniture and rich carpets. It spoke well of the woman's prosperity.

At the top of the second flight Prudence proudly beckoned Laurel into the room that she shared with Sarah and, presumably, the other apprentice girl.

Despite the low, steep ceilings, it was a pleasant room; three tidy beds, a small table and chairs, fresh candles—a luxury, Laurel realized, as opposed to giving the girls a small, smoky, fat-burning betty-lamp, like the ones they had used on the Garrick farm. The room was clean, the girls had a wardrobe for their clothes instead of pegs on the walls, and each bed had a small chest at the foot.

Two of the beds had beautifully made scrap quilts on them; the bed Prudence sat on had a plain coverlet. "I'm going to start a quilt," she informed Laurel. "Mistress Kimball lets us choose the scraps. Betty chose 'Tory Rose' for her pattern, and now she's sorry. I think I shall do 'LaFayette's Orange Peel.' It's meet, I think, with the war on. What do you think, Hope?"

Laurel didn't want to admit that quilt patterns were a mystery to her. "Sounds wonderful. Prudence—I need to tell you why I came. Aside from just to see you, I mean."

"Why, Hope? Oh, I know! You're going to marry Mr. Goodwin, aren't you?"

Laurel hesitated for a moment and laid her hand on the child's silky cheek, thinking how much she had come to care for her in such a short time.

"Actually, Prudence, I've come to say good-bye. Seth has to leave the city, and I've decided to go with him."

Prudence's bottom lip drooped, and she hung her head for a moment. "Must you, Hope?"

"Yes, I really, really must."

"And then will you marry him?" Prudence demanded. "Lawful heart, Hope! You must! I've heard him ask you."

Laurel laughed at Prudence's motherly tone. She sounded like her sister Linda, back home, who had such clear ideas of how other people's lives should be lived.

"I'll seriously consider it, honey."

Prudence appeared somewhat appeased. "And when will you be back, Hope? Will it be a long time?"

Laurel considered lying and decided against it. "I wish I could tell you, Prudence, but I can't. I really have no idea. There's a war on, and we might not be able to come back. Maybe not till the war's over."

"Maybe never?" Prudence's voice was very small and soft.

Laurel took a deep breath. "Maybe never."

Prudence looked at her small, plump hands, clasped tightly together in her lap. "Oh." She appeared to think about that.

"But you're safe here, Prudence. Mistress Kimball has said that you can stay as long as you need to, and that she'll be good. And Prudence . . ." Laurel swallowed, telling herself not to cry, not to make this harder. "I love you. I always will. Remember that, wherever I am."

Prudence nodded, wiping a tear away with the back of her hand. "I'll remember, Hope. And I love you, as well."

Laurel gathered the child into her arms for a hard, quick hug, and kissed the top of her silky head. "Be good; work hard. And don't worry about me. I'll be fine, and so will you."

Prudence raised her chin. "I always work hard, Hope. I'm going to be the best worker here."

"Good for you, Prudence. We'd better get you back to work right now, before Mistress

Kimball puts us both in a pot for dinner."

Laughing at this ludicrous idea, Prudence dashed the last remnants of tears from her blue eyes, and together they went down the narrow staircase.

Laurel left Prudence at the embroidery table, working her needle over patterns of morning glories, her face shining with pleasure.

Laurel resisted the urge to run back for another hug, telling herself firmly that when she got home she could have a good, long cry, but until then she'd better handle it.

She was making her way through the dress shop with her head down, brushing by the skirts of another customer without looking up, when a voice stopped her.

"It's Mistress Garrick, isn't it? Seth Goodwin's cousin from Chadsford?"

Startled, Hope looked up, and recognized the woman from the Williamses' party, who had worn bronze silk with peach ribbons. The one who had been so shocked by the profanity she'd uttered.

"Uh, yes . . . yes I am. How are you?"

The woman smiled, a curious look on her round face. "Oh, well enough. How odd to see you. I'd assumed you'd left the city, with the rest of the patriots."

The shop suddenly seemed silent, the conversation suspended into an eerie, waiting hush.

Laurel didn't like the look on the woman's face. It was sly, self-satisfied.

"And has Mr. Goodwin left the city?" the

woman continued, her voice bright and careless, sharply at odds with the gleam in her eye.

Out of the corner of her eye, Laurel caught the scarlet-and-gold gleam of a British uniform.

The scene before her suddenly took on a dreamlike, slow-motion feeling—the shelves of fabric, the way the cool sunlight shone through the paned windows and lit the powdered curls of the smiling woman before her, the slow approach of the man behind her elbow. There was a loud, persistent buzzing in her ears.

"Lie, Lisa." It was Uncle Jerry's voice, as clearly as if he stood behind her.

Without hesitating, Laurel lied. "Oh, yes. Seth left the city immediately after the party. I don't expect to see him for some time. He's off to the country, he said, until this all blows over."

"Seth, you say? Seth Goodwin?" The voice behind her was cool, with a very precise British accent—one that made Laurel shiver.

"But Seth Goodwin is quite dead, I'm sure. He fell at the battle of Brandywine. I was there."

With a sickening feeling of premonition, Laurel turned.

It was Howard. Images rushed through Laurel's head, memories of Howard, waist deep in the murky green waters of the Brandywine, holding Seth's head beneath the water, watching the way his dark hair floated. Memories of Howard, gasping and triumphant, pulling the lifeless body onto the bank and reaching to search through the dead man's pockets . . .

Laurel stared into the man's narrow eyes, his pale, tense face.

And watched his expression change as he recognized her. It took a moment, for she looked very different in her fashionable city clothes than she had that day on the river, hot and sticky, in a worn dress of brown home-spun, barefoot and with her hair tangled.

"You were there," he said softly, and his voice was cool and dangerous. "You saw him die, didn't you? Why do you say he is living?"

Laurel's pulse was pounding through her veins, so hard and fast that she thought she might faint.

"Lie, damn it!"

Uncle Jerry's voice was so loud that she jumped. The woman from the Williamses' party gave her a curious look. Howard remained unmoving, his eyes glittering and watchful.

"You're mistaken, sir," she snapped. "Of all the ridiculous ideas! You must have the wrong name, the wrong man. My cousin is very much alive—or at least he was when he left the city. As for the rest, I'm sure we've never met. Perhaps the man you're speaking of is another Mr. Goodwin. Perhaps a relative. I'm sure I don't know. If you'll excuse me . . ."

Howard started to speak, but Laurel pushed past him in a rush of petticoats and flowered skirts, her heart hammering against her tightly laced gown. The bells on the shop door jangled as she pushed her way out.

As she rushed past the shop windows, she saw Howard turn to the woman from the Williamses' party and tuck her arm beneath his in a familiar way, speaking to her with an urgent expression.

Panic seized Laurel, a dangerous, ugly feeling. As soon as she was out of sight of the window, she seized her skirts in both hands and started running, her heart thumping in time with her footsteps.

Chapter Fifteen

"Geez Louise!" Grandma exclaimed. "We almost had her that time! Did you see that?" She leaned forward so eagerly that the couch rocked and bobbed in the clouds, like a buoy on the sea.

Nathaniel leaned closer to the TV set, watching as Laurel rushed across a crowded street, where she had just narrowly missed being trampled by a passing horse. "It was close," he agreed.

From the corner of the couch Jerry was watching the screen through his fingers. "Too close. I don't like it. We decided to take them out together, didn't we? And nicely? There's nothing nice about being trampled to death."

Nathaniel frowned. "No. And there's nothing nice about being hanged as a traitor, either, so you two buffoons make sure that girl gets back to Seth's in time to warn him. My grandson doesn't deserve a traitor's death."

"Buffoon yourself," Grandma snapped. "Just pay attention. We have exactly twenty-four hours till we get called in front of the Boss. And we'd better have some good answers. I want everything exactly as it should be. A place for everyone, and everyone in his place."

"I'm a little concerned about where Seth's place is," admitted Nathaniel. "Hope's tampered with destiny to the point of utter chaos."

"Oh, get over it," Grandma told him. She adjusted her baseball hat over her gray curls; neon green with the words *I'm with Stupid* written on the front. Beneath the words, arrows pointed in both directions: one at Jerry and one at Nathaniel. "Chaos, my foot. It's just one little thing that we need to straighten out."

"Pay attention," Nathaniel shouted, pointing at the TV. "There she goes crossing the street without looking again!"

"Got it," Grandma announced, and a passing carriage swerved around Laurel, so close that the wheels brushed against her skirts.

Jerry, who was watching through his fingers again, lowered his hands with a heavy sigh. "Hoo boy. I need a nice cold bottle of Olympia after that one. Anyone else?"

"That was a good one," Grandma remarked watching as the carriage swerved, almost tipped over, and righted itself again. "Let's watch that on the instant replay."

Laurel clattered into Seth's kitchen as if she were being chased by an entire army, almost colliding with Mrs. Avery, the housekeeper, who was industriously cleaning the already clean floor.

She stopped to catch her breath, leaning on the rounded back of a sturdy Windsor chair. The boning in her dress seemed to stab into her sides with each hard breath she drew. She had lost her cap on the way home, and her hair was working its way loose from its tidy knot and hanging in damp wisps around her face.

Mrs. Avery dropped her scrub brush and rose abruptly to her feet, wiping her hands on her apron. Her round face was tight with concern. "Have mercy, what can have happened, child? Is young Prudence ill?"

Laurel shook her head and drew in another painful breath. "No, nothing like that. She's fine. Having a great time. Where's Seth?"

Mrs. Avery indicated the small stairway off the kitchen. "Down in his shop, happy as a king."

Laurel was down the stairs in a flash, and pushing through the heavy door.

Seth was carefully joining together the final drawer of the secretary, fitting the perfectly made notches into each other. He looked, as Mrs. Avery had said, as happy as a king. All around him his tools and scraps of wood lay in scattered disarray, and he looked up at Laurel with a surprised expression, as if he was so involved in his work that he had forgotten her existence.

"Is that done?" Laurel asked abruptly, indicating the graceful desk.

"Yes, almost. Look." He slid the center drawer into place and gave a self-satisfied smile. "Perfect fit, of course. Come give me a kiss."

He didn't appear to notice her dusty skirts or windblown hair. He slid the drawer out again, and then in. "Perfect," he commented.

Laurel stood back, assessing the elegant writing table. In the center of the drawer, the inlaid rising sun shone in pale satinwood, unfinished and white against the darker walnut of the drawer.

"Good. Because you said that you hate to leave an unfinished piece, and we're leaving. Right now."

He looked up, his dark brows raised. "By my foot, we are not! You can't be serious."

"I'm as serious as a heart attack," Laurel retorted. "You're in real trouble here, and so am I. Do you know who was in Mistress Kimball's, as I was leaving?"

"King George," Seth suggested, looking more amused than worried. "Come give me a kiss."

"I'm not joking!" Laurel cried. "Seth, it was Howard. And he knows you're alive!"

Seth's eyes narrowed and seemed to darken. "How does he know? Did you tell him? Are you sure it was Howard? Did he recognize you? Speak to you? Exactly what was said?"

"I'll tell you, if you let me get my breath. These damned clothes are killing me." Laurel sat down on a rough workbench and stretched her legs. "Okay. This is what happened."

She told Seth every detail, beginning with bumping into the woman from the Williamses' party and ending with her own arrival at home. "I'm sure she knew what she was doing," Laurel added. "She seemed to intentionally bring your name up, Seth. I think she might have been there with Howard. He was holding her arm and talking to her when I ran out."

"Tell me again; what did this woman look like?" he asked. His face was tight and dangerous-looking, and Laurel was reminded of how he had led them through dense forests, as wary and agile as a cat. It was like watching him transform from Seth Goodwin, proper and happy merchant, to Seth Goodwin, revolutionary spy.

"Oh, Seth, she looks like every other damned woman I met that night! Small, white-powdered hair, ten-inch waist, and a nice fan. She was wearing kind of a bronze-colored dress, with peach ribbons and way too much lace, and what else?" Laurel thought hard, trying to remember anything unusual about the woman. "Oh! She was really stacked, for her size."

"She was what?" Seth stared at her, utterly baffled.

"Stacked, Seth. Well-endowed." Laurel sighed. "She had a lot going on in the bosom department, Seth."

"Damn," he exclaimed, recognition showing on his face. "Lucy Reed. It must be."

"Boy, that didn't take you long," Laurel observed, not bothering to hide her disapproval. "I should have mentioned her bloozies right away and saved you the trouble."

"Don't be ridiculous," he said automatically, but he was obviously not really listening. He stood as tense as a wound spring, rubbing the back of his neck, a distracted look on his face. "If Lucy Reed's involved with the British, they won't be far behind you. Damn that woman! I should have guessed she'd make trouble."

"Why?" Laurel demanded. "How well do you know her?"

"Not that well. Not as well as she would have liked. But, damn! I never suspected she might be a British agent." He sounded thoroughly disgusted, either with himself or with the duplicitous Miss Reed. Laurel guessed both.

"Come on." He grabbed her wrist, casting a brief, regretful look back at the unvarnished secretary. "Lucy Reed knows where I live. We've got to get out of the house immediately."

Laurel's stomach started another roller-coaster ride.

They were almost to the kitchen staircase when they heard the clatter of hooves on the street in front of the house, and the muffled sound of a brisk voice giving an order to dismount.

"Too late," Seth said, and spun her around. "They'll have both doors covered before we can get out."

Laurel's heart leapt and raced, her mouth dry with fear. She heard footsteps clattering up the front walk, and someone banging on the door.

And Seth was dragging her across the room, behind the tidy stacks of lumber. He threw open the doors of the enormous wardrobe that stood in the corner. It was empty, save for the three broad shelves that lined it.

"Get in," he ordered, shoving her roughly in beneath the bottom shelf.

"Are you nuts?" she hissed. "We're going to hide in a closet?"

Without answering, he reached behind her and slid his hands over the smooth, dry wood and pushed.

The back of the wardrobe swung open, like a door. Beyond it, Laurel could see nothing but darkness.

There was shouting in the house now and the sound of running footsteps, and Mrs. Avery's frantic voice.

With one push, Seth tumbled her into the blackness. For one terrifying moment she was falling into nothing; then she hit the ground hard, her breath leaving her body in a sickening gasp.

She lay there, trying to breathe, and heard Seth climbing in after her. There was the soft sound of the wardrobe doors clicking shut and the sound of the false door closing, and they were in utter blackness.

"Don't speak or move," he whispered, so softly that Laurel could barely hear him. "I'll find you."

She felt him in the darkness next to her, touching first her foot, then her hip, then her shoulders. He helped her sit up, and pulled her tightly against his chest, laying a warning finger against her lips.

The warning was unnecessary. If Laurel had been able to catch her breath enough to speak, she would have been too frightened to do so. Above them, she could hear booted feet crashing from room to room, footsteps thundering down the kitchen stairs and into the workshop above them.

Laurel cringed against Seth as she heard things falling, the clatter of tumbling furniture, and a sound of wood splintering.

The sounds were dangerously close. Laurel heard a horrendous crash and knew it was the pile of stacked lumber in front of the wardrobe. And then, inevitably, the sound of the wardrobe doors opening.

Seth held her tight against him, his heartbeat steady and fast and loud against her ear, and she wondered if the sound was really loud enough to be heard in the other room, or if it just seemed so in the darkness.

"Devil take it." The voice on the other side

of the false door was so close, Laurel's heart missed a beat.

"Thought I might have had them."

"Did you?"

Laurel felt Seth tense as he recognized Howard's voice above them.

"Did you really? Are you such a fool as to think that Goodwin would hide in a closet, and leave himself no way out? We're dealing with a spy, not the village idiot. Keep on with your search."

Laurel could picture Howard clearly—the small, unpleasant eyes and the crisp white braid that hung stiffly from his wig, just grazing the collar of his immaculate uniform.

She didn't realize she'd been holding her breath until she heard his footsteps walking away from the wardrobe, and she exhaled in a long, shuddering sigh.

Then Howard's voice was speaking again. "This little desk is a nice piece of work. After you've done searching the place, have it sent round to headquarters. I fancy having it." Laurel could picture him standing in the middle of the sunny workroom, touching Seth's beautiful little secretary with his pale hands as he spoke. It seemed almost blasphemous.

"I'll see him in hell first," Seth whispered, so softly she could hardly hear him. His breath was warm against her ear, and they were both silent as they heard Howard's footsteps crossing the room and retreating up the kitchen stairs.

Laurel let out a shaky breath and leaned against Seth.

They sat like that for a long time, surrounded by total, unrelieved blackness, holding each other and listening to the footsteps of their enemies above them.

Eventually, Laurel heard the sounds of the search quieting; and then, somewhere above her head, she heard Mrs. Avery's voice, raised in what sounded like great indignation.

" . . . coming in like a great herd of cattle, spilling my wash water and kicking things about. And now mistreating a helpless old woman!"

Laurel thought Mrs. Avery sounded anything but old and helpless, and apparently, whoever she was speaking to agreed.

"Please, madam, cease this tirade. For the last time, tell us where Mr. Goodwin is."

"I'll tell you again and again, for all the good it does me when nobody listens. He left the city immediately after a party last night. He and his little cousin. And that's all. Haven't heard a word from either of them. Now you get your men and their dirty boots out of my kitchen, if you please."

God bless Mrs. Avery, Laurel thought. *She cleans, she cooks, and she can handle herself under fire.*

Mrs. Avery's voice grew quieter, as she was obviously led out of the kitchen, and all Laurel could hear was the distant sound of voices, punctuated by the dull thud of footsteps.

"They don't know we're here," Seth murmured. "If they suspected it, they'd still be searching. They can only know that we're somewhere in the city."

"How long will we have to hide?" Laurel whispered back. Her voice sounded eerie, thin and muffled in the darkness.

"Until we're out of Philadelphia and in American territory. Even when we leave this room, we won't be able to walk the streets openly. They'll post a guard outside the house, if they haven't done it already. It may be close, getting out. Let's just hope that they don't hold Mrs. Avery. It'll make it that much more difficult for us if they do."

"Does she know about this . . . room, or whatever it is?" Laurel asked, still dizzy with all that had happened.

"Yes, she does. And if she's back in the house tonight, she'll let us know when it's safe to come out. If not, we'll have to take our chances."

Laurel shivered in the cool darkness.

"Are you cold?" Seth's voice was low in the blackness.

"No, not really. Just a little scared. I'd feel better, I think, if I could see. It's unnerving, not to know where I am."

"You're with me," Seth answered, sounding defensive.

"You know what I mean. Being in a weird place in complete darkness. And knowing that there are soldiers just a few feet away, searching for us." Laurel's whisper dwindled away to almost nothing.

"I see what you mean. Take my hand and very slowly, very quietly, come this way."

Laurel held tightly to the strong, warm hand that guided her across the stone floor.

"Here we are," Seth whispered, close to her ear. "Feel in front of you. Not there, woman, that's—"

"I know what that is," Laurel was unable to resist answering, with a soft, nervous laugh. "Is that what you wanted to show me?"

"I'll show you more than that, if we get out of here. Now, give me your hand—"

Laurel let him guide her hand and felt the wooden frame of a narrow cot, and what felt like a heavy quilt on top of it.

"Go ahead, sit down," Seth whispered. "I'll find a light."

Laurel felt the cot carefully before sitting on it, huddled in tight around herself. The darkness around her was nerve-racking. If it hadn't been for Seth's presence in the room, she might have panicked.

Be calm, she told herself sternly, *you can handle this.*

She could hear Seth moving around, and the muffled sound of him rummaging through the darkness. Upstairs in the house, she could hear the sound of footsteps, and the low murmur of voices.

How long will we be here? she wondered. *Is*

*there food? Water? What if Mrs. Avery breaks
and tells where we are?*

A few sparks struck in the darkness; and then
she saw Seth's face, the planes and shadows
faintly illuminated as he blew at a tinderbox.
Slowly, patiently, he kindled the faint fire until
it caught. From somewhere in the darkness he
produced a candle, and Laurel breathed a sigh
of relief as the darkness receded, replaced by
the soft glow of candlelight.

"Better?" he asked in hushed tones, shutting
the small tinderbox with a snap.

Laurel nodded, looking around. They were in
a room of smooth white plastered walls, only
six feet square. Above her she could see the
back of the false wardrobe door, the smooth
boards dark against the pale wall.

Seth sat on the floor next to her, an open
wooden chest beside him, and in it, Laurel
could see extra candles, a pistol, and a few
tightly wrapped bundles.

She settled back on the cot, leaning on one
elbow.

"What now?" she whispered. "We wait?"

Seth nodded, and rose to his feet. "Move
over, angel."

Laurel sat up to make room for him, soothed
by the steady arm he wrapped around her
shoulders. She rested her cheek against him.

"I'm sorry for bringing you into this." His
words were whispered, his breath warm
against the top of her head.

"It's as much my fault as yours." Laurel

341

reached up and tugged at his hair, watching the dark sheen of it as it moved between her fingers. "Anyway, I can think of worse things than being locked in a dark room with you."

"Brave girl," he murmured. "Does nothing frighten you?"

Laurel thought about it. "One thing," she confessed. "Losing you."

Her hand trailed down from his hair, over the warm column of his neck and his chest, solid and strong.

"You won't lose me, sweetheart. I won't allow it." His hand covered hers, and he raised her fingers to his lips and kissed them.

"Now, tell me about Lucy Reed," Laurel ordered.

"Damn, are we back to that?" Seth smiled down at her, the hollows beneath his cheekbones dark in the dim light. "There's naught to tell, really. She's some sort of distant cousin of Jane's. She's married to a man three times her age. She tried to seduce me at a party one night. I refused, of course," he added nobly.

"Of course. After you noticed her bloozies," Laurel pointed out.

"Leave off, Hope. At any rate, it would seem that either Lucy is a secret royalist or she dislikes being spurned and has a more vicious sense of revenge than the average woman."

"Maybe both," Laurel suggested. They fell silent as they heard footsteps above them, and the solid bang of the front door.

Seth stared up at the ceiling, almost as if

he could see through it. "Two more gone," he murmured. "Unless I'm mistaken, that would leave four in the house, and Mrs. Avery."

At Laurel's quizzical look, he explained, "I counted their footsteps as they came in."

They sat for a few silent minutes, listening to the sounds above them. Laurel guessed that the upper rooms of the house were being searched.

"Do you know what this reminds me of?" she whispered, rubbing her cheek against his shoulder. "It reminds me of the storm, and the night we spent hiding in the springhouse with Prudence."

"I wish it was only a storm, up there." Seth's voice was soft, regretful.

"What will they do, if they find us?" Laurel asked.

Seth seemed reluctant to answer. He patted her arm in a distracted way and kissed the top of her head.

"I want to know," Laurel said, squaring her shoulders.

He looked into her eyes, his own dark and glowing in the candlelight. His generous mouth was set in a grim line. "We die," was his blunt response. "Unless there's a miracle, of course. We'll either be shot on sight or tried and hanged. If that happens . . ." He took a deep breath and ran his hand gently over Laurel's cheek and stroked her neck. "If that happens, and you're imprisoned and sentenced, plead your belly."

"Plead with my belly for what?"

"No, plead pregnancy. Tell the judge that you're with child. Pretend symptoms if you must, or hope for a miracle. They won't hang a pregnant woman. If you must lie, continue the lie as long as possible."

Laurel sat silently, trying to imagine living in a British prison camp, faking pregnancy. Without Seth. He had no such recourse. They would hang him swiftly.

"No," she told him.

"No, what? What do you mean, no?"

Laurel reached out and put her hands on either side of his face and looked him full in the eyes. "I mean, no, I won't lie. If they hang you, I'm going, too, and as quickly as I can. I don't belong here, and you're the only reason that I'm still here. If you're gone, I'm going."

He shook his head, pulling her tightly against his chest. "You shouldn't speak of dying so lightly."

Laurel gave a silent laugh. "Why not? I've done it before, remember? And so have you, and don't bother trying to deny it. And it wasn't that bad. A little confusing, maybe, but not that bad. Of course, I'd rather go with you than without. Do you think that's possible?"

"I don't know." His eyes were fastened to her face as she spoke, as if he was committing every detail to memory. "But if it is, I'll be with you forever."

She lifted her mouth to his, and he kissed her softly, silently. Their tongues met in a blend of heat and softness, and Laurel moaned softly into his mouth.

He wrapped his long fingers through her hair, rubbing the back of her head, pulling her close against his shoulder. For a few blissful moments Laurel felt perfectly content.

"It does feel much like that night in the cellar," he said, moving his hand across her shoulders in a soothing motion. "I'll never forget waking up with your body next to mine. I thought I'd go out of my mind."

"I did, too." Laurel gave a delicious shiver at the memory.

"Do you remember?" Seth asked softly. "You had your face pressed into my neck, like this . . . and you had your leg over mine, like so . . ." He reached over and slid his hand over Laurel's thigh, pulling it across his own.

"Oh, I remember," Laurel agreed, pressing closer against him. She pressed her lips against his neck and kissed him softly.

"And your hand," he added, "was resting right here . . ."

"Oh, it was not," Laurel protested, trying to draw her hand back from his lap.

"It was. I swear. And I kept thinking, if only you were to move it, just a little, what would happen?"

"Like this?"

Seth exhaled slowly as her hand moved down, over the hard length of him. "Like that." His voice was husky. He turned her face toward his with a firm hand and kissed her, a rich, warm kiss that seemed to go on and on.

"But I couldn't have done that," Laurel reminded him, pulling back. "Because Prudence was there."

"And if she hadn't been, do you know what I would have done?" Seth asked. His eyes were dark with passion; his hand was stroking her shoulders with a warm, smooth motion.

"What?" Laurel asked. Her voice quivered a little as she spoke. Her body was warm and felt soft and slow. Her lips felt full as she lifted her face for another kiss.

"I would have done this . . ." Slowly, he pushed her full skirts up, his hand firm and strong as it moved up her calves, over her thighs.

Laurel pressed closer, her breasts pressing against him, and their mouths met again, their tongues meeting and mingling like hot satin.

"And I would have done this . . ."

She quivered and drew a sharp breath as his hand moved over her hip, and behind. He stroked her buttocks, his hand moving in a hot, sensuous pattern, and then gripped her tightly, pulling her over him.

She knelt over him, wrapping her arms around his neck, rubbing her face in the silk of his dark hair. "Tell me more, Seth. What then?"

As soft and light as a bird's wing, his fingers trailed across her hips, and between her legs, and she made a soft noise in her throat as she felt his hand against her, stroking her with a maddening, rhythmic motion.

"This, I think . . ." His voice was dark and ragged, and when she looked down at his face he was watching her with almost feverish, glittering eyes. "I would have done this, just so. And when I felt you open to me . . . I would have opened my breeches . . ."

Breathless and eager, Laurel moved back a little, her fingers seeking the buttons of his breeches, until she felt him hot and hard beneath her. She moved her hand over the length of him, feeling the smooth, satin skin, the heat and firmness, loving the soft sound of pleasure that he made, deep in his throat.

"Angel," he whispered, and gripped her slender hips in his hands, pulling her down over his waiting body.

She lowered herself onto him, slowly, enjoying the look of almost pained ecstasy on his face when he felt her heat and softness surrounding him. She pressed tightly against him, and his eyes opened, glimmering in the reflected light of the candle.

"I love you," he murmured, and reached up to her neck, pulling her down for a kiss.

All thought of danger fled Laurel's mind, and she lost herself in the flowing heat of her need, the perfectly matched rhythm of their bodies.

Their hands ran over each other, exploring the curve of a waist or the hollow of a shoulder, the silken skin behind an ear or the sharp line of a hipbone, as if their touch could commit the moments of love to memory.

Laurel abandoned herself to the experience, thinking only of the sight of him, the feeling of his body joined to hers, the way his skin tasted and smelled, until her mind darkened and flamed, and she collapsed against his chest, rolling waves of heat shaking her body.

Even then, he wasn't satisfied. He lifted her gently and rolled her body beneath his, moving in her with hot, even strokes. Eventually, her body began trembling and rocking against him again, and when he was sure she had reached her peak for a second time, he released his own passion, filling her body with the heat of his own.

They lay twined together as their breath steadied and slowed, and the only sound in the room was that of their heartbeats, as they touched each other with tender satisfaction.

Exhausted, Laurel fell asleep in his arms, while Seth lay awake in the dimly lit cellar room, listening to the sounds of his home being plundered.

He wondered how long it would be until they could make their escape. He wondered if they would be able to escape at all, or if they had just made love for the last time.

The house lay quiet, the ransacked rooms empty, lit only by the occasional beams of opalescent moonlight that shone through the unshuttered windows.

Beneath the workshop, bolted firmly behind

the secret door of the ornate wardrobe, Laurel lay in Seth's arms as they spoke to each other in soft voices.

"Tell me something else," he asked, as his fingers played in the golden tendrils of hair that hung around her face.

"Anything," Laurel promised, stretching against him like a cat. "What now?"

"Tell me about . . . drills, again."

"I really must love you, you know. Okay, they're heavy, but they work quickly. You just plug them in—"

"Electricity, again."

"Right. And you squeeze the trigger, about this hard—" She caught his hand and squeezed to demonstrate—"and it goes *vvvvmmmmmmm*, and there's your hole, drilled. Or you can change the bit and use it to put in a screw. And *vvvmmmmmm*, it's done. Now, if you get a reversible drill, you can take the screw out with it."

"What a marvel." Seth's voice was almost dreamlike. "And the electric sander. Have you ever actually used one?"

"Once, and I left it in the same place too long and almost wore a hole through the wood. My dad was mad," Laurel added.

Spaceships and skyscrapers aside, Laurel had at last interested Seth in the marvels of the twentieth century.

"Now, about this jigsaw—" In the house above them, they heard a heavy thud, and the stealthy sound of a door opening and closing again.

They both fell silent and lay unmoving, their bodies suddenly taut with fear.

The footsteps sounded through the hallway, loud on the wooden floors, and then were muffled as the unknown intruder crossed a carpet.

Without a sound, Seth reached out and snuffed the candle. Jet black surrounded them.

Laurel guessed by the sound that whoever was above them had reached the kitchen. For one hopeful moment she thought it was Mrs. Avery. But the footsteps weren't those of a woman, and she didn't have to be a spy to hear that.

She heard Seth reaching to the chest beside the cot, and she knew he was taking out the pistol. She could hear the muffled sounds, the metallic clicks as he readied the weapon.

"Stay behind me, whatever happens," he murmured.

Laurel nodded, as if he could see her.

The footsteps hesitated in the kitchen, and then, to Laurel's horror, started down the kitchen stairs to the workshop.

She sat behind Seth, one hand on his shoulder, wondering if this was the way it would end. She wondered if the soldiers had somehow broken Mrs. Avery, wrung the truth out of her. She wondered if they would be allowed to leave alive or if they'd be shot on the spot.

Beneath her hand, Seth's shoulder was tight and motionless, and she could imagine what he looked like, crouched like a cat, his eyes glittering, the weapon in his hand aimed at the door above them.

The footsteps approached the wardrobe doors, and the sound of the latch clicking open was as loud as thunder in the dead silence.

Laurel felt Seth shift slightly as he readied himself.

A light tapping sounded on the false door.

And to Laurel's disbelief, a voice followed.

"Mr. Goodwin? Oooo, Mr. Goodwin?" came a very poor imitation of a female voice. "Did you want tea sent in, sir, or shall we come back later?"

Her heart plummeted from her throat to her stomach, and beneath her hand, Seth seemed to go limp.

"Stephen," he said softly, "shall I kill you now, or would you like to wait till later?"

"Damn," came the whisper back. "How'd you know it was me? Open up, Goodwin, and kill me, if you like. But please, let me get out of this dress first. My mother will never get over it if my body gets sent home in this."

Weak with relief, Laurel felt an almost hysterical urge to laugh and put her hand over her mouth. As Seth stood and slid open the bolt on the false door, she felt, for the first time in hours, hope.

Chapter Sixteen

The bolt slid open, and there was a faint glimmer of moonlight as the door to the wardrobe swung in.

"Can't see a thing," Stephen murmured, and then Laurel heard him drop to the floor with a loud thump.

"Damn. Do you have a light, Goodwin? The house is empty. One guard at the front door, one at the kitchen door, and that's it."

Seth closed the back of the wardrobe and, after a moment, found the candle. They waited in silence until the flame caught.

"What a babe," Laurel said, wiggling her eyebrows at Stephen.

He was dressed in a stiff, panniered frock of jade green, his heavy boots protruding from beneath the delicate lace hem. His golden hair, normally "clubbed," as they called it, in a ponytail, was hidden beneath a cap as delicate and beribboned as any that Laurel had seen since her arrival in the city. Delicate lace lappets hung down on either side of his face, which, at the moment, was uncharacteristically sour-looking.

"Enough out of you," he told Laurel. "If you think this is my idea of a good time, you may think again. How the devil do you women move in these things?"

"Beats me," Laurel admitted. "Don't you hate the way that stomacher cuts off your breath?"

"Actually, I find the petticoats more tiresome—all that weight. And the way the bodice digs in above the hips is—"

"May we save this fascinating discourse for another day?" Seth interrupted. "Not to be rude to such a charming lady, of course."

Stephen sank onto the cot next to Laurel and hurled his lace cap to the floor with a disgusted look. "Go piss and howl at the moon, Goodwin. I can always turn around and leave, if you like. Unless, of course, you want to get out of here."

Seth bit back a smile. "Pray continue, madam."

"That's it," Stephen exclaimed, looking quite put out. "Unlace me, for God's sake." He presented his back to Laurel, who immediately began tugging at the back laces of Stephen's ludicrous gown. "It's dangerous enough, traveling this city tonight, without looking like a dockside jade, I can tell you."

"And not the best-looking dockside jade, either," Seth pointed out, his dark eyes sparkling with merriment.

"Piss off," Stephen returned. "A lot of help you were, tonight. If I hadn't heard your housekeeper being questioned, I never would have thought to look for you here."

"How did you figure it out?" Seth demanded.

"With God's grace." Stephen struggled out of his cumbersome gown, revealing his own shirt and breeches beneath. "The British are camped all over the state house square. Terribly disorganized, Goodwin. Their main concern seems to be securing the Delaware Bay."

"They should have a merry time with that," Seth observed. "There are booms and dams blocking it to the sea, and countless encampments ready to fire at them."

"They know," Stephen told him. "Until they can secure it, they'll have to bring supplies overland. Howe's about to dispatch three thousand men to carry in supplies from the Chesapeake."

Seth digested this information. "Are you sure?" He let out a low whistle. "Three thousand? That'll put a dent in their forces."

"As sure as I am of my name. We've got to get the information to Whitemarsh, and quickly. We should go separately, just in case."

In case of what, Laurel didn't want to think.

"Mrs. Avery's doing well, by the way. They've forbidden her to enter the house

355

until everything's been removed. We followed her to her sister's, and she told me where to find you."

"I wondered how you knew." Seth was digging through the chest on the floor as he spoke, loading a battered-looking leather pack as he spoke. He thrust the pistol into his belt and put on a riding coat of soft buckskin. "I notice you said 'we.' Am I to assume you meant Gordon?"

"Aye, I brought him out."

Laurel sighed with relief. "Oh, Stephen, I'm so glad. How did you manage?"

He raised his brows. "Why, you'd be surprised how much a pretty girl can accomplish."

"They must be drunk," Seth observed. "Did anyone see you enter the house?"

Stephen rolled his eyes. "Aye, and they decided I was too lovely to shoot. Merciful God, Goodwin! What do you think? I came in through a window. There's one guard at the front door, one at the back, and one circling. I timed it well. You needn't have asked."

"Sorry." Seth slung the pack over his shoulders. "Do we have horses?"

"Is King George a horse's ass? Of course we have horses; Gordon's holding them down the street, two doors down east from Ross's."

"You've done well, Stephen." Seth clapped his friend on the shoulder. "I couldn't have done better."

"You wouldn't have looked so good in that

dress, either," Laurel pointed out.

Both men ignored this remark.

"Then, to Whitemarsh," Seth proclaimed. "I think you and Gordon should travel north, and skirt Germantown. The troops will be heavier there, but you're not as easily recognized as Hope and I might be. Given luck, and your skill, you should reach the camp a full day before us. We'll travel southwest, back toward Chester, and ford the Schuylkill at the bend below Whitemarsh."

Stephen nodded. "Let's go. And Godspeed, Goodwin."

The two men clasped hands.

Seth turned to Laurel. "Stay behind us and make no noise. We'll go up the kitchen stairs, and you'll stay inside the door until I call you."

Laurel reached for his shoulder, feeling the hard muscle beneath the soft buckskin of his jacket. "But what about the guard?"

"We kill him," Stephen answered simply.

"Kill him?" Laurel's voice squeaked. "Oh, no."

"It's the best way," Stephen informed her. "If we just lay him low, there's a chance he might get up. We don't need one more man following us."

Laurel clutched Seth's arm. "Oh, Seth. Please don't. I'll get sick."

"This is a war, sweetheart. Do you think he won't kill us, if he gets the chance?"

"Can't we just . . . tie him up?"

"No rope," Stephen objected. "And it would waste time."

"I don't want anything to do with it," Laurel announced. "I can handle a lot, but I simply cannot handle seeing someone killed. I refuse."

"She's got a stubborn chin," Stephen told Seth. "Have you ever noticed that? It doesn't bode well for your future, Goodwin."

"Aye, I've noticed it a time or two." Seth reached out and touched Laurel's cheek, stroking it gently. "Be reasonable, sweetheart."

"The hell I will." Laurel sat on the cot and crossed her arms. "If you're going to kill someone, I'm not going. The end."

"She's trouble," Stephen said, in sympathetic tones. "Or is she a Quaker?"

"No, she's a pain in the—"

"I mean it, Seth." Laurel's voice was firm. "If there's any way out of here without killing, we do it."

Seth raked his hair off his high forehead and gave a heavy sigh. "Very well. We let him live."

"But we hurt him," Stephen amended, "badly enough that he stays down for a while."

"If that's your best offer, I'll take it." Laurel stood up, somewhat appeased.

"Let's go," Seth ordered. "I'll take the guard; Hope, you stay behind Stephen."

He extinguished the candle, and darkness and silence filled the air around them.

For the last time, Seth opened the false

door above them and climbed out into the dark room above. Stephen followed, and Seth reached in to pull Laurel after them. He planted a quick, soft kiss on her forehead as he helped her to her feet.

"Not a noise," Seth whispered, and led the way across the room, slowly, avoiding the tumbled stacks of wood and the piles of papers scattered across the floor. As they reached the staircase leading to the kitchen, Laurel glanced back.

The room lay in utter shambles, a far cry from the organized room she was used to seeing. In the center of the room, illuminated by a beam of moonlight, the walnut secretary stood, perfect and untouched, the inlaid rising sun glowing white in the darkness.

Laurel hoped that Howard would forget about it, that he would never sit and write at its smooth surface, or store his pens and inkstones in its perfect drawers.

Silently, she followed Seth and Stephen's shadows up the narrow staircase, her fingers knotted in the fabric of her full skirts. Through the unshuttered kitchen window she could see the man guarding the house, his back ramrod straight, facing the kitchen door. The moonlight glinted off the deadly bayonet at his side, and she shivered.

Seth crouched down, motioning for Laurel and Stephen to do the same. Approaching footsteps sounded around the side of the house, and they heard the posted sentry greet his fellow guard.

Unsuspecting, the circling guard continued, his muffled footsteps disappearing into the night as he continued on his rounds.

As silent as a ghost, Seth slid to the kitchen door and put his hand on the latch. He shot Laurel a quick, sharp look, and put his finger to his lips.

"Now," Stephen whispered.

With the speed of a jungle cat, Seth threw open the door and leapt out into the night.

"Good hit!" Jerry shouted, jumping up off the couch with the enthusiasm of a football fan whose team has just made a touchdown.

"Huzzah!" Nathaniel added, raising his fist in a victorious gesture. "Replay that one."

The TV set scooted forward through the mist, the screen dimmed and fuzzed. Jerry and Nathaniel leaned forward for a closer look.

They stared as the scene repeated itself in slow motion—the door swinging open, the young, red-coated guard swinging around in the same instant, his wide-eyed, startled expression. He raised his rifle and drew back, the steel bayonet poised to strike.

In the same moment, Seth sailed through the dark doorway, with the strength and grace of a dancer. One foot made contact with the young soldier's weapon, sending it hurtling into the darkness beyond.

As Seth touched ground, his hands reached

out, seizing the young soldier's ears, and with a deliberate, swift movement, he lowered his head and slammed it with a vicious, hard movement square in the soldier's face.

There was a crunching sound as the young redcoat's nose shattered, and he dropped to the ground, unconscious.

"Whew!" Jerry commented. "That hurt!"

"Not for long, it didn't," Nathaniel pointed out. "But I'm sure it will when he comes to."

They watched the screen, unblinking, as Laurel and Stephen raced out of the kitchen and followed Seth across the dark yard.

"Look behind you!" Nathaniel shouted, as if they could hear him.

The circling sentry had appeared around the corner of the house, only an instant before the three disappeared into the night. "Halt, in the name of the King," he shouted, and dropped to one knee, already loading his rifle.

The three fugitives vanished into the darkness. The guard from the front of the house came running, and after a moment's consultation the two gave chase.

"Turn it off," Jerry said. "I just hate these chase scenes. You've seen one, you've seen them all."

"It seems to be well in hand," Nathaniel agreed, waving a hand at the TV with a dismissing gesture. The set gave a little bow and retreated into the clouds.

Jerry reached into the clouds, withdrew a bag of pretzels, and looked over his shoulder.

Grandma sat at the kitchen table, papers spread over its yellow linoleum surface. Her face was set in furrowed lines of concentration. She wore a sweatshirt in an unnatural shade of purple with shining white letters. It read: BECAUSE I'M THE GRANDMA AND I SAID SO.

"How are things going over there, Joyce?"

Grandma picked up a pen, added something to a piece of paper, and settled back in her chair. "I think we've got it, by . . . George. Listen to this. 'We regret that we are unable to attend tonight's conference, as requested. Our duties as guardians have interfered. Hope to see you soon! Respectfully yours, etc. . . . ' What do you think?"

"Send it," Jerry proclaimed. "We're almost home free. By the time we get to His office, everything should be cleared up."

"Send it," Nathaniel agreed. "What do we have to lose?"

Grandma gave the paper a toss, and an unseen breeze caught it and carried it off into the billowing white clouds.

A few seconds later, there was an ominous rumble of thunder. The white clouds darkened and began to boil.

The two men on the couch turned and looked over their shoulders at Grandma.

"Don't look at me like that! It's nothing. Just a little change in the weather."

Jerry and Nathaniel exchanged dubious glances, reached back into the clouds, and

withdrew umbrellas, which promptly popped open.

"Oh, Geez Lou-ise," Grandma exclaimed,
bobbing up from her chair and coming over
to the couch. She settled between the two,
covering her head with a clear plastic rain
bonnet. "Where the hell is that TV? Things
were just getting good."

"Where the devil did this storm come from?"
Stephen demanded, reining his horse over to
the side of the road. Thunder crashed again,
and the animal reared a little and pranced
backwards.

Laurel clung tightly to Seth, her arms
wrapped around his waist as the horse beneath
them shied, nickering softly.

"Damned if I know," Seth answered. "But it
will make our trail harder to follow." He tipped
his head back, examining the sky. Dark clouds
were rolling, thick and fast, blotting out the
face of the moon. A bolt of lightning tore across
the sky, brilliant and blue against the black.

They hesitated on the hilltop for a minute
more. From their viewpoint they could see the
lights of the city, looking small and faint to
the southeast. The black ribbon of road that
wound through the farmland below them was
dark and empty-looking.

"Here we part ways," Gordon said, after a
moment's pause. "I wish you luck, Goodwin,
and you as well, Hope. God willing, we'll see
you at Whitemarsh."

"God willing," Seth echoed.

Another rumble of thunder punctuated his words.

Stephen tipped his blond head back to look at the sky and gave a nervous laugh. "He doesn't much sound willing, does He?"

"Don't be superstitious," Laurel told him with an affectionate smile. "It's only a little storm. We'll see you in a day or so."

"Take care," Gordon cautioned them, squaring his battered tricorn on his light brown hair.

For a moment they hesitated at the dark crossroad. The markers that had once stood there had been removed, in a futile attempt to confuse the invading army.

Slowly, the rain began to fall, heavy droplets that clattered through the leaves and pelted Laurel's back. They shone on Seth's hair like black ink and dripped off the brims of Stephen and Gordon's hats.

"Look," Gordon said suddenly, pointing down the road they had just taken.

In the distance, lights flickered in the darkness.

A feeling of foreboding touched Laurel, like cold fingers trailing down her spine.

"Damn," Seth exclaimed. "We're off." He turned the horse in a graceful circle and raised a hand in farewell. "Ride well; ride fast. Till Whitemarsh, my friends."

"Till Whitemarsh," the brothers echoed, kicking their horses into motion.

Laurel looked back once, as a lightning bolt illuminated the landscape, just as Stephen and Gordon reached the crest of the hill, speeding northwest toward Germantown. They looked very small against the landscape, obscured by the falling rain. As if he felt her eyes, Stephen raised his arm in a final good-bye.

Laurel shivered again. She clung to Seth's back, her face held tightly against him, as they descended the west face of the hill, down toward the Schuylkill River.

The horse felt unsteady beneath her, and frighteningly high off the ground.

Seth glanced over his shoulder at her. Raindrops clung to his eyelashes and dripped down his face. "Are you afraid yet?"

"Not a damned bit," Laurel lied.

"God help us. Do you realize we've been followed?"

The horse shied at a flash of lightning; the rain began falling in hard, driving sheets, hissing through the leaves and grasses that bordered the dirt road.

"I hope the rain will obscure any traces of us," Seth went on. "By the way, can you swim?"

"A little," Laurel answered, not looking forward to the prospect, "but I'd rather not, given the choice."

"We may not have the choice," Seth told her, his voice grim. "Look behind us. I think they have our trail."

Laurel looked back and saw a shimmer of

faint light behind them, slowly descending the hill.

"Shit," she said.

She had no idea how many hours they rode along the road. The horse slowed as the dirt became mud, and Laurel cursed the storm, the wet, cold rain that soaked her skirts and trickled down her neck. She huddled against Seth's back, her cheek pressed against the fragrant wet buckskin of his coat. Every now and then she looked back and caught the glimmer of lights behind them.

"I think they're closer," she informed him. "I hate to say it, and I've been trying to tell myself that it's my imagination, but it's not."

"Damn!" Seth gave her a worried look. "They have light and we don't. Their horses will naturally make better time. If we don't lose them soon, they'll overtake us."

Another bolt of lightning sang through the sky, and a scream choked in Laurel's throat as it seemed to come toward them.

The horse reared in terror, and for a horrible, sickening moment, Laurel felt herself plummeting through the air. She hit the ground so hard that she couldn't breathe. Blackness surrounded her, and silence.

And then pain, shooting through her arm and her back. She wondered what had happened, and slowly, she became aware that she was lying in the mud, the rain pouring over her, a horrible sound filling her ears.

"Seth?" There was no way he could hear

her; her voice had no substance. She trembled, trying to sit, wondering what the terrible shrieking noise was. It filled her ears, made her stomach lurch.

She realized it was the horse. For the first time in her life she was listening to the screams of an injured animal.

A gunshot rang out, and the screams stopped.

And then Seth was bending over her. "Hope . . . sweetheart—how bad is it?"

Relief washed over her. "Not bad," she lied. She drew a painful breath as his hands moved over her, checking for broken bones.

"Thank God. Can you stand?"

A faint rumble stirred the ground, and Laurel heard the distant sound of voices.

"I have to stand," she answered.

Seth pulled her to her feet, supporting her weight with a strong arm. "Come on. The river's this way. It's our only chance. Once they see the horse, they'll be on us."

Still dizzy, Laurel stumbled beside him, pain shooting through her body. He half carried, half dragged her over the mud of the road, and lifted her over a low fence.

"Hurry, angel. As fast as you can manage." His voice was low and urgent.

They moved forward, vines and branches scratching and pulling at them.

"I love you," Laurel said suddenly, looking up at him through the darkness.

Seth stopped; his damp hand seized her chin

and his mouth covered hers. His kiss was hard, urgent.

"I love you," he whispered. "If you're taken, don't forget what I told you. Plead your belly."

"I won't be taken," she answered, her voice fierce. "And neither will you. Come on."

They pushed forward into the darkness, branches breaking in their wake, the rain falling around them with a hard, relentless rhythm.

"Go left," a voice said, clearly and abruptly.

Laurel jumped, her heart lodged in her throat.

Immediately, Seth turned toward the left, pulling her behind him.

"Who the hell was that?" she cried, when she was able to speak.

Seth glanced back at her. "Did you hear it, too?"

"Obviously!"

"I don't know how or why, but this I know. That was my grandfather's voice." Even as he spoke, he stopped abruptly.

They had reached a low fence of stone, and on the other side was a field. A flash of lightning lit the scene, and they saw a farmhouse, dark and silent, ahead of them. Below it, down a gentle slope of pasture, wound the Schuylkill River, a gleaming black snake moving through the dark landscape.

"There we are," Seth breathed. "There's where we ford. Are you strong enough to follow me across?"

Laurel wrapped her arms around his neck and clung to him tightly, as if she could absorb his strength. "I'd follow you through hell, if you asked."

He laughed softly, holding her close. "Let's hope it doesn't come to that. And Hope?"

She tilted her head back and looked at him with glowing eyes.

"When we get to Whitemarsh, marry me."

"Oh, all right. You can quit your nagging."

He laughed again, his dark eyes glittering black in the night. "Come down to the river, Laurel-Hope-whatever-I-should-call-you. We have to move while we have a chance."

"They don't have a chance." Jerry reached out and aimed the remote control at the TV set. The screen went black.

Next to him on the couch, Grandma and Nathaniel sat silently, staring at the blank screen.

The clouds surrounding them were black and dense. Rain poured over them, beading and glistening on Jerry's sweater, making dark spots on the white brocade of Nathaniel's frock coat and striking Grandma's rain bonnet with curious little *ping ping* sounds.

Grandma looked down at her ample lap, and then up again, her blue eyes watery. "Well? Wasn't that the idea? Wasn't that the plan? What are we sulking for?"

Nathaniel sighed, reaching under his white wig to scratch his head. "I don't know. It seems

369

so sad—so much waste. They're so young, and so brave."

"Hooey," Grandma answered, but there was none of her usual spirit in her voice. She simply sounded old and tired.

The three sat in silence, while the rain poured over them.

"Shall we turn it back on?" Jerry asked at last, gesturing at the silent TV.

"Oh, right, Jerry. Like I really need to see this. Geez Louise, why don't we just watch something cheerful, like 'World at War,' or 'Terminal Endearment'?

"Did we handle this correctly?" Nathaniel asked softly. "Do you think we should have gone for help?"

"No way," Grandma replied in alarm. "The less He knows about this, the better. That way, when He calls us to the office, everything will already be taken care of. Problem solved."

"Then why do I feel like such a heel?" Jerry asked, rubbing his nose.

"Because you're an idiot, Jerry." Grandma's voice was harsher than usual, and she went to the yellow kitchen table and began to lay out a game of solitaire, the wet cards slapping against the wetter table.

Chapter Seventeen

The river seemed alive.

It flowed past with an unnatural force, fed by the sheets of falling rain that hissed into its depths as it made its way downstream.

Laurel stood ankle deep in mud, staring at the dark water, wishing there was another way out of their predicament. Every now and then a branch floated by, tossed about by the wind and rain.

There had never been so much water. It soaked Laurel's hair and dripped onto her bedraggled skirts. It puddled in the mud at her feet and streamed in tiny rivulets into the rising Schuylkill River. It fell from the trees, a million shimmering, hissing drops falling from a million leaves. And all the while more fell from the rumbling sky.

The opposite riverbank seemed very far away.

"Ready for a swim?" Seth asked. He sat on the wet grass behind her, stuffing his leather boots into his pack. After a moment's thought he stripped off his shirt, wrapped the pistol in it, and stuffed the bundle deep inside one boot.

"It's almost pointless," he said, glancing up at her, "trying to keep anything dry. But if there's even a small chance, I'll take it."

The rain glistened on his face and ran like tears over his cheekbones. It gathered on the blunt, well-shaped end of his nose and dripped down with a steady, monotonous beat. His hair was slick with water, dripping onto his already wet back.

Laurel looked at the dark water. "I don't like this."

Surprised to hear her complain, Seth looked up. "I don't like it either, sweeting. Not a damned bit. But once we cross the river we're relatively safe. If we stay here, we're dead."

A faint sound caught Laurel's attention, and she turned swiftly, staring up the hill at the dark silhouette of the farmhouse. Faintly, she heard voices, and saw the flickering light of lanterns approaching.

"Now or never," she said softly. "Our friends are here."

Seth swore, following her gaze up the hill. "Move. Keep hold of me and don't let go for anything. Are you afraid?" He leapt to his feet as he spoke, balancing the pack on his bare shoulder.

"No, absolutely not."

He gave her a quick smile. "You've really got to stop lying to me."

The rain dribbled down over his bare chest, glistening in the dark hair, and Laurel was unable to resist running her hands over it. He wrapped a strong arm around her waist and gave her a quick squeeze.

"Stop that. We'll have plenty of time later. We've got to cross now, before we're seen."

Barefoot and shirtless, his hair streaming and wet over his broad shoulders, he waded into the river. One hand balanced his pack safely out of the river's way and the other kept a firm grip on Laurel's wrist.

The river was cold, the rising water stronger than she had expected. Her skirts pulled at her legs, tangling around them like heavy wet blankets.

"Damn. It's deeper here than I thought. We should have gone farther upstream." Seth's face was tense.

They waded in deeper, slowly feeling their way. The river bottom felt slick under Laurel's feet.

The pull of the river was slowing their progress. Laurel glanced back over her shoulder and up at the farmhouse on the hill. The lanterns were there, and she could see the shadows of the men carrying them. She could hear, very faintly, the sounds of their horses.

"Hurry, sweetheart."

The water was around Laurel's thighs, black and cold. Beneath the surface of the water, her cumbersome skirts caught on something, pulling her down.

She was unable to stop her cry of panic, and Seth grasped her arms just as she was about to fall. His pack tumbled into the river and was gone.

A flash of lightning lit the storm-tossed river, and behind them Laurel heard a shout.

"They've seen us," Seth told her, his voice raised above the sound of the storm. His hand gripped her wrist with a fierce strength. "Go down."

With a gasp, Laurel obeyed, plunging to her neck in the cold, swift water.

It pulled at her like a living thing, strong and persistent. She fought against the current, trying to take smooth, even strokes with her arms, kicking against the burden of her skirts. Why hadn't she taken off her petticoats? she wondered.

The water blinded her, filling her eyes and ears. It pushed her downstream, and she felt Seth next to her for a moment. His arm reached out and bore her up.

"Keep going," he shouted. "We're almost halfway." His voice sounded strained.

Over the sound of the rushing water, Laurel heard a new noise: an odd popping, like firecrackers.

Guns, she realized. *They're shooting at us.*

Her heart felt tight; her breath was loud in her own ears. Wet, gasping breaths, coming hard.

Swim, damn it.

Her arms felt weak and frail, useless against the force of the river. Her legs felt like lead.

Thunder rumbled, a crackle of lightning flashed, and she saw the riverbank far ahead. Ahead of her, too, Seth's bare back surfaced, his muscled arms splitting the dark water with a furious motion.

Slow down. Don't leave me behind.

The gunfire was louder, and when she turned her head to breathe she could see the sparkle from the weapons as they were fired.

Fight the river. Keep going.

Thunder drowned out the sounds of the river and the shooting. She kicked with a fury she didn't know she possessed, an energy surging through her body. Her heart was striking hard and fast, like the rhythm of the rain.

Something gripped her arm, and she panicked until she realized it was Seth, pulling her toward him. He must be able to touch ground, she realized. The water cleared from her eyes as he pulled her, and she struggled toward him, wanting nothing more than to cling to his shoulders.

"Almost there," he shouted. His voice was ragged and harsh.

Laurel didn't have enough breath to answer.

She kept her eyes and mind focused on him. Her feet sought the river bottom and found nothing. Her accursed skirts tugged at her, impeding her progress.

The sounds of wind and rain and swirling water and gunfire filled her head. She felt Seth's hand gripping her wrist, the only safe, solid element in the terrible night.

Her feet touched bottom.

"We're going to make it," Seth shouted. "You're almost there, sweetheart."

Something floating by in the current struck her, almost knocking her down. Seth's arm snaked beneath her shoulders, forcing her upright.

The water was up to her neck, and she strained to keep her face above it, each breath she took aching in her chest.

Slowly, fighting the force of the water, they struggled forward.

And then, suddenly, Seth stopped. Lightning illuminated his face. The fierce, determined expression was gone, replaced by a look of gentle surprise.

"I've been hit," he said simply, his voice barely audible over the sounds of the night.

Hit by what? Laurel wondered, but didn't have the breath to say.

Enemy fire. Gunfire. It's not good.

Strange, she could hear his thoughts. Even as she wondered how, she saw the wound, a dark, ugly hole beneath his collarbone that seemed to deepen and grow beneath her eyes.

He didn't move. He simply stood there, the water rushing around his chest, staring in surprise at the darkening bullet hole. His arm slipped from beneath her shoulder.

"*Nooooooo!*" Laurel's scream was torn from her chest, a raw, ugly, animal sound.

She grabbed his arm as he wavered and pulled him with all her strength. He felt leaden.

He was slipping, going down. He was too heavy; the pull of the river was too much. The river was swallowing him, taking him.

She cried out, refusing to let go. His eyes met hers, dark and sorrowful as he slid down.

I love you.

The words were there in the air between them, as solid as if they'd been spoken out loud.

"*Noooooo!*" Her scream rose above the sounds of the rain, the water. She caught him beneath the shoulders as he slid beneath the water.

Too heavy. Dragging me down. Don't let go.

She swallowed water and struggled to lift her head above the surface. She fought, cursing the river, the mighty, roaring force that was tearing his body from her arms.

No. Don't let go. Don't take him from me.

With a superhuman rush of strength she lifted his shoulders from the water and saw his face, still and quiet, looking oddly peaceful. He was too heavy. Dead weight.

She knew he was gone.

She lifted her face to the dark, pouring sky and let loose a primitive cry of grief, pain racking her body.

She didn't see the oak branch, rushing downstream on the force of the river. She was never sure what struck her, dragging her down.

She was only aware of her hand, clinging to Seth's arm, fighting in the roaring blackness to hang on; until she felt his fingers, long and smooth, pulled away from hers, and he was gone.

The smell in her nostrils was sharp and bitter, the smell of chemicals. No, medicine, and bleach. The lights hurt her eyes.

Cool, and clean. Her arms and legs ached, as if she'd been working out all day and then slept in the wrong position on a hard floor.

Someone came into the room with quiet, efficient footsteps. She heard the rustle of paper, the sound of a pen moving over it.

The steady hum of machinery, the buzz of fluorescent lights. The strange, electronic sound of buttons being pushed. Far away, the sound of a telephone ringing.

She opened her eyes with a painful effort, and the light burned against them, blinding her.

She blinked and focused.

White sheets, white blankets. The glossy, fake-wood surface of a night table next to her bed. A bouquet of carnations, lurid red, with a miniature balloon on a stick impaled into the vase. "Get well!" the balloon read, above a picture of a panda bear.

A plastic bag, hanging on a shining chrome

pole, steadily dripping clear liquid down a long, narrow tube.

There was a window, dull orange curtains drawn to show gray buildings against a gray sky.

Her mind felt dull. Something was not right, but she couldn't grasp what.

She saw a movement of white in the corner of her eye.

A nurse bending down, the electric lights reflecting in her glasses.

"Laurel? Can you hear me? Just nod; don't try to speak."

Speaking was out of the question. With effort, she nodded, her head barely moving.

"You were in a car accident three days ago. You're at Harborview Hospital, in Seattle. Do you remember?"

Three days. There was something wrong with that.

No. She shook her head slightly.

"That's fine; sometimes it takes a while. I think your mother's in the cafeteria; would you like me to call her?"

Yes. Laurel nodded her head and closed her eyes.

The sound of footsteps leaving the room, the murmur of voices in the hall.

A jumble of images crowded her mind. She saw Grandma, sitting at a table, surrounded by clouds, her playing cards slapping the linoleum tabletop. Her car, the front end crumpled and twisted, rain falling over the shattered windshield. A farmhouse, standing in the middle of green fields, dense woods surrounding, and brilliant blue skies.

And Seth carefully carving little pieces of pale wood. He looked up from his worktable and smiled, his brown eyes sparkling at her.

And then another image of Seth, the sharp planes of his face glistening with water, his eyes closed, slipping beneath the surface of the river.

Her heart gave a sickening lurch and twisted in her chest. It hurt to breathe; it hurt even more to think.

Don't remember, please don't remember.

She felt as if she were going to shatter. Her mind cried out with pain; her heart was breaking.

"Honey?" Her mother's voice, a soft, cool hand on her cheek.

Laurel opened her eyes and looked at her mother, solid and real, with her neatly cut hair. Her eyes were full of concern.

"Hi there, lazybones. How do you feel?"

If she spoke, she would break. Her eyes felt hot and painful, her throat so tight she couldn't breathe.

"I thought you were going to sleep your life away."

Laurel closed her eyes and turned her face into the pillow. Hot and salty and wet, tears streamed from her eyes.

"It's okay. Everything's going to be okay."

Nothing would ever be okay again.

380

Forever

*   *   *

Three days. She couldn't grasp it. Three days. It seemed inconceivable. In three days she had lived in a farmhouse in rural Pennsylvania and learned to love a little sister named Prudence. She had saved the life of a revolutionary spy and traveled through a war-torn countryside with him. She had walked the streets of Philadelphia, a city she had never seen, and watched those same streets overrun by the British army.

And she had fallen deeply in love with a man she would never see again.

She walked the sterile halls of the hospital, her mind overwhelmed by the constant noise and activity, reliving her experiences.

She suffered through tests and interviews with doctors as they performed X rays and CAT scans, and she thought about Seth and how his thick hair looked in the sunlight, and how the hollows beneath his cheekbones deepened when he smiled.

She sat in bed while nurses checked her pulse and measured her blood pressure, and she thought about his deep voice, and how he had called her *angel* and *sweetheart*.

She smiled when Linda and Tamara came to visit, bearing bouquets of roses and carnations and ferns, and she thought about the way he looked when he carried his long rifle through the forest, tall and beautiful and dangerous.

And every night she lay in her lonely hospital

bed and thought of how it felt not to wake up in his arms, and feel his heart beating beneath her cheek. She thought of how his chest felt, warm and strong, and how she had rubbed her face against the soft, dark hair of it each morning, and how he ran his beautiful fingers through her hair.

Every night, she cried.

"Two more days, pal." Tamara sat in the ugly green chair next to her bed, silver bracelets jingling as she set down a bulging shopping bag. "Are you looking forward to getting out?"

"I guess." Laurel tried to sound enthusiastic.

"Here." Tamara opened the shopping bag and pulled out a deli container. "Chicken salad and crackers. You're looking puny."

"I feel like crap." Laurel set the food on her nightstand, knocking down a few greeting cards.

"I think it might be those hospital gowns," Tamara suggested. "How can you feel good with your butt hanging out?" She opened the chicken salad and dipped a cracker in. "Mmm. Not bad." She chewed thoughtfully for a minute and swallowed. "What do the doctors say?"

"They say I'm depressed. It might be a result of the head injury." *Or not.*

"Geez, I should be a doctor. I could have told you that. Guess what?"

"You saw your astrologer, and she says you're going to med school?"

Tamara laughed, tossing her dark curls. "No, pinhead. I've got a date. And guess who with?"

"A doctor." Laurel stared out the window at the Seattle skyline. A cold, gray drizzle was falling over the buildings and onto the parked cars below.

"Close," Tamara admitted. "The ambulance driver who brought you here. He came in to check on you while you were still out, and we clicked. Remember the night of the wreck? I told you I'd seen my psychic, and she said I was going to meet my soulmate in a tall building? Check it out."

Laurel remembered the conversation clearly. *"Oh, my psychic says you should be careful around water."* She shivered, tears coming to her eyes.

"Hey, I got those books for you," Tamara announced, holding out the shopping bag. "What's the sudden interest in history?"

Laurel grabbed the bag and dumped it onto the hospital bed, scanning the titles of the library books. *Patriots—the Men of The American Revolution. Redcoats and Rebels—the American Revolution. Espionage— A History. American Homes of the Eighteenth Century. Furniture Building in Early America. Pennsylvania.*

There were at least fifteen books, some new, some worn, all bearing the familiar public library smell.

Laurel grabbed the one entitled *Patriots*, and immediately flipped to the index. The words sped under her finger—*Gloucester, VA. Goldfinch, John. Goldsmith, Oliver. Grand Union Flag.*

No Goodwin.

She tossed the book aside and seized the next.

"Hey, pal?"

Tamara was looking at her with wide, puzzled eyes. "What's going on?"

"Nothing. Maybe I got a little addled when I hit my head. It's been known to happen."

"Like you need an excuse. Hey, do you want to go outside and smoke?"

Laurel shook her head, already reaching for a third book. "No. I quit." She found the index, and her eyes scanned the list. *Gladstone. Gloucester. Graham. Grant.*

It was as if he had never existed. For the next day Laurel sat on her bed, poring over book after book. In one book, a history from the British perspective, she saw a picture of Sir Colin Howard, a portrait in full uniform, looking better than he ever had in life.

She stared at the page for several minutes. He had existed. She wasn't crazy, and it hadn't been a dream.

There was, of course, the possibility that she had seen the portrait before, and the name had lodged in her subconscious mind, but she didn't believe it.

"Seth," she whispered, staring out at the cloud-covered sky. "What happened to you?"

*   *   *

She was sitting up in bed, her metal bed table across her lap, eating the last of her turkey casserole, when she saw it.

She was turning the pages of a book on early American furniture, and there it was.

The secretary Seth had built, photographed against a deep blue background, polished and gleaming. Her heart skipped a beat, and she shoved the remains of her lunch aside, pulling the book closer.

She ran a trembling finger across the glossy page, across the image of the rising sun inlaid on the drawer, and down to the caption beneath the photograph.

Secretary of mahogany and satinwood, by an unknown Philadelphia craftsman. Aprx. 1776. Private collection.

She clutched the book to her heart and cried softly, her tears falling like warm rain. It was so hard to accept that this was all she had left.

It was small, cold comfort to know that he had existed after all.

Somehow, she hated to leave the hospital. It was one more ending, the final page in a book.

She moved around the hospital room like a sleepwalker, packing cards and emptying vases, putting on the clothes her sister Linda had brought her.

She slid into her Levi's, remembering how much she had missed them, and then her pale blue angora sweater, thinking of the dress with the velvet roses around the bodice.

Tamara came into the room, a challis scarf thrown around the neck of her dark coat, her car keys in her hand.

"Hey, pal. You're sprung."

Laurel nodded, packing the book on early American furniture into her bag. The library would just have to accept it as lost. She'd never let go of it.

"Have you signed out?"

"An hour ago. I have to come back for a couple of checkups in a week. That's it."

"What about the depression?" Tamara asked, suddenly serious. "Are you going to see someone for that?"

And say what? Laurel thought. *That I'm grieving for a man who may or may not have existed over two hundred years ago?*

"No. I'll get over it." She shrugged her arms into her favorite jacket, a soft brown leather flight jacket lined with fleece, and combed her hair, not really wanting to look in the mirror. Old. She felt old. It had been fun, being eighteen.

Tamara took the shopping bag, and Laurel slung her purse over her arm.

They walked down the tiled hall, past nurses' stations and empty wheelchairs and an open janitor's closet, Laurel blinking back tears.

"Oh, pal, do you mind if we stop on the way out?" Tamara shifted the shopping bag over her arm as she punched the down button on the elevator.

"Stop where?" Laurel asked, not really caring.

"Just down to three, to say good-bye to Seth. I kind of hate to leave him here alone. He doesn't ever get any visitors."

The elevator hummed to a stop, and the door slid open. Tamara walked in, set down the shopping bag, and leaned against the wall.

The doors began to close before she noticed Laurel, still standing in the hall, her face still with shock and one hand across her heart.

"Hey! Hey!" Tamara pushed the doors apart before they closed. "Are you okay, Laurel? What's wrong?"

"Say it again." Laurel's voice was husky. She didn't dare breathe. She stared at Tamara's dark eyes, watching her intently.

"Okay, I said—Hey! Hey! Are you okay—"

"Not that!" Laurel cried, her heart thundering. "Before that! You said, 'Let's go down to three' and see who?"

"Seth. The pedestrian."

"What pedestrian?" Laurel shrieked, grabbing Tamara by the lapels of her wool coat. "Seth who?"

"Good God, Laurel." Tamara pulled her into the elevator, and the doors closed firmly. Tamara reached out and hit the three button. "Seth I-don't-know-his-last-name. And we're assuming he was a pedestrian. He wasn't in

387

the other car, but he got knocked down, some-how, at the accident. Shoulder and collarbone injury. He doesn't talk much, so they're assuming he has head injuries. Amnesia, I guess. Doesn't know his address; doesn't remember a lot. Silly things, like how to get on an elevator or turn on a shower. The police are trying to identify him. He didn't have any ID with him. Personally, I think he might be a little nuts—he says the funniest things. Too bad. He's a real babe."

Afraid to hope, Laurel stepped out of the elevator and followed Tamara down the hall.

They walked around a corner and stopped in front of an open door.

Laurel took a deep breath and stepped into the room.

He was sitting on an unmade bed, his dark hair unbound and falling over one shoulder. The other shoulder was covered with plaster and gauze to the elbow. He was barechested, covered to the waist with the regulation white hospital blankets. The remote control for the TV set was in his hand, his dark eyes riveted to the screen.

"If it's tuna casserole, take it away," he said. "And no milk. I want a beer, by God. A good, strong pint."

"You really are the bossiest man I've ever met," Laurel said softly, a catch in her voice. "I'm glad I don't work here."

He dropped the remote control, turning toward the door with startled eyes. Confusion showed on his face at the sight of her.

"I'm sorry." His voice was uncertain. "I thought you were someone else."

Laurel stepped toward him on trembling legs, tears welling in her eyes. He didn't know her. She was no longer the tall, willowy eighteen-year-old he had loved.

Unable to stop herself, she reached out and touched his cheek, stroking the days' worth of stubble that darkened his jaw.

"I was. That is, I told you I was someone else."

He caught her hand in his and pulled her next to him on the bed, staring into her eyes.

"Hope?" The word was soft, almost fearful.

She nodded, and he caught her in his good arm, crushing her against his warm chest.

She cried hard, her tears running over his skin, and cried even harder when he kissed her, their lips melting in a fevered heat. "Never leave me," he whispered, and his hand moved through her hair in the familiar, soothing pattern she loved.

"Never," she promised, wiping her eyes.

"And Hope?" He placed a firm hand beneath her chin, raising her face to his. "Promise me one more thing."

"Anything. Just ask."

He looked up at the TV set, where the home shopping channel was celebrating Diamondaire week, with great buys on cubic zirconium jewelry. "Can we get one of those? The television, I mean."

Laurel laughed through her tears. "It's done."

"Gee," Tamara said from the door, "I guess you two have met, huh?"

"We're old friends," Seth answered softly.

"You wouldn't believe how old," Laurel added, with the first heartfelt laugh she'd given since emerging from the darkness.

"I'll bid . . . seven." Jerry looked over the top of his cards with a self-satisfied expression.

"Six," Grandma announced, writing the bids on the score sheet. "Nat?"

"Two," Nathaniel muttered, glaring at his cards.

Jerry guffawed.

"I'm still worried," Nathaniel said suddenly, "About the way she took him out of the hospital. Acting Against Medical Advice, the nurse kept saying. Is that serious?"

"It means the insurance he never had won't pay," Grandma snapped. "Geez Louise, quit fussing and play."

Jerry threw down the ace of hearts, beaming.

"And nobody's said a word to us about it," Nathaniel added. "Doesn't that worry you?" He threw a two down next to Jerry's ace.

"Nope," Grandma returned, pulling a bottle of beer from the clouds. "It tickles me pink."

"Amen," Jerry added. "Throw, Nat."

Nathaniel scratched his head beneath his

white wig. "I don't know. It seems so bloody unlikely."

Jerry scooped up the cards and was tapping them into a tidy pile when they heard the soft chiming of a bell.

"Hey—what the hell was that?" Jerry looked around in alarm.

Slowly, with the grace of a falling leaf, a gold-edged paper floated down toward the table.

The three companions exchanged worried looks, and Grandma reached out and grabbed the descending paper.

"What does it say? What is it, Joyce?"

Grandma's eyes scanned the paper, and she let out her breath in a long sigh. "Listen to this, will you?" She waved the paper triumphantly, and read: " 'Situation handled admirably, with grace and intelligence. We extend Our compliments to you. P.S. Did you really believe you were fooling Someone?' "

"That's good!" Jerry cried. "Except for the last part. That was a little high-handed."

There was a distant rumble of thunder, and a downpour of rain began falling from the clouds, dripping over the three friends.

"Jerry, you idiot," Grandma said. She brushed the raindrops off the glittering letters on her new orange sweatshirt. LIFE'S A BITCH, said the shirt, AND THEN YOU DIE.

Chapter Eighteen

Laurel walked up the sunlit path to her front door, balancing a bag of groceries on her hip.

"Mrs. Goodwin! A minute, please!"

Laurel turned toward the voice and offered a smile at her neighbor, who was frowning over the top of the fence, her crisp gray hair still in rollers.

"What can I do for you, Mrs. Martelli?"

Mrs. Martelli looked as if she doubted Laurel's ability to do anything. "It's about your husband. I don't like to complain—"

Laurel was of another opinion altogether.

"But he was out here at six this morning, running that new chain saw. Now, if he wants to saw down every tree in your yard, that's your business."

Laurel glanced toward the back of the house.

The trees did look as if they'd all had bad haircuts.

"But not at six in the morning."

"I'm sorry, Mrs. Martelli. It's a brand-new saw, and he's a little excited about it."

"Last week it was the lawn mower," Mrs. Martelli pointed out. "I've never seen a grown man get so excited about mowing a lawn."

Laurel shifted the bag of groceries on her hip. "I promise to speak to him." She turned toward the house, stepping over a package that sat on the doorstep. She glanced at the shipping label and rolled her eyes as she recognized the address of the TV home shopping network.

Mrs. Martelli gave Laurel a final disapproving look as she turned back to her own house.

"Seth! I'm home!" Laurel pushed through the front door.

The house was alive with noise. Somewhere, a television was blaring, the dishwasher was running in the kitchen, and the phone was ringing, over and over again.

"Seth?"

The answering machine clicked on, and Laurel smiled as she heard Seth's recorded voice.

"Hello. You've reached Goodwin's Antique Reproductions and Restoration. We're unable to answer the phone right now, so please leave a message at the tone. Thank you."

Laurel headed for the kitchen and dumped the bag of groceries on the table. An open box of sweetened cereal sat there, the decoder spy ring prize next to it.

"I hate it when you dig through the cereal," Laurel announced, even though he wasn't in the room.

She opened the garage door, but the work-table lay bare, the power tools silent.

"Seth?" She followed the sound of the TV, and found him in the bedroom, lying across the bed, eyes riveted to the small television set, remote control in his hand. He wore only a pair of faded Levi's and a red bandanna tied around his head, pirate-style.

Laurel reached out and turned the TV off.

He looked up, startled. "Hello, sweetheart. Didn't hear you come in."

"I'm not surprised. Think you had the volume up high enough?" She lay on the bed next to him, reaching out to rub his shoulder. "Seth?"

"What?"

"Why do you have that ridiculous rag on your head?"

He looked offended. "I think I look dashing. I saw it on MTV. I rather thought I looked like that Alex Rose."

"Axl," Laurel corrected. "Axl Rose, honey." She reached out and tugged the bandanna off and tossed it to the floor. "And you don't. You're much more handsome."

"I sing better, too," Seth agreed, looking pleased.

"Well, we'll leave that subject for another day. Seth, what did you do to the trees?"

He pulled her over him and kissed her hard on the mouth. "Trimmed them."

"Don't do that again."

He smiled, looking as if he had no intention of listening. "Do you know what came in the mail today?"

Laurel cringed. "Tell me it's not anything from the home shopping channel."

"No, not yet. Though I'm expecting something. No, look . . ." He reached onto the floor and presented Laurel with a catalog of lingerie. "Why don't you order this? Look, look at this black lace. I think you'd look perfect in that."

Laurel stared at the flimsy garment. "You think so, do you?"

"Aye, without doubt. But you know what you'd look better in?"

"What?"

"Nothing. Right now."

Laurel laughed, and obligingly pulled her sweater over her head and unbuttoned her jeans. "Do you ever quit?"

"I would hope not. You'd divorce me."

He pulled her toward him and trailed a row of kisses across her bare stomach. "I love you."

Laurel reached out and touched his face, marveling that he was real, that he was here. "You'd better," she told him, "or I'll take your new nail gun and give it to the poor."

He bellowed with mock outrage and wrestled her beneath him, until she laughed and begged for mercy. He kissed her until her laughter turned to soft sighs, and she welcomed him into her body, murmuring words of passion and promises that would last forever.

SPECIAL SNEAK PREVIEW!

SWEET SUMMER STORM

by Amy Elizabeth Saunders

A sassy and spoiled French aristocrat, Christianna St. Sebastien has fled the bloody revolution of her homeland, leaving behind the only way of life she's ever known. Arriving in England at a rustic farm, the disheartened noblewoman doesn't know quite what to make of its humble surroundings or Gareth Larkin and his rough-and-tumble brothers. Determined to prove that she too can contribute to the household, Christianna reclaims the forgotten flowerbeds—never expecting that she is planting seeds of desire that will reap a bountiful harvest of love....

**Don't miss *Sweet Summer Storm*!
Coming in June 1994
from Leisure Books—
available at newsstands and bookstores
everywhere!**

"I think she's lost her mind," Geoffery said to Stewart, as they dumped the buckets of fresh milk into the cooling pans in the buttery.

"I always said she wasn't the sharpest knife in the drawer. This proves it."

Gareth didn't have to ask who they were talking about.

"What now?" he asked, almost afraid of the answer.

"She's been out in the garden since sunup, wandering in circles," Geoffery informed him.

"When we went out to do the milking, she was crawling under a hedge, talking to herself," Stewart added.

"In Latin," Geoffery said, in a tone of foreboding, as if this was proof that Christianna's sanity had, indeed, deserted her.

"Crawling under a hedge?" Gareth repeated, wondering if his brothers were right.

"Aye, and when I asked her what she was doing, she said, 'Following where the sunlight falls.' She's a few eggs short of a custard, Gareth."

"Following where the sunlight falls," Gareth repeated, his brows drawing together. "Are you sure that's what she said?"

Geoffery nodded. "Aye. I asked her what she meant by it, and she said, 'Never mind.'"

"And then when we came back, she was out behind some bushes, cursing the blackberries." Stewart dropped an empty bucket to the brick floor with a clatter.

"That sounds sensible enough," Gareth observed. "Blackberries are a damned nuisance."

His brothers exchanged glances.

"Not for 'Her Highness,'" Stewart objected. "How would she know a blackberry vine from a potato?"

Gareth shrugged. "Who cares? As long as she's not cursing me or fainting in the kitchen, let her crawl around in the hedgerows."

"Lost her bloody mind," Geoffery muttered, gathering up the empty milk pails.

"Be that as it may," Gareth concurred, "it's nothing to do with us. I need you fellows in the field. We can't wait for rain any longer; so today we need to load the barrels onto the cart and water the plants."

Geoffery and Stewart looked pained.

"Cheer up," Gareth told them. "We'll all go down to the Broken Bow tonight and get sotted, if you like."

They cheered up at the mention of their favorite pub.

"I haven't seen Polly for a month," Stewart said. "Now that's my idea of a woman. Tough as an old boot and ripe as a peach."

"Not like that little madwoman crawling around the garden," Geoffery agreed.

"Oh, leave off," Gareth ordered. "I'll go find Richard and see you in the barn."

Christianna pulled some weeds, threw them over her shoulder, and examined the thin, spindly stems left in the dirt.

"*Dianthus carophyllus,*" she muttered. "I think. Or bachelor's buttons. We'll have to wait and see."

She took a heavy pair of shears from her pocket and began hacking at a blackberry vine that had twined its way around a spindly, yellowing rosebush. "Die, you ugly thing," she ordered, wincing as the thorns bit into the soft flesh of her fingers. She threw the cut brambles over the mossy brick of the garden walls, stood back, and beamed at her progress.

"Roses," she repeated to herself, picturing the open page of the book Daniel had given her, "must be cut beneath clusters of five leaves to promote new and healthful growth."

She cut the roses more tenderly than she had the intrusive blackberries, taking care to leave the few branches with buds, examining the flowers that had managed to survive beneath the cloak of brambles and weeds that had covered them.

"A weak and pale rose," she quoted, "is one that had not been fed. The manure of cows or chickens should be placed at the base of the plants and covered with straw."

She wiped a hand across her damp forehead. "That should be lovely," she remarked wryly.

She had begun pulling weeds and unhealthy looking flowers an hour ago, and although it was still morning, she was already bathed in sweat. The sun beat down on her back, and her hair was tangled with leaves.

She dropped to her knees and examined a stand of ragged leaves, the tall stalks of the plants bending hungrily toward the sun.

"Delphinium consolida!" she exclaimed triumphantly, peering at the tight buds that showed a hint of deep blue. "Larkspur! You may stay," she told the plant in a benevolent tone. "I'd like a nice dark blue display, next to the pink roses, *merci beaucoup*. But you," she said, turning a stern face on the more common, spiky lupines that grew beside them. "You go. There are quite enough of your kind about."

Ruthlessly, she pulled them up by their roots, and they followed the blackberry vines over the fence.

"Discrimination of the aristocracy over the vulgar masses," a voice said behind her, and she turned to see Richard and Gareth behind her.

"You go to hell," she told Richard pleasantly and resumed her work.

He and Gareth laughed.

"What are you doing?" Gareth asked, stepping forward.

Christianna's cry of alarm stopped him, and he looked down at where her dirty finger pointed to a creeping vine beneath his heavy boot.

"*Nigella damascena,*" she explained, "or love-in-a-mist. Call it what you'd like, but don't tread on it."

Gareth stared at the delicate, fernlike plant, which looked to him like a weed. "As you like," he said at last, baffled by Christianna's sudden interest in the long-neglected garden.

She disappeared behind a stand of thick, bushy leaves.

"Blues and pinks may stay," her voice said. "And red, certainly. But *Calendula officinalis* does not belong in this corner. You'll be too bright; you'll distract the eye. Like carrying an orange fan with a pink gown."

"God forbid that should happen," Richard muttered.

Christianna popped up from behind the leaves, a branch hanging from her tangled hair. "Go away," she ordered. "You're interrupting."

She examined her forefinger, where a thorn had torn the skin, and stuck it in her mouth.

Gareth smiled gently. "Here," he said, pulling a battered pair of leather gloves from the pocket of his breeches and tossing them over the dense foliage to her.

She accepted them without a word and disappeared into the bushes like a rabbit.

"Come on," Gareth said to Richard. "There's a revolution happening here, and I think that the aristocrats are winning."

They turned toward the waiting fields, glancing back at the sound of a triumphant laugh.

"*Fritillaria meleagris!*" Christianna's voice recited. "Checkered lily will grow to the height of six hands."

By evening, a brick pathway had appeared, the blanket of moss and clover that had hidden it carefully scraped away and disposed of. The rows of lavender that bordered it looked thin and scruffy, but they would grow, Christianna told herself, now that the weeds were no longer choking their roots.

The weeds were gone, the tall flowers like larkspur and hollyhocks supported and tied with bits of twine to sharp sticks, driven into the ground, and the earth showed brown and rich between the plants lucky enough to have survived the day's purge. Already, it looked more like a garden and less like a jungle.

Bordering the front of the bed were Sweet Williams, their small heads of pink and rose and magenta peeping from their downy beds of soft green, and violas, miniature violets of royal purple velvet with a dash of brilliant

yellow at their centers. Behind them stood
Coventry Bells, looking like ruffled skirts of
pink and lavender clustered on their gray-green
stalks, and spicy smelling gillyflowers of lilac
and cream and rich, dark wine—round, ragged
disks on their pale, thin stems. Leaning against
the mossy brick wall were bell flowers of soft
blue and white and snapdragons—how funny
the English word felt in Christianna's mouth,
sharp and quick.

She had worked through the day like
a woman possessed, pulling the intrusive
creeping weed and raggedy dandelions and
blackberries, cutting until her hand throbbed,
scraping the moss and clover from the bricks
until her back ached.

But more than pain, she felt a peculiar empa-
thy with the flowers of the garden, marveling at
their will to live despite their neglect; and she
wondered at the strength of the dainty blue
forget-me-nots and delicate baby's breath, so
fragile, and yet striving to survive by reaching
toward the sun.

Like me, she thought, and found that she
wanted the flowers to live—not to show
Gareth or Richard and the rest how useful
or clever she was, but simply because they
were beautiful.

Christianna was exhausted as she sat on the
cool brick pathway, her back against the sturdy
trunk of an overhanging peach tree, unable
to move.

Her shoulders ached, her arms throbbed,

her back felt as if it might break. Her face had burned; she could feel, without looking, the tight, red heat beneath the layer of dirt and sweat.

Her striped skirts of pink and lavender were stained beyond repair with streaks of black dirt and green moss. The lace at her bosom and sleeves was torn by thorns, and her entire body was wet with sweat. She was hungry, but nothing in the world could have induced her to move.

She closed her eyes and imagined the garden as it might look in a few weeks. She tried to picture bursts of color and beauty where the tired and yellowed leaves now stood, but even that required too much effort.

"Are you dead?"

She opened her eyes with considerable effort and saw Gareth standing before her, an amused smile on his face. His hands were slung comfortably in the pockets of his breeches, his full-sleeved, white shirt was open at the throat, showing the smooth muscles of his chest. Behind him, the rays of the sun warmed his hair to a fiery red.

"Go away," she said, her voice sounding more exhausted than angry, and she closed her eyes again.

His footsteps retreated and then returned, and Christianna opened a suspicious eye. He set a wooden bucket at her side and offered her a dipper of water. She accepted it gratefully and drank it without stopping, the cold, clear water from the well sliding down her parched throat like ice.

"You've done well," he said, mild surprise in his voice. "I didn't think that you'd get so far in one day."

Christianna smiled.

"I'll send Geoffery and Stewart up the tree tomorrow," he said, "and have them cut back the branches. You'll need more sun here."

"I hate the sun," she muttered.

Gareth laughed, showing his strong, white teeth. "Your face is red. Where it isn't covered with dirt, that is."

Christianna closed her eyes, and when she spoke, her voice was far away and dreamy. "At Versailles, I had my own bath. It was covered in porcelain, painted with rosebuds and lilies; and whenever I wished, my maid would fill it for me and put half a bottle of jasmine scent in the water. I never had to wash from a bowl or haul buckets of water upstairs."

"But the maid did," Gareth pointed out.

Christianna thought of that. "Poor Therese. And half the time, I forgot to pay her."

"It's a wonder she didn't leave," Gareth said, and there was no sympathy in his voice.

"And after my bath," Christianna went on dreamily, "she would do my hair and help me with my gown, and I'd go to operas and ballets and dances. Or I would just go to see Artois. We would have supper, and sometimes I'd play my violin." She hummed a soft, poignant melody, remembering the golden notes of music that had filled her life. "Albinoni," she explained. "So pretty. How I miss the music. And Artois. I wonder if he's dead."

Gareth said nothing, and after a few minutes, he left.

Christianna let the soft evening breeze play over her face, watching the golden light of the summer twilight fall between the branches of the tree.

After a few minutes, Gareth returned.

"Here," he said gently, and he took her hand and pressed a cake of soap into it. "Mrs. Hatton's best. Lavender and primrose oil."

Christianna raised it to her nose and inhaled the soft, clean scent. She looked up at Gareth and saw that he had a linen towel in his hand.

"If you can walk," he said, "I'll take you to the lake for a bath. There's nothing like a bath in the woods after a hot day's work." He laughed aloud at the expression of mingled longing and suspicion on her face.

"I'll turn my back and keep watch for you. Don't be such a baby. It's cool and clean, and you smell like a piglet."

"Bugger off," she muttered, but she offered him her hand and let him help her up. She followed him from the yard and across the green fields, her aching body unable to resist the idea of soaking in cool, clear water.

The grass of the pasture was drying in the sun, and it smelled sweet and fresh. The sheep looked overdressed in their thick winter coats, Christianna thought.

She laughed with delight at the sight of the lambs and the way they half hopped, half skipped around their stodgy elders.

"How can they bear to jump about so in this heat?"

"Just like children," Gareth answered, flashing his white grin. "Hot sun or ass-deep snow, it's all fun."

He leaped easily over the low stone fence that bordered the field and extended his hand to Christianna. She followed with less ease, her heavy petticoats and cumbersome skirts weighing her down.

"Silly clothes," Gareth remarked. "When our Vickie lived at home, she went about in James's breeches half the time."

Christianna could see why. The heavy, boned bodice of her gown was cutting into her ribs, her layers of petticoats felt like weights around her damp legs, and her back felt slick with sweat. She followed Gareth into the woods, welcoming the shade with pleasure.

"Cow path," he explained, leading the way along the uneven trail.

Christianna was too tired to answer.

"It's not far," Gareth added, "and when you get out of the water, you'll feel wonderful."

"I'd rather lie on my bed and have a maid fill a tub for me," Christianna grumbled. "That's what I think is wonderful."

Gareth gave her an exasperated look. "Sorry, Your Highness. Mayhap you should just be happy with what you have."

Christianna glared at him. "What do I have?" she demanded.

"Apart from a bad temper and an arrogant manner?"

She said nothing.

"You have your life. You have a solid roof over your head, food to eat, a brother who cares for you, and a stupid dolt for a brother-in-law who's taking you for a nice cold swim when he could be drinking beer at the Broken Bow. Though why I am, I couldn't tell you. You're the most ungrateful little wench I've ever had the misfortune to meet."

They stood on the path in the dense green forest, glaring at each other for a moment, until Gareth turned his back and walked ahead.

Christianna gathered her dirty, cumbersome skirts in her hand and followed his long-legged stride. "You don't like me, do you?" she asked after a minute.

Gareth looked over his shoulder, a puzzled look on his handsome face. "You're not very likable, are you?" he answered. He turned his back, and kept walking.

Christianna thought about that. Likable? Had it ever mattered if anyone liked her or not? For some idiotic reason, she felt hurt.

"Pig," she muttered, taking care not to be heard; and that made her feel a little better. She lifted her nose proudly and stumbled over a root in the path, breaking the little curved heel from her stained shoe.

"Merde, merde, merde!" she swore.

410

Ahead of her, Gareth laughed.

"Did you step in some?" he asked. "I told you it was a cow path."

"Never mind," Christianna snapped and hobbled after him on her broken shoe.

The lake was small; the water looked cool and green and inviting. Tall trees and feathery ferns surrounded the soft banks, glowing in the golden sunlight.

Christianna inhaled the cool scent of the water and the dusty, spicy scent of the warm leaves.

"It's pretty," she said to Gareth as she stepped over a fallen log. Twigs crackled beneath her feet.

He smiled. "Yes, it is. Even if it isn't a porcelain bath with lilies and roses."

Christianna stood awkwardly for a moment, fingering the cake of soap.

"I'll head back up the bank," Gareth offered, seeing her dilemma. "And I'll keep my back turned."

"See that you do," she said sharply, her cheeks flushed with heat and embarrassment.

He heaved an impatient sigh. "For God's sake, you really are full of yourself. Do you think that you're so damned beautiful that I brought you here to ravish you? You're not my sort. You're too small and skinny, for one thing, and too sharp tempered, for another. I like my women soft and sweet."

"Good," she snapped, her eyes narrowing. "Go away."

Despite Gareth's promise not to look, Christianna hid behind some bushes to undress, her cheeks burning. With a quick look around to assure herself that nobody was in sight, she slid down the grassy bank and into the water, clutching the bar of soap in her grubby hand.

She sighed aloud with delight as the cool water covered her body, washing away the sweat and dust of the day. No, this wasn't at all like a porcelain bath; it was better.

She waded in up to her neck, laughing with delight as the soft mud squeezed between her toes, soothing her tired feet. She splashed water onto her face and felt the coolness of it against the sunburned skin of her nose and cheeks.

She felt weightless, buoyant. Even her hair floated, the dark strands moving around her neck and shoulders like liquid silk.

She let her arms float up and felt the throbbing pain of her day's exertion subsiding, drifting away into the cool green depths of the lake.

The air was full of birdsong, sweet, high notes like a flute. Fingers of golden light reached between the trees and sparkled on the water, and the cloudless sky looked like a dome of blue above the circle of trees.

Christianna felt like a nymph, a tree sprite in an enchanted wood. She had never felt anything as heavenly as the touch of the limpid water against her skin; she had never felt so light and euphoric.

The softly scented soap felt like silk against her bare skin; and she filled her hair with the clean lather, scrubbing her scalp vigorously before dunking her head.

She laughed aloud as she emerged, shaking her head, sending crystal droplets flying across the surface of the water.

"Are you having fun, then?"

Instinctively, her hands moved to her breasts, even though they were covered by the water. She looked over her shoulder to see Gareth sitting on the bank, his teeth showing in a broad white grin.

"Turn your back," she called, her face hot, a panicky feeling in her stomach.

"Don't be stupid. I can't see a thing. And even if I did, it'd be nothing new." He glanced down at the pile of her discarded clothing and picked up a beribboned garter. He examined it with a good-natured smile, touching the white lace and pink silk rosette. "Pretty," he remarked.

415

Christianna glared, her good mood vanishing.

"You look like a wet kitten," Gareth added, dropping the dainty frippery back onto the pile and turning his attention back to her.

"Thank you very much. Now go away."

"How's the water? Cold?"

Christianna wondered if he was hard of hearing or just enjoying her discomfort. She decided it must be the latter. "The water is fine, thank you. Will you turn your back?"

"Truth be told, I was thinking of coming in."

Genuinely panicked, she sputtered for a minute. "Don't you dare!"

"Why not?" he asked, laughing. "There's enough room, I think."

He pulled his shirt over his head as he spoke, and Christianna's heart fluttered and started thumping wildly against her ribs. He wouldn't, he simply couldn't. She looked wildly about, but there was nowhere to go, except back toward the shallows.

She began backing up into the deeper water, and suddenly, the ground was gone. There was nothing beneath her feet. She flailed wildly, reaching for something solid; but there was nothing there, and the water closed over her head.

She tried to cry out, and water rushed into her mouth, choking her. Instinctively, she tried to draw air and swallowed more water. She splashed wildly, and for a second, light appeared through the darkness and there was air.

She choked and tried to breathe and immediately went down again into the murky green. Her lungs ached, her hands grasped at nothing, and she wondered fleetingly which way was up.

Her lungs felt as if they would explode, brilliant lights were bursting in her eyes, and she felt her body sinking down deeper into the endless expanse of blackness.

When something seized her waist with a terrifying grip, she fought against it, arms and legs lashing out against helplessly against the relentless pull. Then she broke the surface into the blinding brilliance of the light, and she was choking, coughing water and gulping painful drafts of air, still trying in her terror to pull away from the tight grip that clutched her body.

"Stop fighting. I've got you. Stop fighting or you'll go under again. You're out. It's all right."

It took a moment for the words to register.

"Stop struggling and breathe."

She sagged with relief as she realized that Gareth was holding her, and her hands instinctively grasped his shoulders. Blindly, she coughed and sputtered, her ribs heaving painfully as she drank in air.

He pounded her back. "Good, that's right. Slow and steady. Don't gasp so. You'll faint. Try to relax, and breathe slow and deep."

Shaking, she tried to obey. Her vision cleared, the pounding in her head subsided, and she realized that she was naked, clinging to this man like a vine, her arms and legs wrapped around him tightly, her bare breasts pressing against the warm skin of his chest. She froze.

"Good," he murmured, and the pounding on her back was replaced with a soft, slow stroking. "Lord, you gave me a fright. Jumped in with my breeches on. You've got a lot of fight for such a little thing."

His skin was warm against her, and she felt a soft thrill, a gentle wave of heat moving through her body. His voice sounded as gentle as the soft lapping of the water.

"Are you better? Got your breath back?"

She tried to speak, but her throat felt tight—a strange, full pressure that had nothing to do with the water she had swallowed. The gentle hand on her bare back felt like velvet, and she shivered.

"Christianna?"

She couldn't speak. Her nipples tightened and throbbed against the warm skin of his chest, and she was painfully aware that her legs were twined around his hips, the very center of her tightly against him. The cool water moved between their bodies, touching every inch of her skin.

Wondering at her silence, he put his strong fingers beneath her chin and tilted her head back to look at her face.

Christianna stared back, unable to look away

as his expression of concern turned to puzzlement, and then slowly, gradually, awareness.

"Oh, Lord," Gareth murmured as his eyes took in the sight of her flushed cheeks and glowing eyes. "Oh, Lord." His hand moved across her cheek like silk, and his rough fingers moved to her parted mouth.

Unable to stop herself, she closed her lips over his finger and tasted warm skin and lake water. She could feel his breath quicken, a sudden tensing of his muscles. His heartbeat was loud in the quiet of the forest.

He looked down at her and took his fingertips from her lips and traced them along the line of her cheekbones, smoothing a wet black curl back from her face.

It seemed forever that they stayed there, locked together with the cool water sparkling around their waists.

And then Gareth smiled at her, a gentle, soft smile, and his eyes glowed cool and green in his tanned face.

"You want me," he said softly.

He said it as calmly as he might say, "The sky is blue," or "It might rain today."

Christianna wanted to die of shame. And even though her body was clinging to his, and her heart was pounding like thunder, and her breasts were throbbing against the hard breadth of his chest, she lied.

"No, I don't," she whispered. Her voice quavered with the lie, and she drew a deep breath and was about to repeat herself when his mouth covered hers.

If he had been rough, she might have found the strength to pull away. But his lips touched hers with the most incredible sweetness she had ever felt—warm and rich with a gentle persistence. When she felt herself lifting her mouth for more, opening to him, his tongue met hers, and the smooth heat of it made her cry out softly deep in her throat.

As he pulled her closer against him, his mouth trailed to her neck, and his breath was hot against her ear.

"The truth," he whispered.

The truth was that she was trembling with unspeakable feelings, that she thought that he was beautiful, strong and golden from the sun with shimmering drops of water rolling down his arms, and she wished with all her heart that she was a simple country lass whose virtue meant nothing to her.

"I want you to let me go," she answered, the words taking an enormous amount of effort.

He laughed softly. "The truth, I said."

His hand was on her breast, gently teasing the hard bud of her nipple against his palm; and she quivered at the sensation and gasped.

"Is it so hard then, to say it?" His voice was low and soft. "You want me. It's a simple enough thing to say."

"I don't." Her voice sounded strangled, and he laughed again.

"What a stubborn little thing you are. Lie

until you choke, if you wish; but bodies don't lie, Christianna. You opened your mouth to me like a starving kitten. And here," he said, his finger circling her nipple till it tingled and throbbed. "Your lovely little breast isn't lying. Your body knows what it wants."

It did, she thought, almost crying with the indignity of it. Her traitorous body was clinging to him, pulling closer to his touch, her breasts lifting to his hand as her spine arched back.

Easily, he shifted her weight over his arm and bent his head to take her aching nipple into his mouth. His lips were firm and strong, his tongue hot and damp against the sensitive bud. An almost unbearable heat rushed through her body, and she moaned, tossing her head.

At the sound, he pulled her almost roughly to him and took her mouth again, his tongue stroking hers with a fevered, velvet heat. He stopped only when he felt her hands in his wet hair, pulling him closer and deeper into the kiss.

"Lie to me again," he whispered, his breath hot against her cheek, "if you can."

Christianna couldn't speak. His hands were on the round curves of her derriere, pulling her against him in the limpid water of the lake; and she realized that she was pressing against the hard length of his shaft with only the thin fabric of his breeches between them.

She wanted to tell him to put her down, to

stop this and leave her alone, and at the same time, she wanted to feel his back beneath her palms, to tell him to kiss her again, to tear away the fabric of his breeches and let him fill the aching need of her body. His mouth was on her neck, raining soft, fiery kisses against the tender skin.

"Tell me that you want me." His voice was gentle, but insistent. One of his hands was stroking the soft curve of her thigh, and Christianna trembled, even as her body answered him, moving toward his touch. Hot tears trembled on her lashes, and her mouth quivered against the clean, warm skin of his shoulder.

His mouth sought hers again, and he bit her lip gently, as if he was tasting her. Then she cried out into his kiss as his hand slipped onto the soft black mound between her legs.

She was lost. Nothing had ever felt as sweet and exquisite as the firm fingers that stroked her, softly and expertly. She was senseless, caught up in the pulsing, tingling thrills and sparkling, swelling waves of fire that chased through her body.

Shamelessly, she writhed against the insistent heat of his fingers, closing her eyes against the sunlight that sparkled over their bare skin, and when he began speaking softly in her ear, his voice only inflamed her more, even as his fingers teased and stroked the soft, pink petals of flesh. And she opened to him like a rosebud unfurling in the sun.

"That's right, that's good. Aah, yes, what a beautiful girl you are. You're wet for me. Do you feel it? God in heaven, you're so sweet. . . ." His breath flowed like fire against the tender skin of her ear; his voice was husky and low. His fingers stroked her, firm and quick.

"Don't fight it, sweetheart. Just let go. . . ."

She did. A wild cry rose from her throat, a primitive, animal sound; and her body shook with white-hot spasms, wave after rolling wave of heat. Her pulse was like a drumbeat in her ears, her fingers gripped his shoulders, and hot tears flooded from her eyes as she collapsed, shuddering, against the smooth golden skin of his chest.

"Sweetheart. . . ." He was stroking her face, kissing the salty tears that poured over her cheeks.

She shook with shame and anger and disgust at her own animal behavior and pushed his hand away from her face.

"Batard sale!"

Gareth's handsome face was blank with shock at the fury in her voice. He shook his head, flinging the dark, wet strands of hair from his eyes. "What?"

Christianna turned away from his clear, troubled gaze, folding her arms over her white bosom. She was still trembling. She felt exposed and humiliated; and she wanted to strike him.

"Christianna, sweetheart—"

"Don't call me that! Stop calling me that! You

bastard, you stupid, filthy bastard!" She was choking with rage and shame. She struggled to get loose from his grip.

He took her shoulders and pulled her roughly against him, turning her face up with a cool hand.

"Stop it. Stop it right now. Do you hear?" He didn't raise his voice, but there was no mistaking the anger in his eyes. "What the hell is wrong with you? Are you crazed?"

"Let me go." Her voice was cold, her cheeks burning.

He laughed, but it wasn't a happy sound. "What, drop you in the water so that you can drown? Calm yourself, and tell me what is wrong? I didn't force you, for God's sake, you were having fun."

She twisted her head away, humiliated.

"Aaah. That's it, then." He was silent for a moment, and Christianna froze, afraid of what he would say next.

"You bloody little snob."

She glanced up through the curtain of wet black hair that covered her face and stopped at the cool anger on his face.

"You bloody little snob," he repeated slowly. "You can't bear it, can you? If I was an earl or a prince, well, that would be a different story, wouldn't it? You'd be laying your pretty head on my shoulder and cooing in my ear. But you can't bear the fact that you've been twisting and crying on the hand of a bloody peasant, can you? Like any common little wench would."

Christianna didn't know what to say, and her face burned with shame.

Gareth stood silently for a moment, his eyes bright with anger, his generous mouth set in a hard line. He lifted her in his hard arms and carried her toward the shore, where he dumped her abruptly in the shallow water.

"Get your clothes on and go home, little girl. And don't come trifling with me again, because the next time you look at me with your big blue eyes and press your pretty white tits against me, you'll get more than you bargained for. I'm no damned courtly fop to play your games with."

No, he wasn't that at all, Christianna thought, watching him stride back into the water. He looked like a pagan god, with his long, wet hair clinging to the hard muscles of his shoulders and the sunlight dappling over the long, smooth line of his back.

She sat where she was, wiping her tears of rage and shame away with a trembling hand, until he plunged into the water with a mighty splash and began swimming away with long, even strokes.

She struck the surface of the water with her fist, and the resulting splash was only mildly satisfying.

Her grubby gown felt wretched against her clean skin as she dressed; and she swore under her breath as she made her way back through the quiet forest. She wondered how she could ever face him again.

HISTORICAL ROMANCE
WILD SUMMER ROSE
Amy Elizabeth Saunders

Torn from her carefree rustic life to become a proper city lady, Victoria Larkin bristles at the hypocrisy of the arrogant French aristocrat who wants to seduce her. But Phillipe St. Sebastian is determined to have her at any cost—even the loss of his beloved ancestral home. And as the flames of revolution threaten their very lives, Victoria and Phillipe find strength in the healing power of love.

_0-505-51902-X $4.99 US/$5.99 CAN

CONTEMPORARY ROMANCE
TWO OF A KIND
Lori Copeland
Bestselling Author of *Promise Me Today*

When her lively widowed mother starts chasing around town with seventy-year-old motorcycle enthusiast Clyde Merrill, Courtney Spenser is confronted by Clyde's angry son. Sensual and overbearing, Graham Merrill quickly gets under Courtney's skin—and she's not at all displeased.

_0-505-51903-8 $3.99 US/$4.99 CAN

LEISURE BOOKS
ATTN: Order Department
276 5th Avenue, New York, NY 10001

Please add $1.50 for shipping and handling for the first book and $.35 for each book thereafter. PA., N.Y.S. and N.Y.C. residents, please add appropriate sales tax. No cash, stamps, or C.O.D.s. All orders shipped within 6 weeks via postal service book rate. Canadian orders require $2.00 extra postage and must be paid in U.S. dollars through a U.S. banking facility.

Name_____
Address_____
City _____ State_____ Zip_____
I have enclosed $_____in payment for the checked book(s).
Payment <u>must</u> accompany all orders. ☐ Please send a free catalog.

COMING IN FEBRUARY!
HISTORICAL ROMANCE
BITTERSWEET PROMISES
By Trana Mae Simmons

Cody Garret likes everything in its place: his horse in its stable, his six-gun in its holster, his money in the bank. But the rugged cowpoke's life is turned head over heels when a robbery throws Shanna Van Alystyne into his arms. With a spirit as fiery as the blazing sun, and a temper to match, Shanna is the most downright thrilling woman ever to set foot in Liberty, Missouri. No matter what it takes, Cody will besiege Shanna's hesitant heart and claim her heavenly love.

_51934-8 $4.99 US/$5.99 CAN

CONTEMPORARY ROMANCE
SNOWBOUND WEEKEND/GAMBLER'S LOVE
By Amii Lorin

In *Snowbound Weekend,* romance is the last thing on Jennifer Lengle's mind when she sets off for a ski trip. But trapped by a blizzard in a roadside inn, Jen finds herself drawn to sophisticated Adam Banner, with his seductive words and his outrageous promises...promises that can be broken as easily as her innocent heart.

And in *Gambler's Love,* Vichy Sweigart's heart soars when she meets handsome Ben Larkin in Atlantic City. But Ben is a gambler, and Vichy knows from experience that such a man can hurt her badly. She is willing to risk everything she has for love, but the odds are high—and her heart is at stake.

_51935-6   **(two unforgettable romances in one volume)** Only $4.99

LOVE SPELL
ATTN: Order Department
Dorchester Publishing Co., Inc.
276 5th Avenue, New York, NY 10001

Please add $1.50 for shipping and handling for the first book and $.35 for each book thereafter. PA., N.Y.S. and N.Y.C. residents, please add appropriate sales tax. No cash, stamps, or C.O.D.s. All orders shipped within 6 weeks via postal service book rate. Canadian orders require $2.00 extra postage and must be paid in U.S. dollars through a U.S. banking facility.

Name _____

Address _____

City _____ State _____ Zip _____

I have enclosed $_____ in payment for the checked book(s).
Payment <u>must</u> accompany all orders.☐ Please send a free catalog.

TIMESWEPT ROMANCE
TIME OF THE ROSE
By Bonita Clifton

When the silver-haired cowboy brings Madison Calloway to his run-down ranch, she thinks for sure he is senile. Certain he'll bring harm to himself, Madison follows the man into a thunderstorm and back to the wild days of his youth in the Old West.

The dread of all his enemies and the desire of all the ladies, Colton Chase does not stand a chance against the spunky beauty who has tracked him through time. And after one passion-drenched night, Colt is ready to surrender his heart to the most tempting spitfire anywhere in time.

_51922-4 $4.99 US/$5.99 CAN

A FUTURISTIC ROMANCE
AWAKENINGS
By Saranne Dawson

Fearless and bold, Justan rules his domain with an iron hand, but nothing short of the Dammai's magic will bring his warring people peace. He claims he needs Rozlynd—a bewitching beauty and the last of the Dammai—for her sorcery alone, yet inside him stirs an unexpected yearning to savor the temptress's charms, to sample her sweet innocence. And as her silken spell ensnares him, Justan battles to vanquish a power whose like he has never encountered—the power of Rozlynd's love.

_51921-6 $4.99 US/$5.99 CAN

HISTORICAL ROMANCE
HUNTERS OF THE ICE AGE:
YESTERDAY'S DAWN
By Theresa Scott

Named for the massive beast sacred to his people, Mamut has proven his strength and courage time and again. But when it comes to subduing one helpless captive female, he finds himself at a distinct disadvantage. Never has he realized the power of beguiling brown eyes, soft curves and berry-red lips to weaken a man's resolve. He has claimed he will make the stolen woman his slave, but he soon learns he will never enjoy her alluring body unless he can first win her elusive heart.

_51920-8 $4.99 US/$5.99 CAN

A CONTEMPORARY ROMANCE
HIGH VOLTAGE
By Lori Copeland

Laurel Henderson hadn't expected the burden of inheriting her father's farm to fall squarely on her shoulders. And if Sheriff Clay Kerwin can't catch the culprits who are sabotaging her best efforts, her hopes of selling it are dim. Struggling with this new responsibility, Laurel has no time to pursue anything, especially not love. The best she can hope for is an affair with no strings attached. And the virile law officer is the perfect man for the job— until Laurel's scheme backfires. Blind to Clay's feelings and her own, she never dreams their amorous arrangement will lead to the passion she wants to last for a lifetime.

_51923-2 $4.99 US/$5.99 CAN